Acclaim for J.M. Redmann's Micky Knight Series

Transitory

Golden Crown Literary Aw~~ ~~
Lambda Literary Award

"You can count on both Hur.   ite
plots, interesting characters   it,
Redmann turns to the trans co.   ᵤ mystery
whose components all come   ᵤ₁srying ending. So,
once again Redmann knocks o   ᵤ₁ or Washington Square Park as
Micky Knight continues to slouch her way toward oblivion, headed
for what she's not sure. The mystery is interesting, the characters real,
and the setting as seedy as you'd expect. What could be better? Highly
recommended."—*Out in Print*

Not Dead Enough

"Micky is the epitome of the anti-heroine, a woman with serious
flaws who had a hard childhood and who paid a high price for her life
achievements as an adult. The great thing about this character is that
she seems so realistic in her self-deprecation, her sarcasm, even her
loneliness. It's inevitable that your heart goes with her as life gives her
yet another blow. I absolutely love this character with all her flaws and
also her strengths."—*LezReviewBooks*

"The author kept me on my toes, divulging just enough to keep me
in the throes of the various situations arising. When I thought I knew
where things were going, the author changed direction with a few
exploits that enhanced my reading pleasure."—*Dru's Book Musings*

"*Not Dead Enough* offers fresh character insight, a compelling mystery,
and addictive pacing. Through it all, Micky Knight continues to impress.
Sure she makes mistakes—both professional and personal—but she
remains a character readers can champion, and this book proves just
how resilient Micky is. It will be exciting to see where J.M. Redmann
takes her as she heads toward a dozen novels in this first-class series."
—*BOLO Books Review*

"Although the mystery itself is complex and has a big cast, Redmann
juggles the elements with a sure hand, lingering long enough to either
establish or embroider the characters while making sure we understand
how they fit into the larger picture. The complexity builds without you

realizing it until you're as deeply involved as Micky, no matter how much she doesn't want to be."—*Out In Print*

Girl on the Edge of Summer

"Excellent storytelling and a brilliant character. This is one of only a few series where I reread all the books when a new one comes out… FIVE STARS and recommended if you like crime fiction with a heart—you may fall for Micky too."—*Planet Nation*

"The two mysteries themselves are interesting and have twists and turns to keep the reader entertained, and there are the usual fast-paced dangerous scenes…Overall, an entertaining read charged with action."—*Lez Review Books*

"We get to enjoy some well-plotted mysteries, some life-and-death rescues, and some despicably seedy characters. Redmann works through her action scenes with precision and balance, never letting them drag or sputter. The YA characters here are also well-drawn. They sound like teenagers, not forty-year-olds, and they act age appropriately as well. But at the heart of it all is Mickey–mostly smart (but sometimes stupid), looking forward without forgetting her past, and trying to reassemble her life with some bent and abraded puzzle pieces."—*Out in Print*

Ill Will

Lambda Literary Award Winner
***Foreword* Magazine Honorable Mention**

"*Ill Will* is fast-paced, well-plotted, and peopled with great characters. Redmann's dialogue is, as usual, marvelous. To top it off, you get an unexpected twist at the end. Please join me in hoping that book number eight is well underway."—*Lambda Literary Review*

"*Ill Will* is a solidly plotted, strongly character-driven mystery that is well paced."—*Mysterious Reviews*

Water Mark

***Foreword* Magazine Gold Medal Winner**
Golden Crown Literary Award Winner

"*Water Mark* is a rich, deep novel filled with humor and pathos. Its exciting plot keeps the pages flying, while it shows that long after a front page story has ceased to exist, even in the back sections of the newspaper, it remains very real to those whose lives it touched. This is another great read from a fine author."—*Just About Write*

Death of a Dying Man

Lambda Literary Award Winner

"Like other books in the series, Redmann's pacing is sharp, her sense of place acute and her characters well crafted. The story has a definite edge, raising some discomfiting questions about the selfishly unsavory way some gay men and lesbians live their lives and what the consequences of that behavior can be. Redmann isn't all edge, however—she's got plenty of sass. Knight is funny, her relationship with Cordelia is believably long-term-lover sexy and little details of both the characters' lives and New Orleans give the atmosphere heft."—*Lambda Book Report*

"As the investigation continues and Micky's personal dramas rage, a big storm is brewing. Redmann, whose day job is with NO/AIDS, gets the Hurricane Katrina evacuation just right—at times she brought tears to my eyes. An unsettled Micky searches for friends and does her work as she constantly grieves for her beloved city."—*New Orleans Times-Picayune*

The Intersection of Law and Desire

Lambda Literary Award Winner
***San Francisco Chronicle* Editor's Choice for the year**

Profiled on *Fresh Air*, hosted by Terry Gross, and selected for book reviewer Maureen Corrigan's recommended holiday book list.

"Superbly crafted, multi-layered...One of the most hard-boiled and complex female detectives in print today."—*San Francisco Chronicle* (An Editor's Choice selection for 1995)

"Fine, hard-boiled tale-telling."—*Washington Post Book World*

"An edge-of-the-seat, action-packed New Orleans adventure... Micky Knight is a fast-moving, fearless, fascinating character...*The Intersection of Law and Desire* will win Redmann lots more fans." —*New Orleans Times-Picayune*

"Crackling with tension...an uncommonly rich book...Redmann has the making of a landmark series."—*Kirkus Review*

"Perceptive, sensitive prose; in-depth characterization; and pensive, wry wit add up to a memorable and compelling read."—*Library Journal*

"Powerful and page turning…A rip-roaring read, as randy as it is reflective…Micky Knight is a to-die-for creation…a Cajun firebrand with the proverbial quick wit, fast tongue, and heavy heart."—*Lambda Book Report*

Lost Daughters

"A sophisticated, funny, plot-driven, character-laden murder mystery set in New Orleans…as tightly plotted a page-turner as they come… One of the pleasures of *Lost Daughters* is its highly accurate portrayal of the real work of private detection—a standout accomplishment in the usually sloppily conjectured world of thriller-killer fiction. Redmann has a firm grasp of both the techniques and the emotions of real-life cases—in this instance, why people decide to search for their relatives, why people don't, what they fear finding and losing…and Knight is a competent, tightly wound, sardonic, passionate detective with a keen eye for detail and a spine made of steel."—*San Francisco Chronicle*

"Redmann's Micky Knight series just gets better…For finely delineated characters, unerring timing, and page-turning action, Redmann deserves the widest possible audience."—*Booklist, starred review*

"Like fine wine, J.M. Redmann's private eye has developed interesting depths and nuances with age…Redmann continues to write some of the fastest–moving action scenes in the business…In *Lost Daughters*, Redmann has found a winning combination of action and emotion that should attract new fans—both gay and straight—in droves."—*New Orleans Times Picayune*

"…tastefully sexy…"—*USA Today*

"An admirable, tough PI with an eye for detail and the courage, finally, to confront her own fear. Recommended."—*Library Journal*

"The best mysteries are character-driven and still have great moments of atmosphere and a tightly wound plot. J.M. Redmann succeeds on all three counts in this story of a smart lesbian private eye who unravels the fascinating evidence in a string of bizarre cases, involving missing children, grisly mutilations, and a runaway teen driven from her own home because she is gay."—*Outsmart*

By the Author

The Micky Knight Mystery Series:

Death by the Riverside

Deaths of Jocasta

The Intersection of Law and Desire

Lost Daughters

Death of a Dying Man

Water Mark

Ill Will

The Shoal of Time

The Girl on the Edge of Summer

Not Dead Enough

Transitory

The Smallest Day

Women of the Mean Streets: Lesbian Noir
edited with Greg Herren

Men of the Mean Streets: Gay Noir
edited with Greg Herren

Night Shadows: Queer Horror
edited with Greg Herren

As R. Jean Reid, the Nell McGraw mystery series

Roots of Murder

Perdition

Visit us at www.boldstrokesbooks.com

THE SMALLEST DAY

by

J.M. Redmann

2025

THE SMALLEST DAY

ISBN 13: 978-1-63679-854-7

This Trade Paperback Original Is Published By
Bold Strokes Books, Inc.
P.O. Box 249
Valley Falls, NY 12185

First Edition: May 2025

Credits
Editors: Greg Herren and Stacia Seaman
Production Design: Stacia Seaman
Cover Design by Tammy Seidick

Acknowledgments

My first book was published in 1990. I am lucky and privileged to still be writing, still publishing books. Looking back on my writing life—more of it is behind me than in front of me—there are so many people along the way who pushed, cajoled, inspired, and helped me. I cannot name you all; possibly not even remember you all. It doesn't take a village; it takes a city.

I need to thank the writing community, especially the mystery and the queer writing communities. Yes, there are exceptions, but for the most part, we all help each other through the long slogs of writing books. Big thanks to Susan Larson, longtime New Orleans book maven and host of *The Reading Life* on NPR. She supported queer writers like we were real writers long before so many of her other straight colleagues did. Also, thanks to Paul Willis, Executive Director of Tennessee Williams Literary Festival, Rob Byrnes and Carol Rosenfeld of the Publishing Triangle, John, Jeff, Stephanie, and everyone in Queer Crime Writers. Have to include MWA (Mystery Writers of America) and Sisters in Crime. Also, thanks to Michele Karlsberg for her unstinting support of the LGBTQ writing community and for her friendship.

I need to thank all my writer friends who struggle to get the words on the page amidst everything else life throws at us. Greg, Cheryl, Jesse, Kay, Carsen, Ali, Anne, Clifford, VK, 'Nathan, Jeffrey, Rob, Fay, Isabella, K.G., Jerry, Lucy, David, Thomas, Dean, Barb, Margo, John, Jeff, Mary, and I know I'm forgetting some of y'all. Special thanks to Anne Laughlin and Clifford Henderson, for the good times and the support. Y'all keep me sane, or as close to it as I'm likely to get. Also, thanks to the authors who started so many of us on this journey and have been kind and generous to me, Ellen Hart, Katherine V. Forrest, Barbara Wilson, Dorothy Allison—greatly missed, Jewelle Gomez, and so many others. You gave us lesbian heroes at a time when lesbians weren't supposed to be heroes.

Thanks to the best little book club in the world, silverback edition: Marie, Candy, Barb, and Yvonne, for reading a lot of good books together and a few (one in particular) not so good ones. Good times with good friends.

I also need to thank Rabbi Abby Phelps and Cantor Richard Newman for their patience and kind advice. Also, Congregation Sinai for welcoming me when I visited their services and events, a truly great group of people. The book is mine and any mistakes are mine as well.

As always, a major thanks to Greg Herren for his editorial work, and his calm demeanor, especially about those minor details like deadlines. And what happens in New Orleans stays in New Orleans. Unless it makes a good story.

Huge thanks to Radclyffe for making Bold Strokes what it is. Ruth, Sandy, Stacia, and Cindy for all their hard work behind the scenes and everyone at BSB for being such a great and supportive publishing house.

And my partner in life and cat care duty, Gillian. Last and certainly not least in their minds, our cats Sazerac, Rye Whiskey, and Absinthe.

To the resisters, the fighters, the LGBTQ writers who tell our stories fiercely and fully. To many of you too many to name, but I will try. My godmothers of lesbian mystery writing, Barbara Sjoholm (Wilson for her Pam Nilsen books), Katherine Forrest, Ellen Hart—I would not be where I am without the trail you blazed. Also, the trailblazing crime-writing men—Joseph Hansen, Michael Nava, and Greg Herren—the latter two friends and supports. Books make us real; books make us human. Thank you all for the words you have put on the page.

Chapter One

You call that a bodyguard? Safer, I'm not feeling."

I should have been insulted, since she was referring to me, but save for my ego I agreed with her. I'm a private investigator, more suited to trawling through boring stacks of records than throwing myself in front of bullets. Although, as good as the promised fee was, bullets were still above the pay grade. Somebody needed to live to testify at the murder trial, and as the not intended victim, that was likely to be me.

Sarah Jacobson was in New Orleans because it was the place she hated more than any other in the country, swearing that the only time she'd ever come, back in college, was more than enough. Rabbi Sarah Jacobson. She was in hiding because someone had shot and killed her wife, Leah, presumably aiming for her.

"We just need someone for a few weeks," my friend and NOPD officer Joanne Ranson had promised me. "Travel with her, check the surroundings, call us ASAP if you see anything off." When not guarding her, I could continue with my regular cases, meaning I got a few weeks of nice cash flow in my direction rather than the usual sluggish inflow and gushing outflow. I could use it. The summer had been brutally hot—yes, it's always hot here, but we were setting records, days over one hundred degrees, which used to be rare. For most of my life here, summers were low to mid-nineties with a chance of afternoon thunderstorms. Didn't even need to look at the weather report. Not anymore. So hot no one wanted to do anything, and that included hiring private investigators. I needed to have a good fall and winter to catch up.

So, that was why I was at this hotel by the airport, being talked about as if I wasn't there. I chose not to argue in my favor. I could collect my fee for the day, only have to work an hour including travel time, and then be free to go if she rejected me. Who was I to disagree?

Her point was that I was about the same age as she was, only a few years younger, still on the lower side of fifty, and she was two years beyond. She was about five-eight, so my height of five-ten wasn't much taller. She looked in reasonable shape for her age; hard to tell about muscle since she was wearing a too heavy jacket for the weather, but her movements were sharp and quick, her hands were vehemently expressing the same thing her words were saying. Her face would be called handsome, not pretty—strong jaw, high forehead, a few lines of worry across it, wire rim glasses that masked eyes the brown of rich earth. Her hair was mostly gray, a few tendrils of the dark brown it had once been still showing in the tangle of curls, on the cusp of tipping into frizzy instead of wavy.

If she couldn't protect herself, could someone like me protect her?

Joanne was being nice, letting her ramble on about me not being the right bodyguard, how much she hated New Orleans, it was too hot here (take off the jacket, sweetie), and if she could find kosher food. She finally had to pause to take a breath.

"She is a highly trained professional," Joanne interjected. "If you want someone who can win a physical fight, we can arrange that, but it might be better to have someone who prevents that in the first place."

Me? You want me to do that? I kept quiet, still hoping she would opt for the big, burly man.

She suddenly sat down, close to a collapse, and started crying.

Sarah Jacobson was whisked here last night, arriving close to midnight, four days after standing next to her wife when she was shot. The shock and whirl of grief was coursing through her—anger, sorrow, numbness—the person she most cared about gone and her here stumbling through the pain.

Joanne went to the bathroom to retrieve a wad of tissue to hand to her.

There were four of us in the room: the two men who'd brought her, one tall and wiry, the other short and muscled, Joanne, and me. We all seemed lost for words.

Earn the money they're paying you.

I knelt in front of her. "I'm sorry that you're here, and I'm sorry for the tragedy that brought you here. The world is broken in so many places. I can't offer much, but I'm trained—and good at—observing, seeing what's out of place, acting quickly, knowing what I can do and can't do, and being even quicker to call for help. I'll do my best to keep you safe."

She slowly raised her head and looked at me, her eyes red rimmed, glistening with tears. "Keep me safe from what? Going on with a life I no longer see any purpose in?"

"Keeping you safe while you hurt, long enough to see if there is a way through the grief, long enough to see if there is something of life you want to hold on to."

She slowly wiped her tears away, leaving only the red, angry eyes. "Fine, do your job, earn your money. Let time do what it will."

I stood up. *Fuck, you had to be nice, let a crying woman trick you into compassion.* And now I was stuck being a bodyguard for someone who didn't want a bodyguard, didn't want to be here, and maybe didn't even want to live. I looked at Joanne. She was engrossed with something on her phone and avoiding my glance.

Sarah was the rabbi at a liberal congregation in New York City. A wealthy member of her synagogue was covering the costs of her being in New Orleans. I'd gotten few details beyond that. I needed to get Joanne alone and pry everything I could from her.

"Um, we have a plane to catch," the wiry guy said. "You gonna take over?"

"Yes, go ahead," I said.

They didn't do a very good job of hiding the relief on their faces. They got to go home and this was no longer their problem. After the usual placeholder chat—"you guys take care," "any good restaurants in the airport"—they were gone. There are no good restaurants in airports, but even I had to admit that the new New Orleans airport did better than most, with local offerings instead of the same boring chains. Some of the sandwich shops carried Central Grocery muffalettas. You can't go wrong with that.

Sarah excused herself to wash her face. I listened for the sounds of water running before turning to Joanne. "I want to move her someplace else as soon as possible. And then you and I need to have a long chat about everything you know."

She put her phone away and nodded. "You don't trust them?" she asked.

"Don't know them. The fewer people who know where she is, the better." I needed to learn a lot more before I could consider who to trust.

"Fair enough. Where?"

I sighed. "The French Quarter. Lot of tourists, lot of new faces around, hide in a crowd."

"She will hate that," Joanne said.

The water cut off and she came out of the bathroom, drying her face. "I presume you're talking about me?" Her tone made it not a question.

"We're talking about what to do next and, yes, that obviously concerns you," I said. "I think it's safer to move you away from here."

"Away from this charming hotel and scenic freeway?"

"There are other airport hotels if you're truly attached," I answered.

She shot me a look, catching my sarcasm and not liking it.

"The French Quarter might be best," I continued.

"Really?" She turned to Joanne as if hoping she would counter. "I want to go to a calm, quiet area, away from the party pestilence this city is so good at."

"We need to consider where you'll most likely not be noticed," Joanne said.

"Well, damn," she said, collapsing into the chair, no energy left even for this small fight. Then she looked up at me, "How long do I have to stay?"

"One step at a time," I answered. "First, we move from here and get you settled there. Maybe a few days to a week. It's probably best to not stay anywhere too long."

She shook her head. "I hate living out of a suitcase. In my least favorite city. When do I get my life back?"

I couldn't answer that. "Let's get you packed and out of here," I said.

"We'll work on finding some place you feel comfortable," Joanne added.

Sarah washed her face one more time, then quickly packed, easy since she had barely unpacked.

While she was doing that, Joanne and I pulled up a hotel app and booked a room under Joanne's name. She had no connection to Sarah until that very minute. I'd have to take over, and we'd both get reimbursed at some point. At some point soon, I hoped.

From there, we headed back into the city, Joanne with Sarah in her car, since she had a police radio and all the cop bells and whistles. Plus, my beat-up old Mazda could use a cleaning, or at least a vacuuming from helping my cousin Torbin take the cats to the vet when his car broke down. For all I knew she was allergic.

Traffic on Canal Street in late afternoon is not the Ninth, but certainly a lower circle of hell, probably around the Seventh. I opted to park in a lot over in the Central Business District, divided from the French Quarter by Canal Street. I parked at one on Poydras, close to Mother's restaurant. Po-boy on the way home for me.

Then a quick hike back to Canal, weaving through the workers going home for the day. Joanne texted me asking where I was just as I got to the hotel. The lobby was so large I had to text her back to find her. It was a big convention hotel, about as anonymous as could be. Joanne texted, directing me to Sarah, sitting by herself in an out-of-the-way area.

Before approaching her, I surveyed the surroundings. Nothing other than people milling around, groups in the lobby bar, people waiting to check in, for other people, or to leave for the airport. The restaurant wasn't busy, but why would it be? There are world class restaurants only steps away.

I scanned the room one more time, then slowly walked over to Sarah, taking a seat close, but not so close as to connect us. She looked up at me, but I shook my head. Here, in the city she hated, it wasn't likely anyone was looking for her. No one might be looking for her at all. A crime of hate and convenience: the shot fired, killing one person, and the shooter fled, now more intent on not being caught than trying to track down his intended victim. Unless she was his prey, not just hate. He could all too easily find others.

I've been targeted for being a lesbian. Maybe not just being a lesbian, but being tall, not hewing to the conventions of how women are supposed to dress and behave. The cardinal sin, breaking the gender rules, showing how easily they could be broken. I'd been hit once by a drunk young angry man I'd made fun of as I was crossing Bourbon Street. "Spill their drinks quickly, spill their seed quickly," I'd mouthed to the women—barely beyond girls and likely not yet old enough to legally drink—surrounding him as he threw up in the street. He had taken offense, shouting, "Dyke!" then jumping at me, only landing a blow on my shoulder as I twisted away. He swung again, grazing my cheek. The next minute the cops were there, including one I knew. I was told to leave; he got off with a warning.

I remembered the hate and anger in his eyes. The ugly words he used, "dyke," "cunt," "faggot," anything he thought might land a blow. Words hurt; they just don't leave visible marks. The cops blew it off, even the gay cop I knew letting it slide. Not a big deal, not a real crime.

Mouthy dyke, stepping out of her place, drunk white guy responds. No real harm. Except to all the queer people watching, seeing how easily they could be victims and no one would care. I was in my late twenties then. Decades ago. Now I look for the anger, not to appease it but to be aware and consider if it's a battle worth fighting.

Two glancing blows, a faint bruise on my shoulder. No harm done.

Sarah had harm done, brutal, life-shattering harm.

No, it wasn't likely anyone was looking for her here, but it was possible. That was part of the underlying horror—once you're one of the hated groups, you never know when the hate will hit you again. Even if it never does, the constant, nagging worry is always there.

I glanced around the lobby, like I was waiting for someone. Again, everything normal, no sharp glances our way, no one loitering where they could watch us.

Joanne headed toward me. I nodded her to Sarah. She understood, passing me by and getting Sarah, then heading for the elevator.

"Fourteenth floor, should be a nice view," she said to Sarah as she passed me.

I gave them about half the lobby, then followed. They got on an elevator when I was almost there. I waited for the next one and then took it to the fourteenth floor. They weren't in the elevator lobby when I stepped out, but I heard Joanne's voice down one of the hallways. I quickly caught up.

"Do we have to be this cloak and dagger?" Sarah said irritably.

"Short answer, yes. Let's get in the room," Joanne said.

We continued down the hallway in silence. Her room was near the end. Few people should be back in this area.

Joanne opened the door and let us both in first.

Sarah tossed her suitcase on the bed, then flopped down beside it. "So, to my question. What's with the security theater?"

"Not playing games here," I said. Her annoyance was starting to annoy me. "If someone is too interested in you, we need to know. By being well behind, I could observe anyone watching where you were going."

"So, how hunted am I?" she demanded, crossing her arms, anger lacing her words.

I told myself she had the right to be angry. A right to blinding fury, even. I just needed to remind myself it wasn't about me; I was just handy. "All looked normal," I told her.

She sighed and looked away. "Safe enough for me to take a nap? I haven't had much rest in the last few days."

"Sure," Joanne said. She handed Sarah a key card, then one to me as well.

The latter didn't escape Sarah's notice. "So, you get to barge in whenever?"

"Not unless I have to," I said calmly. "But helpful for me to have access as well."

"Are you going to stay and watch me sleep?"

The room had two queen beds, a desk and comfortable seating area, but no separate area other than the bathroom.

"No, not necessary," Joanne said. "We can leave you for a while. Just don't go out by yourself. Text Micky when you wake up. Only open the door if it's one of us."

I would have said the same thing but was glad it came from Joanne. Everything up until now had been hurried, no time for questions, so I wasn't sure what we wanted to accomplish, other than keeping Sarah as safe as possible.

"I don't have my phone. Too dangerous, they said."

"I'll get you a prepaid one," I said. What else was I going to do while she napped? Besides sitting Joanne down and getting as much info as I could. I wrote down my cell number and told her to call me on the hotel phone.

"I'll call you when I wake up," she said, heading to the bathroom. "It may be tomorrow." She shut the door. Our cue to leave.

Joanne and I exited the room, then I waited while she headed to the elevators. I gave her a few minutes, then followed. The floor was quiet, no one else around.

At the elevator, I got a text from her to meet outside on the street.

I again scanned the lobby on my way out, but it was hotel staff and a multitude of tourists in various states of sobriety.

Joanne was waiting off to the side of the entrance.

"So, what exactly have I gotten myself into?" I asked as I joined her.

She sighed. "I'm not sure myself. Late lunch, early supper? Let me eat something and we can talk." I agreed. If she was eating, she'd have time to answer my questions.

We again crossed Canal Street, going to a shabby lunch place for the workers in the CBD. It was mostly empty now and would close in an hour. A throwback to the days of plate lunches and booths with red plastic seats.

"Really good gumbo here," Joanne said. She ordered the roast beef po-boy.

I decided to try a cup of the gumbo.

Once the waiter gave us our water glasses, I gave her an expectant look.

"Sarah seems to have pissed off everyone," Joanne started.

"I can see that."

"The rabbi of a Reform congregation in Brooklyn."

"And she hates New Orleans? Everyone from Brooklyn is moving here."

Joanne gave me a look. I nodded, letting her know I'd be quiet.

"She's a lesbian rabbi and outspoken on social justice issues. That alone gets her unwanted attention. She is also a strong advocate for Palestinian rights, critical of Israel and vocal and active about it. After the October 7 terrorist attack, she defended Israel, stating the terrorists are the ones responsible for unleashing the bloodshed. Pissed off the people on the left. Then back to criticizing Israel for falling into the trap of overreacting. Pissed more people off by blaming both Hamas and the Israeli government, no neat good side/bad side. She can be on the assertive side."

"I hadn't noticed." Full sarcasm font.

The waiter brought our food. We paused to take a few bites. Joanne was right about the gumbo, a rich dark roux.

"Plus, being openly gay, advocating for trans rights, all the progressive causes," Joanne said once she'd finished chewing.

"Okay, she has a right to free speech, even truly annoying and contradictory speech, but why kill her? Just don't listen."

"Too many guns, too many crazy people," Joanne said, taking another bite. Another pause to chew. "The background I got is that no one claimed responsibility."

"Do we even know for sure it was aimed at Sarah? Or was she assumed to be the target because she has a knack for pissing people off? Could her wife have been the real target? Family inheritance and they kill her to make it look like a hate crime?"

"Anything is possible, and the NYC cops are investigating it. I'm guessing they're considering all angles, but so far nothing suggests that. The report indicates Sarah was the target. They were standing facing each other outside the temple. Sarah dropped her phone, bent down to pick it up just as the shot was fired. If she hadn't moved, it would have been her." Joanne continued, "Since we have no idea who might want to kill her, it's a wide investigation—the crazy left or the crazy right."

"Or some crazy in between. So the goal is to keep her alive for the investigation. What happens if they don't solve it?"

"We figure that out when we get there. In the meantime, you get paid to keep track of her and try to keep her from doing anything too stupid. She does have friends and supporters. They're covering the cost, so the only official part was getting her out of New York to an undisclosed location, i.e., here."

"A location she hates, so might help throw anyone looking for her off track."

"That's the thought. You don't need to be with her constantly, just check in on a daily basis, and if she goes anywhere, go with her. It's best if she mostly stays in her hotel room."

We went over the details of the most important things—how to pay for her keep and how I'd get paid. Joanne handed me a debit card to cover most things. It would be audited, and the account had about ten thousand dollars in it. Enough to pay for a few weeks of hotels and meals, not enough to tempt me to cash it out and disappear. I'd get paid by check, with the first one arriving tomorrow. If I needed to communicate with Sarah's benefactors, I'd do it through Joanne. Convoluted, and probably hidden enough to confuse the crazy zealots of the world. If the people out to get her were more sophisticated, like a government, it might not be enough. We were going on the assumption that the good ol' US of A and its federal powers were on our side.

Or didn't care.

Once we got that settled and Joanne called for the bill, I asked, "Could it not be about her specifically, but a hate group targeting the Jewish community? She was outside the synagogue, they saw her and fired."

"Also possible, but no way to know. Until we catch them."

"What else do I need to know?"

"If I knew that, I'd tell you." She put a twenty on the table. I left a ten for my gumbo. Together, it would be a nice tip. "From what I know, this should be babysitting her for a few weeks until the NYPD find the killer. Their guess is it was a lone or small group of fanatics. One located around NYC with enough resources to get a decent sniper gun and drive into the city. But they're not likely to be able to track her as long as she stays hard to track."

"What if they're wrong?"

"No one is paying you enough to shield her with your life. If bullets start flying, you duck."

We got up and left the restaurant.

"I'll keep that in mind and hope it doesn't become an option. If I have questions, can I call you?"

"You can call. I don't have any more answers beyond what I've already told you. If I learn more, I'll let you know. But touch base, let me know how things are going."

My car was in one direction, Sarah's hotel in another, and Joanne turned in another. We waved good-bye and I headed back to the French Quarter, not wanting to watch her walk down the street. I didn't know who else might be watching.

CHAPTER TWO

I stopped at the next street corner and looked at my phone as if checking important messages. I had none, but I did need to consider my next step. I was at loose ends until Sarah called me. That could be in ten minutes or tomorrow morning.

Did I stay around here or go home? On the map, my house in Tremé wasn't far, about a half-hour walk. I could retrieve my car, go home, and come back when she called. But if I did that, I would be at least half an hour away, no matter what. Traffic around here is cruel and unusual punishment, a sludge of big convention hotels, the locals whose work is concentrated in this part of town, and people coming to have fun and frolic in the French Quarter. Walking would leave me without a car easily available. But driving here and then parking, even if I paid the outrageous fee at the hotel, would be a task.

Maybe we should have kept her out at the airport.

Except people can come to the French Quarter and stay a week or two without it being out of place. More than a few days at an airport hotel might be noticed. The big, anonymous hotels are in this part of the city. There are smaller, boutique hotels at the lower end of the Quarter, much closer to my house, but guests at small hotels are more noticeable than guests at the big ones.

You did the best you could in the time you had, I told myself and decided to hang around. It had been a while since I'd rambled in this part of town. I'd give it a couple of hours and check in with Sarah if I hadn't heard from her. We'd have to come up with a schedule so I didn't have to hover around while she napped.

I wandered along Royal Street, gazing in the antique and art gallery windows until I hit St. Ann, then I cut down to Chartres, sauntering back uptown, pausing to listen to a jazz band in Jackson Square. They were good, so I tossed a couple of dollars in their bucket.

They finished and I crossed the square. I heard a voice call out, "Michele!"

Yeah, that's my name, but the people who call me that instead of Micky are not people I want to randomly run into. I kept walking.

"Michele!" Closer now, footsteps behind me.

I reluctantly turned, still hoping for another Michele in the vicinity.

Paulette DeNoux Carter. I hadn't seen her since high school and was happy to keep it that way.

"Michele Robideaux! I'd know you anywhere. You haven't changed a bit. Well, some gray in the hair. But you never did much with your hair, did you?"

"Paulette. Nice to see you." It's possible to be so polite you are rude, which is what I was aiming for. Robideaux was my family name; I had changed it in my early twenties for a lot of complicated reasons, mostly to get away from a family I never felt part of.

She had gained a little weight, but some of it seemed to have come from her now-protruding chest, something she hadn't had in high school. Her hair was a blonder blond now; gone were the brown streaks from her natural hair.

"Imagine running into you here!"

"Imagine that, one of the busiest places in the city."

"I don't get down here much, too many tourists and it can be dangerous if you wander off the beaten path."

"Wasn't there a triple murder out in your neighborhood?" I had no idea where she lived now but doubted she had strayed far from her comfortable, suburban perch. I'd been living with my Aunt Greta and Uncle Claude, who also preferred the supposedly "safe" suburbs. That was how Paulette and I ended up in school together. We had not been friends. In the brutal hierarchy of high school, I was the weird outsider from the bayous, where I'd lived until I was ten and my father was killed. I was even more hated because, improbably, when I was a sophomore, I'd hung with some of the cool seniors, dating Ned, the football star running back. We always double-dated with Misty, a cheerleader and Bryan, the quarterback. What no one knew is that the real couples were Bryan and Ned and Misty and me. They graduated and I still had two years left. And a big secret I couldn't tell anyone. As outcast as I was, if I told the truth—that we were all gay—I would have been cast even farther out.

Paulette had been one of the mean girls, not the leader but first lieutenant, enforcing their rules. Little did they know that their punishment of me, not inviting me to things, making sure I knew I had been deliberately left out, wasn't much punishment. The small sting of being rejected, but all in all, did I want to go to a slumber party and talk about makeup and boys? Tell lies, pretend that Ned had dumped me and I wasn't up to dating, or pretend I had crushes on some annoying jock? Being honest wasn't an option.

I think they finally realized that I wasn't miffed enough, so three of them tried to jump me in the bathroom and push my head in the toilet. Not Paulette, although I was sure she was in on the planning. It was after school, most people gone. I'd grown up in the bayous; my father didn't have a clue how to raise a girl, so he raised me as a person, including teaching me how to fight. "Might need it to get away from a gator," he'd said. We both knew that included the human variety. I was tall for my age, already five-eight in tenth grade. I'd heard them come in. Another thing about growing up in the woods—you know when you're being hunted.

They were standing too close to my stall door. I knew what they were going to do because they'd done the same thing a few months ago; a girl even more outcast than I was, weird, probably untreated mental health issues, short and overweight. She was an easy target.

I took my time. One of them finally yelled, "Other people need to use the stall." A lie, since there were about six stalls and only four of us here.

I waited just long enough to make it clear I wasn't going to respond, then slammed open the door. I burst out, pushing them aside, making gagging noises and covering my mouth with my hand. "I'm throwing up!" I yelled, bending as if I was about to retch up a stream.

They stepped back. No one wants to be covered in someone else's vomit.

I immediately charged through them, shoving the first one aside, tripping the second one. I raised my fist. The third one, seeing it was no longer an easy victory, turned and ran.

I followed her only long enough to get out of the bathroom, then sprinted the other way. A voice of authority yelled at me to not run in the hallways, but I ignored it. Just as they had ignored what had happened to the other girl.

I kept running until I was about ten blocks away from the school, on unfamiliar streets.

They didn't try again. They wanted to fight battles they wouldn't lose.

Paulette standing in front of me brought back all those memories, ones I thought I'd left long behind.

"Oh, that thing. It was blocks away, and anyway, it was domestic stuff, killing his ex-wife, her new boyfriend, and then himself."

Ah, New Orleans. Always a crime when one is needed.

"I was thinking about calling you," she continued.

I managed to not allow the shock to show on my face.

"You're a private detective, right? A private dick? Who would have thought?" She snickered at her joke.

One I've heard far too many times. Yeah, a lesbian dick. Ha ha.

"I am," I said.

"I need to hire a private dick." She giggled again.

"Let's set up a time for you to come to my office and we can discuss it," I replied.

"We can't do it now?"

I gave my best fake smile. "Sorry, I have to meet someone over on Canal Street in about five minutes."

"Oh. Are you sure? It won't take long." She frowned, an expression that showed the lines she did her best to cover up with makeup. Paulette was used to getting what she wanted.

"Sorry." Not sorry. "I'm sure. This is an important client, and I can't be late."

"Oh. Okay." Still not happy, but she needed something from me and had to jump through my hoops.

I gave her a card. "Call me tomorrow after ten and we can set something up."

"Oh. Okay." She put the card in her purse, one large enough that it might never be found again. "Well, it was great to see you again." Fake smile.

"Yes, it was." Even faker smile.

I hurried toward Canal as if I really did have an important client waiting. And to put as much distance between us as possible. I doubted she would call, and that was fine. A part of me was admittedly curious about what she would want to hire me—of all people—for.

A small part.

I swerved around a shuffling group of tourists into the street, then zipped back to avoid a mule-drawn buggy. The mule diapers aren't perfect, and I didn't want to get too close. Between Jackson Square and

Canal is the insane tourist part of the Quarter. Jackson to Esplanade was more residential and included the gay area. I usually stayed in the lower end when I came into the Quarter, with its slower pace and queer vibes.

"Get behind me, Satan," I muttered, having to pivot around another mass of tourists who had paused in the middle of the sidewalk.

I thought about stopping in one of the many watering holes along the way but was worried I'd be unlucky enough to pick the one Paulette was going to. I wasn't willing to take the risk.

Finally, the narrow Quarter street opened to the wide expanse of Canal.

I glanced at my watch. We had moved from later afternoon to early evening, the sky now the final glow of a setting sun.

Damn, I'd told Sarah I'd get her a burner phone. I used my map app to locate a store a few blocks away. Canal Street was once the glitzy shopping area of New Orleans—the whites only shopping district, of course. That changed a long time ago. The old-line stores like D.H. Holmes and Krauss had left, either out of business or moved to the suburbs. For a long time, it was a strip of cheap tourist shops and not the kind of restaurants you came to New Orleans for. In the past few decades, it was changing, with high-end hotels. Although lurching back to respectability, it still had pockets where the old ambience remained. Just off Canal, there were several mobile phone stores, including the kind where you could get pay as you go ones.

They asked no questions, just took my money and I had a phone for Sarah.

It was five o'clock in this part of the world. Past five, in fact. I headed to her hotel, hoping that Paulette had not decided to make it a night on the town and stay there. There was a bar, and I could kill enough time to not seem too pushy knocking on Sarah's door.

One drink and a small bowl of bar peanuts later, it was decision time. I could have another drink, but my car was parked down here and I didn't want to leave it. I also didn't want to drive not as sober as I should be, especially in this part of town. I could leave now, go home, and hope she didn't call until the morning. I could have another drink—at hotel prices—and hang around until she called and I was sober enough to drive, hoping they happened around the same time. Or I could go knock on her door, wake her enough to give her the cell phone, and arrange a reasonable schedule.

The chair was comfortable and the drink, a Vieux Carré, not too bad.

The waiter came and asked if I wanted another.

I said no.

With a sigh.

After paying the bill, I ambled through the lobby like a dawdling tourist. I'd seen so many today I could easily imitate them. Looking around, just to see what was going on. Oh, a drug deal over in the corner. Two khaki pants dudes, acting cool and thinking no one noticed their exchange of a small baggie and cash. I thought about alerting hotel security, but I'd have to tip my hand that I'm a PI. They might help keep Sarah safe; they would be there twenty-four hours a day. They might not care, which would be okay. But they might not like queer people or Jewish people, and that would be decidedly not good. I hate making those calculations: Are the people who are supposed to be the good guys—security, the police, a repair person—the kind of people who hate people like me?

I kept walking, sauntering to the elevators.

The security guard stared at me as I entered the elevator lobby. I flashed my key card. He turned away, still ignoring the dudes in the khakis.

I'm a woman of a certain age, still wearing jeans, a scuffed leather jacket and no makeup. Oh, also a T-shirt that says "Make Levees, Not War."

I let one full elevator leave and was lucky enough to get an empty one.

Just as the doors shut, my phone rang.

No greeting. "What do I do for food around here? Anything kosher?"

"I'm on my way up, let's talk about it when I get there." I would have hung up on her, but she beat me to it.

I got off the elevator but paused long enough to use my phone to search for anything with the word "kosher" in it.

This is not the mecca of kosher food. I found only a few listings, none of them anywhere nearby. I do know Jewish people, but only ones who seem fine eating shrimp and grits.

I slowly headed down the hall to her room, pausing for one last second of peace before knocking on the door.

"Who is it?"

"The person you just talked to on the phone."

"Maybe I talked to a lot of people. Name?"

"Michele Knight. Micky," I added. I was tempted to be Michele with her. But if she was here a week or more, I didn't want to hear "Michele" that often. "Standing out in a public hallway where anyone can hear." No one was about, but a door could open at any minute.

The chain and the lock were undone and the door opened slowly. She was standing behind it, not visible until I stepped into the room. She closed it quickly, relocking all the locks.

She claimed the one empty chair. I looked at the rumpled bed and the desk chair with a pile of books on it. I guess I was expected to stand. I picked up the books and moved them to the desk.

She looked annoyed.

I sat down.

"Phone," I said, handing it to her. "Two hundred minutes. Can get more, but the more people you talk to and the longer you talk, the more likely anyone monitoring the phones of your friends will find you."

"Lovely," she said, in a grumpy tone.

"No, not lovely," I said. "But if we're lucky, it'll be short term."

"We? You mean me. If he's caught. Like that would make me safe. Sorry, Tree of Life took that away. Oh, and that little Holocaust thing. Jews have had targets on our backs for centuries."

"Tree of Life?" I asked. I knew about the Holocaust.

"Synagogue in Pittsburgh. Eleven people murdered. Killer caught and convicted. We're still not safe."

"I remember. I just didn't remember the name. Maybe we should deal with the immediate issues. You're hungry and want something to eat."

"That would be nice."

"There aren't many kosher options in New Orleans," I said, showing her the search on my phone screen.

"Wasn't expecting any. I'm surprised there's more than one. I'm not strict."

"Would room service do? Or I can get you something out in the wide world—within a few blocks' walk."

"It'll have to, won't it?" Her voice was resigned. Not a question, the reality of what was happening to her, what her daily life would be, sinking in. She was stuck in this hotel room for the near future, and I was her link to everything—someone she didn't like and didn't trust.

I rummaged under the books on the desk to find the room service menu, handed it to her. She stared at it for at least a full minute, then tossed it back to me.

"Hamburger. No mayo. Medium."

Like it was my job to call it in for her. I reminded myself we could work on boundaries as we went along. *Maybe she's a nice person when she isn't a target and just watched her wife get murdered.* She picked up one of her books and was reading it. I called room service and placed the order.

"What have you been doing?"

"Saw the sights, not usually down in this end of the Quarter. Got your phone. Peanuts and a drink in the bar here to give you time to nap."

"The bar? Don't tell me you're drinking on the job."

Well, maybe that boundary talk would have to happen now. "Yes, I was drinking in the bar, it's what people usually do in bars. I had already spent a few hours wandering around looking in shop windows, getting you the phone, and it was the only innocuous place to wait. I sipped one drink for over an hour. You can ask for a lot of things, but you don't get to dictate how I do my job."

"Some job, drinking the day away."

"I don't think you heard what I just said—getting the phone, walking around for several hours, checking out people in the hotel. If I have to cover being here by getting one drink, then that's the way it's going to be."

She sighed. "How long for the food?"

"About half an hour," I said.

"What did you get? I presume you're eating on my dime."

"You heard what I ordered, just what you asked for. I didn't order anything. I ate earlier and paid for it myself."

She looked away, stood up, and walked to the window, staring out of it. After a moment, she said, "Sorry, I feel like I'm living in fog. Should I not look out the window? Someone might shoot through it?"

"We're on the fourteenth floor. If they're slick enough to pull that off, they can do anything they want."

"Is that likely?"

"I don't know. Who wants to kill you?"

"If I knew that, don't you think I would have told the police?" she said, throwing her hands up in the air. And walking away from the window. "They could catch them and I wouldn't have to be here. So, no, I don't know who wants to kill me."

"I'm not expecting you to give me a name. But it can help to narrow down where to look. A small cell operating in New York? Not likely they can harm you here. A larger, more organized group? It makes a difference in how protected you need to be."

"And if we can't figure it out?"

"We're not there yet and we may never be there. Right now, get some food, watch stupid TV, rest."

"I hate TV. I'll read. Find the wisdom in the centuries, those who have gone before us."

She picked up a book, one with writing I couldn't read. Hebrew? She opened it from what would normally be the back and started mouthing the words in an undertone I could barely hear and wouldn't understand if I did.

"I'm sorry," I said. "I hate to interrupt but wanted to come up with a schedule that works for you." She looked up but didn't say anything. I continued, "When I should be here, if you want to get out and how to arrange that, getting you food. Something other than room service."

She put the book down. "You're the expert, you tell me." Then she waved her hands as if erasing the words. "That came out wrong. Too New York. Advise me. I've never done this before. Should I leave the hotel room? Can I take a walk around the block? What are my limits?"

"Within reason, you get to decide. For the next day or so, best to stay here as much as possible. I can bring food; let me know what you might like. After a day or two, you can consider what you want to do— stay here for a while longer or move someplace else. If you want to get out, let me know. I'll go with you. Or take you someplace safe—as safe as possible."

There was a knock on the door. She jumped up, frightened by the sudden noise.

I motioned her into the corner out of sight, then, after looking through the peephole, opened it. As expected, a young man in the hotel uniform, wheeling a cart with Sarah's meal.

He started to come in, but I said, "No need, my friend is napping and I don't want to wake her." He nodded and silently gave me the bill. I added a decent tip, then took the tray from him. I pushed the door closed with my foot.

"Only a burger. The current worry is whether they cooked it the way you wanted." I put the tray on the desk, nudging books out of the way to make room for it.

She slowly stood up, shaking her head. "Scared by a knock on the door. Does it ever end? The fear?"

"Over time. It gets better." I added, "I was shot once. Close to twenty years ago. It took a while, but it got better."

She nodded, then said, "You want to go home, right? Maybe come back tomorrow, noon or so. I can do room service for breakfast. Or should you be here?"

"I think you can open the door. Check through the peephole first. Or you can ask if they can leave it outside. I'll come around noon. I'll bring lunch. Call me if you need me."

She nodded again, then mumbled, "Thanks."

I let myself out. I paused for a moment in the hall and heard her lock all the locks.

I was hungry and Mother's was on the way to my car. A reward for being a good girl today.

CHAPTER THREE

I headed for my office, burping fried oysters from last night's po-boy. I needed to cram in the follow-up on my other cases if I was meeting Sarah at noon. Mostly the billing. I had two cases that were done and dusted except for the final bill. Of course, I ask for a retainer up front, but depending on how complicated a case is, it can add up. Especially if they keep changing what they want. The first case was finding a not-so-missing husband. I suspected the wife could have done it on her own, but would only believe it if someone else told her. After I found him, she wanted him surveilled. Not my favorite job—harder to pee in a car if you're a girl—but I reluctantly agreed and got her the photos that would cinch her divorce case. Then she wanted me to serve him the divorce papers, claiming he wouldn't suspect a woman. I even did that, but that was my limit. I made sure I did it in a public place with people around. Then she started flirting with me, like I'm a lesbian, she's a woman, of course I'll sleep with her. That was way beyond my boundary. Because I'd said no, she was slow paying the bill. The other case was one of my regulars, Dominick. He hired me about once or twice a year to find an old friend. He was in his eighties now and wanted to know what happened to them. "You know, so you know the end," he told me. He always paid, but I always had to send him at least two bills. He got a discount, of course, for being a repeat client and giving me cases that weren't hard. This last one was an old work buddy, still alive and kicking, and that made Dominick happy. A lot of them were no longer here.

Just after nine I got to my office, a building I now own in the Bywater section. Below the French Quarter, an area bounded by the river and the Industrial Canal, it had been down at heels when I first opened my office here. It was what I could afford. As the years passed, the area gentrified. I made the leap to buy the building as I saw what was happening. I would either own it or let someone else own it and jack up my rent. So now I'm a reluctant landlord. There's a trendy coffee shop on the first floor, which pays the mortgage, and I rent the second floor to the computer grannies—a group of older women who prefer sitting at a desk doing computer searches rather than greeting customers at a big box store. They get a break on the rent and I get the advantage of their services at a discount. That covers most of the bills, except the big repairs, like the roof from six months ago. I'm still paying that off.

After coffee and a reasonable amount of procrastination, the bills were done. I'd sent both emails, with a follow-up in real mail. I'd even made some order in my files, old cases into the storage room in back and everything else properly alphabetized. When I'm in a hurry, sometimes an R-something case ends up in a random place in R, with an Re coming before an Ra. But now all was as it should be.

Right at ten on the dot my phone rang.

"M. Knight Detective Agency," I said. I was here; I might as well answer it.

"Michele! I'd know your voice anywhere."

Paulette. She had actually called. I was so sure she wouldn't that it never occurred to me she would.

"Can you fit me in this morning? I really need to have a small matter taken care of."

Oh, double duck shit. "I'm booked all morning, in fact all day. Can we do it tomorrow? If Saturday works for you? Around nine?" I was hoping by putting her off, she would decide to go elsewhere. Or not want to come in on a weekend.

"That's great! I've never been to a real private dick's office," that annoying giggle again, "so it will be fun."

I kept my expression out of my voice and gave her my office address. Then I added, "I have to go. I'll see you tomorrow," and hung up halfway through her good-bye.

"Fuck, fuck, fuck." But I wasn't a high school kid anymore, instead a grown woman of almost fifty. She hadn't had the power to really hurt me back then and she didn't now.

I looked at the fitness tracker my friend Danny had talked me into buying. How many steps I take. Like I really want to know? It was lousy at stairs. My office is on the third floor and my bedroom on the second, so I rarely got the credit I deserved.

I felt like I needed to get out of the office in case Paulette was outside watching, having come here in hopes of seeing me and now waiting to see if I really was leaving. She did that kind of thing in high school.

I did need to leave. I was seeing Sarah in just under two hours. I again looked at the list of kosher places. The most promising was out in the burbs. I noted its location, grabbed my bag—not a purse, a roomy messenger bag with everything from PI equipment like a flashlight to aspirin to tampons in case my meno was still considering whether to pause or not—and headed out the door.

Late fall in New Orleans is a gift from the gods of weather—bright sunshine, the humidity of the summer gone, perfect blue skies. Just enough of a nip to need a jacket, not a real bite of chill. It feels like the day has been washed clean and is as bright and shiny as it can get. As I left the building, I glanced up and down the street. There was a new Lexus parked by the far corner, not one I'd seen here before.

You're being paranoid, I told myself as I got in my car. I was parked right out front, so no excuse to wander the block. Yeah, like most regulars, we know each other's cars, my dinged-up Mazda, Rodney's old blue and white truck, the various comfortable sedans of the computer grannies. But there were now a fair number of short-term rentals on the block and new people in and out. I had someone tell me my car wasn't up to snuff for a rideshare, assuming I was there to pick them up. I responded by threatening to run over their luggage.

Someone was sitting in the Lexus, big sunglasses, nose barely peering over a map. No one uses paper maps anymore. Paulette? But too far away to know. I could grab my binoculars out of the bag, but that would be obvious.

I drove away, taking the corner at a fair clip, in case she tried to follow me.

If it was her, that is. I was giving her way too much space in my head. I needed to stick to my vow to leave those years behind.

I took the most direct route to the interstate while checking my rearview mirror more than usual. No sign of a blue Lexus. Even if she was, so what? I was working a paying job.

I hate driving I-10 out to the burbs. Save for the very rare four a.m. foray, it's always packed with drivers who think they're more important than anyone else. Left lane below the speed limit? Weaving in gaps that aren't big enough for thread, let alone a car? Thinking the lane lines don't apply to them? So close to my bumper that I can see the spinach in their teeth? All of the above in a fifteen-minute drive.

I finally—and safely—got to a place called Kosher Cajun. It was early for lunch, so it wasn't crowded. I threw myself at their mercy, telling them I had a Jewish friend in town, she had a refrigerator in her hotel and I needed to get her food for a few days. I got a few warm things—matzo ball soup, a Reuben sandwich—for lunch today and a few other things that would be happy in the fridge for a day or two.

I opted to avoid the freeway to save my sanity, taking the surface roads back. My hurrying away from my office had given me a sliver of time and I was using it on the slow road. Right choice; I got a notice on my watch about an accident on I-10 that brought everything to a standstill.

I decided to park at the hotel—and expense it. I could have saved about twenty bucks by parking in the various surface lots, but I had two full bags of food, including drinks. Plus, in the scheme of things, twenty dollars wasn't much. Especially when it didn't come out of my pocket. I showed the valet my room key, handed him a five, then headed into the hotel.

Again, I scanned the lobby, acting like a confused tourist trying to figure out where to go. The khaki drug dudes were back again, smug like they'd never be caught. I sighed and looked for the security people. No uniforms, but a middle-aged man in a blue sports coat, watching the lobby. I headed for him.

"Security, right?"

He looked surprised, but nodded.

"Two guys over in that corner," pointing with a nod of my head, "are dealing. Here yesterday doing the same thing."

"Cop on vacation?" he asked, a voice too quiet to carry.

"Naw, local PI working with a client staying here."

He nodded. "What should I know about your client?"

"Her family was attacked and she's laying low."

"Who's targeting her?"

I had hoped he wouldn't ask that question, but if he was any good at his job, it would be obvious to ask.

"Right wing hate group." Then I added, "Should be no risk to the hotel. Client's not from here, not likely anyone will follow, and we're going to move in a day or two."

He again nodded, then handed me his card. "Let me know if I need to know anything."

My turn to nod and head for the elevator. Out of the corner of my eye, I saw him slowly ambling toward the khaki dudes, as if he were just another tourist wandering around.

For the most part I think drug laws are useless. We should legalize most of them, tax the hell out of it and use a good chunk of that money for treatment and services. Kids in the good neighborhoods smoke weed in their parents' rec room with impunity; kids in the bad neighborhoods, no rec room, sharing bedrooms, don't have any place to hang out except in the parks or streets. They get arrested and have a record hanging around their necks for the rest of their life.

But I do have lines, and being blatant, stupid, and arrogant are big ones.

I let a full elevator go, then got on an empty one that arrived right after it.

It was just noon, more on time than my morning should have let me.

I knocked on the door. "It's Micky," I said. "With food."

No answer. I waited, debating whether to knock again. Just as I was about to put a bag down to free a hand, the door opened.

She stayed behind it, out of sight. I didn't step fully into the room until I was sure it was her who opened the door. I hated being this suspicious.

I put the bags of food on the desk, having to nudge aside a few papers and books to make room. The bed was made. It also had books on it, as if she had been sitting in bed reading.

"Kosher," I said, pointing to the bags.

She looked drained, her face void of emotion like she was too tired to move even those small muscles. Her eyes were rimmed with red. She was dressed in black jeans and a sweatshirt that was too heavy. Doubtful she'd had time to pack and consider the elements.

She lifted an eyebrow at me. "Where did you find kosher food?"

"Out in Metairie, a suburb. I tried to get enough to last a few days."

She smiled, small and tired, but a hint of what she looked like when she was happy.

"I'm not hardcore about kosher. Habit, comfort, not faith. We didn't keep strict kosher at home. Complaining is about my disgruntlement at being here. We have a great kosher deli right around the corner, and I'm used to getting it whenever."

"You mean I could have gotten you a shrimp and bacon po-boy and avoided going out to the burbs?"

"I'm a stranger in a strange city, and something familiar is a comfort." She looked in the bag and pulled out several packages, examining each. "But shrimp and bacon is pushing it."

"More for the rest of us," I said, moving to the window to look out, giving her room at the desk. It was one of the small side streets, view of the roof across the street with its lines of air-conditioning units.

"Warm food even," she said.

"Thought you might like it for lunch. The rest will be okay in the refrigerator and save me not-fun trips."

"Always the defense. Do something nice, then water it down. Is that how you navigate the world? A protective wall?"

I didn't turn from looking out the window. I didn't need to consider if what she said was true, because I knew it was. I needed to consider whether to admit it or not.

Finally, I said, "Just doing what I'm paid for."

She nodded, opened the soup, then sat down, taking a tentative spoonful. "The other people who got me here were paid as well. They didn't worry about what I was eating. I know you did me a kindness and you don't want to admit it because you don't want people to know you are kind. Why does that scare you?"

I turned from the window to face her. The woman I had met yesterday was broken, in shock, fumbling through a strange day. But that wasn't who she was. She was a rabbi, a leader, ministered to her congregation, willing to say what made others uncomfortable and upset. That was the woman showing through now: smart, perceptive, honest, maybe too honest for her own good. I needed to recalculate how to deal with her. This wasn't about me, and I didn't want to be questioned. I had my flaws and demons, but they could stay hidden for today.

"Is this your defense? Probe other people, make them justify themselves? Don't make this about me, because it's not. Our goal—our only goal—is to keep you safe."

"So that's how you want to play it." She took another spoonful of soup, then unwrapped the sandwich and took a bite. "But you drifted first. Going out of your way to get kosher food isn't about keeping me safe."

"Maybe my version of keeping you safe is being kind to you while you're here. The more bearable it is, the more likely you'll cooperate."

She nodded, taking another bite of the sandwich, and looked up at me. "You aren't eating? One of those sandwiches should be for you."

I was hungry, but this was for her, so she had something for the next few days. "I'm fine," I said.

"Take some of this," she said, placing half her sandwich on a napkin and nudging it in my direction. "With the soup, I can only do half, and it won't be good when it's cold." She looked at me. "Take it."

I wasn't going to get much to eat until I left here, and that might be a while. I took the half sandwich, then propped myself against the windowsill and ate it.

I was done and she was still working on both her soup and sandwich, taking her time, as if living in the present moment for each bite.

I checked email on my phone, mostly deleting junk.

When she finished, she looked up at me and said, "Thank you. This helps."

"It's still hard, isn't it?"

"What?"

"All of it. Being here, a place you hate, only because it might keep you safe."

"I had a dream last night. Leah. She told me it was all right. I don't much believe in dreams, just floating images from our subconscious. Maybe it was her, from the faraway place she's in now, telling me to be strong, to keep on living. Maybe my memory of her, knowing her and knowing what she would do. Maybe it was just what I wanted to hear, a wisp of a lie to make me feel less broken. Then I realized it didn't matter. I tell people all the time you can't change what happened, only change how you react. We didn't love each other because we broke easily; she wouldn't want me to break now."

She gathered her trash, putting it in the garbage, turning her face from me so I couldn't see the glimmer of tears in her eyes.

"It's okay to break occasionally. I'm not judging."

"You're too kind to judge."

"Oh, I can judge and I do, but only the people who deserve it."

She quickly wiped her eyes, then said, "It looks like a beautiful day outside. Is it possible to go for a walk? Even just around the block?"

I did not want to walk around this area; too many people, cars, too busy.

"Why don't we go for a drive? I can take you to a park or the lakefront."

"Isn't that a burden for you? Driving me, when we can just go outside for a few minutes."

"No, it's my job. I'd rather you roam where there are fewer people around. This is pragmatic, not kindness."

She nodded and stood up. "Shall we go?"

"You might want to put on something lighter. It's mid-sixties out there."

She looked down at her sweatshirt. "I don't have anything lighter. This will have to do."

"I'm going to go down and collect my car. I'll text you when they go to retrieve it. Sometimes there's a line, and I don't want you to be waiting."

She again nodded, then moved to give me room.

I headed downstairs. When I got to the lobby, the khaki dudes were gone. The security man saw me and gave a bare nod.

As I had predicted, there was a line at the valet. It was ten minutes before my car and I were reunited. When I was the next one, I texted Sarah and told her where to meet me.

The timing gods smiled on us. She appeared just as my car rolled down the ramp.

"Standard, cool," the parking valet said to me. I handed her five dollars.

"Harder to steal," I replied, waving Sarah to the passenger side as I got in.

I pulled out into one of the narrow French Quarter streets before turning and turning again to get to Canal Street.

Sarah was staring out the window at the carnival of tourists and shops. When we turned onto Canal, a wide street with six lanes of traffic and streetcar tracks between them in a wide neutral ground, she said, "Not quite Times Square, but you are right about there being a lot of people around."

"This is a slow day. You should see it at Mardi Gras."

"No, thanks, that's my idea of hell."

It was slow going moving up Canal, stoplights at every corner and a slog of traffic—tour buses, taxis, and a lot of cars. It was impossible to tell if someone was following me or if we were all jammed together with no place to go.

We finally crossed Claiborne, with I-10 built over it.

"The interstate?" She pointed at the concrete behemoth over us.

"Yes."

"This was a Black neighborhood, wasn't it?" she commented.

"Claiborne used to be a beautiful street, tree lined, major commerce for the Black community. There's talk of tearing the highway down."

"Too little, too late," she muttered.

"Better late than never. It won't help the people of yesterday but might the people of tomorrow."

"But it's already hurt the people of tomorrow. If their grandfather owned a store that was doing well only to lose his business and any generational wealth, they are hurt."

"Not arguing that." She was right, but it was a perfect day and we wouldn't solve the woes of the world on a drive to the park.

I changed the subject by pointing out the sprawling new medical complex, the replacement for Charity Hospital, destroyed in Katrina and even now sitting empty, waiting on promised development. Scars in concrete and metal. The washed-away lives only memory.

She nodded, mostly looking out the window at the unfamiliar streets. It had been a while since I'd driven this way up Canal, and there were a few new places, mostly practical, like gas stations and fast food, that had sprung up. At Galvez, I cut over to Orleans to get to City Park.

"Like Central Park," she asked, when I told her our destination.

"Bigger. One of the biggest urban parks in the country."

I pointed out Dooky Chase's restaurant, one of the few places both Black and white people could meet back in the day, its history with the civil rights movement. Meeting Leah Chase a few times when I'd come in before she left us.

"That's the kind of New Orleans I'd like to know. Any chance we can go there?"

"Maybe. Let me think on it," was all I gave her. It might depend on how long this took. If she left in a few days, no. But if this dragged out for weeks? I'd need to come up with a balance of keeping her safe but not restricted.

City Park covers about thirteen hundred acres. I avoided the more popular areas like the tennis courts and the museum, finding a place on Roosevelt Mall with few cars around. I could park on the road instead of a lot, in case we needed to leave quickly. The area was grass and trees, some sports fields around, but they weren't busy this time of day. It could be busy on a nice weekend, but middle of the week and middle of the day was the perfect middle ground.

I pulled over and parked the car.

"What are the trees?" she asked as we got out.

"Mostly live oak," I said.

"As opposed to dead oak?"

"It's their name, contest it with the biologists."

She nodded and started walking. The temperature had climbed to the upper sixties. I left my jacket in the car. I followed behind her, letting her get a good ten feet in front. She was walking at the pace of someone hurrying through the New York sidewalks. I had gone to college there, as far as I could from the cloying slowness of the South. It had been invigorating and intimidating. I had made friends, some close enough that I still visited them on my trips up there. My closest friend there was Danielle, Danny, both of us from the same place, the languid bayous, living about twenty miles apart as we grew up—the miles and the color line dividing us. But New York had never become home. After graduation, Danny came back here, going to Tulane Law School, and I followed, at loose ends, no real career plans. Drifting, until what I thought would be a fun six-month stint with a private investigator turned into a career. I was my own boss, worked the hours I wanted (well, needed) to work, and could make my own dress code. That, and realizing if I kept flitting around, I'd be in my thirties, sitting in a boring office, making ends meet.

Is that the, if not tragedy of age, the disappointment? Each decision closes off all the other possibilities, dreams bow to reality? A career, a partner, and leave all the other options behind. What if I'd stayed in New York? Who would I be now?

But I hadn't and I was here now. I observed Sarah pause to watch a blue jay, cawing above the bushes. Fussing at a snake? Or just making noise? I slowly caught up to her and decided not to mention the snake.

She pushed up the sleeves of her sweatshirt to compensate for the warm day, then continued walking, still keeping ahead of me.

A car slowly cruised by. I tensed and wondered if I should be carrying my gun, keeping my jacket on. I watched it, not staring but keeping it in my sight, looking for any signs the occupants might reach for a pistol. But no, it looked like two older women, out for a drive and taking it slow.

Old women would be the perfect criminals. No one—including me—would suspect them. Maybe that should be my second career, I thought, as I kept watching them, reminding myself I should be suspicious of everyone. I was now a woman of a certain age, past any possibility of childbearing, hair now more gray than black, enough wrinkles on my face that getting carded was now charming instead of annoying.

The car disappeared and we were left with the cackle of the birds and the wind in the leaves.

Was I really protecting her or were we just putting up a façade? Relying on luck and shuffling the cards? Get her out of New York and maybe the distance will make her safe. Hide her so she can't easily be found and maybe that will do it. Throw in someone like me, maybe I can see something in time. The conundrum of the hunter and the hunted. The hunter chooses his time, his weapon, the place. He rests at home until he's ready. The hunted has to be perpetually prepared, always ready to escape.

There are a lot of hunters out there, ready to hurl a slur, a threat, the invisible knife slashing into a walk down the street, eating ice cream, talking to a friend. Words hurt you because they make you afraid for what might come after the words.

Another car. I hastened to catch up to Sarah, to walk beside her, blocking her from the road. Would they think twice about shooting if another person was in the way?

Loud music, two young women. They didn't look at us. Skipping school? Or did they just look that young because I was so far from being that young?

"You seem nervous," Sarah said.

"My job to be nervous."

"You think I might be killed in this out-of-the-way park?" She bent to pick up an acorn, tossing it in the direction of a squirrel.

"Probable, no, at least that's the theory. Possible...well, can't completely close that door."

"They don't know to look for me here, they knew to look for me there."

"How did they know?"

She looked at me, like it was a stupid and useless question.

"Think about it. You knew you would be there. How did they know?"

She threw up her hands as if exasperated, then said, "I'm always there. I'm the rabbi of the synagogue. They could easily see me coming and going."

"You may have been there often, but you weren't always there. You were outside, right?"

"Yes, outside. We'd finished a Shabbat service and were going home."

"Was there a security guard?"

"Yes, of course. But he was at the door, waiting for a lingering group to leave. Leah and I were walking away, heading for the subway. I dropped my phone, bent down…and they fired."

"I'm sorry, I know this is hard for you—"

"Hard? Hell. May I never know a deeper or darker hell."

"How many people would know you were at the service that day? How many would know what time it was and about how long it would take?"

"Everybody. It's our regular Friday evening service. Does it matter?"

"It might. How they knew might help us find who they are."

"So you think someone in my congregation tipped off the terrorists?"

"No, not at all. But trust and goodwill are tools they use. Did someone pretend to be a friend, ask about you, the synagogue? Maybe a few seemingly innocuous questions over a chess game in the park. Your schedule wasn't a closely guarded secret, was it?"

She walked across the grass to one of the live oaks, running her hands over the rough, gray bark. "No, a lot of what I do is posted on our website. Shabbat is your version of Sunday morning."

"From the police report, they used a rifle, firing from the park across the street. You can't just walk around New York City carrying a rifle."

"No, you can't. We're not a crazy state."

"So, they had to have a plan to bring the rifle, find a place to wait until you appeared, secluded enough to fire and get away. Meaning a car. Possibly an accomplice."

"So?" she looked at the tree, avoiding eye contact.

"Were you wearing anything that would identify you as Jewish?"

"Other than my nose and my hair?"

"Like a clerical collar or something like that?"

"No, I'd taken everything off before I left. The police said it was likely a lone bigot, targeting Jews. I just got unlucky."

"Is that what you think?"

She started walking again, in the grass, farther from the road. "I'm a rabbi, not a terrorism expert. I'm outspoken, at rallies, my picture is around, on our website. Yes, it could be a lone gunman, wanted to kill a prominent Jew. It's easier to think that. And harder." She bent down to pick up another acorn, dropping it as if it had no use in her hands.

"Easier? Harder?" I prompted.

"Easier if it's one person, one vendetta. Stupid and sloppy. Once he gets caught, it's over. Harder...because how can one person, his small hatred, cause so much pain? To me, to Leah's family, her grandmother still alive at ninety-five, a Holocaust survivor. All of us in pain. It should take more than just one person to cause so many people so much hurt." She turned and started walking again. "Does it matter what I think?" she said softly.

"Yes, it does," I said, keeping pace with her, keeping between her and the road. "You lived it more closely than the police did, you know what kind of threats were made against you, against your synagogue, what happened in the past. Gut feelings aren't evidence, but I've known when I was hunted and when I just happened to be in the wrong place."

She stopped and looked at me, then over my shoulder at another passing car.

"About six months ago, the threats changed. We had our share, phone calls, even bomb threats, but these felt more...directed at me."

I glanced at the car. Beat-up old truck, probably working on the facilities here. It kept going.

"Directed at you how?"

"Adding 'dyke' to 'Christ killer.' Mentioned my name."

"Threats to harm you?"

"What other kind of threats are there?" She started walking again, forcing me to catch up.

"True, in general. But there is no Hallmark store for generic threats."

"A lot of the Jewish places—synagogues, community centers, schools—all get the same threats. We compare notes."

"But you said some were specific to you."

"Seemed to be. Being called a faggot or dyke isn't uncommon. If we're one vile thing, we're probably all vile things."

"Bigots in one area usually aren't enlightened in another. Why did you feel the threats changed?"

"Nothing that would be evidence. Just more...as if it was about me."

"Like what?"

"Being married to a woman. I don't hide it, but I'm a Jewish rabbi, not an LGBTQ activist. It's background to my life."

"But something a stranger could know, even with an internet search. Anything else?"

"They sent a video…of what was done to women during the October seventh attack. Said it should have been me."

"Ugly, but they could target any woman that way."

"Said it might cure me of my deviance."

We came to the roundabout, where the leafy mall became one road again. I motioned we should go back the way we came.

"Making the ugly even uglier. And more personal." I walked beside her, nearer the road. "Targeting you would be killing a Jew and a queer. Sending a double message."

"Neither is going to change."

"Anything you can think of that was specific to you?"

"No, just general hatred. I've been a critic of the government of Israel, loud and long. Some people don't like that. I support the people of Israel, their right to exist, to have a land and home of their own, but the leaders can be dumb fucks. Human rights apply to everyone."

"Could it be someone who didn't think you were pro-Israel enough?"

"Not likely. I'm not the only one. And even the crazy ones know it wouldn't do any good. We yell about the meaning of the Torah, not shoot each other."

"Is it possible you weren't the target?"

"If not me, who?" She stopped and stared at me.

"Your wife."

She started walking about, striding away from me. I trotted to catch up.

"No. Just no. Leah was a social worker, counseling cancer patients."

"Sorry, I had to ask."

"No, you didn't. I was standing right where the bullet was supposed to go. A brutal twist of fate."

"Okay, point taken."

"No one would want to hurt her. She was kind and generous and…" Sarah stopped and turned away from me, then walked into the grass to lean against one of the oaks.

I gave her a moment, then joined her, putting a hand on her shoulder.

We survive because we have little choice, but if it had been me, a pivot, and the bullet striking someone I loved—Torbin, Andy, Joanne,

Danny, even, maybe especially, Cordelia, despite the years we'd been apart—how would I live with being here and them gone when it should have been me? Because of one stupid second of fate?

Sarah took a deep breath, then another, straightened, and hastily wiped her eyes. "And it wasn't her getting the death threats," she said. She started walking again.

"I don't suppose anyone signed the notes?"

"No, they're not that stupid."

"Not a personal name, but a group?"

"Oh, yeah, lots of those. 'We Won't Be Replaced' on a lot of them."

"Won't be replaced?"

"'Jews will not replace us.' Like we're trying to take over the world. Hell, we haven't even replaced ourselves. We've still got two million to go just to make up for the Holocaust."

"Police have any idea who they are?"

"Lots. I try not to remember. Only looked enough to see it was ugly. Ask the police."

I nodded. I was going to do that anyway. It was grasping at straws. A never-heard-of name was likely to be small, maybe even one. Known to law enforcement and it was likely to be larger and more organized.

"Anything else you can think of?"

"They fired once. Why not fire again? Why leave me here?" she asked. It was a plea to be out of her pain, the one left behind.

I do security, not grief. We walked quietly back to my car.

I took a long way back, driving along the lake, then down Elysian Fields to get to the river side of the city. I filled space with pointing out what we were passing. Nothing major—this wasn't what the tourists saw, not until we got back below Claiborne, the older section of town. She was either good at being polite or was mildly interested.

I bit the bullet and took Elysian Fields all the way to the river, turned onto Decatur for the slow crawl through the French Quarter to Canal Street and her hotel. As much as possible, I only come to this part of town on foot. It's a zoo with the cages open, traffic slower than cold molasses, mule-driven carts, tourists ambling in the middle of the road. I pointed out the usual places, Café du Monde, Jackson Square. Sarah seemed fascinated and appalled at the density of people and history.

"I do come here," I said, as we halted at another stoplight, "but mostly on the end we entered, not this one."

"What's the difference?" she asked.

"The lower Quarter is more residential, and it's below the lavender line—the dividing line between the straight part and the gay part. It's not this tourist frenzy."

She nodded. "Am I going to be able to move soon? It seems it would be easier for you, not having to go through this to get to me. And I'd prefer someplace quieter."

"Let me talk to Joanne and see what she thinks," I said, letting my coward flag fly. Then to placate her, "We're going to move you in a few days anyway. You're safer not staying put."

She nodded.

I turned onto Canal.

"Let me park the car. Don't get out until the last minute," I told her.

"Why don't you drop me off in front? It's not that far to the elevator."

"Better if I check things out." We were stopped at another red light. Then the light changed, but we were still stuck since three cars too many tried to get through the intersection and were now blocking it.

"And what?" she said over the honking. "What will you do if someone pulls a gun and shoots me? Hotel security will call the police."

"I'll have done what I could do to prevent it from happening."

For an answer, she opened the door and got out, knowing I couldn't follow. She gave me an insouciant wave as she ducked around a tour van. I watched as she weaved through the crowded sidewalk, inching forward when I was able, to keep her in view.

The intersection finally cleared and I caught up as she entered the hotel.

I considered parking anyway and marching up to her room. But the garage turn came and went and I kept going. She was an adult and could make her own decisions. This was a small battle. In the crowded lobby, it was unlikely anyone would pull a gun—there were security cameras everywhere, plus security staff. They would be caught. Given they had run without taking the time to fire again, it seemed they didn't want to be martyrs for the cause.

I glanced at my watch; it was creeping onto five. Time to go home.

The slow traffic reached Rampart, where I could turn and head downtown. Still slow, but not as bad. I turned left into Tremé and the last few blocks to my house.

CHAPTER FOUR

Home sweet home. I'd gotten here enough before five for there to still be parking on my street. When I first moved to Tremé, it was considered a bad part of town—aka more Black people than white. It had become a desirable neighborhood, close to most everything, from the French Quarter to the Superdome. People used it as their free parking lot, making it harder to find spaces. I was lucky to have my cousin Torbin and his partner Andy down the block. We could connive on "stupid" parking, using our various cars to take more space than needed so we could leave half a car length from a driveway, then another half a length between two of our cars, so with a little car moving, a space opened up.

I considered putting my feet up and doing mindless hate-watch house buyers on television, but decided to do my duty instead.

I dialed Joanne.

She answered on the first ring. Either she was busy and in a hurry or she wanted to talk to me.

"She still alive?" was her greeting.

"As far as I know." I told her about Sarah abandoning me in traffic to go to her hotel alone.

"You sure she went in?" Joanne questioned.

"I saw her go through the front door. No idea what she did after that. My bet would be on her going to her room to get away from the hordes of people. I'll call her later."

"She gets to make her own decisions," Joanne said. "You can only do so much." She was more forgiving than I expected. Or maybe, little as it was, her time with Sarah had given her an idea of how assertive she could be.

"True dat. But I was calling to ask if you know anything more about who might have attacked her."

Joanne didn't answer, instead talking to someone in the background. She was still at work.

A minute later she came back to me. "Let's meet. I want to get out of here. Why don't you come over to our place? Danny is joining me."

"No Elly?" Elly was Danny's wife. They had gotten married as soon as it was legal. Louisiana, as usual, dragged its feet on equal rights, so they'd gone to New York.

"She's at a work conference. Cordelia had to go, so roped Elly into it. Something about accreditation for health centers."

"Why I went into business for myself."

"Meet in an hour?"

"Sure, sounds good."

She hung up.

That was interesting. In our small, queer world of New Orleans, we did a delicate dance around who got invited to what. Cordelia and Alex, Joanne's wife, had been friends since high school. Since our breakup, and Cordelia being with a new main squeeze, it was an unspoken rule not to invite us all to the same things. Cordelia and Torbin were also good friends, so our social interactions sometimes resembled a farce with people ducking in and out of doors to avoid each other. If Joanne was inviting me over, it meant that Cordelia's girlfriend was on her own while Cordelia was out of town.

It wouldn't take me an hour to get there, so I called Sarah. She didn't answer.

I called again.

It took four rings, but she answered this time. "I don't carry the phone into the bathroom. Can I at least shit in peace?"

"Right. Just checking on you to make sure you got back to your room."

"And if I didn't? What then?"

"I call every legal authority in town to search for you."

"So, I need to answer the phone whenever you call."

"It would be helpful."

"When can I move?"

"I'm working on it. Talking to Joanne later today."

"You'll call me tomorrow and let me know?"

"I'll talk to you if you answer the phone. Do you have enough food to get you through? Should I bring more tomorrow?" She was persistent, and I wanted to change the subject.

"Am I allowed another field trip? Maybe I can come along to pick my own food out?"

"Let me see if I can figure out the logistics," I said.

"When will you come by?"

Persistent, indeed. "How about around lunchtime? We can go somewhere and then figure it out."

"Okay, I'll see you at twelve noon tomorrow." She hung up.

I sighed. Sarah was not going to be easy to handle. She knew what she wanted and would be direct and forceful about getting it. She wasn't going to just quietly do what I suggested. I needed to be a few more steps ahead of her than I was now.

I went upstairs and put on a comfortable pair of jeans, a T-shirt, and a light jean jacket. It was nice enough that being outside was possible and a jacket might be handy.

I sighed again as I locked my door, knowing I was giving up my good parking spot and Friday night would not be kind. But I was looking forward to the evening. Petty, perhaps, but I was happy I was the included one this time.

Joanne and Alex lived in Mid-City, a few blocks this side of Carrollton. The house was a double when they first bought it, and they rented out one side. But about a decade ago they decided they no longer needed the income and no longer wanted the hassle of being landlords, so converted it into a single, combining the two kitchens into one I envied. Over the years they'd changed the paint color, first from the original sage to a yellow that was Alex's choice. Now it was a blue gray, since Joanne got to choose the paint colors when it was redone a few years ago.

I was able to park in front since they had off street parking. Their cars were there, but Danny hadn't arrived yet.

It was a beautiful evening, perfect to linger on their back deck. I felt sorry for Sarah, stuck in the hotel room. Would it be possible to bring her along? Or too complicated, given the logistics and intermingling a client with my personal life?

Alex opened the door before I knocked. She enveloped me in a big hug.

"Door staying open," she said as she let go, pointing to the just arriving car. Danny.

I edged past her to get out of Danny's way. She joined us at the doorway, hugging Alex despite the six-pack of Abita she was carrying.

"Was I supposed to bring something?" I asked, thinking I shouldn't have asked, just brought something anyway.

"I've had this for a while, it needs to be drunk," Danny said, giving me a one-hand hug.

The three of us headed back to the kitchen to join Joanne.

They now had an eight-burner stove, which I would have been tempted to take home except there was no way I could pick it up. Or fit it in my car. Or my house.

She was rolling out dough on the kitchen island. Alex had gotten into bread making during the worst of the pandemic, and Joanne had discovered that rolling and kneading dough was good stress relief.

She handed me a second rolling pin and motioned to a ball of dough. The island was big enough for us both to work together.

"Can we talk about what I need to talk to you about, or should we wait?" I said softly to Joanne while Alex and Danny were chatting and putting the beer in the refrigerator.

"We can talk. Danny knows and Alex knows some of what's going on from me talking about my day."

I caught up, getting my dough as big as hers was. No, I'm not a competitive jerk. Just efficient.

"She's pushing to move."

"The heart of the French Quarter? People pay good money to be there."

"Not people like her. The tourist zoo isn't her happy place."

"She and I can agree on that."

"What do you suggest?"

"What's the best balance between keeping her secure and happy?"

"Nowhere here, I suspect. Maybe the lower Quarter, the quieter places. Still used to people in and out, so a new person is the usual. Plus, easier for me to get there and back."

"A good a plan as any," Joanne said, giving her dough an extra push.

I did the same, making mine a half an inch bigger than hers.

"What do the police know about who attacked her? Any more info?"

"New York, as I was reminded several times, has a much lower per capita murder rate than New Orleans, and this happening on their patch has them stressed. They're under pressure to solve it, but to be fair, it might be hard," Joanne explained.

"Why? Someone must have seen something. Presumably you can't pull a gun in the densest city in the country without someone noticing?"

"No one has come forward. They're pounding the pavement, but if they've found anything, they haven't told me. Most likely the shooter is from the shadowy network of hate groups, so his—or her—name could have been the one picked to do this, not connection to her. Usually murder is something stupid, like a drunken bar fight, or there's some connection to the victim, love, money. Without that connection, it's hard to find a murderer."

"Sarah said she got a lot of hate mail. Anything in that?" I asked.

"Always possible."

"For her security, it would be helpful to know which is more likely, a lone hater, a small outlier group, or one of the larger, more organized ones," I said, dusting flour off my hands.

"I wish we knew. A lone gunman is possible, but given the circumstances, not likely. This wasn't a country road with no one about."

"Yeah, my thoughts as well. Likely a car, likely driven by another person."

"I don't remember the make offhand, but the gun was a decent hunting or sniper rifle. Not cheap and not easy to get in NYC."

"So likely bought out of state and brought there."

"Which required planning and organization," Joanne said. "Not something impulsive."

"Sounds right. A number of groups have either sent threatening notes to her synagogue or made threats online. Do the cops there have a list?"

"Yeah, I can send it to you tomorrow."

"Any the most probable?"

"Not sure. I'll call and see if I can get you any more info."

Joanne gave her dough one last roll, then put it on the pizza peel. She brushed it with olive oil. Alex joined us with several bowls of various toppings.

"Y'all are being serious over here," she said.

Joanne picked up a container of red sauce that looked homemade—or they cheated and poured it out of the jar into a container. Not likely, but the competitive jerk in me didn't like to think I'd been lazing with store bought.

"Talking with Micky about the bodyguard case I handed her," Joanne said.

"Nope," Alex said, when I reached for the spoon Joanne just finished with. "One red, one white. Yours is fig and goat gouda."

"Not a bodyguard," I replied. "Security, helping keep her safe while she's here." I reached for the bowl with the cut figs and spread them over the dough, then the cheese and a drizzle of olive oil.

Joanne added pepperoni, olives, and mushrooms to hers, as well as a pile of mozzarella.

"She's not a fan of the hordes in the big French Quarter hotel she's in now," Joanne said as she lifted the peel. Alex opened the oven door, and with a practiced slide, Joanne got hers on the stone. "We're discussing where to move her next."

"Is that a good idea?" Danny joined the conversation, handing both me and Joanne a cold beer.

"We shouldn't have her stay in any one place for too long," Joanne said.

"Does she get a say in this?" Alex asked.

"Well, sort of," I answered. "She doesn't know the city or police work or security protocols. Like you seeing a doctor. You get a choice, but they have expert advice."

"But they aren't always right," Alex said.

"We aren't always either," Joanne admitted, "we just do the best we can with what we know."

"Is there any reason she has to be in the hotel and not here, to talk about this?" Alex asked.

Joanne, Danny and I looked at her. Alex had a point; this was Sarah's life we were discussing, not ours.

"Too risky," Danny said first. "If anyone is tracking her, they could follow her here."

"And easier for them to do something in a quiet neighborhood than a large hotel. Danny is right, too risky," Joanne said.

"And we're off duty," I added. "This is personal time, not work time." Just talking about work in our personal time.

"Got it," Alex said, "Still, it has to be miserable being stuck in a generic hotel room alone and going through what she's going through."

Joanne and Danny were both in law enforcement. I was, too, in a different way, but we all looked at it through the lens of solving the case, not taking care of the people involved.

I took a sip of my beer. Alex was right in more ways than I cared to admit. If this were me, I'd much prefer leaving the hotel, joining a group of friends, even as a stranger, having people to talk to instead of walls to stare at. Still, as Joanne said, we make the best decision we can. She was likely safer in a large hotel, behind an anonymous locked door, than taking the chance to leave, get in my car, drive to this quiet house, few people out on the street to notice anyone watching. Safer physically, at least.

"That smells good," Danny said, letting the pizza aromas help her change the subject.

"I know I'm outvoted," Alex said, "but I'm willing to take the risk to let her come here. Even if she can't be around her people, she should be around people."

"We'll consider it," Joanne said, opening the oven. Not quite as deftly, she managed to get the now baked pizza on the peel and out of the oven. She slid it on a cutting board, then put mine on the peel and into the oven.

"What Joanne said," I echoed. "We can chew over the pros and cons. Also, she should have a choice in this. She may not want to be around strangers."

"True," Alex said, taking down plates as Joanne was cutting the pizza. "It all should be her choice."

I nodded and took another sip. So much of this was not her choice, and so much of the next few weeks would not be her choice. Maybe I needed to give her what choices I could.

After the second pizza was done, we debated whether to eat inside or outside, finally deciding on inside since their dining table was open to the kitchen and, Danny pointed out, it was still warm enough for bugs.

I was content to let the conversation drift away from Sarah, even though we hadn't decided on moving her. We compared pothole size in our various neighborhoods, always a lively topic of conversation in New Orleans. No one wants to lose an axle if you can avoid it. Then Danny got a call from Elly, which she put on speakerphone so we could tell her all about our homemade pizza and us sitting around having a good time while she was stuck in a suburban hotel with only a few food places in walking distance.

She gave us enough time to enjoy ourselves but not enough time to truly gloat before saying, "Just wanted to check in. Cordelia and I are meeting for dinner in a bit; there's a sushi place the locals recommended not too far from here," then adding, "Oh, that's her at the door now." Elly narrated opening the door and letting her in, then we all chorused a hello. I added mine in the midst of the decibels. I didn't want to pretend I wasn't here, but I didn't want to be noticed, either. A little more chat, then they were gone.

We had another round of pizza and beer, enjoying the company, letting the conversation wander until we moved to coffee and bread pudding for dessert. I had a small slice, already full from the pizza. I don't have the bread absorption rate I did when I was twenty.

I helped Joanne carry some of the plates back to the kitchen.

"So, what do I do about Sarah?" I asked as she stacked them in the dishwasher.

"Let her stay until her check-out date. I think that's Monday," she said.

I looked at the calendar on my phone where I'd noted it down. "Yes, that's right."

"That'll give you time to arrange for the next place."

"Which should be?"

"Nothing wrong with your suggestion about the lower end of the Quarter."

"Okay, I'll avoid the BnBs. Not a good idea to get chummy with the hosts. I think there are smaller hotels on Esplanade."

"Sounds good."

"Let's hope it sounds good to her. How do you feel about what Alex said? To let her get out more, even join us sometimes?"

"Let me think about that. For her mental health, it might help to not be so isolated. But we have to worry about a lot more than her mental health."

Alex and Danny brought the final dishes, Joanne gave us each a hefty serving of the bread pudding to take home, and we said our good-byes.

It was a little after ten when I started my car.

I glanced at my phone. Sarah had texted me. I hadn't checked it the entire time I was there, leaving it in my jacket pocket hanging by the front door.

I opened my phone.

Letting you know I'm still alive. Finished the food you left. Will do room service for breakfast. Can we go somewhere for lunch tomorrow? I need to stop staring at these walls.

I texted back, *We can go out for lunch. Will move you soon, at your original checkout day. We can talk more tomorrow.*

If she was already asleep, she'd see it in the morning.

I pulled out and traveled a block before hearing the chime of a text. I pulled over again.

Thank you. I'll see you tomorrow. Sarah.

She was lonely, and Alex was right.

I didn't respond. We'd said what needed to be said. I'd have to consider how to balance what she wanted, what she needed, and how to keep her safe.

And what did safe even mean? Maybe she was in no danger here. Maybe.

CHAPTER FIVE

I texted Sarah after I had enough coffee to be coherent. *Check the maps and what to eat around here. See if anything appeals. Not promising, but I'll see what I can do*. It was Saturday, but no weekends off from bodyguarding.

I got in two more sips of coffee before she replied, *Don't know the town. Any suggestions?*

Pick up po-boys and eat on the lakefront? I texted back. I suspected she'd nix that, but it would give me some idea of what she didn't want to do.

I took another big slug of coffee.

My foggy brain remembered that I had agreed to meet Paulette this morning. I regretted my curiosity and wished I'd blown her off. Still, I could charge her my "not friend or family and weekend work" rate and use the money for something that would help me forget the not-so-great high school years.

Sarah texted back. *I don't suppose there are kosher po-boys.*

Right suppose, I responded.

I poured the rest of the big pot of coffee in a travel mug. I needed to be at my office and settled before Paulette arrived.

I heard another *ching* of a text as I unlocked my car. It could wait until I got to my office. I felt sorry for Sarah, but I couldn't be available to her for every minute.

When I got there, I scanned the street but didn't see any cars that looked unfamiliar. I was a good forty-five minutes early for our appointment but still wanted to be careful. Was that bleeding off from my constant scrutiny with Sarah? Normal paranoia? Or a gut feeling telling me to be wary of Paulette? Maybe she had a legitimate concern that a PI could help with and maybe she felt knowing me—as slightly as we did—made it easier. Or maybe she was playing the same games she played in high school, thinking winning meant someone else had to lose.

I climbed the two flights to my third-floor office, glad that I could still do them at a fast clip even as my knees creaked a bit more. Although there were days I had to convince myself it was good for me, and days I used the stairs to justify the fried oysters.

I sat at my desk, took a long sip of my coffee, then checked Sarah's text.

I'll look at the maps, see what I can eat. Will get back to you.

At least I didn't have to run through every eating option in this city—there are a lot of them—to give her more things to reject.

I opened my computer. Time to do a little bit of searching and find out what Paulette had been up to since high school.

It always amazes me the digital trail people leave without thinking about it. My rule is if I don't want the whole world to know, I don't post it online. I have a business webpage and social media presence, of course. Those are strictly for work, the kind of cases I work on— missing people, security, records review, licenses, etc. I have a few personal ones, but mostly for me to see what my friends are up to. I'll post a picture now and then, a river shot, flowers in bloom, occasional food—this is New Orleans, and our food is worthy. I don't post pictures of my house or myself. Sometimes it happens. I'm in a group shot and they post it. But my goal is to keep myself tucked away and as anonymous as possible.

Unlike Paulette. She had several sites, some for her businesses and some personal, with a lot of overlap. She mentioned her businesses on her personal page, mostly to cross-promote but sometimes to complain about work on her personal page, like the paperwork, calling people at insurance companies idiots, about clients that didn't know how to use a phone.

Her main business was Jeffers Medical and Wellness Clinic. It was in Metairie, a suburb in Jefferson Parish. I had to dig on their website, but it was for profit, mostly doing basic medical services, including pain management and physical therapy. She also did what she called Wellness Coaching. Oh, and healthy living classes on the side that seemed to be mostly selling expensive juicers and packages of healthy ingredients to put in them. If you could get ten of your friends to come, she'd go to your house to demonstrate. And presumably sell, sell, sell!

"Stay true to your ethics, Paulette," I muttered as I read more.

Maybe legit, but on the shady side of the street. She co-owned the clinic with two of the doctors there. They had a staff of eight, not including the three owners. A quick look at staff profiles showed only one of them had been there longer than three years.

Being suspicious is a job hazard, but this reeked of making money, not health and wellness.

In high school, it mattered to Paulette that she looked good, and looking good to her meant expensive. Her parents had money, a big house in Old Metairie, new cars every few years, including for their high school kids. She'd gotten used to having things, and nothing had changed.

I looked up her home address. Yep, a posh gated community out in Kenner, the suburb beyond the suburb of Metairie. Her house was big, with a pool and what looked like the car I'd seen in the street. Nice, but not as upscale as the home she'd grown up in. I'd been there a few times, some important planning for a high school thing—oh, yes, the class pep rally. I was asked along because I was one of the better writers and they wanted something funny. Like jokes about how queer the opposing quarterback was.

It was a large French provincial, an expansive patio in back, a pool with a rock waterfall and hot tub. A maid to serve her high school friends.

I managed to come up with a skit that mocked the other team for eating fast food in New Orleans, not knowing how to say Tchoupitoulas, and being unable to catch Mardi Gras beads, let alone footballs. Avoiding any references to limp-wristed quarterbacks.

I never went back. True, I wasn't invited. I'd been useful and I wasn't anymore.

That was the old money part of the suburbs. Paulette lived in the new money part now.

I glanced at my watch and closed my computer. She would be here in a few minutes if she was on time. I knew enough to know what I might be getting into. And enough to avoid getting into more than I wanted. If it wasn't straightforward and legit, I'd turn her down.

She was fifteen minutes late. Late enough to let me know she was deliberately late, not just caught in traffic. Late enough to let me know she was still more important than I was.

She texted when she parked, asking which way in. There were two doors in front, the big double door to the coffee shop and, a few yards away, a single door that led into a hallway to the stairs. I had a tasteful but noticeable brass plate next to the smaller door.

I told her I'd meet her downstairs.

Two can play this game.

I headed down the stairs, definitely not hurrying.

I opened the door, waved her in with "this way," and led her down the hall to the stairs. I took them at my usual pace. Well, maybe a little faster.

When I got to my door, I looked down to see her just rounding the second-floor landing.

She stopped, caught a breath, and said, "You need something more accessible. I don't think this conforms to the Disability Act."

"Old building. Grandfathered in. I can meet clients elsewhere; they don't have to come here."

After she came up the last flight and into my office, I motioned her to the chair in front of my desk.

She sat down, still catching her breath. "That's a workout."

I asked her if she'd like coffee, tea, or water. Her big house must be one level.

"Coffee," she said, as if ordering it.

As was my habit, I'd made a pot once I got here, to sip through the morning. I poured her a cup. "Black okay? I don't have milk or sugar."

"I suppose; I prefer with both. Many of your clients might as well," she said.

"As I said, I don't always see clients here. No point having milk go bad. There's the coffee shop downstairs if you'd prefer something else. I can wait while you get it."

I put the cup in front of her, away from anything it might spill on, since I didn't put that past her. I'd poured a cup for myself as well. I took a sip and waited. She ignored her coffee.

Look at my watch? Sigh? I took the high road and did neither. "You indicated you might want to work with a private investigator," I prompted.

"Yes," she said. "I need to hire you to help with a bit of a mess. Ex problems. I'd like you to start as soon as possible."

I noticed the screen on my phone with a message. The sound was off. Sarah. I'd have to check it later.

"I have to know more about what you want done before I'd consider taking the case."

"From the looks of this, you can use all the work you can get. I thought your office would be nicer."

"Looks can be deceiving," I said. "I own the building, and the rent from the other two floors is a good living." Not giving her a chance to respond, I continued, "Why do you want to hire a PI?"

She started to say something, but thought better of it. Or couldn't come up with the words to do justice to her annoyance. "I was in a relationship. He seemed nice, a real gentleman. A bit younger than me." She giggled there. "I brought him into my business, teaching him a lot of it. I paid him, of course, but over time he didn't think he was paid enough."

"Was he?"

"Does that matter?" Then she added, "Yes, of course. He learned everything from me, had no experience, no skills when he started. I paid him what he was worth. But he started to think since we were together, he should get the same I got. Like it was his business as much as it was mine."

"What kind of business is this?" I asked like I hadn't just looked it up.

"Health care, an accessible clinic for people who don't like to wait in line with all the people who think they can just show up and not pay."

"I didn't know you had a medical background."

"I don't, but I have a business background. BA in business from LSU. You can't do medicine unless you can run a business."

"Isn't that a rather specialized area?"

"Yeah, one I'm good at. I started working in a doctor's office, the usual crap, answering phones, paperwork. But I'm smart and I learned how it works, all the billing, the insurance, all that stuff."

"How long have you been doing this?"

"About eight years. It was hard at first, struggling to get clients, then we brought on the right doctors, ones who could pull in the right patients. We've been doing quite well in the last few years. Just bought a new Lexus and paid for it in cash." She smiled, proud.

"When did your boyfriend start?"

"About three years ago. He applied for a job. It was work at first, but he was cute and flirted with me nonstop."

"What job did he apply for?"

"Office maintenance. My partners didn't think we needed someone full-time, but it was an old building, from the 1990s, and needed work. They weren't the ones who had to deal with overflowing toilets."

"So, your relationship began with him as an employee?"

"Well, sort of. There were sparks in that first interview." Again, the giggle. It had been annoying when she was in high school and girls were expected to giggle. As a middle-aged woman, it needed to be retired.

"What were his qualifications?" I asked. Not really relevant, but I wanted to see what she would say—or when she might tire of talking and realize she was telling me things I didn't need to know.

"Well, how qualified do you need to be to plunge a toilet? He said he did some construction work. He was young and had muscles, could lift things. I didn't have time to interview dozens of people."

"You said you trained him?"

"Well, after we got together, I needed help and he was interested. About a year after he started, I promoted him to office manager."

"What were his duties?"

"Doing what I told him to do. I mean, mostly. Keeping the billing straight, making sure the other office staff stayed in their lane. I oversaw everything."

"I gather you are no longer in a romantic relationship with him?"

"He turned out to be a cheating dog." She stamped her foot. Yep, actually stamped her foot. Call me suspicious, but it felt rehearsed.

"You broke up with him over the cheating? It sounds like you solved your problem."

"Well, yes, we broke up and I fired him. But he wanted to cause problems. Claiming I couldn't do that, telling me I needed to give him half the business or else he'd...um, he'd sue or something like that."

Yep, suspicious. My guess was he threatened to out all the ways she'd cut corners, maybe even in ways law enforcement would be interested in. "I'm not a lawyer. I can't help you with lawsuits."

"I don't need that. He's disappeared. I can't contact him. He took a lot of the paperwork from the office, and he'll only give it back if I agree to his terms."

"You didn't have backups?"

"No, we didn't...that was his job, and he took the backups he made."

Suspicious. No, we only had one copy of the crooked books. "Can't you recreate it?"

"Not easily. He stole this stuff but, well, I just want it back, not to get him in trouble. Which is why I don't want to go to the police."

"They don't charge victims of crime. I cost money," I pointed out.

She sighed. "I know, but I don't want to go that route. Once I have the stuff back, I can just put it behind me. It's not good for our business to have police involved. Plus, it'll be embarrassing to me—our relationship and all that. You know how it is, some hot guy smiles at you and you think he means it and do something stupid."

No, I didn't, but if she hadn't figured that out, I wasn't going to tell her.

"To be clear, what you want to hire me for is to locate him and try to convince him to return everything he took?"

"It's my property. You can retrieve it, right? That's what I need. Not just finding him, but getting everything back."

I do a lot of missing person cases, so finding him was well within my professional scope. If she was telling the truth, the property was hers and she had a right to it. I was pretty sure I could find him. He didn't seem like the kind of guy with the skills to stay hidden. Or the resources. But I wasn't going to get into a fight with a well-muscled younger man to wrestle anything away from him.

"I need to get what I want, otherwise I'm not paying for it," she said. "I pay for results."

We were back in high school; she was the popular girl who was accustomed to the less popular girls doing her bidding.

"Good luck in finding a private investigator who works that way." We weren't in high school anymore. "What you buy—from me or anyone else—is our time and expertise. No one can afford to put hours and days into something only to make nothing. Feel free to find someone else, they'll tell you the same thing."

Her mouth was open, shocked from being spoken to like she was just a client, not the high school cheerleader. She finally closed it, then opened it again to say, "But that can't be right. I can't spend this kind of money to get nothing."

"Maybe he found another well-to-do woman who took him to Australia. Maybe he destroyed everything and is on the West Coast by now. There are too many variables for me—or any reputable professional—to promise a result."

"No, he's around here, I know it. He DMs me every few days, demanding the money."

"Can you suggest he meet you to talk?"

She fidgeted, then said, "I have. He refuses. Says he'll only meet when the money is in the bank. He'll turn over the materials then. After that, he doesn't answer. Only a few days later, with another demand and that time is running out."

"Time is running out? How?"

"Um, he's not going to wait forever. He's, um, going to destroy everything if I don't get him the money soon."

She's not as good as she thinks she is. Yeah, I'm suspicious and tend to look under rocks, but a naïve fifteen-year-old could see through this. "I don't take cases when I'm being lied to. There are a lot of regulations around medical services. At best, you've treated some of them with a wink and a nod, at worst, committed fraud and he has the evidence. He's threatening to turn it over to the cops. You want to get it back before he does."

She stared at me, her face flushed, maybe from her lies being so easy to see through or maybe because she didn't want anyone to know, and now I did. The old high school friend who was never really a friend.

"No, no, it's not like that. It's all legal—I mean, it will be—but there are a few things that are in process and could look bad if someone saw them before they were fixed."

My phone vibrated. Sarah.

"Nothing illegal, I promise," she continued, as if she said enough words she could explain it away. "I just need to get them back. Or… even destroyed. Just so he can't use them against me. If you could find him…then maybe we—I and my partners—could take care of it."

Did I need this case? No…but money is always welcome, and finding a bumbling boyfriend shouldn't be hard. She was ostensibly hiring me to find a disgruntled employee who had stolen company property. Plus, that devil curiosity. If I got a chance, it would be interesting to see how crooked her books were. I don't break the law for clients.

"Okay, I'll take on finding your ex. Once I've done that, I can report back and you can decide what steps to take next."

"You'll take it?" She clapped her hands together as if she was really happy. The same gestures she made back in high school. Maybe more people were fooled by them back then. "I do get the friends discount, right?"

I told her she did. She had no way of knowing what I charge my real friends—mostly nothing. She got the "annoying one-time case" rate. I printed off a standard contract and told her two days' expenses up front. Once I received that, I would start on her case.

"But you trust me, right? You can get started now and I'll get it to you soon."

"I can't start today. I have other clients and cases. That will give you time to get me the money."

She fidgeted, then dug in her purse. "You take credit cards, right?"

I did, and she handed me a gold card. For the business, not her personal card.

Once that was done, I handed her the contract.

"What can you tell me about him?"

"Well, like what?"

"As an employee he would have had to give you his name, address, Social Security number. Birth date. The more information I have, the easier it will be to find him. Easier means less time and less money."

"I don't have most of that with me."

"Name?"

"Elmer Stumbolt."

"What else?"

"Like what?"

"How old is he?"

Again, the telltale shifting of weight. "In his thirties."

Much younger than she was.

"Can you send me a copy of his employee file?" I asked. I didn't have time to drag every detail out of her.

"You're going to start today?"

I thought about telling her the truth—first, I had already started on it by meeting with her, and I wasn't going to waste time searching for what would be in his work file. But I lied. "Yes, I will start today. Please send me the file as soon as you can."

With that, we said good-bye.

The faint smell of perfume lingered, the same one she wore in high school. I was beginning to suspect that was when she was most powerful and popular. Sad when nothing in life was as good as it was when you were seventeen.

I got roach spray and gave a good pump to any places bugs might use to invade. That got rid of the perfume aroma.

I picked up my phone to read Sarah's texts. First was a complaint about nothing to eat in this town. I shook my head. There's plenty to eat in New Orleans. Besides the usual stuff (Creole, Cajun, seafood, gumbo, etouffee, po-boys, etc.), but also Vietnamese to Mexican to Caribbean to hamburgers, we do it all pretty well.

Next text was suggesting a chain restaurant out in Metairie.

That was a hard no from me. The last time I ate at a chain restaurant was when I evacuated after Hurricane Ida, when the power grid would take weeks to restore. I stopped in some place in Arkansas for gas and ate a McBurger Thing. And only because it met what I needed—a gas station, close to the freeway, and the best option available.

Joanne texted me to say she'd just sent an email with the files about the groups that sent threats to Sarah's synagogue. I had another hour before I needed to leave.

I clicked open the file. And spent the next hour in a sewer. Almost every ugly word—some I didn't even know—for Jewish people, Jewish women, women in general, and everyone in the queer community, like we were transgender, sex-crazed gay men, ugly shapeless lesbians, all rolled into one. Many of the notes were anonymous. About ten different groups were proud enough of their handiwork to put their name on, and some even had letterhead. A lot of both denying the Holocaust and claiming it was a good idea—in the same sentence: "It didn't happen, but it should have."

I sat back, wondering how anyone could have that much time and hate to spend their life doing this. Did they actually believe the unbelievable conspiracy theories, from how Jews controlled everything to how they had to grow their hair long to conceal the horns? All garbage designed to turn people into demons, and ones that deserved to be killed.

There are people I don't like—some I hate even. I don't want to kill them; I just want them to leave us alone. Read a little bit more of the Bible they claim to revere, like "love thy neighbor," "turn the other cheek," and "it's harder for a rich man to get to heaven than a camel to pass through the eye of a needle."

There was an additional report with details of what was known about the hate groups.

Another text from Sarah to say she was getting hungry and could I come a little earlier?

Not a bad idea. The report was too long to read in the time I had, and it would keep me from the other task I could do, digging into things I didn't need to know—and probably didn't want to know—about Paulette. I would work on her case when she sent Elmer's file.

I went to the window to check the street. Suspicious about everything, enough to wonder if Paulette was hanging around to see what I did—if I stayed here and ostensibly worked on her case, or went off gallivanting. The street was empty, the usual cars with a few others clustered by the coffee shop, with the fanciest being a newer Honda Accord.

I texted Sarah back and said I would be there in about half an hour. It would get me there not much earlier than the original meeting time, but it's the thought that counts, right?

I got in my car and got another text from Sarah. I checked it just in case she'd changed her mind. Nope. It was to inform me that she'd be waiting out front, so I didn't need to park. I debated texting back and telling her to wait in the room but had no way to compel her. Better I get there sooner, so she wouldn't be waiting too long.

That is what I did, taking the fastest route.

I stopped in front of the hotel, partly in the taxi stand. I scanned the sidewalk for Sarah. Didn't see her. I picked up my phone to text her, resigned I'd have to go around the block if she wasn't there in two seconds.

I'd just hit send on the text and spied a doorman heading my way to tell me to move on when she appeared. She hurried enough to beat the doorman. Seeing that I was about to move, he gave an annoyed wave. I gave a cheery one in return.

"Can we go to that place I suggested? At least I've been there before and know there is stuff I can eat."

I wavered. It would be a solution, although not one I could admit to in polite company.

I edged into the traffic on Canal. "Do you like Vietnamese?" I asked as I cut off a too big truck trying to move forward in a too small space.

"This place has ethnic food?"

"Yes, not the variety of NYC, but we have some that can hold its own."

"I'm skeptical, but willing to try."

"Okay, we're going to a part of the city tourists don't see."

I turned onto Claiborne, and from there to I-10 out to New Orleans East. It's on the other side of the Industrial Canal, along the lake. It took a long time for it to recover after Katrina, and in the further reaches is the hub of the Vietnamese community.

"Where are we going?" Sarah asked as we were driving over the Industrial Canal. Because it's the interstate, it's high enough for ships to go under so traffic won't be stopped.

I started to say my usual throwaway line, "Where we bury the bodies," but caught myself in time. Not appropriate in my present company.

"Out to an area where there's a large Vietnamese community. There are several good restaurants there." I didn't add that it was far enough out in the boonies to be an unlikely place for anyone to see us. We'd have a stretch on the interstate, then surface roads for me to see anyone following.

A burgundy sedan had been behind me when I entered the freeway, and it was still only slightly behind me in the mix of traffic. I was keeping an eye on it, but too soon to worry. This was the interstate and they could just be going east.

Just to be sure, I pulled into the right lane and slowed enough to let them pass.

They pulled behind me.

Then a black "small budget, smaller dick" car shot past both of us, one of those pseudo sports cars with an automatic transmission. "Go faster or it will disappear into nothingness," I muttered.

Once it had sped by, the burgundy car pulled back into the center lane and passed me.

I'm not out here often, so had to guess which exit to take. I went for Crowder and took it to Chef Menteur. It's a stretch of road that has never been prosperous as long as I've lived here. In a long-ago era, it was the highway from east to west, before the interstates. It stepped on the small dots of precarious land as it headed east to cross the lakes and rivers that separated Louisiana from Mississippi. Now it's a strip of necessary businesses, gas stations, used tire shops, and nail salons, many run down and tired. A few hotels of the kind most people don't spend the night in.

"You sure you know where you're going?" Sarah asked.

"No, we're completely lost," I said, with as much side-eye as I dared while driving.

I tried to recall the last time I'd been out here. I remembered the first time, back in high school, an adventure with Ned, Brian, and Misty, the four of us acting like two straight couples instead of two queer ones. Even in a place like this where no one knew us or was likely to see us again. I sat with Ned, and Misty with Brian. Ned suggested it—he was adventurous and wanted to sample Vietnamese fare. He and I liked the food, Brian and Misty, more hamburger and fries types, did not. The two of us promised we'd come back, but like so many promises made when the days seem to stretch forever, it got lost.

I also remembered the last time. It had been a whim, a weeknight, the refrigerator was not promising, so we—Cordelia and I—drove out here. It was a quiet night; the food was good. We didn't have to pretend we were straight.

The past is gone. Or we should be able to banish the past we wanted gone.

I checked my rearview mirror. It's possible there was a double tail, the burgundy car and a second one. I gunned my car to just make it through a yellowish-red light. Another car followed me, through the very reddish light. A dark blue truck.

I turned off Chef at the next light. The truck kept going. So many cars run red lights, I always pause a half second at the green to be safe.

"We're going the long way," I said to Sarah as the only explanation.

"You think someone is following us?"

"No, but better safe than sorry," I said as I turned into a quiet subdivision, ranch style homes from the sixties, many of them now raised, a testament to the waters here. Then another turn to loop back to the larger street and onto Chef.

The pandemic had hit this area hard. Several small businesses were boarded up. It had flooded badly during Katrina. Many of them had finally come back, only to be hit again with COVID.

I drove past the signs in English and Vietnamese. There were fewer restaurants than before.

I did a U-turn, more quickly than I would normally, both to get to the right side of the road and see if anyone else also turned.

I pulled into the place I'd gone to with Cordelia.

I didn't immediately open the door, instead scanning the cars that went by, looking for any that slowed or pulled in after being close enough to see us pull in.

Sarah put her hand on the door but followed my lead, not getting out. Good to know she wasn't reflexively rebellious.

After the cars that might have followed us had gone by, none slowing or stopping, I got out. Sarah followed.

"This is a completely different world," she said. Overgrown save for the places that hewed back the ever-growing plants. "We're not in the city anymore, right?"

"Nope, still New Orleans. The far east reaches, but the city."

I motioned her in front of me and we entered the restaurant, taking one last look over my shoulder at the road and the parking lot. It wasn't crowded. The server pointed us to a table by the window, but I pointed to one in the corner. He shrugged and nodded.

Sarah and I both ordered bahn mi, hers with chicken and mine with beef instead of my usual pork. Deference to her. And to not get the same thing as the last time I was here.

Our orders taken, I told her Joanne had sent me the hate report.

"Do we have to talk about that?"

"We don't have to talk now," I said. "But we should talk at some point."

She nodded, resigned. With an exaggerated sigh, she said, "Okay, so what?"

"So what?"

"The report. What do we need to talk about?"

I pulled up the email on my phone and downloaded the report. I scrolled past the hateful messages—she'd seen them once; she didn't need to see them again—until I got to the list of names that had been culled.

"Which of these do you recognize? Any that stand out as the most threatening?"

She took a sip of her water, shoved her glasses to her forehead, and looked at the list, taking the phone from my hand to see it better. She stared for a long time.

Finally, she handed the phone back to me. "So, you're asking which one of these is most likely to kill me?"

Blunt, but accurate. "Which did you have the most interaction with? Was it just notes, or did anyone ever come by and harass you?"

She again turned the phone in my hand to look at the list. "Is this all of them? It felt like there were more."

"There were; these are just the ones signed with a name."

"So, you think the anonymous ones were just one-off assholes?"

"I don't know. This is the information we have. I need to find out more about these groups and see if any of them are active down here."

"How does that help us? It only tells us what we know, not what we don't know."

"True," I had to admit. "If we know they're in this area, we might know what their tactics are and how to protect against them."

"If they're responsible. That is, as we say in Brooklyn, a big fucking if."

"We say that here, too."

"If they're responsible," she continued, "if they're here as well, if we know what kind of shit they pull, and if they are still pulling that kind of shit."

"Any knowledge is better than nothing."

"Is it? Is it better to know something wrong and have that lead you than not know and keep possibilities open? How many times have we thought we knew something and then learned how misguided we were? Knowledge isn't wisdom."

She wasn't wrong. We knew so little, any or all of it could be completely wrong. "I'm doing the best I can," I said weakly.

She reached across the table and put her hand on my forearm. "I know that. I do appreciate it." To what must have shown on my face, she added, "Really. I know you're getting paid and all that, but you haven't been a big bully telling me I don't know what I'm talking about and I need to do what you tell me. I know you're looking at a very dark place and trying to see enough to know what creatures lurk there."

"What do you want? What would you do if you were me?"

She leaned back, smiled a sad smile. "If I were you, I would do what you're doing. I'd be grasping at straws because nothing else is in reach."

"Should we not bother with these names, stay in the unknown until we know more?"

"What if we don't know more? That's the hell, isn't it," she said softly. "What if we never know and I always have to wait for the bullet?"

"They'll make a mistake. In fact, they probably already have, we just need to find it," I said. Maybe she was right, but I wasn't going to live in that uncertainty until I had to. Until all I could do was say goodbye to Sarah Jacobson and hope a bullet never found her.

"You really think that?"

"Yes. They are blinded by their hate. They have to believe they're right, and that means they aren't good at questioning themselves."

"And if you never question yourself, you never really see yourself."

"Exactly," I answered. "I'm a small part of this. There are many other law enforcement people working on it. Eventually one of us will find something."

"So, why are we doing this? Why not leave it to them?"

"We could, if that's what you want. But I'm the one here with you. It's possible you know something that you don't even know you know."

"Like I saw something?"

"Maybe," I said. "Or a gut feeling, or something that doesn't seem connected but is. Someone in the street that sent a chill down your spine."

"Okay," she said slowly. "I'm in. I don't want to sit around and do nothing. It might be straws, but at least we can grasp at something in the dark." She smiled, the first real smile I'd seen from her. It transformed her face, and I got a glimpse of the joy she brought into the world.

The waiter brought our food.

"Oh, my goodness," she said after the first bite. "This is really good. I had my doubts, with you bringing me out here to what seems to be barely reclaimed swamp, but I'd have to look to get this good in NYC."

I took a bite. Yep, not bad. We're not NYC, but I could get in my car, drive here in about fifteen minutes, park in the lot instead of schlepping on the subway. When I was young, in college up there, it was a lark to get on the subway, ride for an hour, get off and see what was at the other end. The world opening to us, and life was an adventure. But the last time I was up there, it was cold—by New Orleans standards, which are now mine—and we kept our food choices to an easy walk.

We ate in silence, concentrating on the food.

When we were done, Sarah ordered tea and another sandwich to go for her dinner. I joined her in the tea.

"I wish I could talk to David," she said. "He's is our executive director, usually the one to open the letters and see them first. I suspect he may have thrown away some of them, especially early on, before… before it got worse."

The waiter brought our tea. After he left, Sarah, continued, "By worse I mean the bomb threats, ugly words spray painted on the building. At first it seemed to be just words, but I guess words didn't satisfy them."

"They escalated?"

"I guess you'd call it that."

"Did you go to the authorities?"

"We reported the ones that were threatening, but not much they could do with a piece of paper. We immediately called in the bomb threats. Had to. Couldn't take the risk it was real, even though we thought it wasn't. A number of Jewish places all got bomb threats around the same time."

"About when was this?"

She took a sip of tea. "Maybe about six months ago? I had to leave my phone—and calendar—back in Brooklyn, so I don't have access to much of the info."

"You have your memory."

"Memories can be tricky. We remember the sparkly and forget the bland but important."

"True. What's David's last name? Maybe I can contact him?"

She looked at me. "Maybe. David Moskowitz. Not sure how you can call him from New Orleans without it tripping whatever it is that might lead them to me."

"I'm not sure either. I might have to call someone who has to call someone." Or get a burner phone, but I didn't know enough to be sure that would be safe. That was the challenge—until we knew who had targeted her, we didn't know what they were capable of. "Let's work with what we have at the moment—your memory," I said.

She gave a shake of her head, then took another sip of tea. "We can try. I've been racking my brain, not wanting to relive it, but having to relive it, to see if I saw, heard, even smelled anything. But…no."

"Don't relive it. Not now. Think back earlier. Before the time the threats started coming. Someone picked you, your synagogue. If we can parse out what triggered that, it might help us narrow down who."

"Nice theory, but there's a long-standing haystack of hate, and we're looking for a needle."

"True, it's always been there, but that changed when this country elected a demagogue and decided if letting hate loose would keep them in power, so be it. The monster is let out and I don't know how to contain it."

She took another sip of her tea.

The waiter brought her to-go order.

"Okay, let me think," she said. "So much has happened, it's hard to know even where it began." She finished her tea. She started to get up but looked at me. "You done?"

"Almost," I said. I stood up.

She thanked our waiter, told him the food was delicious, and we headed out to the parking lot. We didn't say anything until I had pulled out.

"I got hassled at a rally," she said. "People want black and white answers. You're for or against. One side is right, the other wrong. I have been critical of the government of Israel. Not its existence, not its people, the actions of some of its leaders. I was calling for the rights and dignity of the Palestinians."

"A two-state solution?" I asked. I was woefully ignorant on the issues, only seeing what I read in the papers. And honestly, sometimes I skipped over it, too heartbreaking to stare at and know there was little I could do.

"Yes. Either Israel gives everyone in the occupied lands full citizen rights, including voting, or gives them their own state with full rights. Well, this is a long discussion, with a lot more nuance than I can manage here. Some people cheered; some booed."

"Threats?" I asked, deciding to take the surface roads back— slower, but easier to see if anyone was following. Not many people would take the old highway from here to the French Quarter.

"No, the usual give and take of free speech. But after I finished and was leaving, a guy came up to me and—I'm trying to remember his words—'you want to replace us with the mud people, don't you?' First time anyone accused me of wanting to replace them to my face. I'm used to the 'you're not supporting Israel enough' stuff. To respond, I've got everything from a whole speech to one line—do you hate the U.S. because you don't agree with everything the president does? I think I mumbled, 'I don't want to replace anyone. We all need to be free.' He stared at me, just stared. Then he called me a fucking dyke, and stalked away."

"What stands out for you?" We were stopped at a light. There was a big, black truck behind us. Young white man, with a hat pulled low.

"The anger in his eyes. That he felt safe enough to confront me in Brooklyn in an audience that was mostly Jewish and BIPOC."

"Not too many white faces?" I asked.

"About half and half, so being white didn't stick out. But...as I think about it, he was out of place. Like he was checking out the enemy camp."

"They depend on our decency—that we won't beat the shit out of them because violence is wrong. What did he look like?"

"Young, pudgy face, clean shaven, wearing a beat-up ball cap, hair that I could see was brown. Tall, wearing new jeans, a button-down black shirt. The kind of guy you see and pass because he doesn't look like anything. Unless you look in his eyes."

The light changed. I was gentle on the gas, wanting to see if the truck would pass me. It hugged my bumper.

"What was on his cap?" I asked.

"I have no idea. Some logo, I think, but that's it. Dirty brown."

At the next street, the truck turned, in a huff of diesel smoke.

"Did you see him any other time?"

"Maybe? I don't know. I blew it off. Talked to…Leah about it, and she said let it go. So I did. Until you asked. But yeah, I did kind of look around for him. If he traded in his cap for sunglasses, would I know? Like I said, he was a nondescript man's nondescript."

"Was this before or after the first threats came?" I sped up to keep with the flow of the traffic.

"Not sure. But not far after we got the first ones. Maybe a little after? It's hard to remember."

"But close in time?"

"I'd say so, but this is memory, the unreliable metric. If I had my calendar, I could look when that rally was, and if I could talk to David, I could confirm when the letters came."

"It gives us questions to ask," I said as we crossed the Industrial Canal.

"Is this the Mississippi?" Sarah asked. The bridge we were crossing was much lower than the Highrise, the water easily visible.

I managed to not laugh. "No, it's a manmade canal from the river to the lake. The river is much bigger."

"So, how do I get a look at it?" she asked.

She could walk from her hotel down to the levee and see it there—that would take about five minutes, but I didn't want to suggest she wander around the busy tourist area.

"Next drive, I'll take you to see it," I said.

"It's close to my hotel, isn't it?" she asked. "Yeah, I can read maps."

"Yes, but—"

"Please don't go there by yourself." She cut me off. "You fed me well, I won't."

We were still well out of the scenic parts of New Orleans, now on a more populated but no less down-at-heel area. Budget motels, fast food places to serve them, unrelenting commerce you could find almost anywhere.

"You said you might have seen the man again? Where? What context?"

"You don't give up, do you?"

"I'm paid not to give up."

"No, you're paid to keep me out of sight and out of mind," she pointed out. "This is extra."

"Lagniappe," I said.

"What? Did we just leave English for French?" she asked.

"No, not really. We use that word a lot down here. It means a little extra, like thirteen in a baker's dozen."

The road morphed from Chef Menteur to Gentilly Boulevard, another of those confusing New Orleans street changes. We were in a nicer area, older homes, fewer chain businesses. I then turned onto Esplanade. This was a tourist area, an artery from the French Quarter to Jazz Fest. It was an old part of the city on what passes for a ridge, enough elevation to avoid the worst of the floods.

"A face in a crowd. Him? Someone who looked like him?" Sarah said, looking out the windows at the old homes.

"Did you think that at the time? Or considering it now?"

"At the time. Same build—what you might call Midwestern corn-fed. Tall, broad but soft, a little too much weight, like the linebacker who wasn't working out anymore. But a face, a body in the crowd."

"How many times did you see him?"

"Not sure it was him. Maybe once or twice at most. Oh, and there was another one."

"Same threat?"

"No, not a threat at all, at least on the surface. A young woman who said she wanted to convert."

"What about her?" We crossed Claiborne, with I-10 looming over it. We were now in Tremé, not far from where I lived. I considered swinging by but remembered she wasn't a tourist; I wasn't showing her around. Too bad, I'd had the house painted about six months ago, sedate gray with white trim, but shutters in dark purple and the door about two shades lighter—this is New Orleans, after all—and it looked good.

I also decided to not cut through the French Quarter. Dauphine isn't bad but is one-way and can be slow. Rampart, the line between the Quarter and Tremé, was two lanes each way.

"She was needy, although I'm not sure for what, but in a way that made me uncomfortable. She wanted time with me, said she needed the help. We're happy for people to come to us, so we welcomed her."

"What happened?" I asked as I turned on Rampart.

"Wanted to know too much about me. Asked where I lived. Asked about Leah, too much info, how we met. Nothing to do with learning about Judaism."

"Why does she come to mind?"

"I once joked to Leah that I thought she was a spy. I thought I was laughing away my discomfort, but maybe I was right. She played at it, a way to get access to me. She would miss our Intro to Judaism classes unless I was present. Always with an excuse, ones you can believe the first time it happens. But the pattern emerged."

"She missed everything except the ones where you were there?"

"Yeah. Once I had to cancel at the last minute, so I wasn't there. Abby, who replaced me, said she was annoyed and didn't stay the whole time."

"That does sound weird. About when was this?"

"About a week before the bomb threat."

"In the time frame," I said as we stopped at the light at Toulouse Street.

"At the time it never occurred to me the two were connected. I thought she was some messed-up kid, probably had a crush on me or some other mixed-up emotion. I tried to never be alone with her."

"She made you uncomfortable?"

"Very. I even talked to David and Carol, our cantor, about her. She once tried to follow me home."

"What?" I started to turn to look at her, but the traffic was getting heavy now that we were close to Canal.

"Yes, I caught sight of her as I entered the subway. It was about eight in the evening, too late to be crowded enough to mask her. She hadn't been at the temple, so it seemed odd she was in the neighborhood, but I shrugged it off. Until I noticed she got off at my stop."

"What did you do?"

"Got back on the train just as the doors closed. Got off at the next stop. Waited for the platform to mostly clear, and she wasn't there. I went back to the other side and took the train home, looking over my shoulder the entire time."

"Can you be sure she was following you?"

"Pretty sure. The address she gave wasn't anywhere close. I don't know if you know New York, but it's a big city with a bunch of small neighborhoods."

"I went to college there. And my mother lives there, so I visit often," I cut in. Bare details, but it was too complicated to get into much more. Like me, my mother was a lesbian, deemed unsuitable to raise a child, so forced out when I was five. We had only reconnected as adults. Another rip in my childhood.

"Where did you go?"

"Barnard."

"Really? You must have been smart at one time," Sarah said.

I passed Canal, driving into the CBD. "Yeah, but that was a long time ago."

"Noted," Sarah said. Probably sarcasm but too deadpan to be sure. "We live in a quiet neighborhood backing up to a cemetery. A brownstone that used to belong to my grandmother. She bought it when people like us could buy there. Not the kind of place people go on a whim."

"Maybe she was visiting someone?"

"Like the old Jewish doctors who lived around us?"

"Okay, it's certainly suspicious. Did she do anything else?"

"Disappeared. A few weeks before…"

I was stopped at another light. Not as bad as Canal, but still slow going, with the narrow one-way streets.

"Disappeared how?"

"Stopped showing up. We called to check on her, but it went to voice mail. I assumed she was one of those lost people, searching for something, and she hadn't found it with us. But then she left a message the day after…condolences, said she was so sorry, wanted to see me, asked for a time to get together."

"What did you do?" The light changed, but a timid tourist was too nervous to edge around a delivery van, so we didn't move.

"Nothing. I didn't answer. Why would I? She wasn't family or even a friend. Weird and inappropriate."

The car in front of me honked, so I tapped my horn as well. Green lights don't last long here. "What else can you tell me about her?" I asked.

"Like what?"

"Name? Address? Description?"

"First name was Betty, can't remember her last name. Address was somewhere out in Rockaway, which was also odd that she came to us. We're by no means the most convenient synagogue. Description? Young, desperate. Yeah, I know. Brown hair, long, straight. About medium height, maybe five-five. Pretty, but only in the way that most everyone is when they're young, no lines or worry on her face. Chin pointed, not strong. Teeth that had seen an orthodontist, but drank a lot of coffee or tea."

The tourist car finally edged past the van just as the light turned red. The car in front let out a long, annoyed honk as we waited for a second red light.

Sarah continued, "You can ask David if you contact him. He'll have her info in the files."

"It won't hurt to look into her."

"She may be harmless and needy."

"She may be, but better to know."

The light changed; the first car shot through. I wasn't far behind.

"Is it right? We fish around, scrutinize anyone who seems odd or out of place, pry into their lives," Sarah mused. "If she's harmless, does she deserve this?"

"First, she's not likely to know. There are a lot of checks you can do that people aren't aware of."

"That's comforting." Definitely sarcasm.

"If something comes up that demands more, well, maybe it will help her learn appropriate boundaries."

"But she didn't really do anything wrong," Sarah argued.

"She didn't break the law, if that's what you mean, but she came to you, claiming she wanted to convert and, at best, the kind of lost and indecisive that wasted time. At worst, she was using your decency for her indecent ends."

We made it to the end of Gravier, and I turned back to Canal.

"Okay, you have a point."

"She could have been scoping you out, an actual spy, to learn about you and the synagogue. Could she have known about your comings and goings?"

Sarah was silent for a moment. "Yes, we send out monthly calendars, and she would have received it."

"Let me park the car and walk you in," I said as I turned onto Canal, just making it through the about-to-turn-green light.

"Waste of money for a two-minute walk."

"It's not about the walk," I replied. We were a block away, but traffic was bad enough that walking would be quicker. "It's about you being safe."

"And that gets back to it. What are you going to do if someone pulls a gun and tries to shoot me?"

"At that point, not much. But I might be able to see them in time to prevent that from happening."

"No." She put her hand on my wrist. "No. One person has died because of me. It's a crowded street and lobby. No one will try anything. And if they do…they'll get caught. If I thought you could do something, I'd say yes, but we both know flesh and bone don't stop bullets. Better you work on…work on other things."

Traffic lurched forward, gaining me half a block. I debated whether what she said was true or if I wanted it to be true because I didn't want to park, then unpark and still be here in this traffic mess.

"Go straight to your room. Text me when you get there. If I don't hear from you in ten minutes, I'm coming back to look for you," I bargained. I still wasn't sure if this was the right choice or the convenient one.

"Thank you." She removed her hand from my wrist.

We gained a few more car lengths and were almost in front of her hotel. She took this stop as a cue to open the door and get out.

I watched her go into the hotel, not even noticing cars had started again until the one behind me honked.

It was a traffic slog until I turned onto Rampart. Then it was still slow but mostly from the traffic lights. Once I was past Armstrong Park, it flowed, even with a nice gap for the left turn into Tremé and my house.

It was on the just-past side of midafternoon. I debated going back to my office, but I could work from home—my boss is nice like that—and already be here when the workday ended.

After taking off my shoes and bra and putting on comfy sweats, my first task was to contact Joanne. I needed her to be the go-between for me to contact David at Sarah's synagogue. I got her voice mail.

Until I had a last name, it was pointless to do any searching on my own.

As promised, Sarah texted that she was snug in her room. I responded with a smiley face.

I glanced at my email. Paulette had sent a copy of Elmer's work file. I didn't want to work on her case, though, so instead read the document Joanne had emailed about the hate-wing organizations.

That was happy reading.

I would have thrown it down in disgust, but it was on my computer screen. A few of them seemed to be little more than shadows, like pop-up hate groups, around only long enough to send an ugly threat and then disappear. The analysis said it was likely these were one-man (woman?) operations, a few people at most, with only the capability to send threats. Several of the others were larger, from small groups of ten or so up to about one hundred members. They sent threats as well, but also engaged in street agitation, which seemed to mean being dicks in public places, like showing up to vigils for gun victims, carrying weapons. Occasionally brawling at protests. Four of them were larger, in the several thousands, and spread out across the country, some both regional and even national. They engaged in all of the above, plus cosplaying soldiers by holding what they called training events— playing in the woods and the mud—and also things like protests at drag queen story hours or anything else they didn't approve of. They all seemed to think that they, straight white men, were the endangered species, assaulted on all sides by people of color, us queers, immigrants, and of course, the Jews. Our equality was their persecution.

I thought I might narrow it down to groups that especially targeted the Jewish community and the LGBTQ community. Sarah was the intersection of those. But they didn't make it easy. Too much across-the-board bigotry. Also, they had been investigated as hate groups, not focused on the murder of Sarah's wife. The reports also were dependent on who knew what. Maybe undercover, but also disgruntled members blabbing. A subjective narrative.

I turned away from the screen. Presumably there was a team of law enforcement agencies poring over this, with experts of all kinds. I was spinning my wheels, a lone PI in a small city far from where it happened.

Still, I turned back to stare at the screen. I was the one here with Sarah. I needed to know as much as I could. The NYC cops weren't here to recognize a certain color combination or tattoo walking across the lobby in her direction.

I stared at the screen, looking at the list of groups that signed their threats, proud of their handiwork. Several seemed small, only a few people. I couldn't dismiss them entirely, but they seemed less likely to have the resources to search and find Sarah here. Several more slightly larger, tens to hundreds, again, couldn't dismiss, but not likely to have connections here.

Three of them were larger, hundreds to thousands of members, with some active cells in the South, although it was unclear if any were in the New Orleans area.

They all had a strong antisemitic stance, claiming that Jews ran the world and had a secret plan to destroy America by replacing white Christian people with "mud people and heretics." One even claimed that Jews wore yarmulkes to hide their horns, notwithstanding that horns, should they exist, are closer to the forehead, not the back of the head. But in fiction anything is possible. One of them was more firmly focused on hating Jews, claiming to be active in over twenty states. Two of them had once been the same organization but had split off a few years ago. The schism seemed to be more about personality than ideology—two factions vying for power, and when one lost, they took their toys and went home. They both seemed to be spread over the eastern part of the country, including down the Mississippi River.

Another one seemed to be the more hard-core fanatics, calling for the blood of just about everyone except themselves. They claimed to have members in most states, but the only known location was in the Florida panhandle, close to Alabama. However, it seemed that they had played COVID roulette, not only calling it a hoax but deliberately getting infected to prove it was no worse than a cold. That had cut a swath out of them, with the leader suffering from long COVID and on oxygen. He claimed it was a government black op poisoning him.

They all seemed to have their accessories, red or black shirts, logos that all seemed to be some variation of the Nazi eagle and even outright swastikas. I took pictures of as many of these symbols as I could in case I saw any. A tattoo, a small lapel pin, anything that might tip me off.

Tired of the bile, I closed the file and walked into the kitchen. The breakfast dishes were still in the sink—a coffee cup and cereal bowl—so I washed them.

When I finished, I remained, looking out the kitchen window, the lingering light filtering between my house and the one next to it. This house had been renovated a few years before we bought it, the kitchen moved from the back to the middle. Many of these old houses had kitchens in back, originally outdoors because cooking was open flame back in the day. For many, newer kitchens were put where the old ones had been, requiring you to go through the bedrooms to get there. Not ideal.

I try not to stare at the hate and bigotry, only to engage with patches where I might make a difference. March with BLM, donate to candidates who aren't bigots or nut cases. Reading all that—and knowing Sarah and how it had shattered her life—made me stare at it. The huge ugly pile so many of us had to walk around.

I shook my head and got a can of fizzy water from the refrigerator. It wouldn't wash anything away, but it would ease my dry throat.

I went back to my computer. Next up was where to stash Sarah. Her original stay had been for four days. I scanned the smaller hotels down on the lower end of the Quarter. It was still the tourist area, with people staying for a week, even two. And away from the traffic on Canal. I dithered over which one, then realized it didn't really matter as long as it was decent enough. They all were, as far as I could tell. I finally just called the one that was on my screen. They had no availability—"bridal party, don'cha know?"—but suggested one nearby. I called that one and they had rooms. I could only hope by the time this reservation ended, she could go home.

I didn't really want to read what Paulette had sent me, but I did want to bill her for it. I was too honest to charge for work I only skimmed.

I opened the file.

Elmer Stumbolt seemed like a charming fellow. Managed to graduate high school. A year at one of those for-profit rip-off schools. Business. He did not provide a transcript, which probably meant his grades wouldn't help him on his career path. Then a variety of jobs that mostly required a body—barback, waste management (i.e., picking up trash), construction, driving an airport shuttle, landscaping (which could be digging ditches). Most of those lasted six months to a year or two at max. There were gaps between some, indicating a period of unemployment. Or working off the books. It looked like he had stumbled through most of his twenties in this fashion. Some dates were vague, just a year listed, no month, making it harder to pin down his work timetable. He was now thirty-four, with little to show for those years. Unless he could shake down Paulette.

He was a janitor at a small restaurant when Paulette hired him. His longest job was with her. Maybe he found his niche? Or maybe the nookie was good enough for her to overlook actual job performance?

His listed address was one of those apartment complexes out in Kenner, close enough to I-10 and the airport that the rents were cheap. Probably Paulette had looked for him there, but that didn't mean he wasn't sneaking back at odd hours to sleep in his own bed. I'd have to check if he was still renting it.

His emergency contact was his mother, who lived in Monroe, Louisiana, about a four-hour drive from here. He could also be hanging out there. If he needed money, he wasn't likely to be camped at an anonymous motel, although that was possible. Or at least going there when he needed to feel hidden. But unless he was paying in cash, he could be traced.

Being an employee file, it also had a picture of his driver's license and his Social Security number. Those can be big helps, but given he was trying to hide, they would be less useful, unless he had taken another job and given his real name and info.

The actual application was a photocopied page, filled out by hand. His handwriting was labored, block letters that looked more like a sixth grader than a grown adult.

From there I did a social media search. He was as bad as Paulette about keeping things private that he might not want the world to see. A picture of him with his hunting buddies and a dead deer, boasting about killing it off season. Pictures of a beer party outside what looked like his apartment building. He bragged about pissing against the wall of an apartment where a Black family lived, calling them welfare queens. A snap of him next to a shiny red truck with a Confederate flag in the back window.

Now I knew what his car looked like and even its license plate number, and what his apartment looked like and an idea of which one was his.

I hadn't thought this would be a hard case, but he was making it almost too easy.

If he was thirty-four, that meant Paulette was fifteen years older than him. I don't believe in double standards, so the age gap shouldn't bother me…but it did. It felt too transactional—he got a sugar mama and she got a good looking (by some standards) man. Her house was a big step up from his small apartment, and they'd been together long enough for him to get used to her comfortable lifestyle.

I sat back, rubbed my eyes, and tried to decide whether to be a good detective and continue working or blow it off. It was after five. But I was sitting there and already had him in my search engines.

I was saved from that dilemma by a call from my cousin Torbin. He and Andy, his husband, had just ordered a pizza, but Andy had gotten an emergency call about a computer meltdown—he was a computer geek—and needed to leave. Torbin didn't want the pizza to go to waste. They live down the block from me, mostly convenient but sometimes a little too close; they know if my car is parked in front of my house or not. Torbin had looked out, seen it, and called me.

An evening gossiping with Torbin sounded much better than staring at my computer screen.

CHAPTER SIX

Ah, coffee. Torbin had been liberal with libations last night. He had finally learned how to make a Sazerac, so we had one while waiting for the pizza. Then a new dark espresso stout with the pizza and a final Sazerac for the road. Or was that two?

I was in the breakfast nook, debating whether I needed to take two aspirin or was just waking up fuzzy and could tough it out. Yeah, Sunday, but as long as Sarah was in town, every day was a working day.

Torbin and I were the lavender sheep of the family, bonding over being the ones who never fit in. When we were younger, we knew we were different; by our teen years, we had both figured out what the difference was, although it wasn't until we were in college when we told each other, too afraid to lose our one friend when we were still bounded by families that didn't understand. When he was younger, he had been tall, blond, and gorgeous. Now the blond was shading into a foxy silver and the laugh lines were etched in his face. Even now he was a handsome man. When we went out together and people assumed we were a couple, I suspect they wondered why someone as good looking as him was with someone like me. Oh, I don't break mirrors, but I don't hew to the feminine ideal either. Black hair going gray, defiantly not dyed. I'm more likely to wear makeup at Mardi Gras than any other time of the year. As for clothes, I usually slouch with the boys, comfy jeans and a T-shirt.

Sarah texted me while I was there. I'd ignored it until Torbin took a bathroom break. I was ambivalent about mentioning to him what I was doing. Not to worry him about being a bodyguard for someone targeted for violence? Because I was protecting her and telling as few people as possible? She wanted to know when we would meet. I suggested later morning and firmly told her I'd meet her at her room.

I did ask him if he knew anything about hate groups in the area, making an oblique reference to having stumbled over something on a case.

"Hate groups?" he had mused. "Other than some members of the political class? Sadly, there are a few around here. Not in New Orleans itself that I know of, save for one Mardi Gras krewe hating on another, but the burbs are white flight land. I've heard rumors of a self-styled militia on the North Shore."

"Any idea where?" I asked. The North Shore is the other side of Lake Pontchartrain and rural.

"I can ask. Not sure what I'll find; these are not the people I hang with. But strange bedfellows and all that."

I'd let it lapse and we'd gone on to other gossip. An A-list gay couple who'd had a splashy wedding in the Virgin Islands just over a year ago and were now in a messy split, one of them drunkenly screaming about the other from the balcony at the Bourbon Pub. The lesbian lawyer who'd just won a big class action settlement, making her very well-to-do on top of already doing well. Torbin suggested I look her up, and I told him we'd met once for a drink. She was running late and had her secretary call me to let me know. I, being a PI, tried to chat her up to find out what her boss was like, but while she liked to talk, it was mostly about herself—her long commute from down in St. Bernard Parish, her great life on the water until the oil spill, taking this job because she had to, how she did all the real work, including calls like this. I added that time to the time I allotted for the date. The lawyer, Frances G something—Gauthier?—and I met. We both decided we weren't meant for each other—me silently and her telling me she thought I'd be shorter and not so androgynous looking. Her honesty saved me from having to tell her I had decided no, so we had parted with a hug and a wave and cordially chatted whenever our paths crossed. Torbin moved on to the two drag queens who showed up in almost identical gowns, how they teamed up on the designer who'd told them both it was one of a kind and dumped all the trash in the neighborhood on her front lawn, and then on to who was cheating on whom and how likely it was the other knew. Torbin was the gossip maven's gossip maven.

I decided against aspirin in favor of more coffee and a not-good-for-me toaster pastry, one with sprinkles on it. Ostensibly hurricane food, for no power, when something from a box is handy. But the stock has to be replenished every few years, so I might as well eat them in the meantime. We were officially out of hurricane season, so they wouldn't be needed for a while.

I contemplated my day. I was meeting Sarah in a few hours. I also needed to work on Paulette's case. If I went to the office, I could leave Elmer's info to the computer grannies so they would get it first thing on Monday. That way both they and I could make money from Paulette. They're much better at boring computer crawls than I am.

I sighed, poured the remaining coffee into my travel thermos, and headed out.

When I got to my office, I stuffed Elmer's info into the computer grannies' mail slot, with a note about what I wanted.

Then up to my office.

I made another pot of coffee while finishing the mug I'd brought with me.

There was always stuff to do. Sometimes I contemplated hiring someone to help with paperwork, answering the phones and the like, but there was enough of it to be annoying but not enough to justify the expense of another person. I was also reluctant to have someone in my space, watching when I came and went. Neurotic, perhaps? I never claimed I wasn't.

With a sigh, I did that paperwork now, bills, filing, answering emails explaining that I wasn't the best choice of PI to trace your linage to old European royalty and made suggestions of one I didn't like. I was tempted to write, "why not try for Cleopatra—in for one royal, in for them all." But I stayed professional.

I could—and should—keep working on Paulette's case, but let myself off the hook by thinking I might as well see what the grannies turned up before doing anything more on my end.

The hours passed and it was time to leave to meet Sarah.

Traffic was as annoying as I expected it to be. Valet parking didn't have a long line, but it did have a few people who were slow about getting what they needed from their vehicle before handing over the keys.

I was about ten minutes late when I got to Sarah's door.

My phone rang just as I was lifting my hand to knock.

I looked at the screen, didn't bother to answer and instead said, "I'm right outside."

I heard the locks and the door opened. Like before, only wide enough for me to squeeze through.

She looked tired.

"Sorry," she said. "You're late."

"People from Iowa at the valet. Suddenly decided they had to take everything out before actually giving over the keys."

"So, better we should have met out front and I just jumped in," she argued.

"No, not better. Slower, safer."

"I don't want you near me if someone takes another shot. I can't have more blood on my hands." She sat on the bed, indicating the desk chair for me. "I've been thinking. About my situation. I can't hide forever."

"No, you can't. Nor should you have to. Once the shooter is caught—"

She cut me off. "Even if he's caught, there will be another. The Tree of Life murderer is in jail. It didn't make me safe. Is this really helping? Or is it just making me hide, cower, let their hate control my life?"

"It's your decision. But make it slowly and carefully. Sacrificing yourself isn't going to solve anything."

"I see your point, but my first priority is not myself but making sure no harm comes to anyone else."

"I presume you mean to anyone around you. Preventing harm to anyone else is up to the gods, not us mortals."

"Yes, in this context, in the one small one I have some control and choice in."

"Stay in the hotel and live off room service? That's the safest path."

She sighed. "I know, but even that might put the hotel staff at risk."

"Get a tent and live in the wilderness where no one can find you?"

She shook her head. "I grew up in Brooklyn. Went to camp once as a kid. I did not do well at surviving a lumpy bunk bed where there might be spiders."

"What do you want?" I asked.

"That's the hard question, isn't it?" She gave me a rueful smile. "No offense, but I want to talk it over with my friends, my family, but according to you that might put me—and them—in danger. Calls can be traced, that sort of stuff, yes?"

"It's possible," I said.

"But how possible? Could you do it? Who can track cell phone data?"

"How likely is it that someone is monitoring your cell phone? It depends on who targeted you."

"Let's say a small group of crazies."

"Again, it depends. Who are they? If any of them are part of law enforcement or have access, then it's possible."

"Not helpful."

"Just honest."

"But don't they need warrants and stuff like that? Joe patrolman can't just decide he wants to look up someone's cell data."

"In a perfect world, no. But a rogue cop, spy, sheriff, anyone who could in the right circumstances can also do it in the wrong circumstances."

"So even if it is a small group of fanatics, if one of them can track cell data, they could find me?"

"It could also be someone who works for the phone company. Anyone with access."

"Well, fuck. So even if it is a tiny group of extremists, I have to worry."

"It's also what might lead us to them. If they can trace your phone, the cops can trace them. But it takes time."

"Time. I have so much of it," she said with a frustrated shake of her head.

"What do you want?" I asked again.

"What can I have?" she countered. "I don't want to live hidden in a strange hotel room. I don't want to put anyone else at risk. I don't want to die. How do I meet these needs?"

"No easy or perfect answers. We can make best guesses, decide which risks are acceptable as we wait for everyone else involved to do their work."

"What if they're part of the problem?" she asked.

"The team working on this? Not likely. I mean, they would be right next to the people hunting them."

"Okay, so I should be paranoid, but not quite that paranoid?"

"No easy answers. Maybe we should figure out lunch."

But even that wasn't an easy answer. She suggested going back to the Vietnamese place, but I didn't want to go to the same place twice.

Then the chain restaurant. I vetoed that. I have my pride. Friends in New Orleans do not take friends—or anyone they don't hate—to a place you could go to in Des Moines.

Someone had to make a decision or we'd be debating this all day. "Let's go uptown," I said. "There are a couple of places on Carrollton that are possible."

"Like what kind of places?" she said, but got her purse and put on her jacket.

"You don't need that," I said. It was too heavy for the weather.

"Humor me. I'll leave it in the car."

She insisted on coming with me down to the valet. This time we were lucky and the only ones there. She took off the jacket as my car arrived.

We got in and I pulled out into the usual traffic muck. But we weren't in a hurry, no meetings to get to, so I tried to zen through the mess, limiting myself to one "It doesn't get any greener" without the usual extra words. I decided on the slow but scenic route, going up St. Charles, with its Garden District mansions.

"Beautiful architecture," she commented.

"Where the rich people live," I commented.

"Nothing wrong with being rich; it's how you get there that counts."

"Going through the camel's eye and all that."

"Your Bible, not ours," she answered. "Jesus was a nice Jewish boy."

"A lesbian and a rabbi?" I slowed for a stoplight.

"Sounds like a joke, right? A lesbian and a rabbi walk into a bar."

"What made you choose it? Or have you been asked that too many times?"

"Or not enough. 'God disturbs us to our destiny.' I don't know I was so much called as pushed. The good we do in this life is what matters."

"No heaven or hell?"

"Complicated, but certainly not the way Christians view it. What do I do with my 'one wild and precious life,' to quote Mary Oliver. My grandmother told me that we're all small candles, passing our light on, wisdom, traditions, love and joy. The wonder of the stars, a falling leaf, and a gentle spring breeze."

"Just candles in the wind? Lot of ways to make the world better," I said.

"True. Leah was a social worker. I admired her for doing it, but every day she confronted other people's pain, stark and raw. Not for me. I like reading and thinking and debating; I like people, getting to know them, help them through not only the hard times but the joyous ones."

"How do you reconcile being lesbian in a religion that rejected you?"

"It's complicated. Reform Judaism is accepting. That's the beauty of it. We don't all agree and I didn't agree with that. God made me as I am, who am I to argue? All I can do is be the best rabbi I can be; if they don't like that I'm also a lesbian, they can go to a different synagogue. I gather you're not very religious?"

"Did enough churchgoing when I was growing up to last a lifetime. I don't need old, dead men to bully me." She left a space for me to continue, but I didn't. I'd heard too many sermons that said people like me were going to hell.

"I don't let them bully me. I get to tell them where they're wrong. Synagogues, churches, mosques have been around for centuries; a deep part of people's lives. My congregation welcomes all, trans, queer, immigrant. I get to change it from within, not protest from outside."

"I don't want to spend my life on those fights."

"Neither do I. What I have is a community we have created together. The long traditions of our faith, the rituals and words that have sustained Jewish people through the centuries. Touching our ancestors, the ones who have gone before. Not giving up on it, but adding to it. Many small candles together illuminate the dark spaces and pass the light down the generations."

I had to brake for a car that pulled out in front of me. "What if it's what brought you here?" I asked, then regretted it.

Sarah was silent.

"I'm sorry, I shouldn't have asked that."

"Don't be. It's a question I need to answer. Jews have been victims of pogroms for much of our existence. No place home, no place safe. The Crusades practiced on Jewish communities on their way to the Middle East. If I weren't Jewish and weren't a lesbian, would I be safe? If I hid everything of who I am, would I be safe? You live openly, are you safe?"

"Mostly," I answered, more because I wanted it to be than sure it was true. "I live in New Orleans, not the suburbs, in an area about as diverse as it can be. No one on the block blinks an eye at me."

"The same is true for me. Lot of gay people where we live, New York City, about as accepting a city as there is."

"Is safety just an illusion?"

"No, but it's not perfect. I think my answer has to be yes, that I would do it all again. How do I make the world a better place? *Tikkun olam.* Repairing the world. How do I make it safe for others if I live in fear? My congregation trusts me to lead them, that we all make this world better, even if only a corner of Brooklyn. I'm part of the most important parts of their lives, birth, coming of age, weddings and the end, death, grieving. We live our faith, with a food bank, helping immigrants, a community garden. An astonishing privilege, the life I lead."

I stopped at another light. I looked over at Sarah. She looked as happy as I'd seen her.

Then very softly, she said, "The only thing I would change is for it to have been me and not Leah."

I reached over and touched her hand, but the light changed and I needed both hands to drive. I had no words, no comfort, had shut out what I had heard in church. I wasn't welcome, didn't belong, so none of it said anything to me. If there were words, wisdom from long ago, pulling so many generations through grief, that would help, I didn't know them.

We continued in silence. I pointed out Audubon Park and Tulane University. When St. Charles hit Carrollton, I turned and found a place to park, pointing out the various restaurants around. I suggested the pizza place—no, not kosher, but always good food and better than any chain. She agreed, as if food didn't matter to her.

Sarah was here and not here. At times, she was sharp and attentive, and at others, a distance so far I couldn't tell where she was. Grief, of course, but complicated by having to hide, not able to be with the family and friends who help pull you through the days after loss, being in a void of danger—were we merely playing unnecessary security theater or was she truly at risk? Were we safe here, having a casual lunch?

One of the reasons I had taken the long, scenic route was to make sure no one was following me. As far as I could tell, no one was. No one slowed as I parked, no one paid any attention to us. I had even looked under my car last evening to see if a tracking device was there. Like doing the few things I knew might be enough. The haunting reality was that if someone was determined to come after her, I would be just one more body in the way.

My lateness and slow drive had landed us here after one, so the lunch crowd were paying their bills on the way out. We had our pick of tables. I choose one in the back, against a wall.

Sarah barely glanced at the menu, picking one of the first offerings, a veggie pizza. They are sized for one person. I went with my usual, a shrimp Caesar wrap.

"Were you popular in high school?" I asked. "I wasn't."

She looked at me quizzically. "Middle, had a gang, some still friends today, it wasn't too bad."

"I knew I was lesbian and knew I couldn't let anyone else know. It was a miserable time, saved only by being tall enough and smart-mouthed enough that I wasn't a convenient target. Oddly, I ran into an old classmate of mine; she wanted to hire me."

"You told her no, right?"

"No, her money is as green as anyone else's. Besides, I have a curious streak, one of the reasons I'm a PI. I wanted to see where she ended up."

"And where did she end up?"

"Still in high school. Not literally, she runs a for-profit medical business, emphasis on for profit. She and a younger employee—a guy—had a relationship. She has a much nicer lifestyle than he does, and he didn't like being cut off when she ended it. He stole a lot of their files, which I suspect show the ways they were cutting the corners."

"That's messy to the max. It sounds illegal."

"Maybe, or just on the shady side of legal. What she hired me for is legit—to find him."

"What if she finds him to kill him? Does that bother you?"

"She has neither the brains nor the guts for murder. It's harder than you think to hire a hit man. She wants the info out of his hands so he can't threaten her with it."

"Why are you telling me this?"

"Not sure, maybe because it's such a train wreck that I thought it would be distracting."

"You said she hasn't left high school? But she's your age, and well-to-do?"

"She treated me like we were back in high school, like it's the only way she knows how to deal with the world. She was popular, had her minions do her bidding, the popular girls. I look back at it and think what a fucked-up time it was."

"Sour grapes?"

"No, older and wiser."

"You sure?"

Our food arrived. We were silent. I was glad to notice she seemed hungry, wolfing down a piece.

"Pretty sure," I answered. "At least more experienced, enough to know what a narrow world that was. Not much beyond hormones and next week."

"So, have you found this guy?"

"No, not yet, but it shouldn't be hard."

"Don't be cocky."

"Not. Experience. He's not the brightest bulb on the light string. Getting by, but not much beyond that. She gave me his employee file, so I have more info than usual. He's in the area, since he has to be around for the exchange. Not likely to have the kind of resources to fly in and out."

"What will you do when you find him? He stole files and is blackmailing her, right? That should be the police's job."

"She doesn't want to press charges. For obvious reasons. Plus, it would be a messy case even if she did."

"But what if you do find something illegal?"

"I'm not the police, but I also don't cover up crimes, within reason. I'm not going to turn anyone in because they have a few joints, for example."

"What would you turn in?"

"I'll know it when I see it." I tried to deflect her question with a joke. She looked at me long enough that I answered. "Murder, planning it, bodily harm, assault. Significant financial crime. But people doing those kinds of things are idiots if they hire a licensed PI to look into any of it."

"Okay, that's a decent list. I'm glad I'm not your only client. Like you don't want to be the only customer in a restaurant; makes you wonder if it's any good."

"Thanks for the vote of confidence."

"This pizza is pretty tasty, by the way, not New York, of course, but respectable. I'm moving tomorrow, right?"

"Yes, I'll pick you up in the morning, say about ten? Check-out is eleven?"

"It is. Where am I going? Did you have any luck in talking to David?"

"Not yet, and I'll tell you tomorrow."

She finished a second slice, leaving half the pizza. "This can be for later. But it would be nice to stop at a grocery store and maybe get some appropriate clothes."

"I'll see what I can do," I said, taking a bite of my shrimp wrap. There would be no leftovers on my end. "Your new place is arranged. There for four days. I'm contacting Joanne to see about the other stuff."

I finished my wrap as she signaled for the bill and a to-go box.

When we got in my car, she said, "She had a man with her. Just once, and I don't think she wanted me to know."

"Who? Where?" I asked as I eased into the traffic.

"The woman who claimed she wanted to convert. She said she was single, didn't have anyone, not specifying the gender."

I remembered I promised to show her the Mississippi. I glanced at my watch. Midafternoon. Traffic was light, so I did a U-turn and got back on St. Charles, then cut down to the river.

"Are we going to the zoo?" she asked.

"No, skimming it." The road led past the Audubon Zoo parking lot, snaked down a narrow one-way lane to the Fly, a park between the zoo and the river. It had a walk that fronted the bank, giving a wide view. I found a parking space with no other cars around and pulled in, watching to see if any other cars came behind us.

Once it was clear, I motioned Sarah to get out.

"The Mississippi River," I said, stating the obvious.

She walked toward it. I did another quick look around before following her.

I joined her at the bank.

"Okay, this is pretty big," she said, staring across to the opposite bank. "Maybe even as big as the Hudson."

I snorted. "Do your homework. No comparison. Sorry, New York size queen, but we have you beat. It's two hundred feet deep here. A lot of water flowing by."

"Do people swim it?"

"No, no more than you would swim from NYC to New Jersey. Even without the huge amount of river traffic, the volume of water and the currents would take you under. About every year or so, some drunken idiot tries it and their body is found downstream."

She nodded, staring at the water, small whitecaps where the wind whipped them up, a barge slowly going upriver.

She turned to me and said, "Just keeps rolling along, doesn't it?"

"Long after we're gone."

"The eternal grounds me. Looking at the stars at night, they will be here when we're only dust, will be seen far in the future." She turned away, slowly walking back to the car.

I pulled out and jogged back over to Carrollton, varying our route. New Orleans is bent by the river, and streets can't be counted on to go straight. I took it to Fontainebleau, which turned into Broad, one of the shortcuts I used to avoid the traffic on both Claiborne and Carrollton, and cut across the curves of the river.

"The man. What can you tell me about him?" I asked as we came to the intersection with Broad.

"Not much. Tall, but bad posture."

"White?"

"Yes, pale moon face, I think. Hat, of course. Maybe red baseball cap."

"Not the same guy that threatened you?"

She took a moment before answering, "I never considered it."

I pulled into the parking lot of a small grocery store at Canal. "Think about it. I'll run in and get you some things."

"Let me come with you."

I hesitated.

"Will I really be safer sitting in the car than in there wandering the aisles?"

I nodded, conceding her point. "But let's not linger."

"So much fruit," she said as we entered.

"Remember, we're moving tomorrow."

"Got it." She grabbed a handbasket. I followed as she grabbed a few apples and bananas, bread, cheese, and a bottle of wine. "The nights are the worst," she said softly, as she put it in the basket.

We headed to the checkout, me scanning the store, but it seemed there were only other shoppers there. No men with guns.

Back in the car, she said, "I don't know. I can't say he was the same man, but I can't say he wasn't. About the same height, but not tall or short enough to be unusual."

"Okay," I said as I pulled out. Memory is a tricky thing. If she hadn't connected the two, maybe I was planting something not real.

I headed down Canal Street. I chatted, to fill the time, not press her for details she might not really remember but, being human, would fill in.

I only stopped chatting after we crossed Rampart and I had to pay attention to the traffic or we would die. I didn't know if she was listening to me or thinking about the questions I had asked her. My ego wasn't sure which I preferred.

A U-turn and we were in front of her hotel. I didn't even argue about following her to her room. She gave a wan smile, gathered her groceries, and left. I stayed as long as I could, watching her disappear through the door.

You'd feel bad if you found out that she was shot in the lobby.

I'd feel worse if we both were.

I pulled into the traffic. I'd text her once I got to…wherever I was going.

I debated returning to my office, but it would be evening soon enough. I could catch up with the computer grannies in the morning before moving Sarah to her new hotel. There would be about four hours between checking out and when we could check into the new one. I wasn't sure what to do with her. New clothes and groceries? Where could I take her that wouldn't be too much exposure to danger? Or should I get a list of what she wanted, hide her someplace, and get the things for her? Hide her where? My office? House?

No solution came to mind.

But there was a perfect parking spot right in front of my favorite bar, Q Carré. Without thinking, I grabbed it.

Tomorrow would be another day, after all, and it was five o'clock in a time zone close to here. Besides, I could sit and consider what to do at home, or I could sit comfortably with a cocktail and hope the alcohol could loosen the synapses enough for a brilliant idea to hit me.

I assumed the bar would be slow, but no, a bachelorette party was taking up most of the place.

I gave Mary, the bartender and day manager, the side-eye. She shrugged and leaned over the bar to say softly, "The money is good. They rented the space until seven and they're tipping well." She motioned to Peg, the other bartender, to hold the fort.

She beckoned me to follow her outside to the side yard. It had been partitioned, so the garbage was hidden behind a freshly painted wall and there were now a few tables spread around. Nice, but no more than about ten people could fit out here—if they were friendly. Mary pointed to a newly built staircase. I followed her up.

The building had a second story, but only on the front half, like it had been added on over the years. The roof on the one-story part had been remodeled and was now a nice expanse of outdoor seating.

"Take your pick," she said, pointing to all the empty chairs. "We haven't officially opened it yet, still working on the logistics of serving up here. But if you're willing to run up and down the stairs, you can hang here."

That was an easy yes. I followed her back down to get a beer, my drink of choice since I was driving.

Once I had my Abita Purple Haze, I considered my seating choices. I finally took one that overlooked both the street below and the corner. I liked to watch the world pass by, and this was a good perch for this little patch.

I texted Sarah to make sure she was in her room. She texted back, checking what time I'd pick her up tomorrow morning. I reminded her that we said ten-ish, and I would meet her at her room.

One beer didn't give me any great ideas, so I went downstairs and got a second one. I also ordered a burger, but got it to go. It would be dinner and get me out of here. If I changed my mind, I could always come back up to the roof deck to eat.

I'd taken the first sip of the beer when I noticed someone who looked familiar coming down the street. Odd that Torbin and I had just been discussing her. I tried to recall her name, the lesbian lawyer who'd just won a major lawsuit. Francine? No, Frances.

Rampart had once been a deshabille street, tourists warned to stay away, with down-at-heel bars and businesses, sprinkled between parking lots. But all that had changed. New places sprang up. There was a champagne bar just down the street and several decent restaurants. It was now after five in this time zone, so she was probably going to one of them.

She paused at the corner, waiting for someone, looking at her watch, then her phone. I wondered if she was checking with her secretary about who she was dating tonight. After a minute or so, she looked up and smiled, putting her phone away.

Another woman came into view. I also knew her. I hunched down. If they looked up in my direction, they would see me. As much as I could, I tried to keep the deck railing between my face and their view.

The second woman was Nancy, Cordelia's partner.

I admit I never tried liking her because she had never been friendly to me, treating me like garbage now coming back to visit. Cordelia and I still technically owned the house I lived in. Nancy had long been pushing her to push me to move out and let them have it.

What was she doing here with Frances while Cordelia was out of town?

Asshole that I am, I pulled out my phone and snapped a picture of them together. It was a friendly greeting, a tight hug, but nothing said it was more than friendly.

It doesn't mean anything, I told myself. *You can be in a relationship and still go out with a single friend.*

My phone rang. I silenced it before seeing who it was.

Joanne.

Damn, I needed to talk to her but didn't want to make any noise that might cause them to look up. I dithered long enough that the call went to voice mail.

Frances reached out and took her hand, leading her around the corner. They were gone.

Shit and damnation, I hope they're not coming in here. I couldn't see the Rampart Street entrance from here. I could skip out through the garbage gate—if I wanted to leave my hamburger behind.

Calm down, I'm not the one out with someone not my partner. I'm a regular at this bar and have every right to be here.

I took another sip of beer. Heh, if they were downstairs, I could come over to them, all friendly, "Hey, Frances, Nancy. Fancy meeting y'all here. I like this place since it's so out of the way." Maybe even ask if they wanted a photo. Nah, that would be going too far.

I glanced down at the street again. All clear.

I dialed Joanne.

"Hey, what's up?"

"NYPD want to talk to Sarah," she said.

"We can arrange a phone call," I said.

"No, they're here. They asked what hotel she was staying at." Before I could protest, she continued, "I didn't tell them. Made an excuse that I didn't know, you'd set it up and I'd have to contact you."

"You think something isn't kosher? No pun intended."

"I think we don't need to do it on their timetable and their way. I don't know whether I'm pissed they called and basically told us to do as we're told or if I'm concerned it's happening too fast for me to vet the whole situation. Anyone can say they're a cop."

"Shit, that's reassuring."

"I have a call in with the head of the team to check, but he hasn't called back."

"Possible one of the cops is a true believer? Doing the righteous work of his god?"

"Yeah, possible, but I don't want to think it's likely. I'd be more worried if we were dealing with Texas cops. Or even upstate here."

"I have an idea. Can you get an interview room at your station tomorrow? I'm moving Sarah and have to check out by eleven but can't check in until three. What if I bring her to the station and they interview her there?"

"Yeah, that should work. Will she be okay with that?"

"I suppose she can say no. I'll text her and let her know. I also need a favor from you. She identified a couple of weird people, one a young woman claiming to want to convert, but it could have been a spying mission. If we can contact David Moskowitz, the administrator at her temple, he would have the info."

"Do you have a burner phone?"

"Uh, maybe. If I can find it." I'd gotten one a while back, mostly to see how they worked, thinking it might be handy in some situations. And promptly forgot about it.

"Get one. I can contact him, but it would be helpful if he can contact you."

"I'll either find it or get another," I told her. "But if I have a burner phone her friends can call, why can't she talk to them on that phone?"

"You don't need to tell her. Maybe okay, but if anyone is monitoring their phones, they might see a lot of calls to the burner number and get a location."

I left it at that, knowing it would be hard to not tell Sarah certain things. She was far from a stupid woman and would likely figure it out.

Joanne continued, "I'll let you know the arrangements for tomorrow. Later."

I finished my beer.

Time to see who was downstairs. And get my burger.

Save for the even more raucous than before bridal party, the bar was empty. Mercifully, Nancy and Frances were not queer dive bar kinds of people. I picked up my burger, gave a nice tip, and left.

The parking gods continued to smile on me with a spot right in front of my house, left there because it was the size of a reasonable car, not a big SUV.

I did a quick change into sweatpants and an old T-shirt and settled in the kitchen breakfast nook to enjoy my burger before it got cold. With another beer.

I texted Sarah as I was eating, telling her NYPD wanted to talk to her and our plan to do it at Joanne's station. I hit send, then added that we didn't want to give them her hotel info.

She texted back, asking if she had to do it but then agreeing as if the first was a token protest. I texted back, saying I'd pick her up at the same time.

I finished my burger, cleaned up, and searched for the long-lost burner phone. It proved to be not so lost, only tossed into the least likely junk drawer. The charger was even with it. I plugged it in, then turned it on. Still had over an hour of the minutes I had originally purchased.

Once it was humming along, I used it to text the number to Joanne. A bit of a risk; if they were checking her phone, they might get the number. But she's a cop and she could be getting any number of calls from people with burner phones.

She texted back an OK.

Ten minutes later it rang.

Spam so soon?

I picked it up.

"Hey, I'm trying to reach Michele Knight?" Either a Lower Ninth Ward accent or a Brooklyn one. No, it doesn't make sense, but they're very close.

"Who's calling?"

"David, Sarah's chief cook and bottle washer, executive director on my business card."

Ah, that was fast. "Yes, this is she. Most people call me Micky."

"How's Sarah? We're worried about her."

"She's fine," I said. "Well, as okay as possible given the circumstance. I'm moving her tomorrow to a new hotel and there are police from NYPD down here for an interview. We'll do that between changing hotels."

"Why?"

"We feel it's best to not have her in one place—"

"No, not that. The NYPD talked to her nonstop for two days, right until she got on the plane. Barely let her out for the funeral."

"I don't know. Maybe they came up with more questions."

"Gun jockeys, more impressed with the asshole's shooting ability than worried about the murder. They asked to see a copy of their marriage certificate before they believed Leah was Sarah's wife."

"What? In New York City?"

"We have our pockets, let me tell you. Where are you taking her?"

"I'm trying to tell as few people as possible where she's staying."

"No, don't tell me, then. Better I don't know. Where are they interviewing her? Not where she's staying, right?"

"No, we're doing it at a police station here."

"Which one? If I can, I'll get a lawyer there with her."

I gave him the address of Joanne's station. I didn't argue, but I doubted he would find someone here on such short notice.

I told him why I wanted to get in touch with him. "Would it be possible to get any info on her?"

"Have it already. I've been racking my brain, who, how, why. Had to be someone who knew something about us, schedule, what Sarah looked like, where she might be. So, I looked at anyone around. That woman popped up like a rotten fish at low tide. I can send it to you. Not from me to you, but my second cousin Murray has a print shop, he sends out big files all the time. So, it'll come from him."

I gave him my office contact info. I was impressed with how well organized he was and said so.

"Naw, I'm not the smart one in the family, that's my brother and two sisters, the doctors. I organize stuff, a bit crazy and it drives some people nuts. Not Sarah, she learned what I can do well and how to use what I can do. Like I finally found a weird-shaped hole that fits."

"If you're the not smart one in the family, it's good y'all aren't evil geniuses, or you'd have taken over the world by now."

He laughed. "Never thought of that as a calling. Look, tell Sarah we love her and miss her big time. Let me know what else I can do. Anything."

"An order of good New York bagels?"

"Done!"

I hoped he knew I was kidding. I put down the phone just in time to get a text from Joanne. *Eleven. See you and Sarah then.*

I texted David the time on the off chance he found a lawyer. I didn't know that Sarah needed one—she wasn't accused of anything. Except being queer and Jewish.

After that, I read the latest Greg Herren mystery and put myself to bed at a reasonable time.

CHAPTER SEVEN

A h, Monday. I'd worked all weekend, so it was just another day. I was at my office bright and early, mainly to catch the computer grannies to see what they'd found.

There was a message from Paulette asking for an update. *Not this soon, and the time I take to update you adds to the bill.* I'd contact her later, after settling Sarah in her new hotel.

Or maybe I could tell her I couldn't find him and she should hire someone else.

Once I'd made coffee, I trotted down to the grannies. Lena was there.

"What do you have?" I asked.

"Your boy isn't doing well in life. Has as close to a negative credit rating as possible. Mother had to cosign for both his car loan and apartment. Three credit cards, all close to the max, off-brand ones that charge an arm and a leg on interest."

"Not likely he's hiding in a hotel somewhere, then?"

"No. Checked his social media pages; he put up an ask for a loan, said he would have money soon, but the only responses were 'sorry, no can do,' unless someone messaged him privately. But his circle of friends seems more like the good times and beers type and not the help through hard times. Rotating group, no one specifically standing out."

"Any names?"

"Got a list," she said, handing me a sheet. "Even pulled phone numbers for the ones I could find. They…don't seem like an enlightened bunch."

"What do you mean?"

"Confederate flags, far right memes. Lot of 'we will not be replaced' stuff. Talk of arming for the coming civil war. Nasty stuff."

"I'm sorry you had to look at it. Any mention of specific groups or organizations?"

"No, not by name. They hinted at something, but hard to tell if it's just a bunch of beer buddies or something more organized."

"Anything that might lead to where he is?"

"When he asked for the loan, he said he could meet anywhere in south Louisiana, or even Mississippi. He'd need at least two hours' notice. He also asked to borrow camping gear." She glanced down at what she had printed out. "He had a tent but needed a stove and sleeping bag. Again, no takers in the comments."

"Who loans out a sleeping bag? Not easy to wash."

She laughed. "From what I could tell, he's not the rugged outdoors type. No mention of any outdoor trips, not even day hikes. From the addresses I could find, he lived most of his life around here, mainly in the suburbs, Gretna, Kenner. No military service, a few drug arrests. Nothing more than a slap on the wrist, but still on the record."

"Nice white boy justice."

She nodded. "Reading between the lines, but he had an uncle, now deceased, who was a minor gambling kingpin over on the Gulf Coast. Elmer never worked with him and he tended to keep it in the family. My guess is that the uncle didn't think Elmer was qualified enough."

"Who knew criminals had job standards?"

"He got lucky meeting up with your friend; it seems to be the flushest period in his life."

"High school acquaintance, not a friend. No wonder he doesn't want to let it go."

"Here's everything I found, list of friends, people he knows, about five years of addresses; he moved around a lot. Truck make and model—that was easy, in his employment file. As much financial info as I can give you."

I thanked her and headed back upstairs. I put Paulette's pile of paper on my desk; it could wait.

When I opened my email, I found one from Murray's Print and Post with a big file attached. The email just said, *Hope you like this job and come back for more.*

I opened it. The info on the woman had the usual, name, address, contact info. I wondered how much, if any, of it was true. I saved a copy, sent it by email to Joanne, leaving Murray out of it. I gave her the quick overview of she should be checked out. I was tempted to try the phone number, but a murder is a police investigation and I knew from experience that they don't like PIs meddling. I'd be a good girl and give them a few days before I did anything.

Time to pick up Sarah. I headed out the door. Traffic was still bad as I got into the French Quarter, but at least moving slightly faster than the mule-driven buggies.

I pulled into the hotel just after ten, parked, and was up knocking on her door by a quarter past.

"Who is it?" she asked from inside. The cautious person in me was glad she didn't open the door at a knock.

"It's me, Micky."

The door opened and she let me in. All her bags were packed, a tip left for the cleaning staff.

"I think we can check out on the TV," I told her.

She nodded, moving out of the way.

Of course, it's never as simple as it looks. It took me about five minutes to get it all sorted and her checked out.

"So, no groceries or clothes?" she asked as she hoisted her briefcase over her shoulder. "Just a police station."

"Yeah, likely. Maybe we can fit it in after." I grabbed her carry-on bag and two tote bags on one arm, leaving her the rolling suitcase.

I opened the door and checked the hallway before exiting. When we got on the elevator, it was empty, but it stopped at a lower floor and two men got on. I positioned myself between them and Sarah.

But they seemed intent on deciding which Bourbon Street bar to go to, paying no attention to two middle-aged women. They settled on one of the big tourist traps. I considered warning them, but maybe tourist trap was what they were interested in.

I let them go in front of us after we exited, moving slowly so they could get well ahead. Once they were clearly heading out the main door, I hurried us along to parking. Of course there was a line. Two Midwestern families traveling together, driving because one of the husbands hated flying—yes, they had this conversation in three different versions while we were waiting, as well as complaints about city driving—and one very impatient Uptown couple who were muttering about "the people" they hire.

I was even more impatient, wanting us in my car and moving, but kept my attention on scanning everyone and everything around us while not looking like I was doing it.

Once I got to the valet desk, I handed him my ticket and ten bucks. I gave another ten to the woman who drove my car down. She smiled at me and murmured, "Not everyone can drive stick." She loaded the suitcases in the trunk, and we were on our way.

Our slow way.

The two men in the elevator were lingering on the next corner.

Still debating? Or watching us?

At least we were going to a police station. Presumably no one would try anything there.

Joanne was located close enough to Orleans Parish Prison that I pointed it out to Sarah. Like most of the city, Tulane Avenue is gentrifying, new apartments and businesses, but the area around Tulane and Broad was still dominated by the jail and the criminal court, an imposing art deco building. Only a tourist area if you were stupid or unlucky.

Nor an easy place to park with all the people swirling in and out. I ended up about two blocks farther away than I wanted to be.

"Is it safe to leave my suitcases in your car?" Sarah asked as she glanced around the neighborhood.

"Looks can be deceiving. This place is teeming with all sorts of law enforcement. I have a friend who swears it's the safest area in the city."

She looked at the mix of drab, functional buildings, and the ramshackle houses just beyond, but said nothing.

I pointed us in the direction of Joanne's office, and we were passed by two police cars and one unmarked one as we hiked there.

Like the other buildings in the area, Joanne's office was built for function, not form. Any new building ambience was long gone, walls clearly painted multiple times, sloppy brushstrokes on top of sloppy brushstrokes. This area had flooded badly during Katrina, the water marks long gone, but the destruction had aged the already aging structures.

I let the desk clerk know Joanne was expecting us. It took ten minutes before the inner sanctum door opened and a young officer beckoned us in.

I'd been here several times and was used to it, but Sarah didn't seem like someone who often found herself in cop shops.

"You okay?" I muttered as we were led down a long hallway.

"Define okay," she mumbled back.

I didn't and couldn't.

The officer pointed us to the doorway of Joanne's office.

She was on the phone and waved us in. I let Sarah take the only chair that looked like it could hold weight. I feigned an interest in the beige building outside the window. Joanne seemed to be listening more than talking, so I couldn't even amuse myself by eavesdropping. She finally finished with, "Yes, sir, we take all complaints seriously. I'll pass this one on to my supervisor. Yes, he's a man," she added with about as straight a face as possible. She finally put the phone down.

"The New York boys aren't here yet," she said. A hint of annoyance.

"You mean we could have stopped for coffee?" I bantered.

"Probably coffee and lunch," she muttered.

"Maybe they had a bit of a night, didn't notice the bar didn't have last call to kick them out." I glanced at my watch. It was enough after eleven to be late, not yet annoyingly so.

"Maybe. As backward as we are here, we do have working phones." Joanne doesn't usually let the sarcasm loose while on duty.

I had no such restraints. "If we give them fifteen minutes, can we then hoof it?"

She sighed, "No, better you stay here, otherwise they might demand to go to your hotel."

"You're worried about them knowing that?" Sarah finally spoke.

"I'd prefer unless people really need to know, they don't," Joanne answered.

Sarah just nodded.

Joanne stood up. "Let's go to the interview room, at least there are more chairs there."

She led us down another long hallway and into a room painted a depressing swamp green—swamp green on a rainy day, with a beat-up table bolted to the floor and chairs around it.

"Pick a seat. I'll see if I can find some drinkable coffee." Then with a glance at Sarah, "Or would you prefer something else?"

"Water, please," she said.

"No promises, I'll see what I can do."

Sarah stood by the table, a hand resting on it for support, then glanced at her watch. I did the same. On the verge of annoyingly late.

"You don't have to do this," I said, her reluctance palpable.

"But I do, like a root canal, or surgery, miserable, save for the hope that someday, it will be better."

Joanne came back with a bottle of water for Sarah. I suspected she took it from someone's stash. I got a cup of coffee that looked like bayou water to match the swamp walls.

I sniffed it and took a tentative sip. Its looks were deceiving; I've tasted better bayou water.

There was a knock on the door, and the same officer who had led us in stuck his head in. Before he could say anything, two men pushed past him, flashing their NYPD badges.

Both were burly, intimidating men, dressed in suits that looked like they'd been worn last night for carousing and thrown on again this morning. A mustard stain on a tie.

I'm five-ten and both were taller than me by several inches. One at least six-one, the other about six-two. About as stereotypical as could be, one looked Irish, with red hair going to washed out gray, a ruddy complexion that hinted of many nights of beer with the boys, the other Italian, dark hair, no gray but receding, dark brown eyes that gave nothing out. Both were muscular, their suits tight on both their shoulders and stomachs, like they worked out and went for burgers afterward. What stood out the most was their assumption they were in charge.

"Coulda done this in a nicer location," said Mr. Red Face. "Hate to drag you to places like this," he said with a brief glance at Sarah.

I took it as more about his comfort than hers. Had she wanted someplace else, she could have chosen it.

Red Face continued, "I'm Detective Ian O'Reilly and this is Detective Jerry Guilio."

"Can I get you coffee or anything?" Joanne asked.

"Sure, doll, that would be great," said Mr. Black Hole Eyes, baiting her.

She looked at him and said, "My name is Detective Sergeant Joanne Ranson. New Orleans is progressive enough not to be so openly misogynistic." Not giving them time to reply, she went into the hallway and called for the young officer who had brought them here. She asked him to bring the coffee. I hoped it was the same coffee she'd found for me. They deserved it.

Sarah sat down, indicated the seat next to her for me. The dynamics were clear; we were on one side and they were on the other.

"Who are you?" Mr. Black Eyes demanded.

"Michele Knight. I'm providing security for Rabbi Jacobson," I answered, keeping my answer as simple and neutral as possible.

"Must be nice, hanging out in a city like New Orleans while being paid for it."

"I live here."

"So, how do you stay out of the bars?" Red Face asked.

Joanne saved me from answering by coming into the room, followed by a well-dressed man with the kind of briefcase that said lawyer. He was wearing a yarmulke.

"Who are you?" Black Eyes demanded.

"I'm Lev McDonald, Sarah's lawyer," he said. To Sarah, he added, "Second cousin to David's first cousin on his mother's side." He was in his thirties, glasses, brown hair cut short. He was neither big nor tall, a slight man who looked like he biked or ran. Tortoiseshell glasses on observant gray eyes. I suspected his strength was in his brain, and that was where he fought his battles.

"McDonald?" Red Face asked.

"Yeah, a little Scots crept in along the way. Converted, but kept the name."

"Why do you need a lawyer?" Black Eyes demanded. "Thought you were the victim here."

"The legal system can be confusing," Joanne interjected. "It can't hurt Sarah to have someone who's only interested in her welfare."

The two cops looked at each other. This setup was not to their liking.

"Can we get on with it?" Sarah said. She nodded at Lev. He pulled a chair up to be on the other side of her. Joanne chose the semblance of neutrality and sat at the end.

Black Eyes opened a folder he had brought with him, but his eyes weren't scanning it. He was delaying, regaining control.

"What specific questions do you need to ask Sarah?" Lev said. "As you know, she was extensively interviewed while she was still in New York."

He wasn't letting Black Eyes drive the interview. Points for being a good lawyer. It also meant we could tag team.

"Well, there are a lot of areas we'd like to cover."

"I've covered them," Sarah said. "What do you need to know that I haven't answered before?"

I knew she could stand up for herself, but I liked to think with Lev and me both there, she was more willing to do so.

"You haven't gone over them with us," Red Face said.

"Why is that necessary?" Lev asked.

"Look, I get you're a lawyer and all that," Red Face replied, "but we're cops, so let us do our cop work, okay?"

"We're not adversaries here," Joanne interjected. "We all want the same thing."

"It would feel less adversarial if you would let us do our jobs."

"If you have to be macho jerks who make your disdain for women as clear as you have so far, it's going to be even more adversarial," I told them. I was already tired of these fuckers and had nothing to lose.

"What's your badge number, doll?" Black Eyes asked.

"Private, babycakes. No badge. Ask your fucking questions and let us get out of here."

"Hey, no need to use that kind of language in front of a religious leader," Red Face said.

"I've heard it before. What's your first question?" Sarah said.

"Can you go over in exact detail what happened?" Red Face asked.

"I've done that. There is a video of me doing exactly that," Sarah replied.

"Review it when you get back to NYC," Lev said. "There is no need to put her through that all again. Please move on to the next question."

"But there might be things others missed." Black Eyes.

"Review the tape. If you have further questions, ask them after," Lev insisted.

"You want us to catch this guy or not?" Red Face asked.

"We all want that," Sarah said, "but I have already relived that day more than I can bear."

"It would be so helpful," Red Face persisted.

Sarah gripped the side of her chair, her knuckles white. "Friday, after services. I was tired; we were going home. Said our good-byes to the few people still there. We talked about picking up food. I took out my phone to look for a menu, then dropped it. Heard—heard a crack. Then Leah…wrong, something wrong. Blood. She crumpled, went down. I was next to her, on my knees, desperately calling to her, trying to stop the blood. And…" She paused, looking down, her hand even whiter. "Telling her I loved her. Telling her to stay."

"She say anything to you?" Black Eyes asked.

Sarah shook her head, then looked at them defiantly. "No, she was choking on her own blood. She grasped my hand, tight for a moment, but…she couldn't hold on."

Lev and I put our hands on her shoulders, daring them to ask her to continue.

"Next question, please," Lev said.

Black Eyes again looked at the folder. Again, delay for control.

I reached across the table and snatched it from him. It was a printout from the hotel about where to eat. I looked at it, looked at him, and shoved it to Lev.

"Questions? Really? Or is this pretense an excuse for a junket down to New Orleans?" I demanded.

"Nothing like that," Black Eyes replied. "Yeah, it was fake, but we're good at keeping things in our heads and only use props because people wonder otherwise."

"We were able to reserve this room for only an hour and a half. We started late, so time is short," Joanne interjected.

Black Eyes grabbed the fake folder back.

"Can you think of anything you did that might have provoked the attack?" Red Face asked.

"Provoked?" Sarah replied, anger and shock on her face.

"Did you goad anyone, make them angry?" Black Eyes questioned.

"No!"

"You sure?" Red Eyes probed. "Been too in the face with your lifestyle? Too pushy for some people?"

Lev stepped in. Better than me, as I might have thrown something, like a punch, at them. "No," he said. "Other than exercising her rights as an American to free speech and to live her life within the law. You seem to be saying that if we're victims of a hate crime, it's partly our fault. The responsibility is solely on the person committing the crime."

They gave each other a look.

"Look, Sarah, you got any enemies? Could the attack have been personal? Family feud?" Red Face asked. "Some old boyfriend who didn't like you being with women?"

"That's not what happened," Sarah said tersely. "My last so-called boyfriend was in middle school. We are friends on social media and he is happily married—to a man—and living in Seattle."

"Okay, look, we gotta explore all the options."

"We went over this when I was interviewed in New York," Sarah said. "I thought this was to ask additional clarifying questions, not rehash everything that's already been done."

"We're trying to be fresh eyes, see if we see something others haven't," Red Face said.

"You have no leads and y'all thought a fishing expedition to New Orleans would be fun," I said.

"We got plenty of leads," Black Eyes rejoined. "Takes time to track them all down."

A knock on the door and the young officer returned with a tray of several cups of coffee—the same bayou crap I'd gotten—a few bottles of water and some cans of soda. He put it down in the middle of the table.

Red Face grabbed a coffee and a soda. Black Eyes did the same, grabbing water instead of soda.

I motioned to Sarah, to give her first choice of what was left. Having mostly finished her first bottle of water, she took another. That left a coffee, one water, and a vile lemon-lime soda. Lev reached for the coffee, but I gave a brief shake of my head. He took the water instead.

I could do without either. Joanne agreed with me.

"What about old girlfriends? Any of those want to do you harm?"

"No."

"You sure?" he pushed.

"Leah and I were together for twenty-three years."

"Old grudges that ancient only happen in fiction," I added.

"What about her?" Black Eyes asked. "Maybe she was seeing someone and they wanted you out of the picture? Misfired badly on their part."

Sarah stared at them.

"This is contemptable speculation," Lev cut in.

"No, just no!" Sarah said. "Leah was not like that. I would have known."

"Spouse is the last to know," Black Eyes said.

"Sorry, we gotta look at all angles," Red Face added.

"Maybe you should start with realistic ones, then," I said. "You clearly know nothing about them, not even about relationships between women in general. Maybe men don't notice, but trust me, women do."

"You a dyke?" Black Eyes shot at me.

"Worried I might be your wife's type?"

He started to say something but stopped himself in time.

"We gotta look at all angles," Red Face repeated, like that excused them.

"How about this for an angle," I said. "Hate groups. A lot of people hate the LGBTQ community and a lot of people hate Jews. Sarah's a target for both. Look into the hostile letters, the bomb threats. Which of those groups is active in New York and had the capacity to do this?"

"What makes you think we're not looking into that?" Black Eyes asked.

"Because we've been here for an hour and you haven't asked a single question about it," I shot back.

"We are looking into that," Black Eyes said. "But not likely Sarah would know anything about them."

"Rabbi Jacobson," Lev corrected.

"Really? Like looking at people who claimed they wanted to join but seemed more interested in casing the joint? Even a half-pint hate group would want a look around before acting," I said.

"We're looking into that," Black Eyes repeated.

"What have you found?" Joanne said. "We need to know about any hate groups involved, to be able to monitor their activity in this area."

"Early days," he said. "Nothing to send out yet."

"Early?" Lev asked. "It's been over a week. You have to have something by now."

"I'll check," Red Face said. "I'm not working on that area. Jerry, aren't you?"

"Yeah, which is why I know we don't have much."

"Okay, let's move on," Red Face said.

"How familiar are you with firearms?" Red Face asked.

"What?" Sarah said. "Not at all. I've lived all my life in Brooklyn. We've never had a gun in our house."

"So, no one could have stolen a gun from you to have shot your, uh, partner?" Black Eyes asked.

"Wife," Lev corrected.

"No, of course not!"

"Covering all the angles," Black Eyes said this time.

"Stop fishing," I cut in. "If you have relevant questions instead of bizarre speculation, ask them. If not, we're leaving."

"Hold your horses, doll," Black Eyes said.

"I have no horses, babycakes," I retorted.

He glared at me.

"Anyone you have a strong disagreement with? Didn't you debate with another one of your people and it got heated?"

"I was discussing Israel with several other Jewish leaders and the situation over there. We disagreed, but that's what we do. We can scream at each other about obscure passages in the Torah. No one gets killed over it."

"Never?" Black Eyes asked.

"Not that I know of. Maybe in the heat of the moment, an unwise blow. But that was months ago. I have disagreed with the more conservative members of the Jewish community most of my life. So far, no one has done more than wag a finger in my face."

Black Eyes nodded, but Red Face just shrugged. "Some communities are just more violent than others," he added.

"All those white men who do mass shootings. Very dangerous," I said.

Black Eyes grabbed the remaining cup of coffee, hopefully cold by now. "Random violence like this is hard to solve. If it's not someone you know, well, it's hard to find leads and hard to solve."

"Really? Most of the time these people are zealots, caught up in the idiot beliefs of their cult and unable to see reality. They think their particular god is on their side, so whatever they do is going to work, no matter how stupid it is," I said. I was interested to see what their reaction was. I wondered if I was telling one of them—or both—that they were stupid.

"Oh, and you think your side isn't locked in a cult, either?" Black Eyes shot back. "Like the laws of nature don't apply to you?"

"They do. Haven't escaped gravity yet. Your opinion isn't a law," I replied.

"Final fifteen minutes," Joanne cut in. "Please ask any questions you feel you need to ask before we have to end."

Black Eyes and Red Face looked at each other. Red Face said, "Can we contact you later if we have more questions?"

I was about to say no, but Joanne replied. "Yes, please send them to me and I will get them to Sarah and the answers back to you."

"Be easier if we could just meet," Red Face said.

"No," I answered this time. "We gave you time to ask questions. You showed up late, dicked around with stupid speculation well on the bullshit spectrum. You wasted your time, we didn't. We're not making up for your mistakes."

"Look, doll, you don't get the final say here," Black Eyes said.

"No, but I do," Sarah retorted.

"We can pull you in as a material witness," Red Eyes said.

"Not in this jurisdiction," Joanne told him.

"You gotta come back to New York someday," Red Face said.

"Are you threatening my client?" Lev demanded.

"No," Black Eyes replied. "Would just be nice to have a little more cooperation."

"Two-way street, babycakes," I said. "You treat people with contempt, you don't get cooperation back."

"I take it we're done here," Joanne said. She stood up, opened the door, and called in the young officer. "Please escort these gentlemen out."

"We'll be in touch," Red Face said as his parting remark. Once they were in the hallway, there were a few muttered words, one which sounded like it started with a "c."

Sarah drained her water.

None of us said anything until we were sure they were out of the building.

"Well, NYPD obviously sent their best," I said sarcastically.

"Not even close," Joanne said. These were her colleagues. "I'll contact their lead and let them know this was a total waste of time and money."

"Are they legit cops?" I asked, suddenly wondering.

"They had badges. Checked out with the team up there," she answered.

"Are you all right?" Lev asked Sarah.

Okay, so the straight guy was the sensitive one.

"This would have been hell if it had been just me and the two of them," she said, letting out a shaky breath. "Thanks for…" She didn't finish, instead wiping her eyes.

"I'm so sorry," Joanne said. "I would never have agreed to this if I'd known they planned to do an adversarial interview."

"You mean they weren't just bigoted assholes?" I demanded.

"Sarah is not a suspect," Lev pointed out.

"No," Joanne said. "She's not, and that was uncalled for. Again, I'm sorry."

"Maybe we need to leave, since the time for this room is up," Lev said gently.

"We have time," Joanne told him.

I looked at her. "You lied. This room isn't booked."

She didn't answer, just shrugged. On duty, she wouldn't admit to lying.

"Thank you," Sarah said to her. "I'd like to sit for a few minutes. I do not want to run into them."

"You're good," I told her. "Take as long as you like." No, I'm not sensitive, but I can occasionally fake it.

Sarah nodded, not moving. She stared ahead, but her eyes seemed somewhere else.

After a few minutes, Joanne asked if she'd like some more water.

"Thank you, no. I think we'd all like to be out of this room," she said, standing.

Joanne led us out, saying good-bye at the door.

At the bottom of the steps, Lev gave us both his cards. He asked Sarah if she would like a hug. She said yes. After a good, long hug, he turned to me, arms just open enough to ask, and we hugged as well. Straight guy still winning the sensitivity points.

He made us promise to call if we needed anything, then headed off.

Chapter Eight

Sarah walked briskly. I trailed behind her. I had told her this was one of the safest areas in the city, and it probably was, for run-of-the-mill crime. I didn't want to get mugged, but that wasn't my biggest worry.

We crossed the street to the block where my car was.

I heard a car start, looked to my left to see, but the side street was parked up and no one was moving yet, just an engine down the block.

I sped up, getting Sarah to my car as quickly as possible. Of course, people get shot in cars all the time, but it could move faster than we could run.

Once we were in, I immediately pulled out.

"What's wrong?" Sarah asked. She was too smart to not read my actions.

"Nothing. Yet. A car started as we passed the block. Maybe coincidence and innocent."

"But you're worried."

I stopped at the stop sign. A car nosed around the corner, going the same way.

Still could be innocent—these were one-way streets.

I held my flight reflex long enough to get as good a look as I could. The car was new, dark gray, nondescript. Like a rental car. There were two men in it, both tall. One dark hair, one lighter, maybe reddish gray.

Game on. They thought they could follow me in a city I've lived in most of my life?

I considered really screwing them, going to the bayous where I grew up and getting them lost in the back roads with the alligators. But I reminded myself that Sarah was my priority, and having her in the car for hours wasn't keeping her safe. Lose them and move on.

I sped around the corner, taking the easy right onto Tulane Avenue, but at the next intersection pulling a U-turn. They caught it—I thought they would—but it forced them to be obvious. I headed up Tulane, but as I crossed Carrollton, I veered to the right, made another U to turn left onto Carrollton.

"Where are we going?" Sarah asked.

"It's our friends from NYPD, and we're losing them," I told her.

"Shit," she muttered. "Are they part of this?"

I didn't know and didn't have time to think about it.

I did a quick turn into the Costco parking lot to pass through to Palmetto and away from the busy area. It was two lanes, but not much traffic once you got past the parking arteries. I hit the gas, going faster than I should.

A glimpse in the rearview mirror showed me they were still behind, although they'd slowed in the parking lot.

The road curved. I sped up as much as I dared.

Just before the canal separating Orleans Parish from Jefferson Parish, with bushes blocking the view, I took a hard right into a narrow passage, a utility road for Longue Vue House & Gardens. My luck held and there were no other cars on the narrow, overgrown road. The main road continued over the canal and into a turn. I was hoping they would stay on it and only realize I hadn't when they couldn't find me.

I kept going as fast as the narrow lane allowed. It let out onto Metairie Road and I headed back into the city, taking whatever route was faster. The turn lane to the interstate was backed up, so I stayed on the surface roads, turning off onto Bienville.

"I think we've lost them," I said after another check of my rearview mirror.

"Why would they follow us if not to target me?" Sarah asked.

"Ego," I answered, as we crossed Carrollton. "They wanted to prove they're smarter than we are, find your hotel by following us. Or they're bored; it's too early to get shit-faced, they were sitting in their car licking their wounds, saw us walk by and decided to have a little fun."

A few blocks farther and I turned unto a side street, made a few jogs, and cut over to Ursulines.

"So, you think they're just being assholes?" Sarah asked, her voice tight. She was on edge. "Jewish, queer, not a real enough person to treat with dignity and respect."

I pulled over, parking under a shady oak. "I don't know. Well, I do know they're assholes. I do know once you're safe and tucked away, I'm calling Joanne to lodge a formal complaint."

"Why are we stopped?"

"If, somehow, they managed to follow me, they should be here any minute now. I'd prefer to find out in a random place than our real destination."

She nodded. Her body was tense, her arms crossed. "I'm not used to this. Not like you."

I laughed. "Most of what I do is chase paper, not cars," I said. "If it was this all the time, I'd have a better car."

"But you know, you have some idea of what to do. You spotted them."

"Not what I do on a daily basis, but it happens occasionally."

"Do you carry a gun?"

"Sometimes."

"Ever used it?"

"Yes. A last resort."

"Do you have it now?"

"Yes." I started the car again.

"Don't use it," she said as I pulled out. "I mean that. Too much risk of an innocent person getting hurt. Please tell me you won't use it."

We crossed Broad and I took another side street over to Esplanade.

"It would be a last resort," I said. I don't make promises I can't keep. I turned onto random streets in the Marigny, taking a long, looping and indirect path back.

I finally pulled into the yellow zone in front of her hotel.

"Don't move yet," I told her as I got out, scanning the neighborhood. We were at the lower part of Esplanade, close to the river. A few cars over on Decatur, but it was quiet here. I popped the trunk and took her bags out, giving her a wave to join me.

Sarah seemed spent, only enough energy to do what she had to do, following me in. I checked in under my name, with her standing in the background.

She followed me as we made the way to her room.

"This is nice," she said as we entered. I had booked a suite, so she had a place to sit other than her bed and a limited kitchen. But her words were tired, polite; a nice room was little compensation.

I did my usual, hiding behind the practical. "There's a grocery store not far from here. I'll run get you a few things."

She nodded, not even asking if she could go with me, not moving to unpack, instead a slow wander around the room, without really looking at anything.

Maybe Alex was right, maybe I needed to find ways to do more than just stuff her in a hotel room and leave her alone with her remorse and grief.

No answers came to mind. I settled for the concrete. "What would you like me to get?"

"A new life?" Then she waved her hands, shoving the words away. "Food. Whatever looks good."

I waited a moment to see if she wanted to add anything, but she didn't.

"I'll be back in a little bit," I said as I slipped out.

I hurried back down to my car to get out of the temporary hotel zone.

The store was a short jog up Elysian Fields. Small, but with a good selection of prepared foods. I went for the basics—a turkey sandwich, a pasta dish, fried chicken. I considered a muffaletta, but decided not without asking her first. Then muffins and fruit. A decadent slice of carrot cake from the bakery. A bag of chips. Wine and chocolate. Some fancy water. Enough for the rest of today and most of tomorrow.

As I waited in line, I considered what happened. A hostile interview. Then the chase. Was it them? Or did I want it to be them, instead of other unknown men? From my hasty look in the rearview mirror, it looked like the NY cops, but they weren't close enough for me to be sure. Two big men, white, one darker hair, one lighter. Even if it was them, was I right in downplaying it, calling it ego and boredom on their part? Could the cops be infiltrated?

Does the Pope wear a dress?

I'd talk to Joanne as soon as I could—away from Sarah—and come up with what to do next.

I checked out, did a hasty run by my house and grabbed a couple of my most decent T-shirts, then headed back to the hotel, finding a legal parking space close enough to be a miracle.

Because of the sparkling water, the bags were heavy and off-balance. I put them down while waiting for the slow elevator and then again outside Sarah's door. I tapped briefly, then let myself in. She wasn't in the sitting area. I heard her in the bedroom, her voice a low murmur, as if talking to herself. I busied myself unpacking the groceries, putting the water and prepared food in the small refrigerator, leaving the turkey sandwich, a drink, some fruit, and the chips on the table as a lunch suggestion and the T-shirts on the bed.

I didn't want to leave without talking to her, but didn't want to interrupt.

Her voice stilled. Minutes passed before she emerged.

"El Malei Rachamim," she said. "For Leah." To my quizzical look, she added, "A prayer for the dead. Like the Kaddish, but that should be said with others, but…"

"I'm sorry," I said. I'm woefully ignorant on anything beyond the usual Christian burial customs that were part of my childhood.

"Any chance I could go to a synagogue?"

There are some here, but my answer was "That would be risky. If anyone is looking for you, that would be a place to look."

"Online?"

"Also a risk. If you connect to the internet, the internet connects to you."

She nodded, looking around the room like a prisoner examining her cell. She sat by the food but didn't eat.

"You're not staying for lunch?" she asked. The words were flat, but under them was a request not to be left alone in a strange room with her pain.

I pulled up a chair and opened the chips. "I'll hang for a bit, but I have some things I need to do."

She nodded, unwrapping the sandwich. Instead of eating, she asked, "Why are the New York cops here and why did they follow me?"

"I don't know."

"Honest, I'll give you that."

I ate another handful of chips to stall. "I need to find out more. What I do know is you're safe for the moment."

"Because we're sitting here eating. Next moment, they could be breaking down the door."

"No, they can't. They don't know where you are."

"Until they call all the hotels in the area and ask for your name."

"They don't know my name," I defended. Not quite true, and it was a lapse on my part. I did give M. Knight, but still, for the next time, would have to use a fake name. She sighed, finally taking a bite of her sandwich.

"I'll be back later," I said. "Come up with someplace safe to go."

She gave a weak smile. "Thanks, that would be nice."

I stood up. "I'll call you, will aim to come back around six."

Another weak smile and a head nod.

I left before I could make more promises that might be hard to keep.

Once in my car, I headed to my office. It was past two. My stomach was growling. I should have grabbed something for myself at the store so as not to be at the mercies of what I might have lying around.

Before even seeing what food might be around, I called Joanne. Got her voice mail and left a message to call me ASAP.

My choice of food was a can of tuna or an ultra-processed toaster pastry. The latter, being easier to eat at my desk, won.

Paulette had left two messages. One this morning, the second about half an hour ago. *You are not paying me enough for this quick a turnaround.* I would call her tomorrow.

But I might as well work on her case.

First, I called his number. He didn't answer and his voice mail was full.

Then I tried his mother. She answered after the third ring. Her voice was a wheeze, a long life of smoking or lung trouble. "Who's calling?"

"I'm Michele Perkins. I'm trying to locate your son Elmer. He's won a raffle for a year of free pizza. He listed you as an alternate contact."

"He did, now?" she wheezed warily. "I'm happy to take it for him. Y'all deliver up around Monroe?"

"No, sorry," I said, slipping into the accent I had learned growing up in the bayou. "New Orleans suburbs."

"Damn, too bad. He owes me way more than a year of pizza."

"Maybe if he gets free pizza, he could pay you back," I said in my politest Southern voice.

She coughed out a laugh. "Can't hold my breath much, and I ain't holding for that."

"Well, if you can tell me where to find him, I can suggest he at least send you a pizza gift card for something in your area."

"If I could find him, I woulda found him. I cosigned his truck loan and he's missed the last two payments, so they're coming after me."

"Oh, I'm so sorry. He must be down on his luck."

"He's always down on his luck. It's always next week or next month."

"How do you contact him?"

"I call him on the phone, but he ain't answered since that first missed payment. He might be at his apartment, but no way I'm driving all that way. He might be playing with his buddies in the woods with their idiot soldier games."

"Do you know who any of his friends are? Even a name? I could look it up. If I do reach him, I promise I'll put in a good word for you."

"He was never a popular one. Friends changed a lot. Heard him talk about someone named R.C. Maybe Tilman? Got no last names."

"Any girlfriends?"

"Not that he told me of." She coughed, then spat up, holding the phone away, but not far enough for me not to hear.

She continued without prompting. "Would be nice if he settled down. He seemed to be doing all right for a while; said he had an office job, but didn't like his boss, some pushy broad. So, I'm guessing he quit, like a fool. Thought he mighta had a girl, but guess she dumped him when he lost his job."

"Do you know what his job was? Where he worked?" I was assuming this would lead me back to Paulette, but maybe I'd get lucky and find he'd found something new.

"Something medical. He said they were making tons of money and paying him shit, pardon my French, and working him to death."

She coughed again, covering the sigh that I didn't stop in time at the dead end.

"Do you have his address?" I asked. "I can pop by and see if he's there. Maybe he isn't aware his voice mail is full."

She coughed again, excused herself to look it up, and I heard more hacking in the background. When she came back, she read me the address that was in his employment file.

"You mentioned him playing soldier. Any idea where or who else he's with?"

"Not a clue. He asked me to buy him one of those guns, the ones that can fire a lot, for his birthday and I said no way. Too expensive. He was stupid when he was young, got a drug conviction and ain't supposed to own guns."

"Do you know if he got the gun some other way?"

"Nope, best I not know. Have to hope no one else was stupid enough to buy it for him."

"Anything else you can tell me?"

"I know he's got a good heart, just not so good a head. He gets into things he can't get out of. No sense with money. Hope you find him; he likes pizza." She coughed a good-bye and I heard more hacking sounds as she put the phone down.

Not really helpful, although it worried me he was looking for the gun favored by mass shooters.

I looked at my watch. A little before three. Enough time to run out to the suburb and check out his apartment? Joanne would know to call me on my cell and Paulette would not. Better than sitting here and stewing about what I was going to do with Sarah tonight.

I grabbed my keys and headed to my car.

I braved I-10 to save time. I hate the interstate here; it's people either trying to kill you or not moving. Today was moving and attempted murder. I managed to dodge a pickup with no depth perception who almost touched my bumper when they passed and pulled in front of me and a car that didn't seem to know what the white lane lines meant.

I was happy to pull off at the exit. From there I had to listen to my phone tell me where to go. I'm not familiar with this area, and there are drainage canals that dead end roads. Miss Thing, as I call the navigation voice, since she sounds like a bossy drag queen, still thought one of the roads walked on water and I had to redirect a few times before I got there.

A plane roared overhead. It was close enough to the airport to be noisy and also meant the rents were cheaper than places without the airport ambience. The years—and likely the tenants—hadn't been kind. A boxy 70s or 80s build, with fake stucco, cracked in more places than it should be, three story, but only stairs to get up and down. The parking lot was pitted, with a ditch too close to one end and no barrier for protection. The spots weren't marked, so I pulled into one close to the road, likely less desirable. As I approached, I could hear TVs, music, and a barking dog. Not much noise insulation.

I scanned the numbers, having to guess as some were missing. As I walked to what I hoped was his door, two men came out of an apartment farther down the walkway. They looked at me, wary if not outright suspicious.

I called to them, "I'm looking for Elmer Stumbolt."

They looked at each other, then back at me. "Haven't seen him in a few days," the one closer to me said.

The other one added, "We're not exactly friends."

"Why?" I asked. "He play his music too loud?"

They reached me. He pointed at his face. "He drives a truck with a big Confederate flag in the window."

"He's a racist asshole," I surmised.

"He's okay on his own," the second one said. "I mean, not friendly, but polite and all."

"But when he has friends over and they get to drinking, they want to fight the Civil War all over again."

"Have they been violent?"

"You a friend of his?" the older one asked.

"No, never met him." I took out my PI license and showed it to them. "I've been hired to find him."

They both examined it, more for curiosity than scrutiny.

"He in trouble?" the second man asked.

"It may depend on what he does when he gets found. If he's smart, he won't be. If he's not…" I trailed off.

"Smart is not what he does well. Hey, I'm Phil and this is my cousin, Willy. What do you want to know about him?"

"As you saw from my license, I'm Michele, but my friends call me Micky," I said. "What can you tell me about him?"

They again looked at each other. I may have given them too blank a page. "What kind of interactions have you had with him?"

Phil said, "Not much. Shared a few beers when he first moved in and we were trying to be friendly."

"He drank, didn't offer any in return," Willy added. "We're not here all the time, work on the rigs."

"So, he told us he couldn't really be friends with us, like we'd understand. Said he had no problem, but his friends wouldn't get it."

"No more beers after that," Willy added. "We said hi and all when we passed, but then he got that truck and then his friends started hanging too much."

"Walls are thin," Phil added. "They get loud when they get drunk. So we overheard a lot of shit."

"What kind of shit?" I asked.

"Lot of N-word, lot of talk about the upcoming race war and how they had to be prepared. That kind of shit."

"Deep shit," I said. "They just talking or did they have plans?"

"Both," Willy said. "Just so you know, they trash-talked women, even their girlfriends, calling them useful holes and worse."

"No worries, he's about as far from my type as any man could get."

"Got to the point we tried to time our weekends when we knew they'd be playing in the woods to get some peace," Phil added.

"Any idea where it is?"

They looked at each other and laughed. Phil said, "We have a map. He was stupid enough to come home drunk and leave a pile of stuff outside his door. Out on the walk is free."

"Are you willing to let me see it?"

"Sure, but don't go out there alone."

"Call us first," Willy said. "We were thinking of getting some friends, hiding fireworks all over the place and setting them off." They both laughed.

"Remember they have guns. Stupid and a big gun are dangerous," I cautioned.

"Put up a camera. We'd be gone before they woke up."

I smiled. "If I do go out there, I'll go with y'all. And even bring the beer for afterward."

Willy ran back to their apartment and got the map, plus the rest of the stuff they'd found. They were on their way to meet friends. We exchanged contact info. I also asked them to call me if he showed up.

Then back on the interstate, same insanity, but at least I was going in and most traffic was heading out.

I turned for home, not my office. I had to come up with a plan for Sarah. Joanne had called back, but it was when I was talking to Phil and Willy.

I'd call her back from the comfort of my home.

Once I was inside, I took off my shoes and was about to get rid of the bra and into ragged sweatpants but remembered I had promised to meet Sarah. I stayed decent, got a glass of water and then sat in my kitchen while dialing Joanne's number.

Voice mail. "Tag, you're it," I left as my message.

The sun was sliding into the golden hour, hitting the small patch of flowers in my tiny side yard. Cordelia had planted them. I felt obligated to keep them alive, not wanting to add yet another disappointment to the long list of ones I'd already given her.

My phone rang. I checked it was Joanne before answering.

"What's up?" She was driving, I could hear the road noise in the background.

"Sarah and I were followed after we left the station," I told her. "I can't be sure, but I think it was the NYPD cops."

"You lost them, I'm guessing?"

"How long have I lived in this city?"

"Long enough that if you didn't lose someone from out of town, you should have your driver's license taken away. Why do you think it was them?"

"Someone parked in a side street. We walked past, a car started, and as I pulled out, they came behind us, stayed with us after a U on Tulane. Two men, big guys, looked like them, but I had to look at the road, so couldn't get more than a glimpse."

"They strike you as pros or amateur?"

I took a sip of water. "Arrogant pros or brazen amateurs. They didn't really try to hide. Maybe they thought I wouldn't be able to shake them and they'd get to see where Sarah was staying. Or maybe they wanted to harass us, prove we couldn't just walk away from them."

"What if it wasn't them?" Joanne asked. The road noises had stopped; I guess she was where she was going, which I hoped was home.

"Nothing much changes, other than what to worry about. I still have to assume someone is out there, intent on killing Sarah. Just would be nice if the people I'm supposed to be able to trust were trustworthy."

"Yeah. I'll put in a call tomorrow for my NYPD contact. Ask what's going on. You think Sarah is okay for the night?"

"She's in another hotel, an anonymous tourist one. Physically, yeah. But...she's struggling. I told her I'd pick her up later, get her out for the evening. No idea what I'm going to do. Suggestions are welcome."

"Can't we give her a sleeping pill and have her out for the rest of the day?" Riding over what I was going to say, she continued, "Oh, I know, we can't. And the last thing she needs is to be isolated and alone. But...moving her is a risk. The more she can be behind locked doors, the safer she is."

"Unless someone figures out where that locked door is."

"Yes, it's all a guess at what's best."

A text message chimed. Torbin, telling me he was doing drag bingo at Q Carré tonight, subbing for a queen who'd broken all her heels. Torbin can cheer anyone up.

"You're home, I hope," I said. "Torbin is doing drag bingo tonight. That might be something to do with Sarah."

"Yes, I'm home." She paused, then said, "We can join you, you know. More people to scan the crowd."

"No, stay home." I was touched she had offered. I knew it was to help keep Sarah safe, not because she wanted to go back out after a long day. "It's the Q, easy to spot anyone who doesn't belong. The mohawk biker lesbian bouncers will scare them away before they get in the door."

"If you're sure…"

"I'm sure."

"Call me if anything comes up. I'll let you know what I find out tomorrow."

I turned away from the flowers and finished my water. Bathroom break and then I'd call Sarah.

Chapter Nine

"Drag bingo? That sounds like a really great time." Bold sarcasm font. I had hoped Sarah would be a little more enthusiastic about my idea, because it was the only one I had.

"Okay, not your cup of tea, but it's at a queer bar, well off the tourist patch, so only locals, making it easy to spot anyone who doesn't belong. It's usually a good time. Plus, you can see my cousin Torbin doing drag."

"Why would I want to see your cousin in drag?"

"Because he's very good, been doing it for years."

She sighed, loudly enough for me to hear.

"Or you can hang at the hotel, if you'd prefer," I told her.

Another loud sigh, then, "Okay, but next time can we do something like a museum or a classical music concert?"

I wanted to say, "No, we can't," but settled for a vague "I'll see what I can do." Her suggestions were much larger places, with a lot more people. It was a reasonable assumption that whoever was targeting her would not fit in a queer dive bar like the Q. Her suggestions? Anyone could go. They could wear clothes telling me they weren't the kind of people I wanted to hang around with, but no way of knowing if they just thought it or would take action. True, people with Confederate flag pins weren't typical museum or concert goers, but there would be no lesbian biker bouncers to convince them to go elsewhere. And museums aren't on the lookout for terror attacks; queer bars are.

We agreed I'd pick her up in about an hour. The Q was about ten blocks from her hotel, easily walkable, but driving was safer.

Plus, when I picked up my phone to call Torbin, it rang with him calling me.

"Oh, favorite, most favorite cousin of mine. I need a big boon.

Can you drive tonight and give me a ride home after? Andy is dropping me off, then going to a job for a friend starting a new business and needing everything computer." Andy was Torbin's husband, since they had finally gotten around to getting married. The ride was less for Torbin than for his wigs and dresses.

"Can I drive your Mini? I'd like to be in a different car than mine."

"Oh, intrigue. Who are you evading?"

"It's complicated. I'm bringing a friend from out of town with me, and she's here because for those complicated reasons, she needs to lay low."

"So, you're keeping things from me. You should know by now, unless it is the juiciest of juicy gossip, I do not tell secrets."

"I do know that. Nothing juicy here." I made a decision—Torbin was lending me his beloved red Mini Clubman—and said, "She's being targeted by a hate group. They've already taken one shot at her, killing her wife in front of her."

"Oh, shit, Micky, that's horrible. I wish I could do more than lend you my car."

"You can. Teach you to ask. She is, as you might expect, on a ragged emotional edge. As much as possible, I don't want to jam her in a strange hotel room. It's not likely the kind of people targeting her will fit in at the Q, but keep an eye out, will you?"

"Will do. I'll even hang with y'all between being onstage. If any shooting starts, I'm so padded, it's better than a bulletproof vest."

"Our goal is to avoid putting that to the test."

"No disagreement there. You have my spare set of car keys, right?"

I did a quick look to make sure they were where I usually keep them. "Yep, still here." We have each other's spare house and car keys. Torbin and Andy were out of town once when we had two days of torrential rain, enough that it was prudent to move our cars to higher ground. Since then, we keep all necessary keys at both our places.

I spent a few moments debating whether to carry my gun or not and deciding not. We'd be in a crowded bar. I'm a good shot, do target practice at least once a month, but know that I'd need a movie script writer to make sure I only hit the bad guys in a situation like that.

I changed my blue jeans for black jeans, but that was my only concession for going out. And a decent (for the Q) black leather jacket, a bit too warm now, but the evening would cool down.

I grabbed Torbin's keys and trotted down the block to his car. He had left right after he'd called me. It takes a long time to get into five pairs of pantyhose and all that padding. I consider one pair torture, so a career in drag was not an option for me.

I texted Sarah as I was sitting in his car, trying to remember how all those quaint, cute, confusing controls work. Told her I'd be there in five. Assuming I could get this thing started. I use a key, but this is push button.

A minute of the five was given to pushing all the buttons until I hit the right one.

Seven minutes later, I was in front of the hotel. All the traffic lights were red, and a slow tourist stopped at every corner whether there was a stop sign or not.

I texted *red Mini in front*, since that was crucial info. Clearly waiting just inside, she was out almost immediately.

I pulled away as soon as she closed her door, leaving her to fumble with the seat belt as we started moving.

I didn't drive directly to the bar, wanting to make sure no one was following. I meandered into the Marigny, the neighborhood separated by Esplanade Avenue from the French Quarter. It's mostly one-way streets, so I looped around several blocks before heading back up to Rampart St. to get to the Q.

"We're driving in circles, aren't we?" Sarah asked.

"No, we're taking the long way to give me time to make sure no one is following us."

"No one is, you know," she said. "They want a queer Jewish target, there are plenty of them back in New York. I think I'm giving them more power than they have, thinking they could find me here. A waste of time and money." Her voice was resigned.

"Maybe," I hedged. "Remember, someone followed us."

"The NY cops, pissed that we weren't nice ladies."

"Again, maybe. Or maybe it wasn't them. Even if it was them, one or both of them could have been recruited. Those groups target law enforcement."

She was silent.

I looked for a place to park.

Half a block down a large SUV was trying to pull into a spot they didn't have the skill for. I changed to that lane, then hovered behind them, adding to the pressure. Yeah, I'm nice like that.

After three more attempts, each worse than the previous, they gave up, and sped away in humiliation. I quickly snagged the spot.

"Wait," I told Sarah as I got out. I scanned the street. Rampart is busy, but the cars were moving, no one looking at us. Only the biker bouncer was on the sidewalk, outside the Q.

I came around to Sarah's side and opened the door.

"How chivalrous," she said.

"Safety, not chivalry," I said.

"I can't remember the last time I was in a gay bar," she said as we started walking. I slid to the outside, between her and the street.

"That's okay, I can't remember the last time I was at any kind of religious service. Oh, wait, a funeral a few years ago. Bars, on the other hand, about a day."

"That's the beauty of the world," she said, "we find places to belong."

"It sounded like you were judging."

"No, plenty of sins are committed in synagogues and churches. And good deeds in bars. My not liking is a preference, not a judgment. I just don't like loud places where it's hard to talk. Plus, I can afford a much better bottle of wine if I buy them to drink at home."

I nodded. "Sorry. I was raised in a pious Catholic family, sin and damnation everywhere, except for what they did in God's name."

We were at the door. The biker bouncer nodded at me—I was a regular, after all. I motioned Sarah in, then handed—What was her name? Oh, Debbie—a twenty. "If you see any people who look out of place, let me know."

"Ping me your cell," she said, pointing hers at me.

I opened my phone, stared at it just long enough for her, in her youthful enthusiasm, to grab it from me and make a few quick swipes before handing it back. I would have gotten there. Eventually.

"Now you can call me," she said with a wink. She was cute in her leathers and purple hair. Also young enough to be my daughter, if I'd had children in my reasonable twenties. I do have a few standards. Even for one night, I want someone who's lived long enough to know what gravity and time will do.

Sarah was waiting for me inside the bar.

"Friend of yours?" she asked.

"Acquaintance. I asked her to be on the lookout for anyone who looked like they didn't fit."

I looked around, seeing it how she might see it. A short hallway, wide enough for a bouncer to sit and people to easily get by. The walls painted a dark gray that started out closer to black, but faded over the years. Space where cigarette machines used to be, a faint outline still visible, replaced by racks with flyers, local free papers, some drooping and old. Then into the bar area itself, a large rectangular room, with a long L-shape bar immediately in front of you, wood that had been beautiful, but now had scruffs and scratches. The entrance and bar were up front, then tables to the side and back, with a dance floor and stage at the far end of the room. The storerooms and the bathrooms were directly behind the bar, closing the L. The barstools were newer, a good faux black leather, neatly spaced around the bar. The floor was wood even more scuffed than the bar.

The tables weren't new, broken ones replaced with whatever was available. Mismatched or charmingly eclectic, depending on your view. The dance floor had the expected mirror ball. Beyond that a stage, wood painted black, with a faded red curtain behind it.

Restrooms off behind the bar, both doors marked "Don't Care, Just Wash Your Hands." In the far back, a large storage room that doubled as the dressing area for performers. I imagined things being shoved aside as far as they could go for the drag outfits.

At the back on the other side was a newly done sign pointing the way to the upstairs eating area.

"So, this is it," I said, not waiting for a reply as I led us into the main area. It was starting to fill up, although the show wouldn't start for over an hour. I scanned the crowd, wondering who might be here.

I knew Joanne and Alex wouldn't be. Danny and Elly? Cordelia and Nancy? Not likely. As we'd gotten older, we tended to prefer quiet after the workday. Except for me. If I wanted to have people in my life, I couldn't find them at home. But I recognized only the regular bartenders, Mary and Peg. A new young person I didn't know was also behind the bar. Mary was the manager when Rob, the owner, wasn't around. I didn't see him here. I was disappointed and relieved—I liked to shoot the shit with him. His gossip was second only to Torbin's, but I also didn't want to explain Sarah.

I nodded to Mary and Peg. Again, avoiding introducing Sarah. I couldn't really tell the truth but didn't want to get into a messy lie.

"Shall we get a table?" I asked Sarah.

"I guess. It's loud in here."

Music was playing and people were talking, but I was used to it. "We'll go for the back." I led her to the table nearest the back door that led to the stairs to the roof deck. Also, an exit to the street. One I hoped we didn't need.

"What can I get you?" I asked as she sat down.

"I don't know," she said. Still subdued, resigned. I liked angry Sarah better.

"Beer? Wine? Nonalcoholic? Are you hungry?"

"I still don't know. Wine, I guess."

I waited a beat, then asked, "Red? White? They do have some decent stuff here."

She gave me the barest of smiles, as if to acknowledge I was trying. "Red, a shiraz or malbec, if they have it."

"I'll do my best," I said and headed to the bar.

Mary greeted me. "What can I get you? Nice to see you with someone."

"A friend of a friend visiting from New York. I thought I'd show her some of the places the tourists don't see." That would have to do, vague and in the friend zone. To change the subject, "How much trouble has Torbin been giving you?"

"Not a whisper. He's such a darling. Always so good about reminding people to tip the bartender."

"On his best behavior, I see. I'll go with a beer, whichever decent local you have on tap, and a glass of the best red wine you have."

She nodded and headed off to fill my order. It was still slow enough that it took her only a few minutes. She returned with the wine, showing me the bottle. A decent-looking shiraz. "Rob has discovered the Barossa Valley in Australia. A friend of his now lives there. This should be pretty good."

I glanced at the bottle—I'd trust Rob on wine more than I'd trust myself. Gave Mary a nod. She put the bottle behind the bar, got a pint mug, and pulled my beer. She added a bowl of mixed nuts.

Delicately balancing the three items, I made my way back to the table.

Just as I put the wine in front of Sarah, I felt a hand on my shoulder.

"Do not spill the beer! That's a precious soon to be bodily fluid."

I have no idea how Torbin, in heels and gown, snuck up on me. Blame it on the music and me trying not to drop anything.

He took a seat next to Sarah, much more smoothly than I could possibly have done in heels and a form-fitting gown. Or even in sneakers and jeans.

He held out his hand, elbow-length white gloves and rings on at least three fingers of each hand. "I'm Torbin, Micky's lavender cousin. Anything you want to know about her, ask me. I know all the secrets."

I jumped in. "Sarah is a friend of a friend, visiting from New York. Thought I'd get her out of the tourist zone."

Torbin gave me a brief nod of understanding. "Pleased to meet you."

Sarah responded, taking his hand. He gave it a hearty welcome handshake. "Yeah, uh, what Micky said. Visiting briefly and she's showing me around."

"Let's talk about you!" Torbin said. Then after a pause some might call pregnant, "What do you think of my gown?"

Sarah laughed. Torbin patted his mile-high platinum wig, then ran a hand down his shoulder to his knee.

"I think you wear it much better than I would," she said. "How long did it take you to make it?"

"Me? A phone call and a fitting. Oh, and some glue gun work. Micky, you remember Miss Ruby? She is the world's best seamstress. She can do something from scratch or take a thrift store rag and turn it into a miracle of high fashion. She did this one for me. Oh, I helped with the glue gun, but credit where credit is due."

I sat on the other side of Sarah, a seat giving me the best view of the room.

"What brought you to this?" Sarah asked. She seemed genuinely interested, as if someone she just met and might never see again was important. It was a skill—and a level of empathy—I was still working on.

"Torbin is the name, gender fuckery is my game."

"To play with gender roles? Why?" Sarah asked.

Torbin reached over and took a sip of my beer. Lavender cousin privilege.

"I'm not sure. Oh, probably ten reasons, five of which are true on any given day."

"Tell me one," Sarah said.

"To be with my tribe. With people who understand that the people who called me sissy in fourth grade were assholes. I'm now on a stage, people paying to see me, applauding, while those assholes are home drinking cheap beer and singing the Peggy Lee song, 'Is That All There Is?' I guess that falls under petty revenge."

"No, it falls under living the life you want to live and not apologizing for it. As long as you don't gloat for too long, a little schadenfreude is not out of place."

Torbin smiled, a genuine, deep smile. "Thank you. I like performing, being on the stage. It challenges me, can I be as funny as I need to be, can I give them a good show? The zing of energy for a few hours."

"Audiences need performers. We need our storytellers, our fools and bards," Sarah responded. "Micky says you're very good."

"Micky says I'm good? The heavens have parted."

"You are good at drag. I didn't say you were good at anything else," I responded.

"The planets are in alignment again," Torbin bantered.

"Other reasons?" Sarah asked.

"I can be so many different people, someone new with each wig and dress. So many worlds to explore, my knees will give out before my imagination does."

Sarah reached out and gave Torbin's gloved hand a squeeze. "I hope your knees last a long, long time."

"Do you want a bingo card?" the new employee asked us. "Free, but we appreciate donations."

"Why does a bar need donations?" Sarah asked.

The person—gender was indeterminate—blushed. "Oh, not for us. It's for Pussies Galore, a no kill cat shelter run by a local trans group. They help people with affording pets, vet bills, that kind of stuff in addition to a cat shelter."

Sarah pulled out a ten-dollar bill and handed it to her. "Lead with that. You are?"

"Um, Mel."

"Mel, let people know what the money is for. You're doing good work for a good cause."

Mel blushed again as she took the money. We were two middle-aged dykes, but maybe she crushed on older women? Or maybe she wasn't used to talking to strangers and struggling. She gave Sarah a genuine smile and started to leave three bingo cards on the table, but Torbin waved one away.

"Time to do my job," Torbin said, standing up.

"It was lovely to meet you," Sarah said. "Thank you for telling me a few of the reasons."

Torbin blew her—us?—a kiss as he headed back to the dressing room.

"Torbin and I were the lavender sheep, often huddling together at family gatherings. Now we live down the block from each other."

"You go back a long way?" Sarah asked.

"Yes," I said and left it there, not wanting to get into my

complicated family. Mother disappearing when I was five. Father killed when I was ten and being taken in by pious Aunt Greta. And her husband, my Uncle Claude, but he never intervened about the children. Even when he should have.

"Blood family and found family as well," Sarah said, realizing I wasn't going to say more.

"I'm lucky he's in my life," I said, just as a loud fanfare started, signaling showtime.

We once came close to getting bingo, but close is not a prize. It was fun. Sarah even laughed a few times, especially at Torbin, who was a good performer, and quick on his feet. "Oh, honey, would you do better with crayons?" at one heckler. "Do you need beer drinking by numbers instructions?" to another.

There was a break and Sarah turned to me. "The noise is getting to be a bit much, and I'd like to eat something, if that's possible?"

"Let's go to the roof deck," I said. It was the easiest option.

She nodded.

I took our glasses back to the bar and asked Mary if it was okay for us to go to the deck.

"Oh, it's open now, so enjoy." I snagged a menu, went back to Sarah, and took her up there.

It wasn't crowded; most people were here for the drag bingo. It was also quiet, the air still and clear. Cool, but Sarah was dressed for New York, and I had my jacket. I picked a table where I could see the street but Sarah wasn't easily visible.

"Not Commander's Palace, but decent for a bar. The burgers are good," I said as I handed her the menu.

I explained Commander's Palace to her while she looked over the menu. "Located in the Garden District and one of the best restaurants in the country," I finished.

She decided on a burger.

I stood up to take our orders to the bar, but Mel arrived at our table, order pad in hand.

"I can go to the bar," I told her.

"I like working up here; nice to see the stars."

I sat back down and we ordered, including a beer for me and another glass of wine for Sarah. I offered to help when it was ready.

"They put in this awesome thing, pulleys and stuff, you put the tray in and haul it up," she explained.

"A dumbwaiter," Sarah said. And then had to explain what that was.

"Dumbwaiter, cool," Mel said as she headed off.

"The old is new again," I said. "Hard to imagine what young people don't know."

"I find it easy—so much comes from family, our environment. If it's not there, it's not learned."

"Books. Read a book."

"Not everyone has books. Or likes to read. I try to be gentle in my judgments."

"It's in your job description. Mine is to be suspicious and make judgments."

"In every situation?" she asked. "Like with a young waiter?"

But my attention was on the street. Black Eyes was walking on the other side.

"Stay here, keep out of sight from below," I said as I got up.

"Where are you going?"

"Need to talk to someone." I hastened down the stairs, then out the back way.

Quickly scanning the street, I spotted him a few yards away.

"Hey!" What was his name? "Hey, Jerry!" I guessed.

He looked back, confused.

I trotted up to him. "Hey, remember me?" We were on the side street, but only a bit off the corner of Rampart, with a badass biker bouncer within easy calling distance.

He still looked confused. A few drinks? Trying to place me? Or seeing me here?

"What the fuck with following us?" I said as I came up to him.

"Oh, yeah, you," he replied, his face still befuddled, but stalling to buy time. "We weren't following you." But it was a quick denial, as if planned.

"Yes, you were," I persisted. "I could clearly see you in the rearview mirror. Why? More harassment on top of already harassing us?"

"You're mistaken," he tried again.

"No mistake." I wasn't sure, but I needed to push him.

"Yeah, well, you can't prove it," he retorted.

"If it wasn't you, it was someone. Someone following us through a U-turn and down side streets. That means someone followed you to the station and knew you were meeting Rabbi Jacobson and used that to follow her. That is a big fucking problem."

He looked at the sidewalk to avoid my stare. He shuffled his feet to keep his balance. "Don't be crazy," he muttered. "It was just a game. No harm."

"No harm? A woman targeted by a hate group and a car follows her? You such an idiot, you think that isn't harm? You lost your humanity behind that badge?"

He swayed; probably didn't realize we don't water our drinks here. His eyes evaded mine, looking around for a way out. Seeing none, he finally said, "Look, I'm sorry, okay? Ian was driving and it was his idea. I told him to chill but he didn't listen."

"Oh, yeah, blame it all on the guy who isn't here. And what was with that goddamn interview? Treating the victim like the criminal?" He wasn't sober, and drunken answers can be revealing.

"It was him. He always has to drive, which sucks 'cause he's not a great driver."

"Control freak?"

"Sorta. Likes things his way. I'm sorry about all this. We were told to do a hostile interview, that she might be lying and might have set it up herself."

"What the fuck? No one can possibly believe that."

"It happens, you know. Murder is often a person close to the victim."

"I've spent a lot of hours with her. The woman is shattered, grief stricken, no way she's involved or faking it. No way," I repeated.

He swayed again, then reached for the streetlamp to steady himself. "Look, sorry, I had my instructions."

"What do you mean?" I questioned. "From whom?"

"Ian said he'd been told this is how we do it. Be suspicious and all. Guess he got it from our team lead. Or maybe someone higher up. That's all I know."

"A little cog in a big machine. Never question, never think for yourself."

"Hey, that's not nice."

"No, but from what you're saying, it's accurate."

"Look, I do my job, okay? Yeah, I don't always agree, and if I see something really off, I say something."

"Like tailing a victim to harass her?"

"Okay, okay, I'll bring it up when I get back." He burped, and the air smelled of rum. I was right about too many Hurricanes.

"Find out who gave the order to do a hostile interview. Find out why your partner was so keen to follow and harass her. Find out if they have ties to any of the hate groups."

His eyes widened. "They can't. They're cops."

"Hate groups target law enforcement. Most of you guys are good. A few aren't."

"What are you saying?"

But he knew what I was saying. "It's possible Sarah was targeted by a large, well-organized group. All they need is one person in the right place."

"Look, I don't know. That's a hell of an accusation." Another rum burp.

"Yeah, it is. Ask the questions. If I'm wrong, no harm, right? But if I'm right…" I pulled out one of my business cards and handed it to him. "Just think about it. Talk to someone outside the investigation you trust."

"I don't know…" He trailed off. I was a stranger asking him to rat out his friends. "Look, yeah, maybe I can ask a few questions."

But there was no conviction in his voice, and I doubted he would follow through.

He continued, "I need to get back to the hotel, but I'm kind of lost. Is that the way to Decatur Street?" he asked, pointing to Rampart.

I thought about telling him it was, but a level of basic decency I didn't know I had prevailed. "No, afraid you got turned around." I pulled up a map on my phone, pointed where we were and the direction to Decatur from here.

He decided it was a long way (those Hurricanes can really mess with your sense of direction). I walked him to Rampart, pointed out the taxi stand across the street, and watched to make sure he made it safely across.

I headed back into the bar. Sarah was probably wondering what had happened to me. And my burger would be cold. Drag bingo was over, the music blaring, and people were on the dance floor. I made my way to the back, then up to the roof deck.

Torbin was there and halfway through my burger.

He saw my dagger glare. "I ordered you another," he said as I approached the table. "This one was getting cold and needed to be eaten." He had changed and was now in jeans and an old T-shirt with a large crayfish on it saying "Suck my head!"

I joined them at the table. Torbin had a point, although I wasn't going to admit that. His presence also gave me time to consider whether or not to tell Sarah about my encounter. Were they just cops being suspicious assholes mixed in with common biases—queers and Jews were all suspect? Or did it mean the group targeting Sarah was big enough to have pulled in someone on the investigation team?

I needed to talk to Joanne and Danny, but it was too late tonight. They couldn't do anything until the morning anyway.

I was saved from further talking by the arrival of my newly ordered burger. I was hungry.

"Who were you talking to?" Sarah asked just as I took a big bite.

After slowly chewing to give me time to answer, I said, "You looked at the street, like I told you not to."

She shrugged, then sheepishly nodded. "I wondered why you rushed off."

"I got him to admit that they followed us," I said, then took another bite.

Torbin surfaced from his final mouthful. "Wait, followed you?"

After a quick update to let Sarah know that Torbin knew, we—mostly Sarah, since I was eating—told the story of the interview and the cops following us. She finished with, "That's good to know, right? That it was them and not someone else?"

I nodded, eating a couple of fries to not have to say anything. She was on a ragged edge. I'd tell her if it would help, and right now, I couldn't see that it would.

Pushing his plate away, Torbin said, "About why Sarah is visiting from New York. Andy and I are out of town this weekend, I told her she could stay at our place."

I managed not to choke on the new handful of fries I had just shoved in my mouth.

"If you think that's okay," Sarah said, reading the expression I hadn't managed to hide.

"We can discuss it," I said as I finished chewing enough to talk. Another thing I was going to have to think long and hard about. "Let's keep things as they are for the moment."

Then Torbin started talking about his journey into drag, telling every funny story he could think of, letting me finish eating in peace.

We had another round of drinks. I stuck with beer, since I was driving. Three beers in three hours would be okay. Especially with the burger and fries to absorb it.

Then it was time to transport Torbin and his regalia back to his place. Sarah offered to help—which I debated, but she was as safe helping him haul as walking with me to the car. I retrieved it, pulling in front while they dragged Torbin's wardrobe to the curve.

Torbin insisted on being crammed in the back with his gear, so I drove to his place first. After getting him and everything safely from car to house, I took a meandering route back to the hotel, something I didn't want to do with Torbin pretzeled in the back.

Although I might have if he hadn't ordered me a replacement burger.

When did midnight become late? The Quarter and Frenchmen Street in the Marigny were crowded. I avoided the busy streets but could hear the booming music and hubbub as we circled around.

"No one following?" Sarah said as we circled back to her hotel, an ironic quirk to her mouth.

"Nope, seems safe and clear."

I pulled in front.

"What now?" she asked.

"You hurry in, I sit here and watch as long as I can, then we both try to get some sleep."

"I guess I meant long term. I don't want to put Torbin out but would love to be in a real place, with cats to take care of."

"Give me a bit to consider logistics," I said. "Keep you safe and not put others at risk."

"I'll leave before they return," she said.

"What if they think you're still there?" I countered.

She looked away from me. "Okay." Silent for a moment. "I guess not."

"Let me think about it," I repeated. "I don't want to answer yes or no without thinking things through."

"Okay, fair enough. Will I see you tomorrow? Or am I on my own?"

"I'll take you on a field trip, get you out for at least a while."

"Okay, thanks. And thanks for tonight. I had a better time than I thought I would. No, let me rephrase that. I had a good time. I like Torbin." She put her hand on mine, then quickly took it away.

I smiled and nodded.

She got out and I watched for several minutes, but the street was empty and no one seemed to be about.

I slowly pulled away, pausing at the stop sign to again check the street. Empty.

You'll never be perfect enough to save everyone, I told myself, rolling through the intersection.

I did a lazy loop around Tremé, but no one was following me.

Just as I was heading for my block, I got a text. Didn't recognize the number, so considered ignoring it. But I was at a stop sign with no one around, so glanced at it.

Sorry for so late, but his truck just pulled in. Looks like he's staying overnight.

It took me a moment, but I realized it was from the men I'd met at Elmer's apartment.

Thanks, I texted back. *Still up. If you're awake, let me know if he leaves.*

Will do. Up for a bit to wind down.

I again thanked him, parked Torbin's car and got in mine, then headed to the interstate.

Maybe the hotels had gotten too expensive and he was trying to sleep on the cheap.

The late hour made the traffic light, and I was there in fifteen minutes.

I cruised around the parking lot as if looking for a close spot.

His truck was easy to spot. Bright red, with a big Confederate flag in the back window, parked in a space and a half. There were a couple of other trucks parked near it, with similar signs on them, like a small mustache meant to invoke an insane dictator from the 1930s to a White Lives Matter bumper sticker. One of the tags was from Mississippi, the other two Louisiana.

I drove past. The lights were on in his apartment.

I parked near the exit and got out, not locking my door. I might need to leave quickly. With my PI bag slung over my shoulder, I sauntered across the parking lot, as if tired from a long night of work.

As I got closer, I could hear a faint beat of music and voices but couldn't make out any words.

I came up to his truck, acted like I dropped something, and bent down. Listened for a moment, but only the bass beat, no doors or footsteps. I quickly rummaged in the bag and took out a tracking tag and stuck it under the bumper.

Then stood up, jammed my hand in my pocket is if I'd found what I'd dropped, and slowly headed toward the breezeway.

As I got closer, I could make out words.

It seemed Elmer had some friends over. If it was just him, I might risk knocking on his door. But not with the kind of friends he seemed to have.

I was close enough to hear some of what they were saying.

A harsh laugh. "Yeah, bro, you can stay there, but a bitch without water," a loud voice said.

Another voice. "We didn't get what that idiot did until after at least three people took a dump. Place smells like shit! Like real big man shit!" Again, a chorus of laughs.

"What happened to the water?" a third voice asked.

"R.C. got some dynamite. We thought it would be fun to blow a stick up. Son of a bitch, it was in the field where the camp water line is. Blew it out. Gonna cost a shit ton to fix, so we gotta rig something in the next few weeks."

I heard another door open from an upstairs apartment.

I turned, acting as if I'd forgotten something back in my car, and headed back across the parking lot.

Not bad—in less than fifteen minutes I had put a tracker on Elmer and found out he was looking for places to stay, with his pretend soldier camp lacking running water. Enough of a hardship that he had come back to his apartment overnight. And I'd confirmed that he was running around with not nice people.

I got back in my car. A woman from the upstairs apartment came down, dressed in what looked like a security guard uniform. Probably going to work.

I started my car and drove away.

When I got back, Andy had parked with just enough room to fit my car. I smiled as I pulled in with one maneuver, but no one was around to see.

I walked the empty block to my place.

Chapter Ten

I woke to the sound of rain and a drop in temperature. Fall was usually lovely in New Orleans, but we were heading into official winter, which would be a nice fall in more northern places.

I quickly showered and dressed: long sleeves, jeans, late fall leather jacket, and even a scarf—heavy winter gear here.

With a big travel mug of coffee, I drove to my office.

Despite the late night, I was up at my usual time. I had too much to do for the luxury of sleep.

At my office, I first put on the coffeepot; the travel mug was big, not bottomless.

Then called Joanne. Voice mail. Same with her personal cell phone. I left a brief message, saying I had info she needed to hear. I debated calling Danny as well, but we'd have to circle back to Joanne in any case, since she was the contact with the NYPD.

Paulette had called three times yesterday and once this morning.

I pulled up the tracking app on my computer to see if Elmer was sleeping late.

Nope, he—or his truck—was on the move. Guess he knew Paulette well enough to know she was a morning person and he couldn't linger.

He was out of New Orleans, but to the west, not heading for the waterless camp, which was east and near the Mississippi border.

The phone rang. Joanne.

"What's so important?" she asked.

"I was at the Q last night," I told her. "One of the NY cops walked by, so I chatted him up. He was a few Hurricanes worse for wear. Got him to admit that they were the ones following us."

"Well, that's good to know. Is that it?"

"No. Asked about why they questioned Sarah the way they did.

He said they got instructions to treat her as a suspect, from someone higher up. He wasn't sure who, said his colleague was the contact and also the one who insisted on following us."

"That's interesting." I could almost hear her thinking.

"But is it because they're suspicious jerks mixed in with the usual bigotry or because someone on the team is tainted and part of the hate group?"

She sighed. "That's the question, isn't it?" A pause and she continued, "And you'd like me to see if I can get an answer to it?"

"Got a better idea?"

An uncharacteristic pause. "Sadly, no. But I'm also not sure how far I'm going to get. Yeah, I'm a cop, but not one of their cops."

"Go outside? The feds or something?"

"Yeah, maybe." Again, a slow response. Clearly a mess. "Maybe I can contact someone here at the FBI and see if they have any ideas."

"All I have is the info, I'd have less chance as a PI than you as a cop."

Another sigh. "True. Are you sure he wasn't leading you on?"

"In vino—or rum—veritas. I asked him to ask some questions, but he agreed in the way that told me he wasn't going to. One thing is he doesn't seem to like his partner—didn't say all that much, but admitted he was a bit of a control freak."

"Let me try this, I can lead with what we know—talk to my contact about them doing a hostile interview. Then mention them following you, make at least a strong informal complaint. See if that gets me anywhere. Put in a call to my FBI friend, run it by him to see if he has any advice. Figure where we go from there."

"Okay, let's hope it goes somewhere."

"How's Sarah doing?" The subject was changed.

"I think her being here, isolated, leaves her alone with her loss. Nothing familiar or friendly to pull her through the days. Maybe Alex is right, she needs a balance of being with people and being kept safe."

"Like taking her out to the Q more often?" Joanne asked.

"Maybe. She's not a bar person, although she liked Torbin's act. They got to chatting after the show, and Torbin offered to let her stay at their place this weekend while they're out. A ploy for a free cat-sitter."

"What did you say?"

"Said I needed time to think. Which is what I'm doing now."

"With me doing part of the thinking?"

"Two brains and all that."

"Can we keep her safe there?"

"Well, as long as no one knows she's there, she's safe."

"That's the big if, isn't it?"

"Big. But let's consider. If their goal was to kill her and they knew where she was, wouldn't they have done it already? Likely means they don't know where she is."

"If you're right about someone in the NYPD being part of the hate group, then they know she's in New Orleans and you're keeping an eye on her."

"True." And not a truth I liked.

"Maybe someone else should be the one moving her around."

"Who? They know about you, too," I pointed out. "And someone Sarah would be okay with."

Joanne said, "Torbin," at the same time I said, "Alex?"

She added, "Maybe we should see if we can get several people. Mix up who's with her."

"I guess," I said. I liked Sarah; I wanted her safe. But I loved Torbin and would hate myself if he got hurt because of me. Joanne felt the same about Alex. Or any of our friends.

"Let me think on it. She's at the new hotel, right?"

"Yes, I told her I'd take her out for a bit."

"Give me about an hour or so. I'll get back to you."

The call was over and I put the phone down. I hadn't thought through the implications of someone on the investigation team being compromised. Now I was very glad I hadn't let the cops know where Sarah was. I just needed to keep it that way. It was going to be hard to do that alone.

The phone rang. I stared at it for a moment. Too soon to be Joanne with a plan. That left a stranger or Paulette.

I picked it up. I'd have to talk to her sooner or later.

"Well, have you solved it yet?"

"Good morning to you, Paulette," I said in as obnoxiously cheery a tone as I could. "You were on my list to call this morning."

"What are you doing to earn your money? You're not cheap, you know."

It took enormous willpower, but I did not say, "Unlike you." Outrage would just keep her on the phone longer.

"I've been busy but wanted to be mindful of your money, so focused on finding him, not doing billable reports." She started to retort, but I kept going. "He's still in the area and seems to be hurting for money. It looks like he was staying at his pretend soldier camp until the water line was destroyed by dynamite in the wrong place. He was at his apartment last night, pretty late, but with the kind of friends that made it unsafe to approach him. I have some things in place that should lead me to him, pretty quickly." I ended it there, deliberately not telling her about the tracker. She was likely to demand I take her to him, and I wasn't ready to do that yet. I wanted to use the tracker to get an idea of where he was and what he was doing. If/when I approached him, I wanted to make sure none of his gunslinging buddies were around.

"Well, that's not good enough. I need this done yesterday."

"For three times the amount you've already paid me, I can put all my other cases aside and concentrate on this, but even then, I'd need a day or so to take care of a few things."

That shut her up. For a moment anyway. "Well, I think I'm paying you plenty enough for this simple case. How soon can you wrap it up?"

"Simple case? Finding someone who's doing everything they can to not be found is not simple. Not close," I rubbed in. "I'm not sure how long, but likely within the week." A few days of seeing where Elmer roamed and pinpointing a place to intercept him, easily within a week.

"That long?"

"Yeah, that long."

"Well, I expect daily updates."

"Okay, your money. I'll update you every day. Anything else?" I kept the cheery tone to annoy her.

"I expect to be immediately notified if there are any developments. Is that clear?"

I considered telling her I didn't work for her and could walk away if I wanted. But no, I focused on time management skills, cheerily agreed, and got off the phone.

That was the last of the excitement for my morning. I spent the rest doing the necessary paperwork, shredding old files, bills, billing people to pay the bills. Waiting for the phone.

Joanne didn't call until after eleven, when I was up to dithering about what to eat for lunch—the can of tuna here (should check the date first) or going out and getting something. I had gotten Sarah enough food that she should be good for lunch.

"A plan of sorts," she said. "If she's willing, I'm doing a community thing this afternoon, women in the professions stuff. Lunch included, and speaking after. Not open to the public, but lots of people around.

She'd need to talk for a few minutes about being a rabbi. We had a faith leader lined up, but she broke her leg last night Rollerblading. I can get someone to pick her up and another person to take her back. That work?"

"Yeah, that sounds okay," I said.

"You're in contact with her, so can you set it up? Someone will pick her up around twelve thirty p.m."

"Who?" I asked.

Joanne hesitated. "Another participant."

"Oh. Name begins with a 'C'?"

"Are you okay with that?" Joanne asked to my silence.

"I guess I'll have to be." Cordelia, like Alex, was better at the empathy thing than either Joanne or me. Like Torbin, she might help Sarah feel less alone. "I'll call Sarah back and see what she thinks."

"Okay, get back to me ASAP."

I started to dial but instead looked in my PI bag of tricks for the burner phone. The charge was almost gone, so I plugged it in, then dialed Sarah's number. She answered immediately. I told her what the plan was and asked if she was interested.

"Yeah, sure," she said, then added, "if you think it's safe."

"Other than not coming out of your room, this is about as safe as it gets. Also, someone else will pick you up."

"Not you?"

"No, better if we switch things up a bit."

"The NY cops, right? They know you're protecting me and you might lead them to me."

Damn, the woman was too smart. "It's possible. Better to mix things up."

"Joanne, your cop friend?"

"No, a doctor who is also going to the event and works in that part of the city. She'll be there around twelve thirty."

"So, she will know where I am?"

"Yes, but she's a trusted friend of both me and Joanne. You'll be fine." Something I wanted to be true, desperately. "Joanne is also on the panel, and it's not open to the public. You're replacing someone who broke a leg."

"I'm fine with it, if you think it's okay. And not putting anyone at risk."

"Driving in New Orleans is a big risk."

She gave a small laugh, all that tired joke deserved.

"It'll be okay," I repeated both for her and for me. "Let me get back on the phone and arrange things."

I ended the call and dialed Joanne. Voice mail. I realized I had called her on the burner phone and she might not recognize the number. Switched to my regular phone. Voice mail. Considered calling on my office phone but would probably still get voice mail, since there was a real possibility she was busy.

I looked at the burner phone. I knew the number. What the hell? I texted Cordelia's cell. Left it at *Sarah* and the hotel address.

I got an immediate text back. *Who is this?*

Damn. Busted. I had hoped to remain cloak-and-dagger secret. *Micky. From a burner phone.*

No immediate answer.

I called Joanne again, having switched to my regular phone. Again, voice mail, but this time I left a message telling her what I'd done, so she wouldn't have to play phone roulette.

A text on the burner. *Okay, thanks for letting me know. Will I see you there?*

I stared at it. Finally, *No, too disreputable to be a good role model for women in the professions.*

Not true. Is this your new phone number?

No, using a second phone just in case. I didn't know how much Joanne had told her, although likely most of it. Joanne would be honest about what was going on, letting Cordelia make the decision. *Other one still works*, I added. Not that she would ever need it.

Okay, good to know.

Talk to you later; I have to run. A complete lie, but this was supposed to be an anonymous text from a stranger, not chatting with my ex.

That settled lunch for me. I walked to a po-boy place about five blocks away, far enough to be adequate movement to clear my head. Plus, the decision of roast beef with debris—oh, so good, but oh, so messy—or shrimp. It took a moment and looking at my light blue shirt to decide on the safer shrimp.

Then the walk back and eating lunch while I checked what chaos was going on in the rest of the world. I clicked away from that after the third story about new anti-LGBTQ laws. Hard to be a law-abiding citizen when they keep making our lives illegal.

I finally looked at my watch. It was almost one. Cordelia had picked up Sarah, and they were probably wherever they were going.

When I'd started out the day, I'd planned for several hours with Sarah. Joanne was right; this was safer overall, although it introduced more people into the circle of risk.

I pulled up the tracker on Elmer. He was about forty miles out of the city and, as I watched, pulled off the road and stopped. The tracker mapped his movements, so I looked at where he'd been. Drove out almost to Baton Rouge, but on Route 61, not I-10. That was the old river road, part of the highway system before the interstate. A stop at what was likely a gas station in the early part of his journey. Then a brief pause at a residential area on the outskirts of Baton Rouge. I looked at the neighborhood on street view. Modest, on the verge of run down. Small houses, a few trailers. A friend? Not a very friendly one, since he was only there for about fifteen minutes. Picking up something? Maybe a bunch of water jugs to go back to the camp?

But he was still on the west side of New Orleans, in a little cluster of buildings and businesses along the now mostly deserted highway. I pulled up the map for a closer view. It looked like a little diner, a hole-in-the-wall grease spot.

I had the afternoon to kill. And I wanted to be in motion, not sitting in my office trying to convince myself to finish paperwork and not wonder about what was going on where Joanne, Sarah, and Cordelia were.

I grabbed my keys, my jacket, and my PI bag and locked my office.

I took I-10 to get out of the city. Then I-310 over the swamp and down to 61, the old highway built on the small slivers of dry land in the low area.

There was steady, but not heavy, traffic here, as most was over on I-10, just to the north. For a few miles there were businesses that wanted to be close to the city and the airport, but they petered out into a low road, often cut off by water, emerging into sudden vistas of oil and chemical plants. Cordelia and I had once driven this way—wanted to take the back roads and she'd named them dystopian moon bases. Smoke and sometimes flame flaring from the behemoth metal structures. No people visible, just the light and haze. No wonder this stretch was labeled cancer alley. They were here for the proximity to the river, with their own docks.

Then they flashed away into green jungle. Growth never stops here; the climate is too temperate for anything other than a subtle shift in the shade of deep summer green to more brown winter green. A few more clumps of civilization, the towns where the people who worked out there lived, built on the small patches that were solid ground.

I left those behind and onto long patches of brush and marsh. The glimpses of people were less frequent, small and run down, left behind when the interstate was built. A one-pump gas station, a peeling bait and tackle shop. A bar that looked like it was fashioned from a double-wide. Then more green, only the wires of phone and power hinting this land had been tamed as much as it was going to be tamed.

Then a small cluster of homes and businesses, a fading hotel, an RV park. That blip passed and back to wires and brush.

I almost sped past it, another brief opening, gravel parking lot for both a gas station and the small eatery. Luckily no one was behind me, so I was able to jam on the brakes and make the turn.

The gas station had a Closed sign in the door. Hard to tell if it was closed only for the moment or had been closed for a while. The paint was a dull white, windows dusty, but it wasn't the kind of place that did enough business to be kept pristine.

The diner was only slightly better. A similar shade of once white going gray, a sign that needed a new paint job, but the lettering in the door said it was open. There were two vehicles in the parking lot. One was the red truck, the other a much older, beat-up truck, with a peeling "Edwin Edwards for Governor" bumper sticker on it. That one was old. Edwards was famous for the election slogan "Vote for the Crook. It's Important." Everyone knew he was corrupt, but his opponent was the white nationalist David Duke. At that time, even Louisiana wasn't ready to go that far, and Edwards won. Stole like shit while he was in office and later went to jail for it.

I parked, contemplating what to do. It was a little past two.

He doesn't know who you are or what you look like. I did have his driver's license photo to go on. As long as there weren't several white men well into their thirties and still in denial that getting older required better eating and more exercise, he should be easy to spot.

As I got out, I glanced around. Two beat-up cars in the back, probably staff. But we were the only ones here. That's one of the reasons I keep my now ten-year-old car; it isn't out of place here. A swanky nightclub? Yeah, I'd be directed to the entrance for the help without being asked.

Go in, check it out. A cup of coffee was reasonable. Make decisions after that.

As I entered, two older men, both Black, were paying their bill. I guessed they were attached to the truck. An older woman, also Black, was ringing them up.

She smiled at me as I came in. My mother was Greek, which is where my olive skin and black curly hair genes come from. Just dark enough for the kids in high school to taunt me about it. They lay in the sun for hours to get my shade.

Elmer was in a booth in the far corner, making the mistake of having his back to the door.

"Sit anywhere, darlin'," she told me.

"Thank you," I answered, slipping into the soft tones I'd learned growing up in bayou country. "How's the pie?"

"Best you can find. My sister makes it," she said with a nod back to the kitchen.

"Alma," I said, reading her name tag. "Sounds good. Slice of the apple, and coffee, black, when you have a chance."

She nodded and called out a farewell to the other two men as they left, clearly regulars.

I headed back to where Elmer was sitting.

And made a decision. He was alone, and if it came to it, I was willing to bet the people here would take my side, not his. No doubt they had seen his truck.

I slid into the booth opposite him. It took a long second for him to look up from his phone and grasp I was there. He had a pile of plates in front of him, like he was eating for the whole day. Remains of a burger, the onion and lettuce, a stray fry, a side bowl of mashed potatoes, and crumbs left from a chocolate cake.

He stared at me.

I pulled out my license and waved it at him. "I think we need to talk," I said.

He looked around like a trapped animal.

"I'm a PI. Your friend Paulette sent me to find you," I told him.

"You can't arrest me, I didn't do nothing wrong," he said, still staring at his phone.

I caught a glimpse of it before he remembered to blank the screen. Scantily clad women with cleavage not found in nature. He looked like he had taken advantage of being at his apartment, with its hot water and shower, his face scrubbed and shaven, but hadn't run by the shared laundry there. Sour sweat still lingered. He was okay looking, if your standards were low. Full head of light brown hair, in need of a haircut. Probably about my height, just under six feet tall. Pudgy nose a little too big for his face, the bare beginning of jowls as beers and fatty foods were catching up to him. Eyes a gray-hazel that seemed to have no point of view to them, reacting to the world always a bit too slowly.

"Not here to arrest you," I added. "You're lucky because Paulette just wants back what you stole. She has every right to turn it over to the cops."

"She can't do that."

"Why not?"

"Why not? You kidding? She knows what's in those papers."

"Fraud?" I inquired.

He looked surprised that I had so easily guessed. "Big time. She's going to be in more trouble than I am," he said with a suddenly discovered air of triumph. Like he was smart enough to turn the tables.

"Likely," I said, my tone saying I already knew that. "Mutual destruction. She can get you for theft and extortion, but you get her for fraud. You know how this works. The rich crooks pay a fine, maybe get home detention and a slap on the wrist. The not rich crooks—that would be you—go to jail and stay there for a while. Make wise choices here."

He stared at me, the triumph dripping away as he thought through what I'd said.

He got a minute when Alma brought over my pie and coffee. "Here you go. You sure you don't want any cream or sugar?"

"Nope, I'm good. This pie smells perfect. Thank your sister for me. Oh, this is a friend of an old high school friend, Elmer Stumbolt," I said. "Small world, isn't it?"

She gave me a smile that was more polite than friendly. She'd never seen him before and never seen me before and now we're sitting together? I'd be suspicious, too.

She left, going back behind the counter.

"Why'd you do that?" he harshly whispered at me. "I don't want them to know my name."

"Oh? Planning to skip out without paying?"

Again, the stare like the world was moving too fast and he couldn't keep up.

I sighed. "I'll cover your tab, but you have to answer a few questions."

For the first time, I felt sorry for him. He looked surprised. People weren't kind to him, not the people he called his friends, but now a stranger was bailing him out.

"Okay, yeah, sure." Then almost, sheepishly, "Can I get a slice of that pie as well?"

"Sure. Something more to drink?"

Again, surprise at the offer. "Yeah, sure. A big Coke."

I nodded, got up, and went over to the counter to place his order.

"He's eating a lot," she said.

I pulled out three twenties and handed them to her. "I'll settle when we're done. He's a friend of someone I know, and I'm trying to help him through a spot of trouble."

"You're a better person than I am."

I gave her a conspiratorial smile. "I'm being paid for my trouble. But if any other trucks like his pull up, go ahead and call the cops."

She nodded. She understood.

I went back to the table and took a bite of my pie. Oh, it was good. Long workout tomorrow after this and the shrimp po-boy earlier.

"Paulette won't call the police on me," he stated, lacking his earlier confidence.

"She won't pay you either." I took another bite, then a sip of coffee. "So, you have some hard decisions to make. You're out of money, out of friends who'll put you up. Hard to get a job with either a big gap in your history or claiming a place that won't give you a good reference."

"I'm not going back to mopping floors," he stated.

"If you can't pay for a burger in this place, you don't have many options," I pointed out.

"I can pay, but I need to keep money for other things."

That ended whatever small sympathy I had for him. Beer for his friends and rip off a place like this.

"Give me what you stole. I'll tell Paulette she has to pony up a few thousand to settle this. That way, you have enough for a fresh start."

"No," he said, his face now that of a stubborn toddler. "That's not enough. She had tons of money. We were a couple. I should get half of it."

That was delusional. Even if they had been married, they were only together a few years; the law wasn't going to give him half of what she'd accumulated over decades. This was the hard part—they both wanted to win, and a compromise wasn't winning. The choices were compromise, stalemate, or mutual destruction.

"So, what are you going to do?" I asked.

"She has to see sense. She has to give me the money."

"Told you already, not going to happen. Get a few thousand out of her; that's all that's possible." That would take a shit ton of cajoling on my part, and even then, she might stamp her foot and say no. If I could get him to give me the stuff, I'd hold it until she agreed.

Alma appeared with his coffee and pie. This time she gave me a friendly smile.

When she was again back behind the counter, I continued, "You're a smart guy"—yes, an out and out lie, but telling him he was dumb wasn't going to move things along—"you know you need to leave her behind and get on with your life. Give her the stuff back. That ends her ability to go to the police and you don't have to worry about jail. Get some money from her, pay off bills, get some breathing room, get the hell out of here. Go to Vegas or someplace like that and start again. I hear the casinos are hiring." Probably people to mop the floors, but that would be his problem when he got there.

"No, I can't."

"Why not?"

"I gotta be loyal to my friends."

"They can visit you in Vegas," I suggested.

"No, it's not gonna be like that. Vegas might not survive."

"Survive what?"

He leaned close. I took a sip of coffee to mask the sour sweat smell.

"The race war. You have to know it's coming. I gotta stay with my friends. We protect each other."

I did my best to not react, keep my face neutral. "What do you mean? When?" Acting like I was just asking a question.

It must have been good enough for him, because he continued, "Soon. Within the next six months. That's why I need her money— have to have it to win. She's not likely to survive. She didn't believe me, so she won't be safe. That's why I have to stay strong and get it."

Who knew old Highway 61 had a stop in cloud cuckoo land?

"Your friends who will protect you? Can you stay with them? She's stubborn, and it's going to be hard to get her to pay."

He looked down, slurped a gulp of his soda. "They can't. Not enough room, you know. Only one bathroom and that kind of stuff."

"Sharing a bathroom with another guy for a few weeks should be doable," I said.

"No, R.C. has a new baby. Girlfriend didn't take care to stop it, so they're living together. Markwayne lives with his mother, and she barely puts up with him. Skinner and Reg live in apartments that don't allow people not on the lease. So that doesn't work."

"What about the camp over near Mississippi?"

"You know about that? How do you know?"

"I'm a PI, remember? Digging into things is what I do. Why can't you stay there?"

He shook his head. "No AC, water is messed up, and Boss doesn't like people out there when he's not around."

His face revealed the emotions his words denied. His friends could help him if they were really his friends; but he was convenient, not someone they really liked. I couldn't get him to see what he desperately didn't want to see.

"They're my friends. We'll do anything for each other," he protested to something I hadn't said.

"Except give you a place to stay while you fight for money to finance things for them?" He wouldn't hear me today, but words resonate, and maybe someday they would come back.

"No," he protested, loud enough that Alma glanced our way. I gave her a nod to say everything was okay. "No, it's not like that. I told you, they would but they can't. They don't have nice big houses like Paulette does. Four bedrooms, three bathrooms. A pool, even. She owes me!"

"Sometimes it's hard," I said noncommittally. "You don't have it, you can't give it." Torbin had let me sleep on the floor of his small studio when I was between moving from one place to another. It was so small, we had to tell each other if we were moving and set up a schedule for the bathroom. My experience is that people who don't have much are the most generous; they know what it's like to be so close to the edge.

But maybe I run in a different circle of people.

"What if she doesn't ever give you the money?" He was too desperate to think he had friends to admit he didn't. They had pulled him into a seductive scheme—he wasn't just a thirtysomething loser, but a vital soldier for a greater cause. They weren't just wasting an evening drinking cheap beer, but brilliant strategists planning their victories. It made him so much bigger and better than he was likely to ever be.

"I have a plan," he said.

"What?"

"I'll give the police just a few papers, enough to cause her trouble, then she'll know I'm serious and hand the money over."

That sounded like one of those plans hatched over a six-pack. In a boozy blur, it was easy to think it would work.

"Have you thought about what the police would do? They might arrest her, freeze all her assets while they investigate. She'll have to pay lawyers. Maybe a big fine and restitution. Good-bye money. Or the cops ask her, she claims it's forged by a disgruntled employee, and hello jail for you."

He stared at me, a piece of pie halfway to his mouth.

I swear it took a full sixty seconds for him to decide to go ahead and eat it.

"No, that won't happen," he said while he chewed.

"What won't happen is the police telling her to give you the money or they really will come after her. You don't plan well if you only plan for the best possible outcome."

He kept chewing, washing it down with a mouthful of Coke.

He finally came up with the argument that I couldn't rebut. "God is on our side and God wants us to win. We need this to happen, so God will make it happen."

"Whose God?" I asked.

He stared at me. Finally said, "What do you mean? There's only one God."

"Catholic? Pentecostal? Greek Orthodox? Jewish? Muslim? Hindu?" I persisted.

"Only one," he said, shoving another bite of pie in his mouth. "All others false. Satan."

"Did God tell you this?" I wasn't getting anywhere but was curious to see how far he'd go.

Another mouthful of pie before he answered. "Boss. He knows. He preaches to us. His word is gospel. If we do what he says, we'll be saved."

"So, why doesn't God just let you win the lottery? Much easier."

"God works in mysterious ways."

I took the final bite of my pie; it was too good to leave behind. "Indeed God does. Maybe he even sent me here to help you out."

It was worth a try. He glared at me.

"No, a few thousand isn't enough. Boss says he needs a hundred thousand. I can get it from Paulette. Then I become one of the chosen, one of his top lieutenants."

"You think you can get a hundred K from Paulette?"

He smiled. "More than that. She has lots. Twice that, give Boss what he needs and keep plenty for myself. When it's over, I'll be rich."

I considered asking him what bank he would put it in, since things like that tend to get destroyed during a war, but decided not to bother. Elmer was a simple man, without the ability to have simple dreams to match.

His phone rang—the first line of "Dixie," the most annoying ringtone ever.

"Hey," he said. "What's up?" He was silent, just an occasional "yeah" or grunt.

I took the final sip of coffee, planning to leave the second he got off the phone.

"Yeah, I can be there. I can do that." The call ended. To me, he said, "I have to go. Boss needs me to come over. Said he needs my help tonight. I have to go." He got up so quickly he banged his thigh against the table. "You're taking care of this, right?"

"I've got it. Should you change your mind," I said, as I handed him my card.

He jammed it in his pocket as he turned away, then looked back at me. "Can you give me another twenty? For all the time I spent talking to you?"

I didn't bother to keep the look off my face. But his brain was slow and he paused. "Better hurry, they're waiting for you," I told him.

Sour disappointment to go with his sour sweat smell.

He hurried out, jumped in his truck, almost hitting an oncoming car in his hurry to get away.

I bussed my plates over to Alma but couldn't carry his as well.

"He still in his spot of trouble?" she asked.

"I'd say it's bigger than a spot." We both shook our heads in the way people do when someone is going to do something stupid and can't be talked out of it.

"I owe you some change," she said.

"Keep it."

"It's way too much."

"Maybe a slice of pie to go?"

"You paid for more than a whole pie."

"You need a good tip."

"Good tip included."

"Then I can't possibly say no." That brightened my day. *You have to share it with Torbin and Andy*, I promised myself. Well, if they were home. And hungry. Wasn't Torbin trying to lose a few pounds to get into one of his favorite dresses?

Alma went into the kitchen and brought back a freshly baked pie. She carefully packed it in a to-go box.

"Can I get a receipt?" I asked. "For his food." I was going to charge Paulette.

She nodded and rang it up.

I told her I might have to make a few special trips out here, waved, and left.

I carefully placed the pie on the floor of the passenger side, wedging it in with my PI bag.

Before starting my car, I checked my phone. No calls, no texts. It was a little before four p.m. Their lunch and presentation had to be over. I checked the burner phone as well. Same, nothing. Sarah was presumably back at the hotel by now.

"Nice to keep me updated," I muttered as I turned the ignition. Then cynical me remembered I was being paid by the day, not actual hours worked.

Carefully looking both ways—people liked to speed on these back roads—I pulled out. Traffic was picking up, end of shifts at the various plants along the way. At a stoplight, I checked the traffic and saw that I-10 east was blocked by an accident over the Bonnet Carré Spillway. This road was slower, but moving.

It also crosses the Spillway, a low swampy area used to release water from the Mississippi River into Lake Pontchartrain if the river is running dangerously high. The ribbons of road over it are the only indication of humans in this part of the world. The sun was starting its descent into night, the light turning into a low shaft of gold, the shadows blue. A hostile world, one made passable by concrete and steel. I saw a sere beauty in the swamp, without care; in a few decades, less than a human life, this road would be reclaimed by the ever-growing brush and vine. Even old Highway 61 was raised on piers, no ground solid enough. There were a few fishing camps, reachable only by boat, here until the next big hurricane. We can keep the wind and water at bay when it is kind, but we can't tame it.

With I-10 jammed, more people were here, so traffic slowed but didn't stop. When we got back to the city, most cars cut over to I-10, but I stayed on 61, now known as Airline Highway, since it was built mostly to ferry people from New Orleans proper out to the airport. It was now a commercial strip for the businesses that did okay on the back side of the airport. With the new terminal, the airport was now much closer to the interstate, and the businesses, like hotels and parking lots, had to scramble.

I was in no hurry, so passed the turnoffs that would take me to I-10. It gave me time to think, unlike the kamikaze drivers on the big highway.

Sarah was okay. I would have heard if anything had happened. And even if she wasn't…there was nothing I could do. *Joanne will take care of her*, I assured myself.

I hadn't gotten Paulette's papers back but had confirmed there was indeed evidence of illegal activities in them, so she couldn't go to the police, no matter what. And she had horrible taste in men. Elmer had taken about every wrong road that he could. I doubt he'd been given much help in finding the right ones. He'd become a white nationalist because they'd been friendly.

From Paulette's description, it was several boxes filled with paper files. I could follow him with the tracker and see if he went any place where he might store them. His truck had an open bed and only two seats in the cab, so not there.

Finding them would leave me with the quandary of what to do next. I sighed as I came to another stoplight. The most expedient thing would be to hand them over to Paulette, wash my hands of it and hope I never saw her again. The morally right thing would be to look through them to see how egregious her fraud was and how far I'd be stepping over the moral—and legal—line to help her cover up. Only if I squeezed both eyes tight shut could I claim I hadn't seen what was going on. Claim that Paulette was an old friend from high school, so I trusted her more than I probably should have. That would stink worse than a pile of dead fish on the hottest summer day.

I wasn't sure I could live with the stench.

At the next stoplight, I looked at both my phones. No calls, no messages.

Just as I was moving again, I heard the chime of a text. Of course I was on a stretch where there was no easy way to pull over. I started to slow for a red light, but it turned green and I had to keep going.

The next two lights were green as well. Why are they always red when you're in a hurry and green when you need to stop?

I was back in Orleans Parish, finally stopped by the light at Carrollton.

It was from Joanne, *All is well. S with C back to the clinic to speak to a group. A. will get her later.*

The light turned green. "Damn it, you left Sarah with Cordelia. Health clinics are so well guarded."

Airline Highway was now Tulane Avenue and clogged with end of workday traffic. I didn't want to take it all the way downtown, so I did the first mostly legal left I could.

It'll be okay. At least if they were trying to use me to find Sarah, they were unlikely to think I'd stash her with my ex. Unless they thought I was an evil genius and willing to get Sarah bumped off and maybe take an ex in the bargain.

"You're cynical, but not cynical enough to think that," I muttered.

I was tempted to go where Cordelia worked and wait outside to make sure they were okay, but that was an emotional response, not a rational one. *Go about your day as normally as possible*, I admonished myself.

And normal included pulling into an out of the way lot in a closed business and doing a thorough search of my car. I wasn't the only one who knew about car trackers.

Oh, there it was, at the top of the back passenger wheel well.

"Motherfucker." I kept checking, but that was the only one I found.

I got back in my car, trying to decide what to do. I could remove it and leave it here, but they would notice it not moving. Did I want them to know I knew?

I was close to Joanne's station—not likely she was there, but there would be a bunch of cop cars around.

I smiled as I did a U-turn.

Yep, as I suspected, lots of cop cars, both marked and unmarked. I took a corner and parked about a block away. It was a little after 5:00. I'd give it a few more minutes for anyone leaving to clear away. At 5:20, I got out of my car, strategically dropped my keys near the back tire, and removed the tracker while I was down picking them up.

I selected the shiniest new of the police cars and did the same ploy in reverse. Dropped keys, tracker attached. Keys picked up. I kept walking, going around the block to get back to my car.

Even with that, I took a slow route home.

Did the NYPD cops put the tracker there? That seemed most likely. Or were they working with someone else who did it? Or was it someone else entirely? Annoyingly, I couldn't put it past Paulette doing it to check up on me.

When did they do it? Last night, so they only knew what I'd done today? Or could it have been there a few days? Was it on my car when I'd dropped Sarah at the hotel? There were several in that area, but that was way too narrow a search. Just as well she wasn't there at the moment.

I pulled to the side of the road and did a group text on my burner to Joanne and Cordelia. *Don't take S to the hotel. Found a tracker on my car, might be compromised.* All I could do for the moment. Time to get where I was going.

They'd discover I'd moved the tracker, probably take a day or two, more if I was lucky. The cop car wasn't likely to go anywhere that made sense for me to go.

I decided I couldn't drive around all night, which left my office or my home. The bed at home was far more comfortable, and that was where the Scotch was.

Even so, I parked a few blocks away, by St. Augustine, in the spaces on the street next to their parking lot, to obey the unwritten rule of the neighborhood to not park in front of anyone else's house. I almost forgot the pie but remembered to snag it.

The sun was fully golden now, hanging as if sitting on the trees. A beautiful evening, if I could let myself enjoy it.

It's what we have, isn't it? I thought as I walked home. The small moments when we know how alive we are and how lucky to be able to watch the light as it changes, to gaze at the stars and the moon and the eons they represent.

I turned the corner to my house.

The beauty passed and I glanced around the street, the other blocks I could see. Was I being watched? Someone in a car parked far enough away to not be noticed but close enough to see me go into my house?

My phone chimed from a text. As I was opening the screen, Torbin called to me.

"Hey, you're just in time. We're heading over to Danny and Elly's."

I glanced at my phone before answering him. Saw it was from Joanne. "I don't think I can," I said as I looked back at my phone to read it.

"Probably what the text is about. C.J. is taking her there as we speak."

"Wait, what?" I looked at him and back at the phone. Joanne's text said *D&E, all will be there*. That short meant she'd done it at a stoplight.

"Where is your car?" Torbin asked.

I told him about the tracker and parking away from my house.

"Leave it there," Torbin told me. "Ride with us."

I asked him to give me ten, handed him the pie, and trotted home.

That solved the moral quandary of whether to share the pie or not. I'd come up with something else for breakfast.

Chapter Eleven

I needed a few minutes to see if I could catch the tail of the thoughts running through my head. I also needed to pee.

I pushed it to fifteen, including going upstairs and changing my clothes in case any of the grease or sour sweat smell clung to me.

I added my gun to my PI bag, hiding it snugly in a zipped pocket, and then walked back to Torbin's. He and Andy were lounging on their porch.

"Two things first," I told them. "Check your car to make sure no one is tracking us." I told them what to look for, and we were all on our knees searching under both Andy's and Torbin's cars.

"All clear," I said, then added, "We need to make a stop on our way," explaining Sarah couldn't go back to her hotel, so I needed to get her stuff. Better to do it in daylight, when more people were about, rather than later when we were tired.

We decided to take Andy's car, since it was bigger, and headed to the hotel.

Torbin insisted on coming with me, leaving Andy to sit in the car and move if needed since there was no legal parking nearby.

The room was lived in but neat. I told Torbin to hang by the door and listen for anyone coming, pointing out the fire escape and adding he should run if anything happened.

I packed Sarah's things as quickly as I could. She had more books than clothes, with one suitcase full of them, and the bags was everything else. I put items from the bathroom in a plastic bag before finding her toiletries kit. *Sort it out later*, I told myself, *just get everything packed.*

I put any remaining food in another of the plastic bags, checked all the drawers and even under the bed. Then a quick look in the trash before signaling Torbin. I left a ten as a tip but kept my room key in case we had to come back. She was scheduled to stay another few days. If anyone checked, I wanted them to think she was still there.

I let him take the suitcase with the books.

He called Andy as we were waiting for the elevator to let him know we were on the way.

As we exited, Andy was easing into the loading zone in front of the hotel.

As we pulled away, I scanned the streets, looking for anyone looking at us. The disappearing sun cast long shadows and golden reflections on car windshields.

A car pulled out in front of us.

"Let's take a scenic route," I told Andy from the back seat.

He nodded.

"Turn here," I instructed, as we came to Dauphine, taking us downtown and the wrong direction. I gave Andy a few more turns, looping us around until we got to Claiborne and took that uptown.

Without any prompting from me, Andy turned before the usual street to Danny's place, winding around the residential blocks to take us there. No traffic here; no one following us.

Andy parked near but not obviously in front of their house.

"Don't get out of the car yet," Torbin hissed at me.

Another car rolled past us, parking directly in front. Nancy, Cordelia's new partner (not wife, no marriage license that I could find—no, I'm not obsessed, it was a slow day and I was bored) got out and headed to the door.

"Thanks for the warning," I whispered back to him.

We waited until the door had opened and closed before we got out.

Torbin grabbed a couple of bottles of wine plus some beer left over from another party. Andy had taken some bags of chips they had around. I had my fresh baked pie.

Danny and Elly lived in a house in the Broadmoor area. It had been gutted after Katrina, and when they bought it, they had remodeled it as well, making a new, larger kitchen and an outdoor kitchen and small pool. Because of its size, we often ended up here for get-togethers.

It felt normal, and that normal made it feel jarringly out of place.

We had done a delicate dance around who went where, Cordelia and Nancy for one event, me at the other, mixing only for large groups where we could quickly pass by with nothing more than a polite smile.

This was the smallest gathering we'd been in. With Sarah added. Was I here as her friend? Or as a professional PI, hired to protect her? What was the line between them?

On top of those roiling thoughts were the practical ones. We couldn't take her back to the hotel. Probably needed to find one that was nowhere close to where she'd stayed so far. I knew she didn't like those generic places in the suburbs, but large and anonymous might be best.

Torbin rang the doorbell.

Voices and laughter and then Elly opened it.

"Look what the cat is dragging in," Torbin said as he entered.

"No cats and no dragging," Elly said. "You're all welcome." She ushered us in, to the kitchen so we could put down our bundles.

"Oh, we have pussies somewhere," Torbin bantered.

"As well as drag," I added.

It looked like the others had moved to the back yard. Her pride and joy, Danny had added a large accordion door that opened wide enough to make the outdoor deck an extension of the living room. I spotted Sarah, sitting comfortably in one of the large chairs. She was talking to Alex, Joanne's wife. Cordelia was on the other side, Nancy joining her as I watched, pulling Cordelia's attention to her.

We're not really friends. No murders plotted, at least on my end, although I couldn't be sure about her. She was average height, with hair I'd only ever seen as blond and coloring that gave no hint to what its natural shade might be. Or had been; I'm sure it would be gray by now. Light hazel eyes, height/weight proportional body with just enough time at the gym to keep it that way but not build too many muscles. She cared how she looked, walked on the sporty side of the street, with clothes bought at the nicer stores, in warm shades of peach and pink. She had been a nurse. She and Cordelia met when Cordelia was a patient at the cancer center in Houston. Me, a coward, staying here, only giving up weekends for a quick visit there. I rationalized it by claiming I would lose my business, our income, I'd have to shut down, let my clients go elsewhere. I was also scared she wasn't coming back and I'd be left alone to rebuild everything, not even work to pull me through the day. Life sometimes breaks us more than we can make up for. I had done what I thought was my best and it wasn't good enough.

I turned to Elly, explaining that I hadn't baked the pie but gotten it from one of those hole-in-the-wall places. Making a long story out of it, so I could linger in the kitchen.

Elly listened while she organized things, maybe humoring me or maybe also wanting to delay mingling together.

The doorbell rang. I give Elly a quizzical look. As far as I could tell, we were all there.

She headed for the door. I followed her.

I put out my hand to stop her from opening it, moving in front so I could see who was there.

"Pizza," she said, just as I looked through the peephole to see the pizza delivery person.

I shrugged and opened the door, grabbing the stack of boxes, leaving Elly to give the woman a tip and take a bag of additional stuff.

"Let's take them out to the patio," she instructed.

I did as I was told, depositing them on the table, and followed Elly back into the kitchen. The bag was a selection of salads. "In case some people want to be healthy," she explained.

"Take the wine and beer out," Danny told me as she joined us. "That's your area of expertise."

I gathered the wine bottles and some of the beer Torbin had brought. "Wine is not my specialty," I said, getting through the door before Danny could reply. I put all but the red into the cooler stocked with ice but had to return to the kitchen for openers.

Elly and Danny had put the salads into bowls and brought them out. I started to open the red wine. It wasn't playing nice, the foil tearing, only coming off a piece at a time.

"Here, let me do that." Sarah took the bottle from me. "I drink a lot of wine and have gotten good at this. Just keep the bottle steady," she said, setting it on the table.

I grasped it with both hands as she made short work of uncorking it. She took a whiff of the cork, then the wine. "Not a bad pinot noir."

"Show-off," I groused.

She smiled at me, a happier smile than I'd seen from her. Being around people—other than me—was clearly good for her. In a quiet voice she said, "Thank you for letting me off the leash. I was useful this afternoon. Through all this, I felt like I was only taking. Maybe only a little, but today I could pass on some of that help."

I moved the red wine to the middle of the table, then got the white from the cooler, holding it for Sarah to show off her skill. "I thought opening wine bottles was more a Catholic than Jewish thing," I said, wondering if I was being woefully ignorant and maybe offensive.

"We drink wine in our religion, too," she said easily. "I also like a glass in the evening. But I learned my skills working with an uncle who had a small vineyard in California. Where I developed my affinity for wine. Thought I might follow in his footsteps."

I started to ask, but people were commingling around the table. There weren't enough chairs to accommodate all ten of us, so Torbin and Andy each grabbed food and went back to the lounge chairs, using the coffee table.

"Maybe leave the rosé until we see if people want to drink it," I suggested. I noticed our side of the table wasn't crowded so took advantage to serve myself. My arms were long enough to reach.

"Can you snag me a slice of the veggie pizza?" Sarah asked, joining me on this side of the table. I did, then grabbed a beer and joined Torbin and Andy. Sarah followed, setting down her plate, and went back for a glass of red wine.

That left seats at the table for everyone else.

Torbin and Andy were on one end of a long couch. I had taken one of two chairs that formed an L with the couch. Sarah took the other one.

Danny joined Torbin and Andy on the couch, with a big pile of salad and a small slice. She saw me eyeing her plate. "Some of us are not born skinny. Elly and I have a new rule: The more you eat, the more you sweat."

That prompted Torbin to talk about our workout routine. They had a shed that we'd turned into a small gym when everything was shut down during the worst of COVID. I'd chipped in, so we were able to get a decent elliptical and a rower as well as weights. The good and bad about working out together was that it made it harder to skip or slack off. If Andy was on the rower when I got there, I wasn't willing to stop on the elliptical until he was finished. I used the same size weights as Torbin, even if it meant pushing myself and being sore later.

Of course, we started getting loud and laughing, with Torbin telling the story of him and Andy being trapped in the shed because a snake was on the patio outside, only to have me show up, pick it up, and tell them how lucky they were to have a rat snake around.

"She picked the damn snake up!" Torbin shouted at me.

"It was harmless," I countered. I'd grown up in the bayous and I knew my snakes. I usually leave them alone but couldn't resist toying with them, trapped in their own back yard.

Alex joined us, bringing the bottle of red.

Joanne came over, putting a bottle of beer on the table next to Alex to claim the chair. She didn't sit, instead going back to consolidate the pizza and take it back into the kitchen. Danny got up to help, pulling two extra chairs to the other side of the table, so we could all be together over here.

I was between Torbin and Sarah so at least didn't have to worry about Nancy sitting next to me. Or Cordelia.

Sarah nudged my shoulder with hers and pointed to the wine. Andy passed it to me and I passed it to her.

Cordelia was watching us. Nancy was watching her.

Sarah and I had developed a camaraderie in the time we'd been together, the pressure and seriousness of the situation getting us beyond the politeness of people newly met. It probably made us seem closer than we were. Sarah was a rabbi from New York who hated New Orleans. I was a decidedly unreligious person, having long ago come to the conclusion to not be bullied by old, dead men about how to live my life. As well as she held it together, I knew she was in deep mourning. And a client. Nothing romantic between us, instead comrades in a foxhole.

Well, the truth was the truth, but they could assume what they wanted.

The rearranging of people had brought a quiet spell.

Sarah looked at Cordelia and said, "Thank you for bringing me along. I talked to the group about faith and healing, that some religions recognize us all as God's children."

"It worked out for us, as well," Cordelia replied. "We have a support group for trans people who are struggling with finding acceptance. One caught me in the hall afterward and said how helpful you'd been."

"A lot of people, especially queer, have been hurt when some use religion as a weapon."

"You're a preacher?" Nancy asked.

"A rabbi," Sarah answered.

"How did you get from wanted to be a winemaker to being a rabbi?" I asked the question I wanted to earlier.

Sarah thought for a second. "Callings have their particular demands. Wine demanded following the seasons and the land, and I didn't want to be that tied down. I liked drinking it more than making it. In my late twenties, I didn't really know what I wanted to do, except to live an ethical, purposeful life. Leah had just gotten her degree in social work. Then a funeral, a loss, Leah's grandfather. They were close, so I helped her with her grief, sitting shiva, being accepted by her family, of course, but also the rabbi and cantor there. I never thought a radical lesbian could be a rabbi, but they helped me realize I could. And I should."

That led to questions of how one becomes a rabbi, the training, what it was like being a woman and a lesbian. Sarah answered them easily, questions she had probably answered multiple times. She was an extrovert, although I had seen little of it in our time together. First with Torbin and now with my friends, I was seeing the open, curious person she was. I looked for the hidden, the danger in people. She was the opposite, looking for the kindness and the strength, decency and compassion while carrying her sadness so closely.

She was clearly a better person than I am.

"So, how long have you been dating?" Nancy asked Sarah.

Sarah looked confused.

I understood the question, so answered. "We're not. We're friends. Sarah is visiting, and I offered to show her around." I could tell from their expressions that most of the people here knew that was a lie. I didn't care; it was the answer she deserved.

Sarah put her hand on my arm, asking for space. "Micky and I are friends," then with a brief glance at me, "at least, I'd like to think we are."

"We are," I affirmed.

"But I'm not here as a visitor. There was an attack on my synagogue, someone tried to kill me. They…they…instead killed…" She faltered and stopped.

"They murdered her wife Leah in an attempt to kill Sarah. A hate group," I said. "Sarah is here as a precaution until the killers are tracked down. She claims to hate New Orleans, so she decided this was a place to hide where no one would look."

Torbin refilled her wine glass. "You're not driving, you can drink the whole bottle."

She gave him a wan smile, then took a sip. "Thank you, I might. Thank all of you. It has been hard, and it's comforting to be around people and not lost in…"

"If there's anything we can do," Alex said, "ask. Please ask. As you said, sometimes small things can make a difference, and it helps us to be able to make even that small difference."

"Thank you," Sarah said again. "There is one thing. In the Jewish tradition we have mourning periods, with people around. I'll keep it short, but would you allow me to recite the Mourner's Kaddish?"

"Yes, of course," Danny said. "Tell us what you need from us."

"It's usually said with a minyan, ten Jewish adults…but not possible right now. Still, I want to do what I can for Leah. Don't worry, I'm Reform, nothing too onerous," Sarah said. "Can I ask people to stand?"

"Oh, don't worry, honey, I've been to full tilt Baptist funerals," Torbin said as he got up.

"Yes, Great-Aunt Eula's when the AC broke," I added.

"Be respectful," Elly said.

"They are. We mourn and we celebrate, and laughter is part of celebration," Sarah said.

Sarah spoke, words I didn't understand, a distant language.

Her voice was strong, knowing these words, knowing what they symbolized in a place in her soul. How hard it must be for her to say the prayer that others should be saying for her. Saying them to strangers in a strange place.

What would it be like? The grief from a ripping loss too soon, flesh and blood stolen by abstract hate. They could have, should have had thirty, forty more years together.

I'd be screaming at the moon and the stars and the sun, not able to hold my grief the way she was.

A phone rang.

"Oh, I'm sorry, I have to get this." Nancy. She took her phone out of her pocket, then moved into the house, away from our hearing.

New girlfriend with all the money? I was enough of a cynical asshole to think that.

Cordelia managed to keep what she was thinking off her face. Too bad, because I wanted to know what she was thinking. She merely shifted, to bridge the gap between her and Joanne.

Sarah spoke a little longer, words I could only dimly understand through inflection and tone.

"Thank you all," she said. "It's getting late. I should probably go back to my hotel." She sat down and finished the wine in her glass.

"About that," I said. "There may be an issue."

She shot me a look.

I explained about the tracker on my car. "No way to know if it's connected to you. It could be a not happy former client or even a current one who is demanding results yesterday and wants to know what I'm doing to earn the money she's paying me," I added. I didn't want Sarah—or anyone else—to be worrying more than they needed to.

"We were thinking about that," Torbin said. "Sarah can stay with us. She's going to be staying there over the weekend anyway, so this will give us time to school her on the quirky ways we've organized the kitchen."

"No, we can't do that," I countered.

"Why not?" Torbin asked.

My brain scrambled for reasons other than being afraid for my friends. "No way to get her there. I'm riding with you, and if she comes with us, if anyone is watching my place, they'll see us together."

"I can take her," Alex said. "Different time, different car."

"Yes, great plan," Torbin agreed. "I can give you our keys and you can go first."

"But they might see Sarah, and that would not be a good thing."

"Hat, glasses, scarf," Alex said. "Every New Orleans house has a Mardi Gras costume closet."

"It's settled," Andy said.

"No, it's not," I retorted with a look at Joanne to back me.

She shrugged. "We can take her to one of the hotels out in Metairie, far from her last one. But…there is a trade-off. If she's with Torbin and Andy, they come and go as they usually do, bring food, she can cook, so no need for you to get groceries. Plus, if LEOs are involved, they can check hotels. They can't check private residences."

Damn. Joanne had a point. If we were being rational and all that crap. It didn't do much for the emotional toll this was taking—these were my friends, and I had brought them into danger.

I sighed, making it clear I wasn't fully on board.

"It's okay," Sarah said softly, "we can do it your way."

I looked at her. She was letting this be my decision. I knew she'd much rather stay with Torbin and Andy. The sterile hotel might not make her safer—it would only take the danger there instead of so close to home.

"Joanne is right. It might be better for you to be in a place no one expects you to be and where getting you food is part of the routine of the people living there."

Andy took the house keys off the ring with his car key and handed them to Sarah.

"Saints hat and scarf," Danny said, as she got up. "We have a few."

"I can take my glasses off instead of putting any on."

Elly, Alex, and Cordelia started clearing up, taking the dishes to the kitchen, putting the leftovers away.

Danny came back with a Saints baseball cap and a long, winding scarf and handed them to Sarah. She put them on, modeling them for us. It changed how she looked, especially with her glasses off. I hoped the change was enough.

I went through the kitchen to the front door.

Joanne got there first. "Going to check the street, I presume?"

"Better safer than sorry."

"Let me. I can do it and cover with getting something from Alex's car and moving it to mine."

"I'm the one getting paid for this. I should be doing it."

"Take us all out for a nice dinner after this is over," Joanne answered as she slipped out.

It was done. Sarah was now decked out as a fanatical Saints fan. She and Alex left together.

Only now did Nancy reappear, having taken her call to the spare bedroom. She looked like it had been a good conversation. I reminded myself I was filling in what I wanted to believe. In truth I didn't know her well enough to read her expression.

Elly tried to give them one of the leftover pizzas, but Nancy refused on their behalf. "We have to watch our weight."

I put out my hand to take it. The pie would have been better, but pizza is a perfectly adequate breakfast food.

Then it was hugs at the door, Joanne lingering by her car as we all pulled out. I watched long enough to see her get in and drive away.

"We need to do something normal and in character on our way, to give them plenty of time. I suggest a drive-through daiquiri shop," Torbin said.

"It's a weeknight," Andy replied, but it was a weak protest. "But I guess I can make the sacrifice."

We decided to hit Melba's on Elysian Fields instead. No drive-through, but they had gallons and half gallons to go.

I spent most of the ride looking out the back window, trying to see if anyone was tailing us and telling myself all the ways this would be okay. We had checked for trackers, so they could only know where we were going if they were following us. As far as I could tell, no one was. I hoped as far as I could tell was good enough.

Torbin went in to get the booze.

He came back with a half-gallon jug and also a big go-cup, which he handed to me.

"We're not sharing?" I asked.

"No, sadly not. We're dropping you off at your house all by yourself," he told me. "No contact with Sarah."

Much as I didn't want to be alone, he had a point. If I was how they could find Sarah, better not go where she was.

I remembered to take the pizza and large daiquiri—my consolation prizes—my bag on my shoulder, and waved good-bye.

They drove to the other end of the block and took enough time getting out of their car to make sure I was behind locked doors.

Once inside, I checked the whole house, gun in hand. But all was locked and quiet.

It was late, but I wasn't going to waste a perfectly good daiquiri so stayed up, first trying to read, finally admitting I couldn't concentrate, and tried to think things through so I wouldn't stay up all night doing it.

On the strictly practical side, having Sarah change who she was around and how she was moved would make her safer. I had checked the block as best I could short of walking the entire length and looking in each car. I recognized most of them and didn't see anyone in any of the others. There were a few people outside the little bar at the end of the street, but they were the regulars and one of the reasons this block felt safe—people around and watching. Anyone observing me would see me go home, by myself.

Tomorrow, I could stay away from Sarah entirely, so if anyone was following me, they couldn't follow me to her.

I tried to think how I had failed. *One person can't be perfect*, I reminded myself. The looming question was who put the tracker on my car and why? The NYPD cops? They'd be able to look up my license plate. Because they were pissed I'd lost them? Or because one or both of them were working with or even part of the hate group targeting Sarah? As far as I knew, they were the only people who knew I was with Sarah. Or just the most obvious ones? The two men who had dropped her off the first day? They came across as two guys doing a job they wanted over with. I don't remember even being introduced to them, so did they know my name?

Others? I trusted the people I knew—Joanne and Danny were in law enforcement and we'd known each other for decades now. Torbin was a gossip, but I'd trust him with my life to keep his mouth shut. Same for Andy. Elly and Cordelia were medical people; they were used to not talking. Nancy? Okay, I didn't like her, but couldn't see her involved. Could see her treating this as just something interesting and talking about it, but it wasn't likely she would be hanging out with white supremacist bigots.

Some of the people Sarah knew back in New York? Save for her assistant David, who knew I was connected to her? He might have told his cousin, but he could also have asked him to send me the file without telling him why. I had told him my info, and he knew I knew where Sarah was. But…she trusted him. Maybe I needed to trust her trust.

That got me to the bottom of the daiquiri.

Go to bed. Hope the alcohol puts you to sleep.

That's what I did.

CHAPTER TWELVE

The booze had gotten me to sleep, but not kept me asleep. It was a night of tossing and turning. Things were moving too fast and I wanted to slow them down and I couldn't.

I finally gave up and got out of bed a little before six. Cordelia had kept those hours and I'd done my best to ignore them. Now all I had to ignore was my alarm clock.

I considered working out—and needed to—but felt like I had to deliberately stay away from Torbin and Andy. We could go for days without seeing each other, sometimes weeks with little more than a nod if I slipped in the side gate to work out or we drove past each other on our way to and fro.

A long shower to wake me up, pizza for breakfast, and a big mug of coffee. Even more coffee in my travel mug and a couple of slices packed as lunch, and I was out the door.

I gave the street a glance while trying to look like I wasn't before remembering my car was parked elsewhere, so hiked there. No one followed me that I could see. I was out earlier than usual. If they had kept tabs on me for a few days, they might not expect me this early. I kicked myself—metaphorically—for not having checked my car.

Not a mistake I'd make this time.

Clean. Either they hadn't figured out I'd moved the tracker or hadn't located mine parked where it was.

The earliest the NYPD cops might have done it was after the interview at Joanne's station. They didn't know who I was before that. They could have looked me up as they left, seen my car, and tagged it then.

If it was them.

I got to my office and it was barely 7:30 a.m. Blasphemy.

The coffee shop was busy, smells of caffeine and freshly baked goods wafting about.

Fortified with my pizza, I hurried up the stairs to my office.

I thought about calling Sarah to check on her. But it was early; it had been a late night for them as well. I doubted they had let that daiquiri go to waste either.

Maybe I should get a second burner phone to make the calls seem more random. Except they would have to know she had a burner phone as well and have traced it to see who called her.

"Damn, too many unknowns to know what the hell is the best thing to do." *They're all okay*, I told myself. *I live at the other end of the block; I'd know if something happened.*

Time to focus on my other cases. I pulled up the tracking app to see what Elmer had been up to.

After he left the restaurant, he'd hightailed it back to New Orleans and stayed for several hours in what looked like a nice area in Old Metairie, the well-to-do suburb just west of the city, close to the country club. The area where Paulette's parents had their house. Several houses were possible; the tracker could be off by that much. Boss was doing well with his true believers supporting him.

Elmer was there for about four hours. Maybe mopping floors for Boss?

He left around dinnertime, heading back the way he'd come. Stopped at a fast-food place in LaPlace, then a gas station next to it.

Then down a side road and a stop for about half an hour in a residential area. I pulled up the street view. Far more run down than where Boss lived. Small houses, a few trailers. The road narrow, the edge sloping off to the ditch with dirt driveways built over it.

One of his so-called friends? But he didn't stay long enough for beer and visions of glory. Dropping off something for Boss? Picking up something?

From there, a stop at another fast-food place, then back down to old Highway 61 heading west until he stopped at a motel. A small U-shaped one, painted a pale green, close in color to the swamp that surrounded it. A parking lot of oyster shell, with a rut near the turn in that would be a surprise if you didn't go over it slowly. Cheap, but presumably it had hot water.

He was still there.

Apparently, I was the only early riser in this bunch.

The big question was where was he keeping the boxes he'd stolen from Paulette?

My plan was to see if I could figure out where he stashed them and somehow get them. If he left them somewhere that could be easily, shall we say, accessible? A friend's garage with them out? Back at his apartment? I could probably pick the lock. Yeah, he was stupid, but was he stupid enough to leave them in a place Paulette knew about? Out at the camp or places people were around would be hard. At worst, I could tell Paulette where he was and let her deal with the problem she had created.

I closed the app. I'd track him for a few more days.

It was barely past 8 a.m. and I wasn't sure what to do with my day.

Until last night, I had assumed a chunk of my time would be with Sarah, getting her food, or clothes more appropriate for the weather, or just getting her out enough to keep her sane. I hadn't planned on it being the opposite, staying away from her and having no contact.

Read through everything again, I told myself.

First the info David sent me. I hadn't heard yet from Joanne whether they had looked into the woman claiming she wanted to convert. Bettina (Betty) Collingwood. I ran her name. It being New York, there were a number of possibilities, but none of them seemed to fit. Too old, too far away—no one in the Bronx would go to Brooklyn for religious services. One was too dead. If you're dead, it's too late to convert. Probably a fake name.

The name of a dead person. I looked back at that one. She'd died about a year ago. A common ploy in identity theft: Take the name of someone who'd recently died.

But even that only got me back to her using a fake name. That likely meant she was there for something other than a sincere desire to convert to Judaism. Most likely to spy on Sarah, learn her routines, when she was there, scope out the location. Which meant she was connected to the terror group.

What would happen if Sarah called her? From her real phone?

I dismissed that idea. It would be using Sarah as bait, and that was too dangerous.

Besides, Joanne had her phone. Maybe I could ask her about it. It might help us locate the woman.

Or I could forget it. Remember that I was a lone PI in New Orleans, far from the scene of the crime, without the resources of the law enforcement agencies. I could stay in my lane—protect Sarah while she was here.

I glanced at my watch. Just before 9 a.m. People were awake, but still early to call unless I had a good reason. Joanne wouldn't have had time to talk to her counterpart in New York, so no update on either the two cops down here or if they had done anything with the information on the woman claiming to convert.

That sent me back to Paulette's case. I again looked over what the computer grannies had found.

A list of his friends. As usual, the grannies had been thorough. Not just names but a reasonable amount of info about them. Addresses. Workplaces. I first looked for an address that might be Boss, but nothing matched where Elmer was yesterday. Okay, not friends. No surprise. I doubted Boss would hang out with the riffraff he commanded. Not good to let those you are cheating to know too much about you.

One address was in a slightly more upscale apartment complex just off Veterans Highway in Metairie, the long strip of worship to the commercial gods. It had a covered lot and a swimming pool. Another was in an apartment in the same area, with a pool but no covered parking. The two friends who said their leases didn't allow anyone else? Another friend lived on the North Shore, the other side of Lake Pontchartrain. It's twenty-four miles of a bridge long enough that you can't see either shore for a good part of it. He lived in a single-family house, barely a step up from a double-wide.

Then an address near where he stopped yesterday, well west of the city. I pulled it up on the map. A house next to a trailer. It had been painted recently, but the small yard in front was overgrown, although who knew when this street-view picture was taken.

Worth a drive?

To do what? I asked myself. See if Elmer had stored any boxes there? More likely to get shot at than find out anything.

Get out of the office and drive so I would have to pay attention to the road and not the ramble in my head.

Good enough. I got my stuff and headed out.

On a whim, I stopped at the computer grannies and gave them Betty/Bettina Collingwood's name. They weren't likely to find more than I did, but a slim possibility was better than none at all.

I did a quick check of my car.

Damn, another one. A different wheel well, but pretty much the same place. I left it. I wasn't going anywhere near Sarah, and this jaunt would be out of the way enough to confuse them. I'd ditch it before I headed back.

I opted for I-10, since it was enough after rush hour to not be too crazy.

Whoever it was knew where my office was and had to have planted it while I was inside. The coffee shop had parked up the spots directly in front, so I was a little way down the block, out of sight of the coffee shop and my front window. Not that I had been looking.

I'd seen no obvious cars or people on the block, but there was no need for them to hang around once they'd affixed the device. I'd been in my office for several hours; plenty of time.

I'd hoped it was the NY cops, done to prove I couldn't escape them. Maybe it still was. They could easily look up my work address. Maybe they were still pissed that I'd lost them, then trolled them by putting the tracker on a NOPD car.

Much as I wanted to think that, it didn't feel quite right. The tracker was a cheap one, available at any online spy shop. Placing it in a convenient location that was easy to find instead of a more hidden spot—that had a whiff of amateur about it. Elmer and his pretend soldiers? But he knew me only in the context of Paulette, not Sarah. And where and how would he or his gang have managed to track my car twice?

He didn't know who I was until I sat at his booth in the restaurant. His phone had been on the table, so it wasn't likely he could have alerted anyone to my being there. Of course, it was still possible Paulette had done it. She would get a cheap one and put it in the most obvious place.

Piss, shit, and corruption. If it was someone after Sarah, going out to LaPlace would throw them off. If it was Paulette, she probably wouldn't know what to think. If it was Elmer or someone connected to him, going near where one of them lived would not be a good thing to do.

I exited the interstate at the airport.

I've done the route to the old terminal so many times, I probably had it memorized, but was still adjusting to the new one. They had built a new facility on the north side of the runways, leaving the terminal on the south side behind. After some hurried lane changing, I pulled into the short-term parking. After driving around a couple of floors, I pulled into an out-of-the-way spot.

I got out and removed the tracker. Considered for a moment whether to put it on another car, then decided the best place was next to a concrete pillar, as unnoticeable as possible. All the cars around me were civilian, not police like the last time. Best to leave them out.

That done, I checked my phone—both of them—but only a text about a boil water advisory in New Orleans East. Annoying, although it didn't affect me, since I don't live there. Our water system has been a mess since Katrina, with so many breaks from the flooding that a drop in water pressure means the water is no longer pushing out of the breaks, and letting things in.

I also checked on Elmer. He was still at the motel. Unless he'd figured out I was tracking him and left it there. I closed the app. Maybe I'd drive by and see if his truck was still there.

I headed out. At least I could make them pay for multiple trackers.

I got back on the interstate, since there are only a few routes over the swamp and it was the most convenient.

I overshot LaPlace and took the next exit.

After a bit of squirreling around, I found the motel. It was a little after eleven in the morning. It was a back road, so I could slow enough to see the red truck with the awful flag was still parked there. Looked like Elmer was sleeping late. And presumably staying another day, since he should be checked out by now.

I headed back to LaPlace. First were neighborhoods of modern ranches, no more than thirty years old, just over the edge into middle class. A few more turns and the houses were older. Smaller, wood instead of brick. The road was narrower, only black asphalt, no line in the middle. A place for the men and the women close to the bottom: store clerks, janitors, those deemed to have little skill save for a body that could lift and haul.

I drove by the house. The yard was still overgrown, not left to its own but only mowed sporadically. It had been painted in the last few years, but a layer slapped over the old one, a quick job to give the house a veneer of newness.

No cars were visible, not in front, not in the short gravel driveway. No garage, only a carport, also painted white, but the rust from the supporting poles was already creeping through.

I rolled past it—this was only idle curiosity, after all—and kept going.

I turned at the next block, but it led to a cul-de-sac with no other way out.

I headed back that way.

As I got near the house again, I saw a woman pushing a stroller head up the walk to the porch. Still no cars. A small plastic grocery bag hung off one wrist.

I pulled over, parking my car only half off the road to keep it out of the ditch.

"Excuse me," I called, trotting to catch her before she went inside. A gamble that the man of the house was off working and we would be woman to woman.

She turned to look at me, surprise and an edge of fear on her face.

"Yes?" she said tentatively, her hand clutching the stroller as if I might snatch it away.

I pulled out my license, waving it at her as I joined her on the porch. She made no move to take at it or look closely, so I put it away.

"We haven't done anything," she said hurriedly.

I don't like scaring people—well, unless they deserve it or I need to. "I'm just seeking information. Do you know Elmer Stumbolt?"

She chewed a fingernail that didn't have much left to chew on. "Um…why?"

Not a blank denial, which meant she did know him but was stalling for time. "We need to question him about the removal of property from his previous employer."

"He's more my husband's friend than mine," she said quickly.

"You need to tell me everything you know or you could be considered an accessory."

She hesitated, weighing what would get her in more trouble.

"I won't reveal anything you tell me or let anyone else know it came from you," I said, bargaining she wasn't worried about Elmer but R.C., her husband.

She looked both ways up and down the street. Only when seeing it was clear, in a rushed tone she said, "We didn't know. Thought we were doing a favor to a friend, okay? He left a few boxes here for about a week. He and R.C. hang out a lot, so just being nice, okay?"

"Where are they?" I asked. Could it really be this easy?

No, it couldn't.

"He took them yesterday. Said he couldn't leave them out. I mean, they were under the carport, but with the rain and all that…So, he got them. We didn't know, we're not in any trouble, okay?"

"You're not in any trouble. You couldn't know. Any idea where he might have taken them?"

"With him, but I don't know where." Her hand loosened on the stroller and she put the bag down on the porch. Diapers and milk.

"Where might he take them? To the land near the Mississippi border?"

"To where?" The hand gripped tightly again. "No one is supposed to know where that is."

"Land transfers are public record. The man you know as Boss," I said, making it up as I was going along.

"No, he said he needed to keep them inside, and it's rough out there. Shed with one shower and a toilet, all in the open. Rest is tents, an outdoor shower that no one uses because they found a water moccasin there. Elmer was hinting hard he needed a place to stay, like we could put him up again."

"Again?"

She looked down, then at me. "Yeah, but he stays here, he expects me to clean up after him, like he's the man and I'm the woman and that's how it works. I already got one damn man who can't be bothered to pick up his socks. All that's my job, like I don't gotta walk way down the road to clerk at the Gas 'n Go. Have to change the diaper right before I leave and change it when I get back 'cause he won't do it. House stinks of shit and he won't do it."

Ah, girl talk. "They can be such jerks," I said, like I'd had to put up with it way too much. "No idea what it takes to do all the cooking and cleaning."

"Yeah, so he stayed a few days and that was enough. Him always hanging out in the living room with the TV on. Asking me for a beer or a sandwich. When I told him to get it himself, he said he didn't know where things were and he didn't want to mess up my kitchen."

"Like you hide the beer someplace other than the fridge."

"What'd he think, we put it under the house?" Then she snorted a laugh. "He'd tell me to shut the baby up, it's annoying him."

"Jerk," I said. "Babies cry, and if he didn't like it, he needed to be the one to leave."

"Yeah, so he left, stayed up at the camp for a night, but no water and too many mosquitos. All brave and that until a tiny insect buzzes around. So I told R.C. that he couldn't stay here no more."

"Good choice," I told her. "A small place like this, you need to be a really good guest. So, if not the camp, any other place you might think of? Any girlfriends?"

Again, the snorting laugh. "He's only good looking enough to get one date. He got some weird ideas of what he wants."

"Like what?"

"Now, Elmer wanted someone who would have a job to bring home money but also do all the cooking and cleaning and always let him do whatever he wanted whenever he wanted it. Said 'she can't refuse me, women have to please their men.' So I asked him if he liked doing it when we got the curse, with blood and all. That grossed him right out."

"Once a month, it happens." I laughed along with her. "You got any other ideas of where he might have the stuff? Anyone else I can talk to? We mostly want to get it back. If that happens, he gets a slap on the wrist."

"Not sure. You can try Derwin. He might talk to you. He goes out with them but once told me he thinks they're a bit crazy, spending so much time and money on things."

"Derwin? Last name?"

"Bergin. Lives over in the city."

The name was the one in the apartment without the covered parking. "Thanks. Don't worry, I won't say I got it from you. What do you think?"

"Think?"

"About what they do in their spare time."

"I mean, maybe they're right. I don't much follow the news and stuff, okay? I know we gotta secure our borders to keep us safe. Can't let them take our guns away. But I don't know, okay? Another big civil war? Too many of us and we have the guns. Those people, the gays and all those immigrants and people that aren't really American. We outnumber them too much for them to fight, okay?"

I kept my face politely neutral. Maybe she was crazy or maybe she just lived with crazy, but there was no point in arguing. "You're right, I doubt there will be another civil war. One per country, right? Listen, thank you for your time, and you don't need to let anyone know you talked to me. I won't tell, and if you don't, no one needs to know."

She nodded as if that was a good idea.

I looked at the bag on the porch. "You have enough of those?" Then I took out two twenties and handed them to her. "For your time."

She blushed and mumbled a thanks.

I went back to my car. With what I hoped was a friendly wave, I drove off.

The money was partly a bribe—and one I was tempted to expense to Paulette—to help keep her from telling anyone. Also, pity. She'd only gotten a small package of diapers, one I suspected was all she could afford. I could argue she made her choices, but how many choices did she have? Maybe she finished high school, maybe not. Clearly not college. She had a baby and was stuck with a man who preferred guns and beer to her. Likely a divorce in the next five years. A brief conversation, but they seemed to be two people living in two separate worlds with a lot of resentment in those large gaps.

Maybe she'd use the forty I'd given her for bus fare to a woman's shelter. And maybe I'd given it to her out of guilt, an offering for the grace that I'd avoided her life.

I headed back to I-10.

I told myself it wasn't a completely wasted trip. I had confirmed that Elmer was still where my tracker said he was, so he hadn't found it. I also found out he did have the material in the area; he hadn't stashed it up with his mother on the other side of the state or out at Camp Crazy. It was likely he was now carrying it around, probably jammed behind the seats of his truck.

Maybe I could run by the hotel when he was out and see if the boxes were in his truck. If I was really lucky, maybe he would think he didn't need to lock it out in the boonies. I knew I was focusing on Elmer and Paulette to avoid worrying about Sarah, Torbin, and Andy.

My dating life had been more off than on. It felt like I'd look around, see the same losers—I mean, people who I wasn't compatible with and had nothing in common. There is a possibility that I'm the crazy one. A sarcastic loner who takes a long time to trust anyone. Like doing criminal background checks before meeting for coffee. A bit much, but better than finding out after your wallet is stolen. Nancy had made the assumption that Sarah and I were dating. She was age appropriate, intelligent, and compassionate. Clearly strong and resilient with what she was going through and how she handled it.

She was also a client, someone dependent on me in a way that gave me power over her. She was a very recent widow, her emotions caught in the loss and what had been. Maybe she would be ready to move on, but it would be long after this was over and she was back in New York. And really, I couldn't see myself as the wife of a rabbi. And even more really, I couldn't see someone like her having any interest in someone like me. If our lives hadn't thrown us together like this, we would have taken one look and kept on walking.

I decided this was not going to be the week of watching my diet, so I stopped by Parkway for a roast beef po'boy, one I'd eat at home since it was messy. The pizza could wait for later.

I ordered fries with it, promising that I would work out an extra fifteen minutes every day before conveniently remembering I couldn't work out while Sarah was staying with Torbin and Andy. It's the thought that counts, right?

I stopped at home to eat. I had hoped that eating a very messy po'boy would be all the temptation my phone needed to ring, but it stubbornly resisted.

Lunch was done, and now I had to decide whether to stay here or go back to my office.

Office, I decided, with a sigh. Here, Sarah was less than a block away. Too tempting for a quick check-in, run by their place to work out. My office was a good twenty blocks away.

I moved slowly but got myself there.

Checked with the grannies to see if they'd found anything, but it was, as I suspected, too early.

Then up to my office to stare at my computer screen.

I did a search for news articles about hate groups in this area, but there wasn't much. Nothing about a plot of land used as a militia playground near the Mississippi border. A couple of stories about foreign plots, people trying to cross the border to attack America, but little about domestic terrorists. Or nothing that labeled Americans that way. Some stories on fights about book banning, with the banners hiding under the guise of being concerned parents. A drag queen story hour canceled due to what the newspaper called "pressure." Was any of that pressure threats of violence?

My office phone rang.

I was bored enough to pick it up.

"Well? Where is my daily report?" Paulette.

I glanced at my watch. Almost three p.m. "I usually do daily reports at the end of the day," I said. Not adding that I usually don't do daily reports, so don't have a usual way of doing them.

"Well, it's close enough to the end of the day now."

"Sorry, I meant the end of the business day, which would be around five p.m., two hours from now." Yes, I was deliberately being annoying.

"Well, I'm down in this part of town, so I'll stop by and you can update me."

"That's not necessary." I stalled. Phones you can hang up, but dislodging her from my office would require me to heave her downstairs, and "she deserved it" is not a good legal defense for bodily harm. "I'm expecting a client soon," I lied.

"No problem. I just pulled up in front. We can be quick." She ended the call.

"Shit." I quickly dialed the computer grannies. Lena answered the phone. "Can one of you come up to my office in about ten minutes and pretend to be a client?"

"Um, let me see who's around."

"You'll be fine. No time to explain. She's coming up the stairs. Or be yourself and say you have info I have to see immediately."

"Yeah, okay. Me or someone else will be there."

I heard footsteps on the stairs. Paulette must have been right out front.

I put the phone down just as she opened my door—without knocking—and entered.

Okay, back to high school intimidation games. If you're bossy enough, the nice girls cave. Or we cave because the battle is so small it's not worth fighting. Either way, she gets what she calls a win.

I made the wrong choice in coming to the office.

Now my cell phone rang. Joanne.

"I have to take this," I told her. I answered as I headed to a back room I used for storage. It had once been a bedroom. I lived here when I was first starting out, but now it was mostly file cabinets and old furniture I planned to someday do something with—like donate—but hadn't gotten around to it.

I shut the door, then moved into the far corner. I kept the phone to my ear, not putting it on speaker. I wouldn't put it past Paulette to listen at the door.

"Yeah, hey, I'm sorry," I said. "I have a client I don't want listening in."

"Have you been in contact with Sarah at all today?" she asked.

"No, why?"

"Good. Just checking."

"Have you?"

"No. I assume that Torbin or Andy would let us know if there were any problems."

"As long as they all aren't dead, they would probably call."

"Stop borrowing trouble. They're fine. You live in a dense, urban neighborhood, with houses barely an arm length apart. Too many people there who would report a fight or gunshots."

"Okay, you're probably right." Torbin lived just across from the neighborhood bar, and usually by the afternoon the old retired folks were already sitting around. They knew the place and watched who came and went.

"I can't talk long. Why don't we meet after I get off? A couple of things to get caught up on."

"Yeah, we can do that. Where?"

"I have some books I borrowed from Andy. I can drop them off and we can meet there. Might as well include Sarah."

"Is it safe for me to be there?"

"Coin toss. If you stay away, is that suspicious? You should go there as you normally would. As long as Sarah remains unseen, it should be okay."

"Makes sense. What time?"

"I'll try for around five thirty, maybe a little later."

"I'll call Torbin and make sure it's okay."

"I already did. See you there."

Well, of course she had. Joanne wouldn't suggest it this late in the day otherwise.

I considered walking back to the door, still talking, and babbling on about something fun, like an arranged assignation or big bank heist. My only hesitation was that Paulette was gullible enough to believe it and call the cops on me. I watched a full minute elapse before reentering my office, where Paulette made a point of huffily looking at her watch.

"This is a business. If you want my undivided time, you have to make an appointment, not just show up when I'm busy." *Not playing your game, lady.*

"You'd do more business if you were more accommodating to clients," she retorted.

"I have plenty of clients, as you might have noticed. One on their way here and that was another on the phone." Sort of. Sarah was a client and Joanne was calling about her. Now I glanced at my watch. She started to say something, but I kept going. "I've tracked down the more recent places Elmer has been. He left the files with a friend out in the LaPlace area but just picked them up yesterday, telling the friend that they shouldn't be stored in a carport, with no real protection from the weather."

"What? They got rained on?" she demanded.

"No, they were covered, but the carport had no walls. He moved them because it's supposed to rain in the next few days. As I was saying, he now most likely has them in his possession."

"I knew that," she interjected.

I ignored that. "He didn't have them in his possession until now. He can't leave it at the place where it was until yesterday. He can't leave it out at the land over by Mississippi—"

"What? How do you know about that?" Paulette was used to being listened to, not being quiet and listening.

"I'm a PI. Finding out things is what I do. They had an incident playing with dynamite and blew up the water line, so there's no running water, so it's highly unlikely he'll go there or leave anything." I started to ask how she knew about it but guessed Elmer's idea of pillow talk was to boast about his outdoor prowess. Killing five mosquitos in one blow.

"But you should check it out, since you know where it is."

"Too unlikely to be there," I told her. Plus, it was where armed men who never met a wack-a-doodle conspiracy theory they didn't like run around. I've taken risks in my life, even foolish ones, but this was where even fools don't go. "Last night he stayed in a hotel to the west of the city. The night before he snuck back to his apartment and crashed there."

"What? I put a bug in it. I'd know."

"Are you sure it's still working? That he didn't find it? Remember, he and his friends are paranoid soldier boys. Or if it was battery powered, the battery might have died."

The look on her face told me she hadn't considered any of these possibilities.

"Well, I guess, maybe."

"If you do things like that, you need to be smart. Don't buy the cheapest crap you can find from some online place you've never heard of."

"I asked someone what to use," she huffed.

"Elmer?"

"No, someone else." But the few words meant she was being evasive. Not Elmer, so it had to be someone she didn't want me to know about. A new boy toy who was even younger?

"And you need to be smart about where you hide it. Like putting a tracker in the ever so convenient to reach wheel well of a car. So easy to find. Both times."

A guess, but the look on her face told me it was an accurate one.

She hastily coughed and covered her mouth with her hand. "What?" But it was a second too late for a real reaction. "What are you accusing me of?"

I stared at her. "I parked my car out at the airport and picked up a rental. Which I'll trade in for another one tomorrow. So quit your shit."

"I don't know what you're talking about." But she was the worst actress in the high school plays that were badly acted. "I don't know about those kinds of things," she continued.

"The lady doth protest too much. You just told me you placed a bug in Elmer's apartment," I told her. Then I looked at my watch. "Do you want to finish the update or argue? I only have time for one."

"I saw your car out front," she said, attempting a subject change.

"You saw a gray Mazda. Lot of them on the road. A barista at the shop downstairs has the same car. That would be the one you saw." No Oscars in my future, but I can tell a decent lie.

Her face settled into a frown, one that would leave hard lines on her face. We all get them, but I hope mine will be from laughing. "I'm a paying client, and you shouldn't accuse people who pay you good money…"

She was still talking, but I stopped listening. I stood up, looked at my phone, and said, "Sorry, that's all the time I have. I'll send you an update tomorrow, since you've already got all the update you're interested in for today."

She stood up as well, her mouth in an angry O. "You're lucky I gave you a chance, given what a loser you were in high school—"

A knock on the door. I grabbed it open. Lena was standing there with a big file. "I know you said you needed this as soon as we could get it and how important it is, so I wanted to bring it up right away." Not great acting, but so much better than Paulette's that I was sure she'd be fooled.

"Thank you so much," I said, ignoring Paulette. "This is very important. I'll run it over to Joanne right now." If I left, Paulette had to leave.

"What about your client?" Paulette demanded.

I held up my phone. "She just texted and asked to meet at her office. I really have to go." I again thanked Lena and held the door open expectantly for Paulette.

Lena, having done her duty, headed down the stairs.

"I need to go to the restroom, can I at least do that?" she asked.

"There are bathrooms in the coffee shop. You can use those and not hold me up." I made a motion with my hands that she needed to go out the door.

"Horrible customer service," she grumbled as she swept past me.

I quickly grabbed my PI bag, hurriedly locked up, and was right behind her. Her nice house was a ranch and she wasn't in stair shape.

"When am I going to get the results I'm paying for?" she demanded, although more as an excuse to pause for breath on the second floor landing.

I crowded her as a hint to not linger. "As I said before, likely in the next few days. A week at most."

She started moving again. "That's way too long. When I pay for something, I want results."

"You'll get the results you pay for," I told her.

Finally, we were on the first floor.

"Which way to the—"

"That way," I cut her off, pointing down the back hall where the coffee shop restrooms were.

The frown settled into her face and she headed there. I had suspected her request was more about making me wait, but it looked like she really needed to pee. At least here, I won't have to clean the bathroom after her.

She tried to open the door without knocking, but someone was in there.

I smiled, working on those laugh lines, at her having to wait.

I strode out the door.

Her Lexus was parked in front of my car, too close to my front bumper. Hard to know if she was being obnoxious or just not good at street parking.

I walked around to the passenger side and opened it, putting my bag on the seat. As I was bending down, I rummaged around in it. Two can play the tracker game.

I found what I was looking for and, with a quick glance back at the coffee shop door, walked as if I was examining my front bumper, then bent down to look at something and was able to easily reach under her too close rear bumper to put the tracker on the underside of her car.

Then I stood up, got in my car, had to jigger a bit to get out of the tight parking spot, and drove away.

Home was the obvious destination, but I took a few side streets, stopped at the food coop to buy bare necessities like bread and chocolate before heading home.

Even with my slow traipse, it was still only a little after four when I got home. In true paranoid fashion, I drove around the block before finally parking.

Once inside, as I was putting things away, I let myself be angry at Paulette. Her fucking entitlement—she was paying me; in her mind I was merely hired help, not a paid and skilled consultant. That gave her the right to insult me, boss me around, and even spy on me. Just like she treated the unpopular kids in high school, occasionally useful and then disposable. Probably the way she'd seen her parents treat the people who cleaned their house and cooked their food.

"We're not in high school anymore," I growled.

I could tell her where Elmer was and that would be the end. The only reason not to was because I was curious to see what was in those files. If I could get them easily enough—i.e., not going anywhere that armed men might be running about—I would do that.

Then I'd have to ask myself if I was looking for justice or revenge.

As annoying as she was, she'd revealed it was her, not the hate group, tracking me. If it wasn't the hate group, that meant Sarah was, if not safe, at least safer. It meant I didn't need to avoid her and leave her safety to my friends, whom I also wanted to keep safe.

I looked at the Scotch bottle on the shelf where we—where I— kept the liquor. Cordelia had decided that was the place and organized everything. It worked and I was used to it, so hadn't changed it.

I started to reach for the bottle, then stepped back. Not tonight.

Or at least not until later.

The gap of time before meeting Joanne was enough for me to clean the kitchen. Which it needed more than I liked to think it did.

Then, in the ultimate sacrifice, I put the good, crusty loaf of bread I'd just bought and a triple cream brie I'd been saving in a bag and walked up the street to Torbin and Andy's. I didn't see Joanne's car as I scanned the street, said hello to several people sitting outside at the bar, and knocked on the door.

CHAPTER THIRTEEN

Andy opened it. He smiled when he saw it was me.

"I bring gifts," I said, hoisting the bag for him to see.

"Very kind of you," he said, also waving at the people across the street. "Any reason?"

"You know some other people are coming over?"

"I'm sure Torbin was about to tell me," he answered, ushering me in.

Andy led me back into the kitchen, leaving the brie out to get to serving temperature. He called out, "Honey, how many people are we having over for dinner? Helpful to know since we've only got leftovers."

Torbin appeared, looking about as sheepish as was possible for him, which is to say, not much. "Sorry, sweetcakes, sort of last minute get-together."

"Too last minute for any grocery shopping, I take it?"

"Anything at your place?" Torbin asked me.

"I brought bread and cheese and that emptied my larder."

"How many?" Andy asked.

"All I know is that Joanne asked to meet here," I answered. "We might be able to do a bread and cheese catch-up and leave it at that."

"There might be a few more," Torbin admitted slowly. "Joanne, but she's not leaving Alex at home, and Danny is a good idea for legal stuff, and she's bringing Elly."

"So, Cordelia and Nancy as well?" Andy asked.

"No, not this time, it's mostly to update all the major players."

In other words, we were again doing the dance of who got invited. Fine with me. Life was complicated enough.

Sarah emerged from the guest bedroom. She smiled when she saw me.

Being with people was doing her good. She looked more rested and happier than I'd seen her. Finding what I couldn't give her, kind, caring people around to help her through the abyss of grief.

"Hi. Good to see you," she said to me. She even gave me a hug.

Andy got us back on track. "So, eight people and no food in the house."

"Pizza?" Torbin suggested.

"We had pizza last night. How many nights can you have pizza?" Andy argued.

"No more than five," Torbin answered, "so we're well below the threshold."

Andy shook his head, both amused and annoyed.

Sarah got to witness a New Orleans ritual, talking about food as if it were the holy grail and respected at all costs.

Andy finally settled it with, "Okay, I'll run to the Roberts on Elysian Fields and get hamburgers. We can grill out back."

"I'll go with you," I offered, but Andy asked me to start the grill instead. "If you get hot dogs, make them kosher," I told him.

He nodded.

As he was leaving, Danny and Elly arrived. They brought more beer.

I went out to the back patio. They had a largish yard by neighborhood standards. Mine went back maybe ten feet, enough for a few chairs and a small garden. Torbin and Andy had a space large enough for a generous bricked patio, with a large grill and a comfortable sitting area. The exercise shed off to the side took up most of one corner, a high privacy fence made more private by banana trees on one side and azalea bushes on the other.

With Andy going to the store and Torbin opening the door—and presumably making drinks—I was the obvious one to start the grill. I'd done it enough times.

Sarah joined me as I was getting the coals going.

"Do you need help?" she asked.

"Naw, I've got it."

"Any clue as to what we're all here about? Am I to be released from jail anytime soon?"

"You consider my cousin Torbin and Andy jail? Or did you mean me?" It didn't come out as funny as I intended.

She looked taken aback. "No, not you or them. You are all people I'd happily see. It's the circumstances." She paused, looked at the ground. "You've all been kind, more kind than I'd expected. More than I hoped for. And brave. There is danger here."

"You're the brave one," I told her.

She gave a bitter smile. "I've had no choice. The only bravery I have chosen is with words. Arguing for causes I believe in, even unpopular ones. Thinking the worst would be being cursed by conservative rabbis for criticizing Israel's government, saying Palestinians deserved respect and dignity and their own state, arguing for the dignity and worth of transgender people. I thought I was brave enough to be hated and vilified as long as it was with words. Not the shattering of bone and blood so close to me. If I had a choice…I don't know what I would have done if I'd known, been told be silent or the bullets will fly. To risk harm, death for what I believe. I'm here because my grandmother survived the Holocaust. Whatever bravery I managed will never match hers."

I put the grill cover down to let the coals get hot. "I'm so sorry." Then helplessly, uselessly, "There just aren't words."

She reached out and took my hand, but I let go to check the coals again.

"Raised sin-and-guilt Catholic. I've left as much as I can behind, but can't leave everything." I reached out and took her hand. Damn the rules, damn my raging brain, Sarah needed human contact. She would never hold Leah's hand again and a stranger would never be the same, but my hand was warm and could hold hers.

She smiled at me. "There are words. Imperfect, ephemeral, stumbling. There are words. The words of ritual that have taken people through centuries of sorrow. Those words have helped us get through ours. My grandmother got through the loss of almost all her family. Only a cousin also survived. All the rest—mother, father, two brothers and three sisters, aunts, uncles, the three cousins who lived next door—all gone. The words we spoke, from the Kaddish to admiring the flowers on the side of the road, helped her carry that unspeakable burden."

"I know, yet the words feel so weak."

"Say them anyway. Imperfect words are better than silence."

The back door opened. Joanne and Alex came out.

I moved away from Sarah, letting go of her hand.

"We were being philosophical," Sarah said. "Words and grief. The words that have been said for so many losses help me to get through.

My friend here," indicating me, "calls me brave and I appreciate it, because I think she knows what the word means. She has put herself next to me, to protect me. A very brave thing to do."

"You forget, I'm being paid to do this." The words—those imperfect words—were out before I considered them, a reflex to bat away praise, defect it with a joke.

"Not well enough," Joanne said. "You are brave. Also, sometimes foolish, rash, hotheaded, obnoxious—"

"Enough." Alex cut her off. "We're all here as friends and need to keep it that way." She came over and hugged Sarah, then me, with Joanne following her lead.

Torbin came out with a plate of bread, crackers, and several cheeses, including the good brie I'd sacrificed. Danny and Elly followed. And a large pitcher of something that I hoped was alcoholic.

I lifted the lid to check the coals—they were nicely glowing—then cut a slice of bread and smeared it with the brie. I might as well have a taste before it was all gone.

Andy wasn't back, but Torbin could catch him up later.

"I discovered a very annoying client left the tracker on my car," I told them between bites.

"Wait, what?" Torbin said.

"We went to high school together. She was popular and, well, I wasn't. Her attitude hasn't changed since. She's paying me, so I need to jump whenever she expects. She bugged her ex-boyfriend's apartment, so knows enough about these things to track me to make sure she was getting her money's worth."

"Well, that's rude," Torbin said. "Anyone I might have met?"

"I hope not. Paulette DeNoux Carter."

Torbin shook his head. He'd only met the people that were my friends, the few I had in those difficult years.

Joanne picked up on the obvious implications. "So, no relation to any possible hate groups stalking Sarah?"

"That seems to be the case. Her ex, whom she hired me to find, seems to dabble in playing soldier with a Confederate flag on his truck. But the IQ points were on a long lunch break when he was being made. He and Paulette are not in contact, to put it mildly."

"Well, shit," Danny added. "All that worry for nothing."

"And not only borrowing our car, but making us get on our hands and knees to check for doohickeys under them," Torbin seconded.

"Safe than sorry and all that," I said.

"Good that you found out." Joanne settled it. "Now we don't have to worry that it's something else. I have a few things. I contacted the NYPD. They were cagey, but reading between the lines, seemed surprised that Sarah had been given a hostile interview. They did say those two were authorized to be here. When I said they'd followed you, they first wanted to know if we were sure, then deflected, saying they would talk to them and see what's up."

"Elephant shit cake with bullshit icing," I said.

"But why?" Sarah asked. "Aren't we all on the same side? Murderers should go to jail."

"The gap between the ideal and the real," Danny said. "The law and justice."

"We have to have evidence that stands up in court," Joanne said.

"With rules for evidence and what can be submitted. A far from perfect system," Danny added.

"I'll give them a day or two and call again," Joanne said. "I had more luck with the local FBI office. If someone is targeting Sarah down here, it's an interstate crime. He seemed interested, said he'd do a dive into hate groups here and see if any have connections with those operating in New York."

"If anyone tries anything down here, they can get involved?" Sarah asked. "Nice to know, since I'll likely be dead by then."

"No, you won't," I said. "We're not going to let that happen. They're not masterminds; they've made mistakes and will make more. Time will trip them up."

"How much time?" she asked. I saw the distress on her face, the question that controlled her life. How much longer would she have to live like this, hidden, unable to do the mundane tasks, take a walk, go to the grocery store, go across the street for the Friday fish fry the bar put on? How long did she have to live in terror?

"Way too much, even if they solve it tomorrow," I answered.

"That would be nice," Sarah responded, with a rueful, sad smile.

"I'd give it another week or two," Danny said. "This is a complex case. Most murders are people who know each other or are connected, and it's easy to follow the threads. The connections are here, but more spread apart, so they'll take longer to run down."

"Speaking of which," I said, "did you ask about the woman who claimed she was trying to convert?"

I got up and poured myself a drink. It was past five enough for a double. A sip told me it was a Cosmo. I took another sip.

"I did," Joanne said. "Didn't get much more than they would look into it."

"What if we called her using Sarah's phone?" I asked.

Joanne gave me a look that said I should have run this by her before bringing it up here. My bad. I wanted to get this solved.

"What would that accomplish?" Sarah asked.

"I'm not sure," Joanne said.

"She might answer," Danny added. "If so, it might be possible to trace her through the phone."

"Like get her real name?" I asked.

"You checked?" Joanne said, not a real question.

"That's all I did. I ran her name. A fair number in the NYC area, but none that fit her. Except for the dead one."

"We can think about it," Joanne said. "If the NYPD doesn't find anything."

"But why use a fake name if she was who she claimed to be," I argued.

"I don't know. Tell you what," she said. "I'll run it by my FBI friend. If we do call, we want to make sure we have the best tech available to track it down."

I couldn't argue with that.

Andy popped his head out the back door, holding several grocery bags for Torbin. "Chips, buns, hot dogs," he said as he gave one bag to Torbin. "Condiments, pickles, cheese, lettuce," as he handed him the other one. "Hamburger that I'll make into patties, drumsticks, grapes and strawberries that need washing in the kitchen." He went back inside.

Once everything was out, chip bags opened, plates, buns, lettuce, and the rest all arranged, I went back to the grill. I could start the hot dogs since the hamburger patties should be out any minute now.

Just as I got them on, Andy arrived with the burgers and a platter of drumsticks.

I womaned the grill. As big as it was, I was able to get everything cooked in two batches, unlike the five or so it would take on mine.

"Can I help?" Sarah asked me as I turned the second batch.

"Yes, relax and eat. That's what this is about."

"Are you sure? I need to help when I can."

She wasn't just the new person in a group of old friends. She knew she depended on me, on us, for all the levels of safety she needed, physical and mental. She wanted to find her way as someone who could help ease our burden rather than be one.

"I'm almost done here, but there will be much cleanup later. I'll happily give you my share."

She smiled at me. "Okay, sounds fair."

"Just leave me one big, juicy burger," I told her.

"That should be easy since we have plenty." She went back with the others and fixed her plate.

I finished grilling duty and joined the others.

Conversation flowed over the usual topics, what to watch on TV, the state of potholes in New Orleans and which of our neighborhoods had the biggest. "Y'all live near the French Quarter," Danny argued. "You are not in the competition." Torbin's upcoming drag performances. We didn't talk about the kind of hate that had brought Sarah into our lives.

I let Sarah, Torbin, and Andy do most of the cleanup. My part was bringing a few platters back to the kitchen, grabbing the holy trinity of grilling—a hamburger, two drumsticks, and a hot dog—to take home with me. And a go-cup for the last of the Cosmo pitcher Torbin had made.

Andy walked us to the door and watched everyone get into their cars as I ambled down the block to my house. He was still at the door, watching, as I put the key in my lock. We usually kept an eye out for each other, but his expression was more serious than usual.

I put the food in the kitchen, checked my house, made sure windows were secure and locked, glanced in the closets, the downstairs bathroom, all the places someone could hide. Better safe than sorry.

I went down to the kitchen and properly put the leftovers away.

My phone chimed a text.

From Sarah. *Thank you. I appreciate you sharing your friends with me. I can't tell you how much it means to not be alone in a hotel room. And you are brave in ways I wish I could be.*

I stared at it, taking a long sip of my drink.

I texted back, *There are many ways to be brave. We will get through this. Sleep well.*

Imperfect and small words.

CHAPTER FOURTEEN

I could hear the promised rain outside my window. The gray and wet did not inspire me to jump out of bed. I pulled back the curtains to look out the window, watching drops slide down the glass.

You had too many Cosmos last night. That's the problem with a pitcher, you can top off your glass and not know how many you've actually had. Torbin and I were the ones drinking. Half a pitcher was a good reason to not want to get out of bed.

Still, I slowly stood up and dragged myself to the shower.

From there downstairs to the kitchen and coffee and wondering if a leftover hot dog or hamburger was a more suitable breakfast.

It took a few sips for the caffeine to hit. I found a bagel in the freezer, letting it thaw and toast at the same time.

I looked at my phone. No more texts from Sarah. She had a few glasses of wine last night, so she might be moving slowly as well.

Then I looked at the tracking app. First for Paulette, just to see what she was up to. Ah, at work. Or at least in the vicinity. They were medical, so they kept those early medical hours, appointments starting at 7:30 a.m. I glanced at where she'd been before that. After she left my office, she stopped at a high-end gourmet grocery uptown, one whose tiny parking lot could lead to gunfights. Then back to the burbs and work. A stop in Old Metairie, probably to visit her parents, then home, where she stayed all night.

I flipped to Elmer's. I could call this work, sitting in the kitchen sipping coffee.

Ah, Elmer was again at the run-down hotel outside the city.

I reviewed where he'd been yesterday. Left the hotel to a donut place late morning. Then he headed upriver, crossing at the Sunshine Bridge, from there to a back road that seemed to be in the middle of nowhere. Satellite imaging showed a few scattered houses. It looked like he stayed there for about an hour. Leaving his packages with another friend?

I pulled up the address cross reference. I could look up the address, see what names were connected to it. The houses were sparse enough for the tracker to pinpoint it. Next door was half a mile away.

First, I poured some more coffee.

I jotted down the names that came up. Nothing looked familiar, but when I went to the office, I could check them on the names of Elmer's friends.

He stopped at a fried chicken chain for lunch. He stayed about half an hour, which did suggest that he wasn't friends enough with whoever he visited to be offered food. This is the South—if we're somewhere around lunchtime, you get fed.

From lunch, he went back into LaPlace and stopped at a grocery store. Eating his feelings? Then stops at a gas station, a pizza place, and back to the hotel.

I wondered how he was paying for it. He'd seemed pretty broke when we'd spoken. This place wasn't high on the hog, but was a lot more than the twenty he'd tried to get from me. If he needed that, how could he afford this?

He hadn't left the hotel since then.

I walked around the kitchen to stretch my legs from sitting and looking at small screens. It was decision time. Stay here and make another pot of coffee? Or go to my office?

I looked at the weather map. A small break in the clouds suggested this would be a good time to go.

The parking gods smiled on me as someone pulled out as I was getting there, leaving me a space almost in front of my door.

I trotted upstairs, let myself in, and locked the door. If Paulette tried to ambush me again, I wouldn't be here.

Another pot of coffee was the first task. I don't drink coffee all day; I stop at five p.m., because then it's cocktail hour.

Waiting for the coffee, I again pulled up the tracking app, this time on my computer screen. Both Paulette and Elmer were where I had last left them.

Now what?

I remembered the pile of paper Lena had given me. I wasn't sure if it was just a prop, a stack left for recycling, or one of the things I'd asked for.

They had done a better job than I had. My dead name theory was dead in the water. A Bettina Collingwood had moved to New York from California about six months ago. No official change of address, but the grannies dug deep enough to find social media posts about her new life in the Big Apple, including a picture of her with her new boyfriend. Possible fit for the description Sarah gave of the man who'd threatened her after her speech. But he also looked like just about every other slightly beefy white man in his late twenties, face clinging on to the soft rolls of youth before settling into the face he would have, those chubby cheeks turning into heavy jowls. Brown hair under a Jets ball cap. Couldn't tell the eye color from the snapshot. I printed it out to show to Sarah later. The grannies had screen-captured some of her posts. There were a wide range, from bragging about drinking too much with friends to her spiritual journey, perhaps to repudiate her upbringing in a mainline Protestant church, one she didn't name but alluded to, calling it "closer to the country club than to God." She'd tried Buddhism out in California, then some sort of hot yoga place, but left them because the rules were too strict. The grannies had done a good job, more than I wanted to read. She sounded possible for the woman Sarah described, more like a person floating around trying to find meaning and, to paraphrase, of all the synagogues in the world, she had to walk into Sarah's.

Time for another cup of coffee. There was no point reading through any of the rest of it, unless Sarah confirmed it was her. And even if it was? She sounded more like a flake seeking peace and love than a crazy bigot.

Then I saw they'd also added more information to Elmer's file.

Hunting license, expired recently. His high school transcript. How do you get a D+ in shop? The rest of his grades made that look like the height of academic achievement. Summer school, repeated classes, finally barely passing enough to graduate. An undiagnosed learning disability? Or did the drug arrests explain it? Two, both after he was eighteen, but a juvenile record was sealed.

I skimmed it. I knew where he was and the two likely places he was hiding his stolen goods, and that was all that really mattered. Elmer was more sad than interesting.

I looked at my watch. A little after eleven. Not close enough to lunch to eat, no matter how much I wanted a distraction from reading files I had no real interest in reading.

Another glance at the tracking app. Ah, movement. Paulette was on Veterans Highway, the long commercial strip in Metairie. Her workplace was located there, in the East Jefferson Hospital area. Maybe it made the services seem less sketchy than they were. She was heading away from her office and into the city.

I smiled. At least I could see where she was and if she was coming this way with time to avoid her.

Elmer was also back at the donut shop.

Paulette hadn't mentioned him contacting her. If he wasn't pressuring her for the money, what was his game? I'd bring it up in today's report. I didn't trust her to be completely honest. She might try a side deal and not let me know. Or she'd done something stupid and didn't want me to know that either.

At least her retainer had cleared. That might be the only consolation I'd get. It would cover about another hour, and then I'd have to bill her. That would be fun.

She was back in Old Metairie. I wondered if her parents were ill. That didn't make me like her more, but it did allow for a soupçon of sympathy. I'd met them a few times. Her father seemed typical, confidence and control at all costs, but more interested in his sons than his daughter. Her mother was always well dressed, always looked like the wife of a successful man. Once when I'd gone into the house to use the bathroom and the others were still out around the pool, she stopped me in the hallway and said, "It gets better. People are barely themselves in high school, often captive to what their friends think. It's better to be outside, as painful as it may feel now."

I'd just smiled and nodded.

A text. Torbin. *You are on call for cat sitting duty, aren't you?*

I sent back a *?* Sarah was there.

Like usual, he texted back. *Cats don't like a change in routine.*

He had a point. When they were out of town, I usually did cat-sitting. Highly unlikely anyone was watching that closely, but if they were gone, I'd be expected to go there a couple of times a day for cat duty.

Got it. Cats hate to have their routine disrupted. I forgot you're going away tomorrow.

Age will do that to you. Ta.

I'd text back something appropriate. When I could think of it.

The day loomed.

I tossed my pen across the room, then got up and retrieved it. I'm not good at this middle part, unsure what to do next, dependent on other people doing what they might or might not do.

I refilled my half empty coffee cup. Took a walk around the office, sat again at my desk.

Pen—still working despite its flight—and paper. Heading of *Sarah*—no known local threats. NYPD cops still a question mark. Waiting on local FBI for info on hate groups in the area. Well-hidden and safe, with logistics to keep her out of public view. My job wasn't to solve the murder but to keep her safe.

Second heading—*Paulette and the Curious Case of the Bad Boyfriend. Client not trustworthy.* I underlined that. Three possible locations for materials. I had to decide whether to tell Paulette where he was or if I wanted to have a look at them first.

That was super helpful. Not.

I looked out at the rainy day. An excuse to stay in my office and not go out in it.

A glance at the trackers. Elmer had left LaPlace and come back into the city. Heading to his apartment? Just a guess, since he was still on I-10. Or more work for Boss? Paid work could explain him having money. Moving to a new hotel and had to kill time?

Paulette was on the move again; she hadn't stayed long at her parents'. I watched for about a minute, and she was heading into the city. There are multiple reasons to cross from Jefferson into Orleans Parish besides coming to see me again. But that was one of the possible reasons and not one I wanted to deal with today.

I looked at the map to see how far it was to the place Elmer had gone yesterday. About forty minutes.

I was mostly wasting time, giving myself an excuse to get in my car and drive instead of sitting at my desk. I could expense the gas to Paulette.

Traffic was kind, an accident on the other side of I-10, but my direction was flowing about as well as possible for a rainy midday.

Over to the West Bank. At the foot of the Sunshine Bridge, there was the usual commercial strip, hotels, gas stations, fast food, but it receded into a two-lane blacktop, with worn yellow lines in the middle and long stretches of cane or other crops the only scenery. The houses were scattered and far apart.

I pulled to the side of the road to get my bearings. I also put my dash cam up. I was unsure I'd be able to risk more than driving by, so at least I'd have footage.

The rain was clearing, the skies still cloudy, but lighter in the west.

As I got closer, I slowed down, making sure there were no cars behind me. The house was back from the road, barely visible through the tall brush surrounding it. It was a weathered white ranch from what I could see. Probably built in the sixties and painted once since. The roofs of several outbuildings were visible over the shrubs. I angled the dash cam to the side to get a better view.

A gap in the overgrown brush was the only way in.

Just as I got close, a dark truck shot out of the driveway.

I jammed on the brakes to avoid hitting him.

He screeched to a halt. Young, dirty blond hair, a scruffy beard, the hair almost the same color as his skin, making his face look lumpen and off-kilter. A snarl on his face. He flipped me the bird, then sped off.

I considered returning the favor, but the gun rack in the back window dissuaded me.

"Only the finest people," I muttered as I started up again. I could still see him in my rearview mirror, so didn't want to be obviously looking over the place. I kept going for about a mile, just to see if there were any other places Elmer could have stopped. But the only options were empty fields.

Off this road were ruts that the map called streets, but were barely one car wide gravel tracks. They looked like I could do a long block around, but I wasn't willing to be that isolated, even if it meant I'd go the long way home.

As I got closer to Bayou Lafourche, there were more houses and businesses.

I stopped at a gas station. I'd been a few feet from a bad accident, and with his big truck and my small car, it would have been worse for me.

I filled up my tank, then went inside. Old bladders don't handle that kind of stress well.

That done, I picked up a candy bar and a bottle of flavored water.

I smiled at the woman at the register.

"You got all you need?" she asked.

"I think so," I said. "Almost got run over by a big truck. He came out of his driveway without stopping. Or even looking. A big, dark truck with gun racks and some of those signs on the back." He had a big

Don't Tread on Me on his front bumper. And a small one with 88 on it, a Nazi reference, on his back.

She rolled her eyes. "Know the one you mean. Comes in here and bargains on beer prices. Said if he's buying three six-packs, he should get one free."

"Like you can do that without it coming out of your pocket."

She smiled. "Yeah, like I'm working this cash register because I own the place. He takes one look, sees a Black lady back here and gets pushy. Dave tells me he's just joking, but Dave is an old white guy and I bet he doesn't try that with him."

"I bet you're right. Men see how other men treat them and think that's the way it is. Any point in reporting them?"

"You should…but I wouldn't. Snakes. With lots of guns. When I told him he had to pay full price, he gave me a creepy smile and said it would be too bad if someone drove by here one night and shot the place up."

"He threatened you?"

"He said it was just a friendly warning. With that nasty smile."

"Friendly as a rattlesnake rattle."

She handed me my change. I put it in the tip cup.

"Any idea who he is?"

"No, but I got his wife's name. He used her credit card."

"So manly of him. What is it?"

"Why do you want to know?" Still this side of friendly, but letting me know she knew I was asking for something she shouldn't give me.

"I have connections to law enforcement. Could pass the info along."

She smiled again. "Just a sec, let me look it up. He was just here a couple of hours ago. Four six-packs and all the beef jerky in the place." She looked at the screen on her computer.

"Got it. Paulette D. Carter."

I hid the expression on my face by jotting it down on my phone. I looked up at her and said, "I don't think that's his wife. Likely it's a stolen card."

"Well, damn," she said with a shake of her head. "Figures. Can you get your cop friends to look into it as quick as they can? I don't want to be the one to refuse him service."

"I'll do what I can. If he comes back, just go ahead like normal. Not your problem to take on."

She thanked me and I left.

In my car, I opened my drink and the candy bar. If I followed the bayou, I could loop around into Donaldsonville and back to the bridge. The other option was the way I came.

That was an interesting plot twist. Was that how Elmer was getting by? Using cards he'd stolen from Paulette? Was he not quite stupid enough to use them himself, but passing—or selling—them to his confederates? Another way for him to get money.

Did Paulette know? Based on what Elmer told me and what I suspected, she would be reluctant to go to the police. Maybe she'd bargained that a few hundred on her cards to be able to track them was worth it.

I wondered if I should put it in my report to her. She would likely pretend she didn't know even if she did. If she didn't know, she'd demand I do something, in which case I'd have to argue with her to cancel the card or report it to the police. Which I doubted she wanted to. Nor had she hired me to handle this mess.

Elmer was willing to break the law. To be sure, he was an accessary for whatever Paulette was pulling, but it's one thing to go along with your boss (and well-to-do girlfriend) and something else to instigate. Maybe he'd gotten so used to living in her corner-cutting world, it blurred the lines for him.

Traffic was not kind on the way back. The rain still lingered over the metro area, and some people drive like they've never seen rain before and have no idea what slick roads do at high speeds. It was close to four by the time I got back into the city.

Office or home?

I decided on a quick run by my office. The demanded daily report to Paulette was drudgery, and I didn't want to do that at home.

I did a quick check of the tracker apps at a stop sign before I got there. I didn't want to find she was parked in front. All clear—the tracker showed her at her home.

Once in the office, I hastily typed, *Elmer may have left the materials with a friend in the Donaldsonville area. Will have to investigate further. Most likely he still has them in his truck, and I will follow up with more when I can safely assess the situation. Do you have a list of what he stole? He doesn't seem to have any means of support, so you might want to consider if he could have tapped into financial accounts or credit cards. Will report again tomorrow at the end of day.*

I put my agency watermark on it, then saved it as a PDF that couldn't be edited easily. *Don't trust this client* was the top of my list for this case. I attached it to an email and hit send.

While there, I also uploaded the footage from my dash cam, clipping about three minutes that showed the house and the almost accident. I saved a still, the best shot I had of his face. I hoped to never see it again. Wasn't sure what to do with it. Giving it to Joanne and letting her make any law enforcement decisions seemed like the best option. I did have pretty good evidence that he was using stolen credit cards. And was a reckless driver.

I checked where both Elmer and Paulette were. She was still home. Elmer had been on the move, seeming to go to Boss's place, stayed there for a few hours, back to the run of junk food places, and had just returned to the same hotel. He hadn't gone by his apartment, so I'd been wrong about that. Smart on his part to avoid it, not smart to stay at the same hotel.

Maybe tomorrow I could go there and see if I could bribe the desk clerk to let me in his room while he was away.

I turned my computer off. Time to go home.

CHAPTER FIFTEEN

Torbin left another text while I was driving home, telling me they were leaving. How did it get to be Friday already? I was to do the pretend cat feeding. Oh, it was only Thursday; they were taking a long weekend.

I parked and went into my house. I'd have to go out again in about an hour, since six was the official cat feeding hour.

While waiting, I called Joanne. The sooner I dumped the stolen credit card thing off, the less I had to worry about it.

"I was just about to call you," she said.

"Be still my beating heart."

"I doubt it. I talked to Teddy—Theodore, my FBI friend. He wants to know if we can meet tomorrow. He has the info on hate groups and wants to see what you know. Ten in the morning? At your office? Not quite official, so better outside our offices."

I pretended to look at my busy calendar and said, "Yes, that's fine. I also have something I want to pass on to you." I caught myself in time to not say "dump." I told her about running into what was likely a stolen credit card.

"Not my jurisdiction," she answered. "Let's talk about it tomorrow. I have no contacts out there, but maybe Teddy does."

And that was that. Paulette could check her credit cards and cancel them if she chose, assuming she wasn't using them to track Elmer. Not very effective, since she could only see where he'd been, not where he was. Plus, nothing to stop him from buying a motorcycle, ditching the too-easy-to-spot red truck, and leaving her with the bill.

I scanned the street as I headed over. Two cars I didn't recognize, one old and beat up, the other a shiny new BMW. I'm lucky to live on a stable block, with mostly homeowners and no short-term rentals, but there were some in the area. Being just a few blocks out of the French Quarter meant people parked here, so strange cars weren't out of place.

I let myself in, just like I would do if this was a normal cat feeding, calling out, "Don't worry, kitty cats, your daddies have abandoned you, but I'll feed you." I do talk to them, but not usually on the doorstep when other people can hear me. Absinthe, a black and white cat who was either angelically asleep or causing chaos, came to greet me. It usually took food noises to get Sazerac, a black cat and Rye, a tabby, to join the fun.

Sarah was in the kitchen and already had their bowls out.

She smiled as she saw me. "I can feed the cats," she said.

"I know," I said, "but better if things stay normal. If I'm not feeding the cats, it means someone's here to do it. If I come over to feed them, it looks like no one is here."

She nodded. "Makes sense."

"Unless you don't want my company," I joked.

She looked at me and smiled. "I like your company. I'm happy to see you. I'm better with people around. But you've done a lot, and I don't want you using time you can spend elsewhere." She turned back to the kitchen island and started spooning the food into the small cat bowls.

She's lonely, I realized. The insecure voice in my head added, *Has to be if she wants your company.*

Rye and Sazerac joined us, a chorus of meows until the food was put on the floor.

"What do you need?" I asked. Realizing it sounded abrupt, like material things were all I could offer. "I mean, other than the end of all this?"

"I...I think I have enough food," she said slowly.

I knew where Torbin kept their wine, so found a decent Malbec and opened it without asking. I poured us each a glass and sat on their comfortable couch. Sarah joined me, sitting at the other end.

"Food, yes," I said. "That's important, and I can bring in anything you especially like. Also, need to replace Torbin's wine. Is there anything else I can do?"

She took a sip of her wine. "I love the cats. And Torbin and Andy. Don't take this wrong, but I feel like I have a place here, not just some strange visitor. I can see inviting them and the rest of your friends to come stay with me in New York. Not something you find in hotels."

"No argument there. I hope you know my reluctance wasn't about you, but…"

"The situation," she supplied. "I could be in danger, and that means anyone around me could be as well."

"Yes, I'm sorry. It wasn't…wasn't that I didn't want you to be around people, but always a balance," I finished lamely.

"You barely know me, and these are your friends, people you've had in your life for a long time. Of course you'd choose them over me."

"I didn't…I mean…"

"You did. As I would have. As anyone would have," she said. "I've lost someone I loved, loved with more than my life. I scream at God asking why her and not me? I think I should tell you to put me back in the hotel but am too weak to get the words out."

"You're welcome here," I said. "My friends chose. I was wrong."

"Doing what you think is best is not wrong," she answered, lifting her wine in a salute to me. "May all the forces on earth and heaven keep us safe, but if anything happens, I will walk into the bullet to keep it from anyone else."

"I will not let it come to that," I said.

She gave me a sad, distant smile. "Promise me, if it does, let me go. I cannot live with your death or the death of any of the people close to you because I brought the danger."

I took a sip of my wine, then another.

"Promise me," she said softly.

Another sip. "I promise to do everything I can to make sure no one is hurt."

"Ah, no promise. Brave? Or foolish?"

"Both. Also obnoxious, hot-tempered, sarcastic, and a few I'm probably not aware of." To change the subject, I pulled out a picture. "Is this the woman who wanted to convert?"

Sarah looked at it. "Yes, this is her. How did you get this?"

"PI. It's what I do. Hard to know about her. She seems to be searching, trying various other spiritual homes." I showed her the picture of the man. "Recognize him?"

She again looked at the photo. "Maybe, but I'm not sure. The man I saw had deep anger on his face; this face is bland. A lot the same, but could be said of many men."

I took the photos back.

Sarah went on, "I do have one request. Your friend Cordelia invited me to meet other LGBTQ and friendly faith leaders. An afternoon meeting at a place uptown. Is it possible to go?"

I wanted to say no. That was the easiest answer.

But was the answer only about safety? Or avoiding an awkward situation?

"Cordelia said she could pick me up," Sarah added.

"Maybe," I said slowly. "Let me take a little time to think about it."

"I could get a taxi back. Not involve you at all. Or maybe a ride with one of the other people there."

That was a no as far as I was concerned. Taxis keep records, and the other people would either have to be told what was going on or take a risk they hadn't agreed to.

"Let me think. Can I get back to you tomorrow sometime?" That way I could also run it by Joanne.

"That's fine, but I'll need to let her know by late morning." A pause and she added, "Or would you prefer I not be around your ex?"

I looked at her.

"I'm not stupid," she said to my expression. "That energy is not hard to spot."

My glass was empty. She still had half of hers. "That's not it," I said hastily. "We've moved on."

Now it was her turn to sip her wine instead of answer.

"It's been a few years. It really is past," I continued.

She watched me, then said, "Are you protesting—"

"Too much?" I sighed. "Maybe, but the past is past."

"What happened?" She asked it kindly, leaving me room to answer or refuse as I refilled my glass.

"I wasn't brave enough. She had cancer, went to Houston for treatment. I stayed here. Weekends there, of course, as much as I could manage. But…I was too terrified to give up everything here to be there."

"You would have had to give up your work?"

"Yes. If I closed down for the months she was there, I would have lost most of my clients. Back to basically starting over. What if she died and I didn't have anything to come back to?"

"That's a hard decision. But you were there every weekend?"

I took another sip of wine. "Most of them. As many as I could."

"So, you worked all week and then had to travel on the weekends? Flying, I'm guessing."

"Flying and driving, both. It's about a six-hour drive. Flying may be shorter if there weren't delays." Another sip of wine. "I should have done more, found a better balance."

"Did you know how long it would be?"

"Are we doing therapy?" I brought the glass to my lips but caught myself before taking another sip of avoidance.

"No, I'm not a therapist. Just a new friend who wants to know more about the people around me. And I suspect you haven't talked to many of them."

She was right, I hadn't. Cordelia was friends with most of my friends, and I didn't want anyone to feel they had to take sides. Maybe I avoided it because I was the one in the wrong, for the most part. "No, I mean, not exactly. First, it was maybe a few weeks, but that was at best. It ended up being a little over three months. And, uh, she met her new partner there. Nancy was her nurse."

"Convenient. She could be there and get paid for it."

"Also, her sister, Cordelia's stepsister came and stayed with her. Her husband makes enough for her to not have to work, so she was able to be there full-time. She never liked me. Well, she didn't like Cordelia being a lesbian but was tolerant about that because she's a doctor."

"She didn't think what you do is respectable?"

"A PI? That's a job for cheap mystery novels, not real life. Especially not for a woman."

"I find you respectable. Professional and competent. So, the two of them were there and you weren't. Do you think they tried to break you two up?"

"Does a rattlesnake bite if you step on it? Yeah, likely…but in the end it was her decision. She left Houston, went to Connecticut, where her sister is, and worked there. Came back here a few years ago when a great job opened up. My friends have had to dance around us ever since."

"Would you get back with her if you could?"

"Is there any point in staring at a closed door?"

"Depends on what's on the other side. You said it's been a while. You haven't found anyone?"

"No." Another sip of wine.

"Have you tried?"

"Yes, sort of. But most people who are my age and still single are that way for a reason. Probably including me. Maybe we only get one."

She looked down in her glass. "Maybe we do. I was more than lucky when I found Leah. Life without her…part of me is gone as well."

"I'm so sorry. I should take lessons from Torbin on avoiding depressing topics. Keep things light and gay."

"Light and gay is good, but life balances. We need both. To laugh and to talk about the hard things. Like a breakup that requires you to navigate through the friends you have in common."

"What clued you in? I thought we did a good job of hiding it."

"I will say you do, and therefore give me high marks for discernment. It was less the two of you but Nancy, how she behaved."

"In what way? I suspect it's pretty clear we're all friends except us two."

"I noticed that but didn't know if you just didn't like each other—there is always someone who has a partner not everyone likes. More than that, she makes a point to always be near Cordelia when you're around."

"I hadn't noticed. Of course, I'm never around when I'm not around."

"I don't know her well, obviously. She was the least friendly to me. It felt like she was weighing if I was important."

"Not useful to her," I muttered.

"Maybe, looking at me as cost versus benefit. One side, I had helped Cordelia and been welcomed by their circle; on the other, I was a outsider who brought danger. I think what tipped her over was that you were responsible for me being here."

"Tipped her against you?"

"I may be guessing, and honestly, it doesn't matter to me. I don't need to be friends with her to remain in touch with the rest of you. I just wonder…how long a relationship like that can last."

"I suppose it would be too cynical to take bets on it."

"It would be for me. Rabbi and all that. But I see nothing blocking you from doing so."

"Finding someone to bet with."

"Leah would have done it. She had a wicked sense of humor. I could see you and her…I think you would have liked her." Sarah looked down at her wine glass.

I reached across the couch and took her hand. "I know I would have liked her. Just knowing you tells me that."

She squeezed my hand We pulled back and picked up our glasses.

She finished hers, refilling it and emptying the bottle. "See, we can do light and gay to scandalous gossip to…the hard parts of life. Thank you. I prefer company to silence. Leah's death is now a fact of my life.

Not talking about it doesn't make it go away. I want to be able to bring her up whenever I would have talked about her before. Remembering the way she laughed and her dark humor."

"As long as you remember, she is here."

"'May her memory be a blessing.' A standard line, but one I think resonates. Memory can be such a blessing." She managed a brief smile. "The small moments are so important. The small days, even the smallest day, the one that doesn't seem important, are the gift of memory. Catching a falling leaf together, the brush of our hands while cooking. So many small moments that will keep her with me as long as I have memory."

"Like now. Imperfect words and the things we say with them."

"I will always remember that moment with the leaf, a brilliant yellow, falling unexpectedly in front of us, both reaching for it, laughing as it drifted away from our hands, finally letting us catch it. I will hold those memories as my last conscious thought, if God gives me that grace."

"If you have any line to up above, let God know I want to go in my late eighties, still in fine fettle, with a glass of really good Scotch, which I've just finished."

"No promises. But when you're in your early eighties, I'll buy you a good bottle of Scotch every year."

"Damn, we're being serious again."

"I'm the one that started this conversation."

"Yeah, you did, but it's good. Not like I can moan about it with our mutual friends."

"Understood. You talk to those who can carry the load. I have my own grief but have to be there for Leah's mother. I'm her rabbi. So, find my strength from others. Thank you as well. You are my oldest friend in this new group of friends. Odd, I know, since we've known each other such a short time. You are the one who knows the most about me, seen me in bad moments. I've done enough funerals to know it's hard to talk about death and loss. The Jewish tradition does it well, sitting shiva—seven days surrounded by friends and family. Then a month of mourning. With services at the year. Markers you can hold on to, in a sea of grief."

"I like the New Orleans traditions. The jazz funeral. A brass band, with a parade out in the street, not hidden away in a funeral home. Somber music going and joyful, a celebration of life, coming back. When I go, that's what I want."

She smiled at me. "May it be a very long time from now."

We finished our wine. I considered opening another bottle before remembering I was only supposed to be there to feed the cats. I took my glass to the sink. "Thank you for…words. Imperfect, precious. Now I should go on with my pretend cat-sitting duties, which would mean going home about now."

She got up as well. "I can wash the glasses. And play with the cats."

"Look at us, agreement. I'll let you know by lunch tomorrow, if not before."

I gave her a hug, then told her she needed to stay well out of sight of the door. It needed to be just me and the cats.

She hid back in the living room and I left.

When I walked home, both the beat-up car and the Beemer were still there. Probably both partying in the French Quarter.

I locked my door, poured a glass of Scotch, ate leftovers, and read the rest of the night.

CHAPTER SIXTEEN

Coffee, a slice of toast with the last pat of butter, enough calories to call it breakfast. The rain had brought cooler air, so I had to adjust my wardrobe. A nice pair of black jeans, a light gray top, long sleeves, and my leather jacket. I wanted to balance looking respectable, but also clearly not a cop like Joanne or FBI like Teddy.

Of course, a quick run by for the putative cat feeding. Sarah was in the shower, so I left a note saying I'd been by.

I wanted to get to my office early, to neaten up and get enough coffee in me before they arrived. The coffee at home was enough for me to safely drive. The rest turns me human.

At least last night's wine and Scotch had been the good stuff. I'd tossed and turned. Maybe from the alcohol, maybe from the worry. Giving up, I had gotten up a little after six, earlier than usual. Hence the early hour at my office.

I still hadn't come to any decision about whether to tell Sarah she could go. It was chilly, so she could wrap up in a scarf like a real New Orleanian when the temp falls below sixty.

Talk it through with Joanne. She was the one who'd okayed letting Sarah stay with Torbin and Andy.

After the office pot of coffee was made and I'd put away a few good gulps, the first thing I did was clean up. Not that it was bad, but when it was just me, I didn't notice dust on the windows behind my desk. Or do a great job of cleaning in the hard-to-reach places. I should do this every week, I told myself, knowing that would slip to every two weeks to every month.

More coffee. Sitting down, I checked the apps for Paulette and Elmer.

Elmer was still at his favorite hotel, presumably sleeping off the fried chicken and pizza. I caught myself. *Well, aren't you judgmental.* Like I didn't eat fried chicken or pizza. Is this how we learn to hate each other? Applying judgments to others that we let ourselves and our friends slide on? "Who in this room had wine, Scotch, and a leftover hamburger and hot dog last night?" I had rationalized them both as needed to absorb the alcohol.

Paulette was at the Old Metairie location. Staying the night with her parents? I wondered if her room was just as it was when she was in high school, an altar to the glory days of cheerleading and the homecoming court (only a maid, never the queen).

They were both where they should be.

I reviewed where they had been. Elmer had briefly left the hotel for a stop at a convenience store, then a burger place before heading back. Paulette had been at work, then her house for about an hour before heading to Old Metairie where she stayed the night. She hadn't responded to my report and she wasn't here to bother me. Although it could be fun if she tried to walk in while I was meeting with an FBI special agent and a homicide detective.

A little more dusting and neatening up before 10 a.m. rolled around.

Teddy arrived first. He was tall, more lean than muscled, in shape, as I heard him lope up the stairs, and he wasn't breathing hard. His brown hair was thinning on the top and styled in a way that made no attempt to hide it. I guessed he was in his early to mid-forties. Suit and tie, of course; a sedate gray, navy tie and white shirt.

"Hi, I'm Theodore Warren. But Ted or Teddy works better. I can't believe I beat Joanne here." He reached out to shake hands.

"Michele Knight, but the same, I go by Micky." His grip was strong and firm, but not trying to prove anything.

"Thanks for agreeing to host us. Always good to have an excuse to get out of the office. Okay if I take advantage of being early to run down and get coffee?"

"I have coffee here, although not as fancy as downstairs."

He smiled. "It's fall and they have pumpkin spice. Have to admit, I'm one of those. My wife hates the smell, so I avoid it at home."

"I can't offer more than black or with milk."

"Be right back. Can I get you anything?"

I assured him I was good and he went back down the stairs. Joanne arrived while he was out.

"I got here before Teddy?"

By the time I explained she hadn't, he was back with a pumpkin spice latte for himself and one for Joanne.

She thanked him and took it. "Once every fall. I can't let Teddy drink alone."

I raised my black coffee. "To each their own."

Teddy retrieved a stack of papers from his briefcase and put them on my desk. "Joanne let me know what's going on. Would have been nice if we'd gotten a heads-up sooner." With a look at Joanne, he said, "From the NY folks. They're treating it as a murder under local jurisdiction, which it might be. But when the target flees to another state, we'd like to know."

"You know now," Joanne said.

"How is Rabbi Jacobson doing?" he asked.

I was impressed he asked. I told them I'd seen her last night and she'd seemed okay, as much as she could be, and mentioned her request for a field trip tomorrow.

Joanne and Teddy looked at each other before Joanne said, "Let's look at what Teddy has, then consider it."

Teddy nodded. "Since Joanne told me what was going on, we've made it a point to monitor known channels to see if there's any chatter about her. So far, nothing. These people are slippery snakes. There are lone nuts, but most like company, and some are organized in multiple locations. These are the ones we know of in this area." He handed me a list.

I looked at it. Three names were the same as those who'd sent threats to Sarah. I pointed them out to Teddy. "What do you know about these?"

"Not much. Snippets of chatter on monitored internet sites. Threats that were hard to trace back to one person. They go old tech, print out a flyer and stick it up in the middle of the night. Vandalism of two gay bars, windows broken, paint thrown on the buildings. Their few open activities were all law abiding, protesting drag queen story hours, supporting book bans, and other forms of protected speech. They often obscure their features, sunglasses indoors, hats, bandanas on their face. A few have stepped over the line; one caught on security camera vandalizing a Black church that openly supports the LGBTQ community. Another pushed a librarian down the steps at a book banning protest, so he's wanted in the Philly area. We'd love to get them in custody. Sometimes jail time makes a man question his choices."

He handed me a grainy still from the church cameras. Young,

white, with a tattoo on his neck. I didn't recognize him but gazed long enough so I would if I saw him. Then a still from a cell phone of the book-banning altercation.

I looked at it. "I've seen him."

"Really? Where?" Teddy perked up.

"How?" Joanne asked. "Near Sarah?"

"No, a different case." I explained what I was doing for Paulette, eliding over her not going to the police by saying she didn't want to press charges against her ex-boyfriend. I had suspicions, but no evidence she was committing fraud. She was a paying client, as she so often reminded me, and short of hard proof, my reluctant loyalty was to her. I admitted putting a tracker on Elmer's truck.

"You're not a cop, and you don't have to play by our rules," was Joanne's comment.

I pulled up the still I'd taken on my dash cam, turning the computer screen so they could see it. I gave them the license number I'd jotted down from memory.

"Well, hot damn, sure looks like him," Teddy said.

"And it's likely he's using a stolen credit card," I added. I told them about my conversation with the gas station attendant.

Teddy was scribbling notes. He was so busy he almost forgot to drink his coffee.

And the cherry on top of this rancid sundae, "Do you know they have property over by the Mississippi border?" I asked.

"Holy shit," Teddy said. "You have been busy. We knew they likely had someplace where they trained but haven't been able to locate it."

"I have a map." I made a copy and handed it to him, telling them the story of Elmer being drunk and leaving a pile of stuff outside his apartment.

"Not the brightest wattage," Teddy said.

"Certainly not Elmer Stumbolt," I agreed. "He mentioned someone he called Boss who seems to be the ringleader. Likely also making money off his recruits. I suspect he lives in Old Metairie." I pulled up the records for the tracking app for Elmer and showed them the location.

"That could be any of about five houses," Joanne commented. "Both sides of the street."

"It does narrow it down," Teddy said. "We can find out who lives there and see if anyone is a likely candidate."

I started to say I could visit Paulette's parents and ask them if they knew who lived there, it looked to be only a few houses away, then stopped myself. Not my case, not my role to find out anything more. Although maybe I should try to see her mother, let her know I remembered her kindness and how much it meant to a messed-up high school kid.

"This has been super helpful," Teddy said, standing up and gathering his things. "I need to organize a raid of that property as soon as possible. Be nice to catch one of them before they move on."

Joanne stood as well. I stayed seated.

"What about Sarah? Her going out?"

Teddy remained standing, but Joanne sat back down. He said, "It's private, right? How will she get there?"

I told him the person who invited her offered to pick her up. That I would get her after.

"So, private event, going and coming in cars," he confirmed.

"Yes," I replied. "I also know the isolation is hard on her."

Joanne looked first at Teddy, then me. "She's been mostly confined since she got here. Scarf, hat, sunglasses, only out briefly to get in a car and get out. I'm inclined to say yes."

"We have no information that says they know she's here," Teddy added. "I'll ask the tech whizzes to check in real time, just in case something comes up."

It was settled.

"Keep me updated," Joanne told him. "Especially if you find anything in the raid that we need to know."

"Will do. Thank you, Ms. Knight. If I ever need a PI, you're first on the list." He trotted down the stairs, coffee in one hand and briefcase in the other.

I looked at the pile of papers he'd left on my desk. I'd go through it, but it was either old enough or vague enough to give to civilians.

"I'd pick her up, but we've got to replace Alex's phone and the account is in my name."

"Another perk of being single. But thanks." I pulled out my phone and swiped through the pictures until I found the one I wanted. "What do you know about this?"

"Spying?" she said, but still looking down at the picture, so it was hard to read her expression.

"No. Was up on the new roof deck at Q Carré and saw them. PI habit to take pictures of things that are interesting."

Joanne handed my phone back. "Yeah, this is interesting. Do you know who the other woman is?"

"Yes, Frances Gautier, who, according to Torbin, just won a very lucrative lawsuit." I gave her a quick description of the one date we'd gone on. "Do you know her?"

Joanne shifted, then drank her coffee before answering. "Yes, both Danny and I know her. She's a good lawyer, but…some of her clients have been people I'd love to arrest."

"Like who?"

"A priest accused of child sexual abuse. Church stonewalled and sued for defamation, and she was one of their lawyers. Defended a chemical plant trying to evade responsibility for a leak that killed one person and injured several others. When she thought she could make more by defending the little guy, she turned around and did that, which is how she ended up on the right side of this settlement."

"She gets about a third of it, right? That's a lot of money."

"Something like that. She recently bought a big house just off Prytania in the Garden District. To give her credit, she donates to a lot of good causes, especially queer ones. Involved as well, on the board of more things than I can keep track of. A point person for a lot of the LGBTQ support things going on, like the thing Sarah is going to, plus the big march coming up."

"Are they having an affair?"

Joanne shrugged. "No clue. Could be that Frances likes company, Nancy likes nice restaurants and ordering two-hundred-dollar champagne."

"I wouldn't mind trying champagne that good."

"You could go on another date with her," Joanne suggested.

"It would be the only reason, and that's not good enough." I decided to step on the dynamite. "Do you think Cordelia knows?"

"I'm not sure what there is to know. Nancy has friends and hangs out with them. Why do you suspect more than that?"

"Well, I don't need to tell you I might be biased, but the energy between them was more flirty than friendly."

"You are biased; doesn't mean you're wrong. But with only that to go on…there isn't anywhere to go."

"Tell Cordelia?"

Joanne shook her head. "No. You and I are suspicious by nature. No evidence of anything other than friends meeting. And…better to let happen what will happen."

"I debated just deleting them. You're the only person I've shown them to. Or will."

"Keep it that way. This isn't enough to tell anyone anything." Joanne stood up. "I need to get back to work."

She finished her coffee, threw it in my trash, and left.

I started to pour more coffee but decided I'd had enough. Because of the social dance, I've rarely been around Nancy and Cordelia, not enough to observe their interactions. I didn't like Nancy and would root for them to break up for that reason alone. Cordelia and I still jointly owned the house I lived in. I'd paid the mortgage since we split, but she had put up most of the down payment. Nancy had pushed for me to either move out and let them move in, or sell it and split the proceeds. It would be nice to get that complication out of my life.

Did I want anything more than that? I shook my head to chase the thoughts away. Too many what-ifs. Did I want to get back with her? I didn't know. We weren't the people we'd been when we were together. Would she want to try again with me? No way to know. If she'd broken up with me once, well, she had reasons to.

I got up, paced around the office, took a bathroom break, and sat back at my desk. I texted Sarah, *You're on. Wear the scarf, hat, sunglasses whenever you're out. I'll pick you up, let me know the address*. She texted back her thanks and would let me know when she got the details.

I decided to focus on the cases in front of me.

I checked the trackers. Elmer was still at the hotel. Since it was after check-out time, presumably he would stay there another night. Paulette was where she was supposed to be, at work.

I picked up the pile Teddy had given me and started plowing through it. Interesting, like looking at a deadly snake. I wondered what they would do without the hate? That seemed to be their motivation. Fear, too, but these were mostly men, and the only emotion they were allowed was anger. They hated queers, immigrants (especially brown-skinned ones), Jews, the libtards, women, religions that didn't affirm their version of God, and even each other if they weren't pure or dedicated enough.

Most of the information was from social media, but also some monitored private channels. One long thread to plan the protest at drag queen story hour. No actual names, of course. Two were doing most of the organizing, with others chiming in, expressing dislike of drag queens in terms they could only use anonymously online. Others did the online equivalent of grunting agreement. Also, their ignorance, claiming all drag queens were trans and lots of repetition of the ugly grooming lies. Their definition of grooming was us existing openly and living our lives. Another long chat about work and how much they hated working for "the man," complaining about having women and/or gay bosses. More crude language.

I forced myself through it, reading some and skimming the rants.

I realized my stomach was grumbling when I finished.

I again checked the trackers. Paulette still at work. Elmer at the hotel—no, wait, he was leaving, heading east.

It would take me about half an hour to get there. He might just be going out to get lunch. But if he was gone for longer, it would be my best chance to get into his room. My half-baked plan was to flash my license at the clerk, with a few twenties thrown in, to see if I could look in his room. And watch the tracker app to make sure he wasn't about to return.

Two granola bars eaten in the car would have to suffice for lunch.

It took me about forty minutes to get there. I drove past, turned into the lot of an abandoned gas station, and checked the tracker. Elmer was on I-10 heading into Slidell, a town across the lake to the east of New Orleans. Heading to the camp? Well away from here, and it would be forty minutes to an hour before he could get back.

I pulled out and went back to the hotel.

It did need a paint job, but there'd been an attempt to spruce it up. Flowers planted in front of the office. A new sign, promising free Wi-Fi and coffee in the morning. The walkways swept. There were only a few other cars in the lot. I parked in front of the registration, a squat building not attached to the motel, a long U shape of about twenty rooms. It was painted mint green, not new, but more recent than the rest of the hotel.

An older woman was behind the desk, with years and pounds weighing on her. I'd put her as late sixties or early seventies, in the kind of flowered dress that was never either in or out of style. She smiled at me, hopeful for a paying customer.

"I'm wondering if you could help me," I said.

The smile wavered. Not asking for a room meant not a paying customer.

I took out my license. She was smart enough to take a look at it.

"So, what's a lady private eye want out here?" she asked.

"Is this man staying here?" I pulled out a photo of Elmer, the one I'd copied off his driver's license. "He goes by the name of Elmer Stumbolt, but might not be using it."

She looked at the picture, glanced at her register, a very old-style ledger book. "Someone going by the name Elmer Smith was here. Looks like him."

I pulled out three twenties. "I've been hired because he, let's say, borrowed something from where he used to work and they would like it back. All I want to do is look in his room and see if I can find it. He can't call the police on you, since it's stolen."

She shook her head, then laughed. "He's gone. We had a couple come in late last night. Fightin' and screamin' just an hour ago. Called the cops. Don't need that kind of trouble. Mr. Elmer whatever his name is pulls in right around then, sees the flashin' cop lights, spins out, and takes off like he's seen a ghost. Doubt he's coming back."

Damn. If he was hiding out at the camp, no way I was going to be able to get Paulette's stuff there. "Well, thank you for your help."

"Not done yet. He paid in cash for the first night, then said he was waiting on getting paid and would get me the rest soon. Not full, so thought I might as well let him stay; he might pay. Don't think that's goin' happen now."

"You think he skipped out?"

"The way he ran from the cops? He's not coming back. So, if you want, pay what he owes and you can do whatever you want with what's left."

There might be nothing but dirty underwear in there, but this wasn't the Ritz, and I could pass the cost on to Paulette.

Total was $189, including tax. I put it on my agency card, to have a record, and added the sixty as a top. She did take it this time. She gave me the key. I thanked her and left.

I pulled my car in front of his room, got out, and let myself in. I grabbed a couple of pairs of latex gloves from my PI bag to protect my hands in case of dirty underwear. I tried to not gag at the thought.

It was a typical motel room, reddish-brown carpet in style about twenty years ago, worn near the door, but clean save for recent crumbs. Neatness was not his superpower. There were two double beds, a chair that didn't scream comfortable next to a desk. Across from the bed a dresser with a TV on it, sink in the back open to the room, with the toilet and shower behind a door. I checked there first, to make sure no one was hiding. Wet towel on the floor, a glob of toothpaste on the side of the sink, and whiskers splattered around the bottom. What I guessed was the usual array of male products. A manly black and silver deodorant and matching aftershave. Toothbrush, razor. I did a visual scan only, was not touching anything.

There was a shallow closet on the other side of the sink, a sheer curtain for a door. I glanced in, but only a small person could hide there.

Then down on the floor to check under the beds, but they were solid, nothing could be lost under them.

Satisfied I was alone, I looked around. One of the beds was unmade and the other was piled with clothes. Two ratty duffel bags were on the floor between the bed and the chair.

I put the gloves on and moved the clothes around to make sure nothing was hidden under them. There was a big hunting knife at the bottom. Cheap and dull, using size to make it look menacing. I grabbed the bags and put the clothes inside, checking each to make sure there were no notes or anything else useful or dangerous. Packing them would help with cleaning, but I did it to make sure I checked everything. I had to hold my nose a few times; laundry wasn't his priority. I wondered if that was all he had or if he'd only brought what he needed. He was not a well-dressed man. A newer camo T-shirt was the best of the bunch. I left the knife out in the open for people to see before they touched it. Maybe the woman in the office would like to keep it on display behind her.

There were two boxes shoved into the space between the dresser and the outside closet wall.

I did a quick look at the tracker app. Elmer was still heading away, off the interstate now and heading to the backwoods of the camp.

I quickly took photos of everything in the room, where the boxes were. Not sure if they had any purpose, but I wanted to show where I'd found the stolen material. I could include it in what I hoped would be my final report to Paulette.

The boxes were sturdy ones, used for transporting files. They were taped shut, but it wasn't a secure job and I easily got them open. Piles of paper, also several computer external drives. One of the documents had Paulette's business logo on it. Bingo.

To be thorough, I also checked the closet. One cheap windbreaker, one button-down shirt in a color that almost matched the carpet with a paisley design on it that screamed the wearer either was going over-the-top ironic or had no taste.

There were two more cartons hidden there, regular cardboard boxes, also taped shut.

I hefted those over to the door, then retrieved the other two. I opened the door and did a quick look around, but saw no one. Leaving the door open, I unlocked my trunk and put the boxes in.

I went back in the room, doing one last walk-through, opening all the drawers, checking the narrow shelf in the closet, but they were all empty. It looked like Elmer's idea of unpacking was to dump everything on the bed.

I got back in my car to drive across the lot to the office to get away from the room I'd just taken stuff from. Legally, more or less. He hadn't paid, so it was all abandoned.

I popped back in the office, gave the woman the key, told her I'd found what I wanted, but he'd left some clothes and other things.

She nodded, expecting it. "Well, not a bad day for either of us, then. You got your stuff, saving us from moving it, and I got the room paid for and a nice tip. You take care, now."

I thanked her and left.

Time to get back to civilization. I felt like I had to keep looking over my shoulder. If Elmer was smart—which he wasn't, but still— he'd get one of his friends to do what I'd done. I couldn't depend on him being too stupid to think of it. The sooner I was long gone, the better.

My stomach argued about the two granola bars, but I told it to shut up and I'd feed it later. I didn't want to stop until I was over the Orleans Parish line.

When I finally crossed that border, I had to decide what to do with the boxes. Take them to my office? More appropriate, but also two flights of stairs. Or to my home, which was only the five steps up from the street.

I glanced at my watch; a little after three. I decided on my office because it was the place I worked, not the place I lived. I could leave the boxes there, lock up, and go home. Besides, hauling them up the stairs would make up for the workouts I hadn't had.

It was late enough that the coffee shop wasn't busy, leaving easy parking. I was able to pull in right by my door. I first moved the boxes to the foot of the stairs. They were heavy enough I had to do one at a time, then up to the second-floor landing, then the landing outside my office, and then into the office, shoving the last two with my foot as I was too tired to lift them up. I got my workout.

I retrieved a bottle of water from the fridge and collapsed at my desk long enough to catch my breath.

I finished the water before considering what to do next. Look through all the boxes, of course. I bargained I'd done enough for one day. No way I could do more than start today, so I'd have to come back here tomorrow anyway. Better to be fresh for the task of plowing through what would likely be boring financial documents.

Almost out of habit, I checked the trackers again. Elmer was at the camp, as far as I could tell. Not a great signal out there, but he'd gone that way and nothing showed him coming back.

Paulette was in Old Metairie. I'd have to give her decent person points for being so attentive to her parents.

Cue my suspicious nature. I pulled up the map of her neighborhood. Went to street view to look at her parents' house. Everything looked well maintained. It had a different color of paint, so it didn't look like the house I remembered. The elegant brick had been whitewashed, windows and shutters now had black trim, very up to date. Were they selling? Or had they passed away and Paulette was getting it ready to sell? Again, suspicious, she hadn't mentioned anything to me. Not as friends, which we weren't, but as an excuse for why I needed to work harder for her. She was good at playing the pity card.

I searched for her mother to see if she was still alive.

She was. Living in Atlanta. Had divorced Paulette's father about twenty years ago and remarried.

I looked up her father.

He had died eight years ago. Survived by his new wife. I looked her up. Remarried and living in Houston.

I looked at the tracker again. It's close but can be off by several hundred feet. She could be at what had been her parents' house. Had she inherited it? But what about her two brothers? Her parents clearly weren't there, so why was she?

What was his name? The football star, a running back all the girls (not me) had crushes on. He lived just around the corner from Paulette; they had been friends as kids and dated for a while. I hadn't kept up so didn't know what had happened. I knew she had been mooning over wedding dresses in high school with him as the groom.

Barry Jenkins. How in the hell did that name slip back into my brain?

I looked him up. His father made money as a car dealer and he'd followed in his footsteps, opening a dealership before inheriting his father's. He lived in the house he had grown up in. The one Paulette was parked suspiciously close to. He'd gotten divorced about six months ago. Paulette an easy and willing rebound? She had alluded to a new man in her life. He seemed likely, given her movements. I felt a spurt of anger. She had probably mentioned me in their pillow talk. "You know the weirdo, the loner? I hired her as a PI. Guess she couldn't get a real job." They'd laugh, just like they did in high school.

Back to street view. His house was a large corner lot, with the front door on the cross street, but his back yard abutted their side yard, with his driveway and garage back there. Paulette's car would be close enough to look like she was at her parents' old house.

Near where Elmer had gone to see Boss. I pulled up his tracking data again, zooming in on them both as much as I could. Close, but not the same. As best I could tell he was several hundred feet away from where Paulette was, so not parked in the driveway. Did they even let people park on the street, or was there a rule against it?

I didn't like it but didn't know what to make of it. Are there so many white supremacists that one can be found in any neighborhood? Old Metairie was a very nice, well-to-do area. We were in the same school district, but I lived in a far less grand area, solid middle-class ranch houses. It was the safe suburbs.

I sat back and stared at the screen. It was late enough that I could justify going home. Instead, I did a quick and dirty search on Barry Jenkins. LSU undergrad. Law degree at Loyola but never practiced, moving into the guaranteed job with his dad. The lottery of life—who your parents are—had been good to him. Married right after law school. Two kids, both girls, one in grad school at UT-Austin, the other a senior at LSU. The divorce wasn't friendly, her accusing him of hiding assets and him claiming the car business had taken a hit during the pandemic and he was in the hole. He kept the Old Metairie house and she got a big mansion on the North Shore of the lake and ownership of one of the car dealerships, which she promptly sold to his biggest rival. One big happy family.

He was active in the usual places, deacon of his church, the board of a cancer charity, coached a Little League team. Nothing to suggest he was even mainstream political—although that can certainly veer into crazy in this state—and nothing to hint he might be far enough beyond that to hang out with the likes of Elmer.

But whoever Boss was, they were neighbors.

"Not your case," I said firmly and shut my computer. I opened it again and typed a quick report to Paulette. *Have a promising lead and think I might be able to get your material back in a few days.* Hit send and the computer was shut again.

I needed to go home and pretend to feed the cats. And have a good dinner. And finish the laundry so if I keeled over suddenly, no one would have to paw through unwashed clothes.

I got up, locked up my office, and slowly walked down the stairs, my muscles not forgiving me for carting those heavy boxes around.

The coffee shop was doing early evening business, people stopping for takeout. I considered grabbing a sandwich to go, but then I'd be helping them pay rent to me, and either my ethics or my stubbornness won that battle and I headed home.

Tomorrow would be a long day. If I was going to look through those boxes, I needed to do it as quickly as possible. Monday morning, Paulette would knocking on my door, and I needed to know before then. Plus taking a break to go fetch Sarah.

At home I had to ignore my stomach again, since I needed to do the cat feeding. I paused long enough to put my bag down, then headed back out the door.

I let myself in and then heard voices in the living room. No one except Sarah should have been there. I recognized her voice. Then Torbin's.

"What are you doing here?" I asked as I joined them.

"Got to our nice beach resort, there two hours, and the water went out. Broken pipe, something to do with next door renovating," Andy said.

"No water, no coffee," Torbin added. "We managed a night in a hotel, which we had to pay for, and when they said it would take a few days to fix, we gave up and came back."

"Could have let me know so I didn't have to drag my weary bones over here."

"Just got here. You were on the list," Torbin replied.

"I'm making cocktails," Andy said. "Will that help?"

"It will if food enters the picture in a timely fashion."

Torbin, Sarah, and I decided on what to order while Andy made cocktails. Sazeracs, in honor of the cooler weather. We went with Thai food from a place close by and were lazy enough to have it delivered instead of picking it up.

After catching up on Torbin and Andy's adventure of the broken pipe, the argument about getting a refund, the gamut of tourists where they stopped for lunch—"They were having a contest to see who could walk the slowest, swear to gawd"—I was able to ask Sarah about the event tomorrow, time, place, purpose.

She started to answer but we were interrupted by the arrival of the food. Once we got that sorted and were eating, she said, "We're gathering for an informal lunch around twelve thirty. Cordelia said she'll pick me up a little after noon."

"You got roped into that?" Torbin said. "Bless your heart, as we say."

"What is it?" I asked.

Torbin ducked the question by taking a bite, leaving it for Andy to say, "I don't need to tell you there's been a lot of anti-LGBTQ stuff happening, bills in the legislature, protests about queer books, threats at drag queen story hours. So, community members have been organizing, trying to build coalitions to fight it."

"They're having a meeting of religious leaders tomorrow," Sarah added. "Creating a network of congregations who can present a united voice. I'm involved with a similar program in New York. I mentioned it, and Cordelia asked if I would help them create something similar here."

"Religious rapid response," Torbin added. "Showing God is really on our side."

"I don't go down that road," Sarah answered. "Too many sins have been committed because some people believe God is on their side. I don't pretend to know. I only know the words I read from the centuries of wisdom. *Tikkun olam*. Repairing the world. One of the core tenets of my faith."

Politics is about consensus and working together, not my strong points, so I haven't been as involved as I should be. Happy to cheer from the sideline and donate when I can, but I haven't done much with any of the local groups.

"Cordelia has been pulling together people from the medical world," Andy said, "Doctors and researchers who can speak against the garbage they're putting out. Some helping out in other areas as well. Getting organized for the big march coming up."

I lifted my almost empty glass and said, "Let the good work go forth. I appreciate everyone but don't think I have the temperament for it."

"'Why the fuck aren't we getting the pitchforks now?' isn't the best attitude for coalitions," Torbin said, attempting to mimic me—badly, I might add.

I ignored him, because he was right. "Where is it and how long will it be?" I asked.

"I'm not sure," Sarah said. "I have it written down somewhere."

"I can tell you," Torbin said. "They asked me to do a ten-minute drag introduction."

"Which led to us being away for the weekend," Andy said.

Torbin waved his glass at Andy, a signal that our glasses needed a refill. Andy pointed to his plate, indicating he would do it when he was finished eating.

"Look, I do a lot of events for community groups, fundraisers, free stuff. But it takes a long time to put on all that drag."

"He does a lot," Andy seconded. "But a brief introduction, for free, isn't worth it. I was the one who suggested we go on that beach weekend we've been talking about."

"I get it," I said. "So where is it?"

"Big house just off Prytania. You know her. That lawyer who recently won a big settlement? She's hosting," Torbin said.

Andy grabbed our glasses and took them to the bar, picked up his phone, and read off the address.

I slowly chewed the last of my roti. Sometimes my suspicions were right and sometimes they were wrong. If Cordelia was involved, Nancy could be as well, and that could explain her meeting with Frances.

At least I had shown those photos only to Joanne and not shared them more widely. I had intended to show them to Torbin but was glad I hadn't.

We finished dinner, had another drink, gave the cats all the attention they wanted, and called it a night.

CHAPTER SEVENTEEN

I had rolled into bed after I'd gotten home from Torbin's—three Sazeracs will do that. But somewhat early to bed meant somewhat early to rise, which was just as well. Today was a long working day for me.

Shower and coffee and I was out the door. Well, clothes, too. I did remember that I had to pick up Sarah and would likely see other people, so I couldn't go with the paint spattered jeans and baggy sweatshirt I first picked out. Instead, decent jeans, no holes or paint, a gray cotton sweater, and my most upscale leather jacket.

I broke my rule and got a big, gooey cinnamon roll from the coffee shop. And a pumpkin spice latte. If you're going to break the rules, you might as well break all of them. We don't get much fall here, no glorious changing of the leaves, only a slight shift in temperature, from very hot and muggy to not so hot and muggy. Other harbingers of fall had to suffice, like pumpkin spice coffee.

Then I was up in my office with four big, ugly boxes of paper staring at me. I gave myself the reprieve of eating the pastry before starting.

Once my hands were washed, I hoisted up the first box, the one I'd opened.

Two hours later, I stood up, my neck stiff from being hunched over all that paper. I'm not a forensic accountant, but I know enough to recognize two sets of books. Clients got a discount if they paid in cash. That cash only showed up in one set of books. A spot check of other transactions showed lower amounts in the official books and higher in the second set. Skimming the top off legit transactions. A hasty estimate of about six months showed that she was hiding tens of thousands of dollars in income.

I finished that box a little after eleven and started on the next one. I was just glancing through the papers. I hooked up one of the computer drives to an old laptop. It showed more of the same, also indicating she was in cahoots with one of the doctors and they were hiding it from the others.

By now I was no longer looking for evidence of crimes but something indicating she wasn't as much of a crook as she appeared.

The second box was older and indicated she had started slowly, a few cash transactions not reported. A quick spot check showed she got more brazen as time went on. She got away with it, so she assumed that she would continue to get away with it. Bad luck that Elmer entered her life. Bad decision, really. First to sleep with a much younger subordinate, second to let him in on the scam during the lust bubble. She was old enough to know the odds were stacked against him being the happily ever after prince. She might have gotten away with it for a few more years. Eventually one of the other partners would get suspicious; insurers would notice something off.

I finished the box, just to make sure I'd at least glanced at most everything. Unless I was way off about the amounts, this was major felony territory.

Now my moral dilemma was whether to pretend I'd never looked and let fate eventually catch up with her. It would be easier. I give her the boxes back; she pays me and I stay as far away as I can. She was cheating people, mostly her other partners—who were doing well enough—and insurance companies. A nice rationalization. And, alas, not one I could sell myself. Also cheating patients, using their trust to gouge them. I'd tell Joanne, who would tell the appropriate law enforcement agency.

I taped up the two boxes and put them back on the floor.

It was noon. Cordelia had probably just picked up Sarah.

Having already broken all the rules, I went downstairs and got a sandwich, tuna melt on fancy whole grain bread. And a cookie, a big chocolate chip one that people raved about. I deserved a cookie for going through those boxes.

I took my sandwich and went back upstairs. Their agenda was lunch from about 12:30 to 1:30, then on to the actual meeting, which was expected to last to about 3:30.

I opened the third box. It had nothing to do with Paulette. It was a collection of memorabilia meaning something to Elmer. A pile of birthday cards from when he was a kid. A high school yearbook, him famous for most wild and crazy, eating a lizard for a bet, jumping into a swamp bog with no idea what was in it. Anything to get attention. A trophy from sixth grade for being most helpful cleaning up after gym. A sad, small pile of memories. I closed the box and taped it shut. If I couldn't get it back to him in any other way, I would mail it to his mother. Maybe with a coupon for free pizza. Spending ritual money because I didn't live his life.

The last box. Did I even want to open it? So far nothing good had come from them. Like Pandora's, maybe I should have left them shut.

With a sigh, I hefted it on my desk and opened it. I jerked away. Right on top was a Nazi swastika. Instinctively, I put on gloves. Then thought maybe I should call Joanne or Teddy and hand this over to them.

Curiosity—and fear—kept me going. They hated people like me. As distasteful as it was, I needed to know how dangerous they were. Smoke and noise about banning books? Bad enough. Planning violence? The gay bars? Community groups? If I called Teddy now, it would be hours, if not days, before anyone looked through this.

In a few days there would be a large march from City Hall to Armstrong Park to protest all the hate being spewed out. Could they be planning to attack that?

"I get to drink all the Scotch I want tonight," I said as I dug into the box.

Like the mementos in the previous box, Elmer collected the items that told him he was important. They gave fancy certificates, office box store variety, for achievements. He got one when he joined, a little over three years ago. For going through "military" training; the dates indicated it lasted a weekend. His promotion to corporal. Pictures of these ceremonies. A mug with their group name on it: Swamp Boy Squad. A nice—for this bunch—camouflage jacket.

There were printouts of email, when he'd been praised or recognized, or just mentioned. Most were proof of the banality of evil—about how many hot dogs and hamburgers they would need for their retreat, about making sure there was enough toilet paper "for the sissies who won't use poison ivy," making the trains run on time. Some were chilling, lists of all the people who needed to be eliminated, like we were a laundry list. A contest to see who could use the most disgusting words to describe us. Also, an inadvertent contest to see who could misspell the most words. None of their recruits knew how to proofread.

At the bottom was a metal box, a fireproof one you store important papers in. I pulled it out and opened it.

A list of names. Several hundred. A list of affiliate groups. I glanced at it; several in the New York area were on it. A thick notebook titled *Operational Manual*. I flicked it open. It was the rules and regulations they lived by, a hodgepodge lifted from the military and fringe stuff, like no one could be vaccinated. For anything. Too late, since one of the reasons they were alive today was because they got vaccinated for all the things that used to kill children. One ominous rule was that actions were not to be written down but communicated orally (misspelled as "orely") or on secure communications.

I put it aside. Next was a list of online channels. Attached to that was a handwritten list of usernames and passwords.

At the bottom was a battle plan, a list of targets when it was time. Libraries and universities at the top. A list of locations: the Main Library downtown on Loyola, Tulane University, government offices, especially those in the deep blue island of Orleans Parish. As I looked it over, it looked like they were listing easily accessible addresses. There was no detailed plan of attack for destroying Tulane, for example, save for vowing to shoot all the professors. No operational logistics, like when/where faculty meetings took place. Maybe their god being on their side was all they needed.

I scrabbled on my desk for the info that Teddy had given me, then checked the web channels with what Elmer had on his list. Two were on Teddy's list; three were not.

I sent a group text to him and Joanne, giving them a brief rundown of what I'd found.

Teddy texted back almost immediately. *Out in the country, at the place you mentioned. A little tied up, but will get with you asap. Your friend wasn't there, but some of his friends were.*

They were in the middle of the raid on the bad driver's place.

I looked at the list of usernames, considering if I wanted to use one to see what was going on. I hesitated, because if I picked one who everybody knew or who was already online, it would be a big red flag they had been compromised.

I checked the trackers. Paulette was at Lakeside Shopping mall, a big, trendy one out in Metairie. Elmer was parked by what I thought was Boss's house.

I looked at my watch. A little before 2 p.m.

Then I looked again at the usernames. BigGuns, HHLove,

TruePatriot—all versions of bragging. Ah, LadyBlaze. A woman member? Then two more: PinkPatriot and BigMomma. Maybe three women. Could I try one of those?

It's the weekend, I remembered. *Maybe they're doing what everyone else is over the weekend and taking a break.* Except most of them probably worked, and this was what they did in their spare time.

I was supposed to pick up Sarah around 3:30. Plenty of time for me to swing by where Elmer was. It would be easy to recognize his truck and see if I could pinpoint where Boss lived. Paulette being so close nagged at me, but I couldn't see how they were connected. Unless she was part of the group. She didn't seem the type, not a true believer in anything other than herself. Still, she loved pink.

I made a copy of the usernames and channels and packed everything back in the box, still wearing gloves. There might be fingerprints; best to not add my own. I sealed the box securely and hid it in my storage room.

I looked again at the usernames and passwords. On an impulsive move, the kind that sometimes gets things done and sometimes gets me in trouble, I signed in to the top channel using PinkPatriot's password.

I held my breath until the screen appeared. A few old posts, nothing in the last month. The old posts were about getting beer for the next meeting and sharing a few "own the libs" memes. They seemed to like to complain about work, with a long one about their workplaces, HHLove for killing all the bosses, BigMomma about her liberal gay boss who looked down on her, TruePatriot about his boss being Catholic and not really Christian. I stopped reading after that.

I quickly logged out.

Was Sarah safe? This group could be part of the one that targeted her in New York. Paulette had put a tracker on my car, and she was seeing someone who lived close to the ringleader of the group. Most of my recollections of Paulette and Barry were from high school, dim memories of who they were. Could Paulette know I was in contact with Sarah? I hadn't mentioned it to her, obviously. The tracker could have told her some of the places I was, but most weren't related to Sarah. Who could know? The NYPD cops that had come down here. Sarah's assistant David. Lev McDonald. My friends. But as far as I knew, none of them had met Paulette.

Just because I couldn't see the link didn't mean it wasn't there.

Joanne texted us back. *What T. says. I'll be in touch later.*

Okay, I texted back.

I couldn't just sit here. I grabbed my PI bag, added the list of usernames and passwords, made sure my gun was snugly tucked in a secure compartment, and headed downstairs.

The coffee shop was busy and the street was parked up, with people prowling for a space. I let a lucky person have mine and drove a few blocks to a slow side street, pulled over, and checked my car for tracking devices, including under the hood and in the trunk. I couldn't find anything. Maybe it really had only been Paulette and her controlling nature.

I looked at my watch—a little before two thirty—then at the tracking app on my phone. Paulette was still shopping, and Elmer still parked where he had been.

I got back in my car and headed to Old Metairie.

Saturday afternoon is traffic stupidity time. People stopping at nonexistent stop signs, pulling in front of me just to go slowly. It was close to three before I was finally on Metairie Road and crossing the parish line.

I rarely came here. The people I'd known in high school weren't my friends then, and the years hadn't changed anything. The house I'd lived in with my aunt and uncle had been sold a few years ago, Uncle Claude long dead and Aunt Greta now in a retirement community on the other side of the lake. I didn't visit her. She might want me to, but only to see if I'd changed my sinful ways—I hadn't—and to tell me I was going to hell and let me know how hard she had worked to tame me from the bayou rat my father let me be. Sometimes you have to let go of as much of the past as you can. It can always come back and grab you, but you don't need to hold on and make it easy.

I turned down the street to Paulette's old house. The bare outline of the place I remembered, new landscaping, new paint, an expanded front porch. Only the bones and memories left.

I drove past slowly. Right beyond the side fence was the driveway into Barry's house. In a neighborhood of ostentatious houses, it was the most ostentatious, with a four-car garage and a large lawn that was, as they say, an entertaining dream. A lush swath of grass separated the garage from a large swimming pool and a huge patio with an outdoor kitchen. At least, that's how it was the one time I'd been there. The fence was new, high for privacy; a tall person would have to stand on their tiptoes to see over it.

The red brick house was also massive, a veranda running around the whole place, two-story columns on every side. When she was dating him, Paulette bragged about it being over six thousand square feet, giggling and saying, "Big enough we can make noise and his parents don't hear." I suspect she was wrong. They heard, but he was a boy, so they didn't care.

The side of the house was on the same street as Paulette's, with the official front around the corner. Most of his friends came in the back; that's where they parked. Paulette liked to brag about her access.

I turned the corner.

Elmer's truck was parked right in front of the house.

That was the distance, him parking in front and Paulette way in the back.

I had stopped. I realized I needed to keep moving, not look like I was paying too much attention.

Barry Jenkins was Boss.

Paulette knew me, she had put the tracker on my car. She was back with Barry. But how could she know about Sarah?

I willed myself to not turn around and go by again to make sure. I turned at the next corner and the next, not even sure where I was going, needing to get away from anyplace they could see me.

I pulled out and texted Teddy and Joanne, *Boss is Barry Jenkins*, adding his address.

Teddy quickly replied, *Got it.*

Joanne wrote, *Damn. See you soon.*

I took that to mean she would meet me when I picked up Sarah as extra protection.

Sarah said she would text me a half hour before I needed to be there. She hadn't texted yet. I'd left both my regular phone and the burner on my seat, just in case.

I picked up the burner and then the list of usernames. I logged in again as PinkLady, my fingers ready to disconnect in a hurry. The screen opened. There were several conversation threads. I quickly scanned the usernames in case she was already logged in. One conversation was about who was going to buy more ammo for the upcoming practice at the camp. One was about proof that Michelle Obama was trans. So tempting to sell them some prime waterfront property. A pile of how evil drag queens, queers, immigrants, Jews, the global elite, etc., all were and a debate on whether to kill us outright or put us in camps. Several people suggested bringing back slavery as the proper place for us. A short thread was buried among them. It had the title *Importent info*. The first message was from late yesterday afternoon: *Found out someone we been looking for is here.*

"Shit," I muttered aloud. I kept reading. Several others asked the usual who, what, where, but the original poster didn't reply for several hours, and then only adding, *Let you know soon. Be ready for action.*

I switched to my regular phone, took a picture of the list of names, passwords, and channels, and texted it to Teddy and Joanne, adding *something is up.*

Joanne texted back, *On my way to meeting place. Talk there.*

Teddy's was *Will get someone on asap.*

I looked at my watch. It was just after three. I picked up my burner phone and texted Sarah. *Do not leave the house until we get there.* The place she was in was large, set back from the street. She should be about as safe there as possible.

Try the third channel. I logged in again as PinkLady. Two messages from this morning: *Big one today* and *Thanks to BigMomma for her help.*

"Fuck and shit!" I pulled out. Frances's assistant. The one who had called me to tell me Frances would be late. She'd said, "I'm the Big Momma of the office." The one Frances had hired to help her out from an earlier settlement from the oil spill. BigMomma complaining about her gay boss. To me, gay is male, and I had assumed the boss was a man. But gay to them could mean all queer people.

If, so many ifs. Someone in New York found out Sarah was here. Likely one of the NYPD cops. They told the group here to check on me. Barry/Boss is bonking Paulette, who tells him all about hiring me, and he already knows I'm also protecting Sarah but hasn't been able to find her. Then a lucky break: Frances is organizing the community thing and lets her assistant do the work and she finds out Sarah is part of it.

The light was turning yellow and I sped up, red by the time I was going through it but no time to waste.

The next light was too red to risk, but I used the time to phone Teddy. Bless him, he answered. I hurriedly told him what I knew, that they were going to try again to kill Sarah, and maybe everyone else there.

His professional response was "Shit." He got the address and said he'd get people there as quickly as he could.

As much as I hate the interstate, I chanced it, getting on at Metairie Road and off at the St. Charles exit, the fastest way to get from Old

Metairie to the Garden District. One advantage of Saturday was no work traffic.

I had to remind myself to breathe as I pushed the lax limits of what's allowed in New Orleans driving, passing a slow driver in the turning lane, stop signs a mere suggestion. Once off the interstate, I headed uptown on Prytania. Too many streets were bent by the river, and they didn't all go all the way through. I crossed Jackson, heading into the heart of the Garden District, the large old houses, lush yards, wrought iron laced balconies, the grand dames of the city.

Another turn, then a stupid loop around because the streets here were all one way, and finally on the right block.

Frances's house was in the middle of the block, and the street was parked up, with tourists and locals taking advantage of a beautiful weekend to stroll amongst the impressive houses. Her home was gleaming white, set off by the fresh black paint of the iron work and shutters, guarded from the street by a matching iron fence, tall enough to discourage wandering on the lawn, but the spears didn't block the view of the wraparound galley and the perfectly landscaped yard. A brick walkway led to the generous veranda. Late fall flowers were in bloom, a cheerful splash of red and yellow against the stark white of the house.

A black van was illegally parked in a driveway across the street.

I stopped as if gawking at the houses, taking time to get my gun out.

Two men got out of the van.

From the driver's side, the man who almost ran me over, his stringy blond hair easily identifiable. The other, still on the passenger side, was tall, dark brown hair, a doughboy round face. The man Sarah described? The one in the pictures I'd seen with the convert? He was in the van's shadow, and it was hard to see him clearly.

It didn't matter. They both had guns, ugly assault weapons.

They wore bulletproof vests.

Ugly Blond raised his gun.

I blared my horn and drove, closing the gap between us.

He turned to look, swinging the gun barrel at me.

I hit the accelerator and threw myself down across the seats, one hand still on the steering wheel to keep the car aimed at him. My head was on the passenger seat, and I couldn't see anything except its fabric. Maybe I should have opted for leather, since this might be the last thing I'd ever see. Too late now. The engine might protect me. For a moment.

The thunder of a gun roared and the glass of my windshield exploded, shards cascading over me.

I kept my foot on the gas and heard the solid thud of what I hoped was him against the front of my car. I caught a bare glimpse of a shape careening off my hood and slamming into one of the parked cars.

I jammed on the brakes, sliding to a halt with my hood angled into the next driveway, the rest of my car blocking the street.

Blood was dripping down my face, covering my left eye. From the glass, I told myself. All I had time for was to hurriedly wipe it away, crawl to the passenger door to keep the car between me and them. Grab my gun on the way.

I opened the door, sliding face first and rolling to my side to get my feet under me. I stood up into a crouch, peering over the hood.

Ugly Blond was moaning, his left leg splayed at an unnatural angle. Blood was coming out of his nose, and his right arm was badly scraped. I brushed the blood out of my eyes and scanned for his gun. It was several feet away. I hoped he was too hurt to get it. A wounded man can still pull a trigger.

Still squatting behind my car, I looked to see where Dough Boy was. He was in the middle of the street, a pistol at his waist and the rifle at his side. He glanced briefly in our direction, dismissing his fallen comrade and me before turning to the house.

I clicked the safety off my gun and wiped the blood away again. Damn, head wounds bleed a lot.

The front door of the house slammed open.

Sarah.

"I'm the one you want!" she yelled. "I'm here. Take me!"

He lifted the rifle to fire.

"No!" I screamed. I pulled the trigger. The roar, the harsh jerk of the recoil in my hands.

Another shot, then another. Too many.

I had only fired once.

I stood up, throwing away the protection of the car. I would empty all my bullets at him, give him the death he so easily gave others.

I violently jerked my head to get the blood out of my vision, both hands on my pistol.

Sarah was crumpled at the foot of the steps.

The man was on the ground, blood pooling around him.

Voices. Shouting. I saw multiple people moving, darting behind cars, coming this way.

The black van tried to reverse down the street, but an unmarked car screeched up and blocked it.

A swarm of people in tactical gear. Police. FBI.

I pointed my gun at the ground and slowly took the grip between my thumb and forefinger, keeping my finger away from the trigger, and put it down on the trunk of my car. It would be too ironic to get shot by the people saving us.

Five officers surrounded the van, the barrels of their weapons jammed in the windows, yelling at the occupants to get out. I heard a whiny voice from inside begging, "Please don't shoot."

Motherfuckers.

I wiped the blood away again, the adrenaline ebbing, pain surfacing. "It's just glass," I muttered.

"Don't move," one of the officers yelled.

Sarah was running to me.

"Don't shoot!" I yelled at the officer. Foolish of her to move with so many nervous people with guns around.

She started to grab me in a hug, then realized I was covered in shattered glass.

"You're hurt!" she said.

"Nothing major, just some glass," I said. I leaned against my car, staring to feel woozy. "Are you okay?"

"Terrified. Shaking, but...okay, physically okay."

"I saw you on the ground," I said. "Are you sure you're okay?"

"I told you I'm a coward. I saw that barrel aiming at me and flattened myself." She took my hand, the only part she could safely touch. "You broke your promise," she said softly.

"Didn't make that promise. Just the one I kept, to do everything I could to keep people safe."

A woman wearing an FBI jacket come up to me. "We need to move this car, that okay?"

I looked at my poor battered car, most of the windows shattered, the hood riddled with bullet holes. "By my guest. Key's in the ignition." She nodded, then called to several other people. There were sirens in the background, voices over them, officers checking every car, every bush. Some of the people from the house had come onto the porch, now that it seemed safe. Two pastors I recognized from the news and events they had spoken at. Several others I didn't. A tall woman behind them. Cordelia.

Safe, they're all safe.

Sarah, still holding my hand, pulled me off the road, sliding between parked cars, out of the way.

I leaned against the fence, then slid to the ground. I needed to sit down.

"Damn it, how badly are you hurt?" Cordelia knelt beside me, opening a first aid kit.

"Glass, I think," I said. "Some bleeding."

"Lot of bleeding," she said. "Let's see if we can get it stopped."

Sarah moved out of her way but still held my hand.

Cordelia gently dabbed my forehead.

"Ouch!" I yelped. The embedded glass was painful.

"A nasty sliver of glass," she confirmed. "The sooner I get it out, the sooner we can get you bandaged. I'll be slow and gentle, see what I can do before the EMTs get here." She took out gauze and tweezers from the kit.

I tried to ignore how much of my blood was covering me.

"How did you know?" Cordelia said.

Joanne knelt in front of me. "Asked the question for me."

"Detective work," I answered. I was so tired. "Lots of paper and talking to people. When I'm not bleeding to death, I'll tell you the story."

"Fair enough," Joanne said. "I saw the black van, called in the plates and as much backup as possible. Then saw you turn the corner."

"And you sensibly waited for backup," I murmured.

"Sort of. Was making my way behind the parked cars. Fired at him when I realized he was about to shoot."

I nodded, too tired and in too much pain to talk.

Cordelia removed the pieces of glass causing the worst of the bleeding. She was gentle, but it hurt. Halfway through, Sarah gave my hand a squeeze and went with FBI agents to be questioned. One of them asked to talk to me, but Cordelia waved them away, going full doctor on them. I was grateful. I wasn't up to answering.

One of the ministers, the regal Black woman, looked at the man on the ground and said, "May God have mercy on his soul. I'm going to have to do a lot of praying before I get there." Several of the other faith leaders chorused an "Amen."

An ambulance arrived. The first took Dough Boy, the most seriously injured.

The second one was for Ugly Blond Boy. He was in good enough shape to curse and moan and demand to only be treated by white people.

The older Black woman in the lead said, "Fine, you can stay here for the next few hours. Too bad we only got Black people here who can give you pain meds."

She came over to check on me, leaving him to curse.

"I don't care if you're purple, green, and queer as everyone at Southern Decadence, happy for the help," I muttered.

"All the above and gold, sweetie. We're going to take care of you," she told me.

Cordelia briefed her on what she had done.

They decided I needed to go to the ER. I'd hoped for just a few more bandages, some good painkillers, and a ride home.

Joanne told me she would take care of my things. My gun and car would be evidence.

I nodded and let the purple, green, and gold people take me away. I was aware enough to see that Ugly Blond was still waiting. The population of Orleans Parish is over 60 percent Black. He might be waiting for a while.

Frankly, my dear, I didn't give a damn.

Chapter Eighteen

After that, everything was a blur. Probably the painkillers they gave me in the ER. And me not wanting to pay attention as they tweezed out small slivers of glass.

Torbin and Andy picked me up. I have a vague memory of arguing that I wanted my own home and bed and not waking up groggy with no idea where I was. Torbin caved and agreed to stay in my guest room. I managed the briefest of showers, forcing myself to wash the blood off.

I called Sarah. "Are you okay?"

"Maybe," she answered. "Ask me a few weeks from now. You?"

"Mostly," I replied, not sure how much of it was a lie. "I just wanted to check."

"I mostly don't believe you," she said, "But glad and angry at what you did. You could have been killed."

"Same with you. But we're not. You get to drink a good bottle of wine tomorrow. And the next day."

It was late, we were tired, we said good-bye.

Then I collapsed into bed.

The pain pills put me out but didn't keep me asleep. I woke up several times, my heart racing. It was hard to let go of the fear. The worry about other men with other guns.

I knew by the slant of the sun that it was well into the morning when I woke up. I first chugged a pain pill—it had worn off over the night—then gave it a few minutes to kick in before dragging myself out of bed and into a proper shower.

I threw on sweats and stumbled downstairs.

The smell of freshly brewed coffee greeted me.

"I heard you moving," Torbin said, poking his head out of the kitchen.

I gratefully accepted the coffee and the assortment of baked goods that had arrived for breakfast. He joined me in both.

"If you're up to it, we're meeting later at Danny's and Elly's to—what's the word you lesbians use?—process things."

"Y'all have been busy while I was napping."

"You were conked out like a tourist who shouldn't have had that third Hurricane, let alone the fourth."

"Getting old, not able to keep up like I used to."

"No, you're not. Not yet. If you're getting old, then I'm getting old, and we both have too many good years before us for that to happen."

I nodded, too old and tired to argue. Plus, there was coffee to drink.

A slow breakfast, caffeine and sugar, helped me revive. I checked the local news, but so far it was only "shots fired in Garden District."

We were all safe. I wondered about Ugly Blond and Dough Boy. I wanted to know how the story ended. I didn't want them dead, just out of my life and not able to ever hurt anyone again.

I gave myself extra time to get dressed, still sore, still moving slowly. I had to find a new jacket, since the nice leather one I had been wearing wasn't nice anymore.

Andy drove Sarah, and I went with Torbin. Just in case.

When we got there, there were a number of cars already parked along the street.

I glanced at Torbin, but he just shrugged.

As we walked to the door, Teddy arrived. His hair was still wet from a recent shower and probably as casual as he got, khaki pants and a light blue shirt with the sleeves rolled up.

"Good to see you!" he called. "Boy, this is an interesting case."

Elly opened the door. First hugs, then I introduced Teddy.

There were a lot of people here, some I knew, some I didn't. Joanne and Alex. Joanne looked tired and Alex was smiling, but I knew her well enough to see the concern behind her eyes. Several of the faith leaders were there as well. Cordelia. Nancy. Frances. Lev McDonald was talking to Sarah.

She saw me and pushed her way through the crowd, throwing her arms around my neck.

"So glad you are okay!" she said.

I held her in return, aware of all the eyes watching us. I didn't care.

We finally let go, and I turned to Teddy and asked, "Updates?"

He agreed, but Danny decided we needed to be organized, so

she herded everyone to the patio and got us seated, drinks in hand. Sparkling water for me because of the pain pills.

Once we were arranged, Teddy turned to Joanne and said, "You first or me?"

"Let me go," she said, taking a sip of beer before starting. "George Hopkins, the man killed yesterday, was the son of a police officer. He was the one who sent Ian O'Reilly and Jerry Guilio down here. When I questioned the NY team about the interview and the chase, they started looking into it. No evidence that he was directly involved, other than being a garden-variety bigot who believed Jews owned everything and queers wanted to groom all children."

"The apple didn't fall far from that tree," Teddy interjected.

"His son lived at home, and Daddy wasn't as secure with things as he should have been. Hopkins was able to access his computer and see the report from the NYPD cops about Sarah being here and protected by Micky."

"Which is how they knew she was here," Danny added.

"How did you figure it out?" Teddy asked me.

I told them about Paulette and her case, with an aside to Joanne that she might want to look at what I'd found. Barry aka Boss had learned about my connection to Sarah through his hate network and got Paulette to put the trackers on my car. Maybe he manipulated her into it, or maybe she was in on it. Elmer was a pack rat, and when I recovered what he'd stolen, I also recovered his terrorist box with the hidden channels and usernames.

"I put the final pieces together," I said, "seeing Elmer's truck in front of Barry's house and realizing he was Boss. The username BigMomma and her complaining about her gay boss." I looked at Frances. "You gave her a list of who was going to be there, right?"

"What?" she said, taken aback that we had suddenly veered into her lane. "We had name tags and place settings. What I thought was a simple admin task. How was I supposed to know Alma Reiner was crazy?" She crossed her arms and looked outraged. Like a lawyer posturing before a jury. Nancy put a hand on her shoulder, then let it drop.

She had a point. Sometimes you only know someone is a snake when they bite you. I was secretly relieved I wasn't the one who led them to Sarah.

Teddy took up the narrative. "She alerted her confederates. They passed it on. Hopkins got the first flight down here. He brought his special rifle with him, so he had to check his luggage, and that's why they only got there when they did."

"Micky had just figured it out, called me and Teddy," Joanne said. "I called backup, Teddy called backup, and we got there as quickly as we could."

"Hopkins died at the scene?" I asked.

"DOA at the ER," Teddy replied.

"We're still looking at footage," Joanne added. "Every house on the block has video security."

"My office has been going over it," Danny said. She looked at me. "No, you didn't kill him. You hit him, the bulletproof vest. You can see him jerk from it, knocking his aim off."

"Slowed him the fraction of a second we needed to get him in our sights," Teddy added.

"We'll need to do the autopsy to know for sure, but likely it was the SWAT team that took him out," Danny said.

"May God rest his soul," the regal Black minister said. "The Lord must have wanted him off this earth before he could do more harm."

"Amen to that," Teddy said. "Buddy Fellows was not at his place when we raided it because he and two others were picking up Hopkins at the airport. Pain finally got to him. He took the next bus, even though only one of the EMTs was white."

"That and being told he might lose the leg to infection," Cordelia interjected. "Probably hearing from a white doctor, albeit just a woman, was enough to hurry him along," she added dryly.

I was considered the funny one of the two of us, but Cordelia had a sly, dry humor. She had to be professional most of the time, so I mostly saw it at home.

"The ambulance crew thanks you," Danny said, echoing what we all were thinking.

"How many people have you arrested?" Frances asked.

I was a good girl and didn't ask if she was looking for clients.

"Still in process," Danny replied.

"We are executing search warrants in multiple places," Teddy said. "At the moment, we have the core group, those at the compound out to the west. They had guns, drugs, and bogus credit cards. The two men in the van, Buddy Fellows, although he's still in the hospital, but handcuffed to his bed."

"He has some broken ribs, shattered knee, possible concussion," Joanne said.

"Once he's well enough to leave the hospital, he's going to jail," Teddy added. "We're still digging into their dirt pile online, but it looks like we'll have enough evidence to put them away for a long time."

"Were they targeting Rabbi Jacobson or all of us?" the regal Black woman said. She put her hand on Sarah's shoulder.

Teddy, Joanne, and Danny all looked at each other. Danny finally answered. "Still gathering evidence. We believe their initial target was Sarah, but…they had no qualms about how many they killed. They called reverends, pastors, rabbis, etc., who considered LGBTQ people to be human the devil's spawn."

Teddy said, "We're working with local and national offices. This was a terrorist plot starting in New York and spreading here. We've broken a lot of their codes, know who many of them are now. Likely some of those will do a plea deal to not have to spend the rest of their lives in jail."

"So, we're as safe as any of us can hope to be," Sarah said, with a small, sad smile.

"Until swords are beaten into plowshares," the Black minister said.

Amen to that.

Joanne grabbed me to go to my office to retrieve the boxes. Teddy tagged along. Once there, I gave Joanne the ones with the evidence of Paulette's fraud, and the terrorist box to Teddy. Joanne gave me a ride home.

Torbin retrieved me later to come over to their place. They had stopped at the good po-boy spot on the way home and, of course, got enough for me.

"Not like I can run to the grocery," I said as I sat down. I was hungry.

"We can let you use our cars until things get settled," Andy offered, passing out plates as Torbin put the pile of po-boys in the center of the table.

They drank a really good bottle of wine; I was allowed a sip, but water otherwise. Torbin promised that as soon as I was off my pain pills, he'd make up for it.

It wasn't a party, instead a gathering of friends to get through the hard times. We ate, they drank, we talked of the safe things, weather, religion, politics.

We got up to put things away, the signal the evening was ending.

"Can I walk you home?" Sarah asked me. "I guess I'm free enough to be on the street."

"Yes, that sounds lovely," I agreed.

As we headed down the block, she slipped her arm through mine.

"I've booked a flight home tomorrow," she said.

"So soon?"

"I've been away too long."

"Stay a few more days. Let me show you the city. Go to some of the places we could only drive past."

"I have to go back to my grief, where my life is, to find who I am without Leah. I need to mourn my wife, our life for every day over twenty years, my Leah. Visit the places we loved. Sort through her things, give away what I can bear to. Cry. Cry a lot. The hollowing heartache has to be faced."

"I understand," I said. "It's just…it would be nice to…do this," I said, using my free hand to encompass the street we were walking on, the gentle night air, the stars above.

"It is lovely," she agreed. "I'm relishing every step."

The block was short and we were at my doorstep.

"Would you like to come in?" I asked.

We stopped and faced each other.

"No. I'm still married to Leah. I can't think of any future until I say all the good-byes I need to say to her. Ask me again in a year." She put her hands on my face, leaned forward, and placed a gentle kiss on my cheek. "I am honored you asked. Good-bye, Micky Knight. When I look at the stars, I will think of you as a shining light in my darkness," she said with a wistful smile. She turned to walk back down the street.

I watched until she was back inside.

Chapter Nineteen

Sarah left the next morning with a good-bye at Torbin and Andy's doorstep. "I hate hurried good-byes at the airport."

We were there, coffee and beignets, an allotted hour before the taxi arrived. Torbin, Andy, Danny, Elly, Joanne and Alex. Cordelia, without Nancy. The words were the small words, safe travels, promises of visits. The words weren't important, only the meaning behind them.

Then Sarah was gone.

Cordelia looked at my forehead as she was getting ready to leave. "I'll come by in a few days to check it."

I was polite and told her she didn't need to.

"You saved our lives. It's the least I can do." She got in her car and left.

Much as I wanted to be my own boss and call in sick, I had to meet Teddy and Joanne to give official statements. Both were long and tiring. Yeah, important, glad to do my civic duty and all that, but they needed to build in more bathroom breaks, especially given how much coffee I had to drink to stay alert.

The debriefings stretched into the next day.

Time moved both slowly and quickly. The days passing with me catching up on my work, security at bars, new cases, insurance, and car shopping—mine was totaled.

Bettina/Betty Collingwood was a pawn; George Hopkins aka Dough Boy egged her on about converting to Judaism. He acted interested in her and her life, asking detailed questions. She was lost and needy, and he used her. He had fired the shot in NY. His gun jammed and there were too many people around for him to take even a minute, so he ran. After missing Sarah, he became obsessed with her. His father, a police leader, was part of the larger team that dealt with terror attacks. He wasn't specifically on Sarah's case, but close enough and friends with Ian O'Reilly, so he got informal reports. He thought his son shared his standard bigotry but was a good boy and "wouldn't be crazy" about it.

Hopkins/Dough Boy contacted the local group down here. He talked to Boss/Barry, who remembered me from high school (I'm so flattered; I didn't know he knew I was alive). He and Paulette had already hooked up, so he asked if she had kept up with me and, jackpot, she'd just hired me. He talked her into putting the trackers on my car. Between the trips I made for Paulette and messing with them by removing the tracker, they didn't get the data they needed. But luck favored them again. BigMomma, aka Alma Reiner, had been hired by Frances, their secret spy in the gay community. She had been the client on one of Frances's previous lawsuits, a juicy oil spill, but there were hundreds of clients, so they only got about twenty thousand each, nice, but not enough to live off. When Alma moaned about how she was going to live, Frances offered her a job. She claimed she did a thorough background check and knew Alma was part of a Confederate reenactment group but said she believed in free speech, etc., and was only concerned with the job Alma did. Which seemed to be doing anything Frances asked, without question, including calling her female dates when she was late and the boring work for the various causes Frances got the glory for, including making the list of names for the Faith Leaders for Human Rights. Sarah's name was on it. Alma recognized it. She let Boss know, who contacted Dough Boy, who demanded to be included. He'd flown down the next day. Ugly Blond joined in, as well as two others. After the raid on their place outside Donaldsonville, Teddy told me they were into just about everything, drugs, gun running, financial fraud. "More crime than all the immigrants in the area" was my comment. Boss/Barry had been arrested that evening, his house and the camp searched. He wasn't a great businessman, spending more money than he made. He was charging his militia members to use the camp, to be part of the group, with rank handed out to those who could pay the most. A nice side hustle. When some of his followers found out, they turned on him, splitting the group in two. This led each side to implicate the other in as much illegal activity as possible. Elmer had been picked up. He'd be spending a few years in prison.

"I think we cut a good chunk of the rattles off the snake." Danny summed it up. "The people in this group, both here and in New York, won't hurt anyone else. But we didn't get rid of all the snakes."

I had to send in my final report to Paulette. A brief email: *Elmer was involved with a domestic terrorist group and had information about them stored in the pile of boxes he was carting around. I had to turn them all over to the FBI. You can retrieve your property once they have cleared it as not related.*

I got a panicked email back demanding I go get her stuff right now and that I had no right to give them to anyone but her.

I responded, saying that unless there was anything illegal in them, she had nothing to worry about. Both of us knew she had a lot to worry about.

I reminded her I was legally compelled to turn over any evidence that might be linked to major crimes.

I didn't hear from her again. She didn't pay me. I didn't bother sending her a bill. I considered our debts paid. Justice? Revenge? More of the latter than I liked to admit.

I heard from Sarah a few days after she returned to New York. A text message. She said she was doing okay and included a picture of her and Leah, taken on their legal wedding day. It was beautiful, not posed, taken as they were walking, both laughing, open joy on their faces as they looked at each other. "Love" would be the only caption needed.

I honored her wishes, sent a text back, telling her we were all doing well.

A week later, I caught up with Torbin and asked if he had heard from her. He, too, had only gotten a text saying she was okay and to pet the cats for her.

Her life was back there.

He took my hand and said, "Are you in love with her? She's a special woman."

"Yes, she is. And…maybe. But could you see me as the wife of a rabbi in New York?"

"I could see you happy, I could see you being loved and cared for," he said and pulled me into a hug. I tried not to cry and didn't do a great job.

If we had met when we were young, our lives still finding their directions, maybe we could have made it work. I wondered briefly, foolishly, what would have happened had we met when I was in college in New York. But that past was gone, closed. Now she had her life there and I had mine here and for anything to happen, one of us would have to give up everything. I'd already proven I wasn't good at that. Love matters, but it isn't always enough.

As promised, Cordelia came by to look at my stiches. Torbin and Andy were over, having just arrived with a pitcher of Cosmos. I'd noticed they were making a habit of dropping by most evenings.

"No, don't do that here," Torbin protested. "We just ordered pizza, and I am not looking at gory wounds when I'm about to eat red sauce."

We retreated to the office at the back of the house.

"You're going to have a scar," she said as she removed the gauze pad.

"There goes my chance at Miss USA, old dyke category."

She smiled, then got medical things out of her bag. She was tired, I realized. We no longer saw each other daily, and the small changes were more noticeable. The lines at her eyes more pronounced? Different shampoo? Different perfume?

Different person?

"Hold still, this won't take long," she said as she started removing stitches.

It didn't. Maybe a minute. "That was quick. Especially since I didn't have to wait for half an hour at the doctor's office."

"Benefit of having a doctor for…a friend," she said.

"Are we?"

"Friends? Yes." She turned to put her equipment away. Then she said, "I miss you. I'd like to find a way…for us to be okay around each other."

"I'd like that," I said. I reached out and took her hand.

Torbin shouted from the other room, "Hey, pizza's here!"

We held hands for a moment longer.

Cordelia joined us for the pizza and a Cosmo—only one since she had to drive home. We said our good-byes at a reasonable hour. I watched Torbin and Andy go in their door and Cordelia get in her car and drive away.

I went out on the back patio to look up at the stars. The same stars that Sarah and Cordelia would see if they looked up. The lights we all see.

Maybe I was in love with both of them. Love enough that I didn't want anything from either of them, other than they be okay. If Cordelia was happy with Nancy, I wanted her to be happy. If Sarah never came here again, I wanted her to find everything she needed and deserved, in New York.

And me? I had saved a few people's lives, gotten a dashing scar that I would claim was from a duel over a beautiful red-haired woman, many years ago under the spreading oaks in Audubon Park, just as the sun barely kissed the morning sky. A small measure of what I would call justice, not revenge, from the long-ago sins of the high school mean girls. Got a few bad men with hate and guns off the street.

"The smallest day. The memories that become a lifetime." I recalled what Sarah had said.

The sun was setting, the last strands of light disappearing. Even on the smallest day, the stars will shine.

About the Author

J.M. Redmann has published twelve novels featuring New Orleans PI Micky Knight. Her first book was published in 1990, one of the early hard-boiled lesbian detectives. Her books have won numerous awards, including three Lambda Literary awards. *Transitory*, the eleventh book, won the Publishing Triangle's Joseph Hansen Award, a Golden Crown award, and was nominated for a Lambda award. *The Intersection of Law & Desire* was an Editor's Choice of the *San Francisco Chronicle* and a recommended book by Maureen Corrigan of NPR's *Fresh Air*. Two books were selected for the American Library Association GLBT Roundtable's Over the Rainbow list and *Water Mark* won a ForeWord Gold First Place mystery award. She is the co-editor with Greg Herren of three anthologies, one of which, *Night Shadows: Queer Horror*, was shortlisted for a Shirley Jackson award. Her books have been translated into German, Spanish, Dutch, Hebrew, and Norwegian.

Books Available From Bold Strokes Books

Discovering Gold by Sam Ledel. In 1920s Colorado, a single mother and a rowdy cowgirl must set aside their fears and initial reservations about one another if they want to find love in the mining town each of them calls home. (978-1-63679-786-1)

Dream a Little Dream by Melissa Brayden. Savanna can't believe it when Dr. Kyle Remington, the woman who left her feeling like a fool, shows up in Dreamer's Bay. Life is too complicated for second chances. Or is it? (978-1-63679-839-4)

Emma by the Sea by Sarah G. Levine. A delightful modern-day romance inspired by *Emma*, one of Jane Austen's most beloved novels. (978-1-63679-879-0)

Goodbye Hello by Heather K O'Malley. With so much time apart and the challenges of a long-distance relationship, Kelly and Teresa's second chance at love may end just as awkwardly as the first. (978-1-63679-790-8)

One Measure of Love by Annie McDonald. Vancouver's hit competitive cooking show *Recipe for Success* has begun filming its second season, and two talented young chefs are desperate for more than a winning dish. (978-1-63679-827-1)

The Smallest Day by J.M. Redmann. The first bullet missed—can Micky Knight stop the second bullet from finding its target? (978-1-63679-854-7)

To Please Her by Elena Abbott. A spilled coffee leads Sabrina into a world of erotic BDSM that may just land her the love of her life. (978-1-63679-849-3)

Two Weddings and a Funeral by Claudia Parr. Stella and Theo have spent the last thirteen years pretending they can be just friends, but surely "just friends" don't make out every chance they get. (978-1-63679-820-2)

Firecamp by Jaycie Morrison. Going their separate ways seemed inevitable for two people as different as Fallon and Nora, while meeting up again is strictly coincidental. (978-1-63679-753-3)

Coming Up Clutch by Anna Gram. College softball star Kelly "Razor" Mitchell hung up her cleats early, but when former crush, now coach Ashton Sharpe shows up on her doorstep seven years later, beautiful as ever, Razor hopes the longing in her gaze has nothing to do with softball. (978-1-63679-817-2)

Fixed Up by Aurora Rey. When electrician Jack Barrow and artist Ellie Lancaster get stuck on a job site during a blizzard, close quarters send all sorts of sparks flying. (978-1-63679-788-5)

Stranded by Ronica Black. Can Abigail and Whitley overcome their personal hang-ups and stubbornness to survive not only Alaska but a dangerous stalker as well? (978-1-63679-761-8)

Whisk Me Away by Georgia Beers. Regan's a gorgeous flake. Ava, a beautiful untouchable ice queen. When they meet again at a retreat for up-and-coming pastry chefs, the competition, and the ovens, heat up. (978-1-63679-796-0)

Across the Enchanted Border by Crin Claxton. Magic, telepathy, swordsmanship, tyranny, and tenderness abound in a tale of two lands separated by the enchanted border. (978-1-63679-804-2)

Deep Cover by Kara A. McLeod. Running from your problems by pretending to be someone else only works if the person you're pretending to be doesn't have even bigger problems. (978-1-63679-808-0)

Good Game by Suzanne Lenoir. Even though Lauren has sworn off dating gamers, it's becoming hard to resist the multifaceted Sam. An opposites attract lesbian romance. (978-1-63679-764-9)

Innocence of the Maiden by Ileandra Young. Three powerful women. Two covens at war. One horrifying murder. When mighty and powerful witches begin to butt heads, who out there is strong enough to mediate? (978-1-63679-765-6)

Protection in Paradise by Julia Underwood. When arson forces them together, the flames between chief of police Eve Maguire and librarian Shaye Hayden aren't that easy to extinguish. (978-1-63679-847-9)

Too Forward by Krystina Rivers. Just as professional basketball player Jane May's career finally starts heating up, a new relationship with her team's brand consultant could derail the success and happiness she's struggled so long to find. (978-1-63679-717-5)

Worth Waiting For by Kristin Keppler. For Peyton and Hanna, reliving the past is painful, but looking back might be the only way to move forward. (978-1-63679-773-1)

All For Her: Forbidden Romance Novellas by Gun Brooke, J.J. Hale & Aurora Rey. Explore the angst and excitement of forbidden love few would dare in this heart-stopping novella collection. (978-1-63679-713-7)

Finding Harmony by CF Frizzell. Rock star Harper Cushing has to rearrange her grandmother's future and sell the family store out from under her, but she reassesses everything because Gram's helper, Frankie, could be offering the harmony her heart has been missing. (978-1-63679-741-0)

Gaze by Kris Bryant. Love at first sight is for dreamers, but the more time Lucky and Brianna spend together, the more they realize the chemistry of a gaze can make anything possible. (978-1-63679-711-3)

Laying of Hands by Patricia Evans. The mysterious new writing instructor at camp makes Grace Waters brave enough to wonder what would happen if she dared to write her own story. (978-1-63679-782-3)

The Naked Truth by Sandy Lowe. How far are Rowan and Genevieve willing to go and how much will they risk to make their most captivating and forbidden fantasies a reality? (978-1-63679-426-6)

The Roommate by Claire Forsythe. Jess Black's boyfriend is handsome and successful. That's why it comes as a shock when she meets a woman on the train who makes her pulse race. (978-1-63679-757-1)

The Blessed by Anne Shade. Layla and Suri are brought together by fate to defeat the darkness threatening to tear their world apart. What they don't expect to discover is a love that might set them free. (978-1-63679-715-1)

Seducing the Widow by Jane Walsh. Former rival debutantes have a second chance at love after fifteen years apart when a spinster persuades her ex-lover to help save her family business. (978-1-63679-747-2)